"Why don't you get rid of the stiff and come up to my room?"

Tempted as she was, she wasn't going out like that. "No. I have a date."

Slowly, he edged closer. Reaching behind her, he flipped the lock on the door, the click echoing in the empty bathroom. Sucking in a deep breath, she waited, anticipating his next move.

His fingers flitted across the hem of her dress and he inched it up a bit. Kneeling down, he slipped his hands under her dress and slowly pulled her underwear down. She held her breath.

"Step out of them," he ordered in a low, deep voice.

Bracing her hands on his shoulders, she stepped out of her lace panties. He stood up, tucked the thin material inside his suit jacket, and pulled out a tiny key card. He placed it in her hand and closed her fingers around it. "Room 1179," he murmured, his lips a mere breath away from hers.

The click of the door brought her mind back to their location and her eyes popped open. She opened her mouth to speak, but he placed a finger over her lips.

"Shh. Try not to think about what I'm going to do to you while you're on your date." Swinging open the door, he walked out, whistling along the way.

She hated him—in the best way.

ALSO BY ELLE WRIGHT

The Forbidden Man

HIS
ALL NIGHT

An Edge of Scandal Novel

ELLE WRIGHT

FOREVER

NEW YORK   BOSTON

Copyright © 2015 by Elle Wright
Excerpt from *Her Kind of Man* copyright © 2016 by Elle Wright
All rights reserved. In accordance with the U.S. Copyright Act of 1976, the scanning, uploading, and electronic sharing of any part of this book without the permission of the publisher constitute unlawful piracy and theft of the author's intellectual property. If you would like to use material from the book (other than for review purposes), prior written permission must be obtained by contacting the publisher at permissions@hbgusa.com. Thank you for your support of the author's rights.

Forever
Hachette Book Group
1290 Avenue of the Americas
New York, NY 10104

hachettebookgroup.com
twitter.com/foreverromance

Printed in the United States of America

First Edition: November 2015
10 9 8 7 6 5 4 3 2 1

OPM

Forever is an imprint of Grand Central Publishing.
The Forever name and logo are trademarks of Hachette Book Group, Inc.

The Hachette Speakers Bureau provides a wide range of authors for speaking events. To find out more, go to www.hachettespeakersbureau.com or call (866) 376-6591.

The publisher is not responsible for websites (or their content) that are not owned by the publisher.

ATTENTION CORPORATIONS AND ORGANIZATIONS:
Most HACHETTE BOOK GROUP books are available
at quantity discounts with bulk purchase for educational,
business, or sales promotional use. For information,
please call or write:

Special Markets Department, Hachette Book Group
1290 Avenue of the Americas, New York, NY 10104
Telephone: 1-800-222-6747 Fax: 1-800-477-5925

To my mother, Regina. You are missed.

ACKNOWLEDGMENTS

His All Night was a lesson in humility for me, an outlet to put down on paper very real emotions. I feel so grateful for this journey. I'm blessed to have love and support from so many people.

I'd like to thank God, first. Without His Grace, I would not be here.

To my husband, Jason, you are my rock! Thank you for riding with me for 16+ years. I love you.

To my children, Asante, Kaia, and Masai; I love you with all my heart. It seems like yesterday I was changing diapers. Now, I'm getting ready for baseball games, driver's education, prom, and high school graduation. You are amazing, inquisitive, and hilarious. Thanks for keeping me on my toes.

To my father and my brother, thank you inspiring me through your lives. I wouldn't be me without you. I love you.

To my sisters, LaDonna and Kim, thanks for your unwavering support. Love you.

To my friend, Crystal, thanks for making yourself

available and just being you. You loved the book before I did, and I'm ever grateful. I'm glad to call you my friend.

I don't want to forget all of my friends, my critique partners, my beta readers. Thanks for everything, for dropping what you were doing to read a chapter, for calming my nerves, for being #TeamElle: Christine, Danielle, Kimberley, Sheree, Andrea, Shannon, Stacey, Nana, Danette, Lisa, Tasha, Autwan, Kristina, LaKeeta (you sure did let me vent multiple times), and Marleta. *His All Night* would not have happened without you all.

To all of my friends and family, I can't name you all. There are so many wonderful people in my life, people who've encouraged me to keep writing and keep dreaming. Love you all.

To my agent, Sara, thank you for your calming presence. I definitely had some moments with this book.

To my editor, Megha, thank you for EVERYTHING! You've inspired me to dig deeper and I can't thank you enough.

Thanks to all the many author friends that have been such a support to me; authors that have supported me, given good advice, written a blurb; you've all inspired me to keep going. I'm ever grateful.

I also want to thank the book clubs that have shown me love, especially Sharon Blount and BRAB (Building Relationships Around Books).

I hope you enjoy Calisa and Red's story! It's definitely a ride.

Thank you!

Love,
Elle

HIS
ALL NIGHT

CHAPTER ONE

This has got to be the worst date ever. Calisa Harper stabbed at her overdone pasta, twirling it around her spoon. For a minute, she felt guilty even thinking that. Joshua Clayborn was one of the most eligible bachelors in the Detroit area, with his dark skin, firm body, and long money. There were hordes of women waiting in the wings to get to him, but he'd picked her. Still, having dinner with him was akin to watching golf or, better yet, sticking a thousand needles in her eye. One word—no, make that three: boring as hell.

She glanced at her phone, torn between opening up her current game of Candy Crush and browsing through her e-mails. This couldn't be the life.

"Why are you so quiet?" Joshua asked, his dark eyes on her, assessing her.

Eyeing the door, she shrugged. "You seemed like you weren't done talking." She smiled at him. "About your house, your car, your job," she muttered under her breath, not even caring if he heard her.

He reached across the table, picked up her hand in his. Rolling her eyes, she forced herself to at least pay attention to the man. It wasn't every day she was treated to dinner by a hot millionaire. *Hot* was the only thing good about Mr. Clayborn, though. What was the use of having a good face but all the charm of dry paint? At least with paint, she could choose her own color.

"Calisa, you're so beautiful," he said.

She could agree with that, she thought with smile. Her black, low-cut, form-fitting dress left just enough for the imagination, stopping at the knee. Long layers fell down her back like ocean waves. Topping off her look with a pair of five-inch, red-bottomed pumps, she knew she looked good.

"Thank you, Josh. You look good, too."

"What do you want to do tonight?"

"Red." Her eyes widened, mortified that she'd actually said that out loud. Scrambling to cover up her mistake, she tried to think of anything *red*. Red rover, red robin, red... "Redeem my points at the casino," she lied, shifting in her seat.

He seemed to accept her answer because he ticked off the casinos in town and mentioned his preference. Nodding, she agreed to go to the MGM Grand. *Maybe I can lose him on the floor?*

The sound of boisterous laughter sounded in the restaurant, and her attention shifted to the bar. Her body stiffened at the sight of a group of men in business suits and the harem of women surrounding them. One in particular stood out, with his smooth golden skin, short wavy hair, and dimpled smile. He chose that moment to look up, locking eyes with her across the room and tipping his glass in her direction.

Knowing he would be in the city and actually seeing him were two different things, since the Detroit-Windsor area boasted a population of 5.7 million. Jared Williams was hard to miss, though. He had a way that drew her to him. Cool, calm, and collected with an irresistible swagger. No wonder

she wanted to do him. It seemed as if that was all she ever
wanted to do. Only they had strict rules; rules she tried to
never break.

Joshua went on and on about his contacts and his con-
tracts in the city and she...watched as "Red" charmed all
the women around him. She gulped down the rest of her
wine, bothered that the sight of him getting so much female
attention made her stomach burn. It was a feeling she'd been
getting used to, especially over the past year.

Jared and Cali had known each other for a long time.
After all, he was her best friend's twin brother. Sydney had
been more like a sister to her from the moment they laid
eyes on each other. Red came with the package, except that
the underlying attraction between them prevented her from
ever viewing him as a "brother." About five years ago, they'd
acted on that desire and entered into a *no-strings* type of
relationship. They had fun, then they had sex, then they went
home.

When Cali saw one woman slip her card to Red slyly, she
stood up abruptly, bumping into the table. "I'm sorry," she
said, interrupting Joshua mid-sentence. She rubbed her sore
knee. "I have to use the restroom." She dropped her napkin
on the table, grabbed her clutch, and limped off toward the
ladies' washroom.

Closing it behind her, she leaned back against the bathroom door. She did a quick glance under the stall doors
to see if she was alone. Once she was satisfied that no one
could hear her, she groaned out loud and let out a string of
curses. Exhaling, she turned to the mirror and pulled out her
compact.

She heard the click of the door latch behind her, but continued to touch up her make-up.

"How's your date?"

Whirling around, she nearly toppled over when she lost

her footing. Shocked, she rushed to the door and swung it open, peeking outside. She closed the door and turned to face a smirking Red. "What the hell are you doing?" she hissed. "This is the ladies' room."

He shrugged, his hazel eyes raking over her body. "I was just checking on you. You bolted from your table so fast, I thought something was wrong."

"How is it that, of all the places in the city, we end up at the same restaurant?"

"Coincidence," he told her. "Holiday party. The firm likes to go all out."

"Really? Red, it's not even December yet."

"They did it early this year," he explained, brushing a piece of hair behind her ear. "They're calling it a harvest party."

"Why didn't you tell me you were coming here?" She forced a frown onto her face even as her insides were melting at the smell of his cologne.

"Didn't think I had to. But since you're here, you could always join me." He traced the vee on her dress, sending shivers up her spine. "Why don't you get rid of the stiff and come up to my room?"

Tempted as she was, she wasn't going out like that. "No," she breathed, suddenly feeling very...hot. "I have a date."

Slowly, he edged closer to her. She retreated until the hard doorknob dug into her back. Reaching behind her, he flipped the lock on the door, the click echoing in the empty bathroom. Sucking in a deep breath, she waited, anticipating his next move.

His fingers flitted across the hem of her dress and he inched it up a bit. Kneeling down, he slipped his hands under her dress and slowly pulled down her underwear. She held her breath, wondered what he would do next.

"Step out of them," he ordered in a low, deep voice.

Bracing her hands on his shoulders, she stepped out of her lace panties. With a smirk, he stood up, tucked the thin material into the inside pocket of his suit jacket, and pulled out a tiny key card. He placed it in her hand and closed her fingers around it. "Room 1179," he murmured, his lips a mere inch away from hers. Closing her eyes, she took in the smell of cognac on his breath and leaned closer.

His soft laugh brought her mind back to their location and she opened her eyes. She opened her mouth to speak, but he placed a finger over her lips.

"Shh. Try not to think about what I'm going to do to you, while you're on your date." Swinging open the door, he walked out, whistling.

She hated him—in the best way.

* * *

Jared Williams flung his hotel room door open, surprised when Cali burst through it straight into his arms. He kicked the door closed as she kissed him deeply and passionately. As they backed up toward the bed, touching and kissing along the way, she undid his tie and slid it off. She flung it over her head and went to work unbuttoning his shirt. Grunting when the backs of his knees hit the frame of the bed, he felt for the hook to her dress. It had a line of tiny buttons going up the back, and he struggled to undo them with his big fingers. *To hell with it.* Frustrated, he gripped the end of it and pulled, sending buttons flying into the air.

"Fuck, Red," she grumbled, shoving him back. "You ruined my dress."

"Sorry," he said, but he wasn't. Wrapping an arm around her waist, he yanked her back to him.

Her head fell back as he nipped at her neck, pushing her dress down to the floor. Pausing, he stepped back to appreciate her. She was standing before him in a black push-up bra and a sexy-ass pair of *do-me* pumps—and nothing else. She was perfect. Her brown skin seemed to glow in the dim light and he hardened at the sight of her.

She tugged on the waistband of his pants and unzipped them, freeing his straining erection. "Step out of them," she said, with a wink and a smile.

Doing as he was told, he kicked the pants behind her and pulled her into another wet kiss. They fell back on the bed, her on top. She straddled his lap and eased herself down onto him. He closed his eyes, gritting his teeth. He wanted to make this last. They stayed like that a moment, staring at each other. Soon, she was moving those hips, grinding into him in a way that often made him forget his name. She was truly the best he'd ever had and he couldn't get enough of her. He wanted to possess her, claim her in a way he never had before, and make sure she knew that she'd never find another man that would mean as much to her as he did. Gripping her hips, he flipped her onto her back and pushed himself into her harder, enjoying her yelp of surprise.

He looked down at her, taking in her long, dark hair fanned out on the pillow, her lips between her teeth and her eyes on his, and slammed into her again. They moved, each of them matching the other, settling into a rhythm that seemed innate—like it was meant to be. She wrapped her arms around him and whispered, "Don't stop."

Hooking his arms under her knees, he thrust into her—deeper, harder each time until he felt her constricting around him. Knowing she was close, he slipped a finger between their bodies and pressed down on her clit. Her body stiffened, and she screamed out his name as her orgasm shook through her. Soon, he was right with her.

Arms and legs tangled together, they lay there panting, trying to catch their breaths. Lifting his head, he ran a finger across her cheek, smiling at the light sheen of sweat across her brow. Her hair, once flowing down her back, was wet with perspiration.

Being with her was the highlight of any day. The need to touch her, feel her against him had him making up excuses to end up where she was. Yet, ending up at the same hotel that night had been a happy coincidence. And he took full advantage of it. He brushed his lips over her shoulder and rolled off of her, onto his back.

She turned to him, propping herself up on her elbow. "You are so naughty," she whispered with a giggle. "You know I couldn't concentrate the rest of the night, right? Imagine Joshua's surprise when I ended our date before he had the chance to bore me with more details of his life."

He chuckled, turning to face her. Seeing her with another man had irritated him more than he ever thought it would. And the knowledge that she'd ended her date to be with him made him want to puff out his chest with pride. He slid a hand over her hip and squeezed her thigh. "Mission accomplished, then."

Red pulled her into the crook of his arms and kissed her brow. Moments like these were hard to come by with Cali. She was determined not to be *his* girl. But it was all he could think about. He wasn't sure when it had snuck up on him, but he wanted Cali to be more than his *no-strings* booty call. Hell, she was already one of his closest friends.

"Why don't you stay the night?" he asked softly. He already knew the answer, but he couldn't stop himself from asking.

"I can't." She brushed her lips against his chest. "I have an early meeting."

Although he wasn't surprised, it still stung. There was something irresistible about Calisa Harper and he wanted to take advantage of their time together. He wanted this night to stay. But she always put up the walls, always found a reason to pull back.

Leaning in, she kissed him and then scooted to the edge of the bed. She picked up her dress and held it up to him. "You are so going to reimburse me for this dress." He watched as she pulled it up and stuck her arms into the sleeves.

"I wish I could say I was sorry and mean it," he admitted.

"Ha-ha." She put on his shirt and buttoned it up. "I'm taking this home."

"Guess you can add it to your collection, huh?"

Over the course of their…relationship, Cali had managed to stockpile many of his clothes, always making up an excuse why he couldn't have something back. He supposed it was par for the course.

"You don't have to leave, you know," he told her. It was the same thing, different day. No matter how much fun they had with each other, she'd always leave him wanting more.

"You know the rules. No sleepovers." She walked over to him and kissed him again, holding his chin with her hand. "I'll call you later!" she shouted as she flung open the door and walked out of the room.

CHAPTER TWO

Two days later.

Cali slammed the bathroom door as she exited, and tightened the belt on her robe. Dread seemed to fill every cavity of her body as she paced the hallway. The solace of her normally quiet home was interrupted by her loud thoughts. She nibbled on her thumbnail, or what was left of it. Glancing at her watch, she hurried to the front room and pulled her iPad out of its case.

"This sucks," she grumbled to herself as she tried to figure out how to work her new tablet. "Ugh." She shook it, flipped it over, and pushed a few buttons. "That damn Red. I told him I didn't want this one. It's too complicated." Tempted to fling the damn thing across the room, she took a deep breath and tried again. When it finally powered on, she sighed with relief.

Calisa scanned the preloaded apps and tapped the Skype button. After she punched in the address, she dabbed her eyes with a Kleenex, angry at the tears threatening to fall. She could not be teary-eyed when she talked to her best friend. It was bad enough that she was crying in the first place, and over a guy, no less. And not just any guy. The one man that could ruin everything she wanted to accomplish, with his hazel eyes and perfect everything. *Ugh.*

Although Cali and Red had been sharing each other's beds for years, they had yet to set expectations for each other—and that was the way she liked it. She didn't want or need a relationship because she was perfectly content with her life the way it was—no complications, no demands, and no stupid lovesick declarations.

But after she'd left Red the other night, she couldn't get the look in his eyes out of her head. Something had changed in him—and her, if she was being honest. It was in his eyes, in the way he talked to her and the way he treated her. The sex felt more meaningful than it had in the past. It had been more than scratching an itch. That's why she'd left so quickly, even before room service arrived with the dessert she'd ordered. Red had a sweet tooth and she'd arranged for a huge piece of cheesecake, fresh fruit, and a bottle of wine to be delivered. The original plan had been to spend the evening getting it in with Red, enjoying his company. Instead, she'd paid the front desk for the dessert and left the hotel. She couldn't shake the feeling that things were going to change between them if she didn't put the brakes on it. After all, she couldn't afford to risk her heart and her livelihood, even for him.

Then there was the despair she felt even thinking about ending things with him. All in all, she was a walking contradiction.

Sydney finally appeared on the screen and Cali sighed, grateful to see one of her favorite people. "Syd! You're a sight for sore eyes. I miss you."

Syd tugged at her one-size-too-small shirt then burped. "Oops. Sorry. Bad indigestion, Cali. What's going on? Are you crying?" she asked, her hazel eyes fixed on Cali. Even though they were miles apart, Syd always knew when something was wrong. They had a sister soul-tie.

"Allergies," Cali lied. "How are you?"

"This baby is kicking my ass," Syd answered, shifting in her seat. "Literally. My butt actually hurts."

Cali smiled at her very pregnant friend. "You look so pretty, Syd." She was always beautiful, but she seemed to have a glow. Her light brown skin was flawless and her normally wavy hair was straightened and hanging down her back. "You don't have too much longer."

"Please," Syd said, waving her hand. "Two months is too long. And Morgan won't leave me alone. It's like this baby is a magnet. He's all over me."

"That's not a bad problem to have, babe."

"Yeah, I guess not, but my body is on fire. My ankles look like logs and I waddle. Can you believe that? Look at this." Syd tilted the screen and lifted up her leg to give Cali a look.

"Wow, they are huge." Calisa laughed when Syd frowned. "Maybe you should prop your feet up. What are you doing?"

"Packing," Syd said. "I have to make sure I have everything I need."

Wanting to prolong the inevitable, Cali told her friend, "Stand up and show me your belly."

Syd rolled her eyes. "Hell no! You'll see it tomorrow."

As happy as Cali was to connect with her best friend, her thoughts kept drifting back to her problem. She wiped her eyes again when Syd's attention turned to something else. She truly missed her friend. It had been months since Syd had packed her bags and moved to Baltimore with her boyfriend, Morgan. As a result, Cali was forced to try and form new friendships; and she was not that interested in breaking in someone else.

Syd folded up a shirt then focused her attention back on Cali. She narrowed her eyes. "You look pale. Are you sick?"

"Thanks, Syd," Cali said with a pout. "Way to make me feel pretty."

"You know you're a stone cold fox," Syd said. "By the way, I love those highlights."

Normally, she'd agree with that. Modesty wasn't her strong suit. "Thanks. I was a little nervous about going so light, but I like it."

"What's going on?" Syd asked, munching on a bag of garlic bread-flavored chips.

Cali guessed she probably did look a little unhinged. Looking down at her attire, she wondered what Syd would say if she saw her outfit. She was wearing brown pajama bottoms and a black t-shirt with white polka dots. Her hair was pulled back into a messy ponytail.

"Girl, let me see what you have on," her friend said, as if she'd read her mind. "Polka dots? And what's with your hair, girlfriend? Do we have to schedule a spa trip when I get back?"

"I'm taking a sick day." Cali absently tugged on her loose shirt. The migraine that had kept her up half the night was finally gone, but she still felt like crap. Probably because her headache was the least of her troubles. "Don't judge me."

Syd dipped a potato chip into a bowl of…

Tilting her head, she tried to make out to the contents of the bowl Syd was currently dipping her chips into. "Is that ice cream and chips? Yuck. Now, I see why you're waddling,"

"Don't hate," Syd scolded through a mouth full of nastiness. "This is some good stuff. It would taste even better if I had a cheesesteak hoagie with extra, extra cheese. I can't wait to get to Gabriel's when I get there."

Cali frowned. Just the thought of a hoagie was doing all kinds of weird things to her stomach. Which was part of the reason she'd called her friend in the first place. Any other time, she would have perked up at the prospect of eating the famous sandwiches. Gabriel's was a staple in Sydney's hometown of Ypsilanti, and it was one of the few places to eat that was worth the drive from her home in Troy, Michigan, about fifty miles away.

Cali bit down on her lip. "Syd?"

Syd bit into a pickle and moaned. "This is so good."

"Syd?" Cali's voice rose to pull her friend's attention away from the array of odd food pairings.

"What's up?" Syd wiped her hands with a napkin and focused her attention on the screen. "You seem troubled. And you're crying and lying about allergies. I'm a little concerned. You know I'll be there tomorrow, and you still wanted to Skype tonight. I wasn't going to say this, but you're kind of scaring me. Is everything okay?" Syd gasped, alarm growing in her hazel eyes. "Is it Red?"

Yep. "I'm not sure if everything is okay, but I can't talk to you about this when you get here because Red will be with us. And this is a girlfriend conversation."

Red had already made plans for his sister when she arrived the next day. It would be a full day, starting with lunch at Gabriel's, then shopping for the baby. He was excited to spend time with his "little" sister, and that's why Cali knew she'd never be able to get a moment alone with Syd. And she needed one.

Leaning back, Syd smoothed a hand over her growing belly. "Shoot, do I have to brace myself for this? Just spill it."

"Okay." She clutched the tablet and blurted out, "I made love to your brother."

Her friend arched a finely shaped brow at her. "Is that supposed to be a news flash?"

"Without a condom," Cali added, bracing herself for her bestie's reaction.

Syd gaped at her.

After a few nail-biting seconds of silence, Syd cleared her throat. Rolling her eyes, she said, "Do you think you're pregnant, Cali? Because if so, that would be so freakin' awesome!" She screamed in delight. "My baby would have someone to play with."

Cali glared at her friend, horrified that she was actually excited when she was so miserable. "I'm going to need you to dial it down a few notches. In whose world is that awesome?"

Syd covered her smile. "I guess we're not happy about this, huh?"

"Why would I be happy?" Cali shouted incredulously. "In case you've forgotten—although I don't know how you could—I don't have a man. So why would I be happy about a possible pregnancy?" The thought of being pregnant mortified her.

"But Red—"

"Is not my man," she repeated. "We're fuck buddies." Okay, so that was the lie of the century. She could classify their relationship as many things, but that wasn't one of them. Sighing, she continued. "Syd, I'm not pregnant. I had my diaphragm in. But we've never had sex without double protection."

She was tempted to take a test, though. Just to be sure. In fact, there was one sitting on her bathroom sink, but she'd decided not to waste it.

"But that's not the point," Cali continued. "Did you hear what I said?"

With a confused look on her face, Syd frowned. Shrugging, she asked, "Can you make it plain? Pregnancy brain. It's a real thing."

Cali bit her lip, hesitant to reveal the rest. But she needed to get it out. "I just told you I made love to your brother and you don't know what the problem is?"

Syd's eyes widened, realization dawning on her. "Made love? Without a condom? You lost control."

"Exactly. That's the problem," Cali said. She'd never actually had sex with anyone without protection, even though she always wore her own. It was actually something she prided herself on. There would be no accidental pregnancies unless Jesus made it so. "The lines are blurred. And your brother is going to ruin my life."

"So you've graduated from booty call to something more with Red. It was bound to happen, and it's not the end of the world."

"It is when I don't want it," Cali argued. "I like things the way they are. Every time I'm with him, he asks me to stay or he wants to stay. Everything in me is screaming to end this *thing* between us before it destroys our friendship."

"I thought I was the dramatic one," Syd muttered sarcastically. "Cali, you're overreacting. And you're running. If Red makes you happy, why not be with him?"

That was an easy question. The answer was much harder and one that Cali had been struggling with for months. "We want different things in life. Shit, I have goals; career goals."

Cali was an event manager at one of the largest hotel chains in the area. She'd also arranged events for many of the top politicians in the Detroit area and had recently been in talks with their other best friend, Allina, to combine their resources and open a niche store, specializing in wedding planning. Well, that was until Allina had up and left the state to follow a man. Even so, Cali was determined to step out and go into business for herself.

"Relationships complicate things. You should know that more than anybody. I don't want to give up what I want for anyone."

Syd pouted. "Why? I get the feeling that you think I'm selling out by being with Morgan and having this baby."

It wasn't that long ago that Syd had been in the precarious position of possibly being pregnant by her ex-fiancé's brother. Syd had spent years with Caden, until he'd cheated on her months before their wedding, leaving her heartbroken and devastated. Caden's brother Morgan had been there to pick up the pieces, and they eventually fell in love and took a chance on being together. Her poor friend had been through so much. Looking at Syd, though—beautiful and pregnant and happy—Cali knew that it was worth it in the end.

"Syd, no," Cali insisted. "I think you're incredibly brave to go after what you want. It's just not me. I know you'll be a great mother. You love kids. And I think you can have it all. I don't think it's in the cards for me. I have anxiety whenever I spend more than twenty minutes with the little rugrats. I don't want kids. I never did."

It wasn't because she didn't *like* kids. In fact, it was the opposite. But there was a huge difference between loving a niece and having a child of her own. Diapers and throw up was not what's up. Neither was being in a committed relationship, sharing a life with another person. It was a risk, a chance she didn't want to take. She'd already given her heart to a man who didn't deserve it and she'd vowed to never do it again. Red was supposed to be easy, but now he terrified her on so many levels. She found herself wanting to be with him, despite her fear of being hurt—or hurting him.

"Fine." Her friend gulped down a big glass of water. "So what are you going to do?"

"Things were fine until this hotel romp the other day. I was so intent to be with him, I left a date to meet him in his room. What the hell was that?"

"Okay, calm down." Syd popped a chip in her mouth. "It's going to be okay." She touched the screen. "This is me, holding your hand."

Cali closed her eyes, tears threatening to spill. "Thank

you. I had to tell someone. I know what I have to do, but the thought of doing it makes me feel sick to my stomach."

Syd burped, then giggled. "Sorry," she murmured. "When do you plan on talking to Red? If every instinct is telling you that your friendship will be ruined by continuing with your little arrangement, then it should be sooner than later."

"I don't know," Cali said, frowning at Syd. Her friend had tried to hide the smirk on her face by turning away and faking a cough. "Why are you smiling and I'm on the verge of tears?"

Syd wiped her face. "I can't help it, Cali. I think it's funny... and cute. You think I can have it all, but you can't. Why?"

"Because I'm not the settling down kind." Cali crossed her arms over her chest.

"You could be."

Rolling her eyes, Cali muttered a curse. "Stop trying to make this something it's not."

"No, I think it pretty much is," Syd said, her hazel eyes fixed on hers. "You want him. But you're not ready to admit it. That's fine. But I just worry that when you are, it'll be too late."

Cali couldn't say that Syd was wrong. In fact, she was pretty sure her friend was right. But *that* was a chance Cali was willing to take. It was better than the alternative. Jumping in headfirst and knocking herself out when it didn't work.

"I'm a little stressed," Cali said, preferring to sidestep the conversation about her true feelings. "I don't feel good."

"Okay, I know when you're changing the subject," Syd groaned, pulling her hair back into a ponytail. "It's not even like you to be this dramatic. That's *my* thing. You must really be scared."

"I'm terrified," Cali admitted, standing up and pacing the room. Tears pricked her eyes and she finally let them fall. Unable to stop crying, she grabbed a towel from the mound of folded ones sitting on her dresser and sobbed into the soft material.

"Cali, talk to me," Syd said, concern in her voice.

Gripping the edge of the dresser, she tried to get her breathing under control. "I do hear what you're saying. I've gone over all of the reasons to just give in and be with him, but our differences are not simple things to get over. I feel like I'm being overly dramatic but there are so many things running through my mind. Like the fact that Red wants kids and I don't. "

"That is definitely something to consider," Syd agreed. "I know my brother. He wants children. He wants the chance to be a father."

Syd was right. Red had a daughter that he'd yet to meet. The mother had vanished into thin air. He'd never seen his little girl and it tore him up inside. He'd been looking for her for months. He deserved to be a father and Cali knew he wanted it more than anything. It was a major hurdle to a potential committed relationship with him and more proof that long-term wasn't in the cards for them. They should never be more than friends with benefits.

"Syd, I need to stop sleeping with your brother." She plopped down on her bed and picked up the tablet so she could see her friend. "We're fundamentally different people. It makes no sense to continue down this road with him."

"As much as I hate to admit it, you have a point." Syd grimaced as if she were in pain and let out a long sigh. "And a decision to make."

"Are you okay? You look like you're in pain."

"I told you my butt hurts," Syd said simply.

Cali laughed out loud and it felt good. "I love you, and

I can't wait to see you tomorrow. Too bad you can't have a glass or two...or three with me."

"I hear wine is good for babies," Syd said, giggling.

"You will not have Morgan trying to slay me for giving you any alcohol."

Morgan Smith was head over heels in love with her best friend and willing to fight the world on her behalf. He wouldn't think twice about cursing Cali out if she gave Syd anything that could potentially harm her pregnancy.

"He won't be there. I can have a little sip," she insisted.

"Nope, but you can certainly watch me."

They burst out laughing together. After a few minutes of small talk, Cali disconnected and tossed the tablet on the bed. She shuffled to the bathroom to check her face in the mirror. At the sight of all the snotty tissues on the sink, she picked up the small trashcan and swept the tattered pieces into the bag. She pulled the bag out and tied it before she opened the bathroom door.

"What have you been doing in there?"

Calisa let out a yelp. "Red! You scared me." Gripping the bag tightly, she prayed he wouldn't ask any more questions.

He gestured to the bag. "What's in the bag?"

"Nothing," she said. "I was emptying the bathroom trash."

"Since when?" He cocked that left eyebrow up, signaling he was skeptical. "You always ask me to do it. What's up?"

"I told you. Nothing."

"You've been crying," he said, tilting his head.

Damn. "Red, stop badgering me. I'm not being cross-examined here."

"Fine. Is your headache gone? Were you able to get some sleep finally?" He peeked in the bathroom.

Cali nodded. "Headache is gone, but I haven't had any rest. I'm glad I stayed home from work, though."

He stepped inside and picked up the home pregnancy test sitting on the bathroom sink. "Why is this out?" He turned to her.

She waved him off. "No reason."

His eyes were fixed on her. "Do you think you're pregnant?" Red asked, his voice low but stern. She'd seen him in action in the courtroom. He was giving her his *work* voice.

"Boy, please. No." He seemed to accept her answer because he put the box down.

She watched as he bent down to pick up a piece of tissue she must have dropped. She couldn't help but admire him. Not only was he extremely intelligent, he was fine as hell. His tall frame, sculpted body, and jewel-toned eyes always made her heart skip a beat. Which was why she wanted to put off the inevitable conversation that would end their fling.

"I guess that's good," he finally said, folding his arms across his chest. "Would you tell me if you were pregnant?"

She wasn't sure why he'd even ask her that question. They'd never had a problem talking about anything before, even uncomfortable subjects. But his tone and the way he was looking at her gave her pause.

Gripping the plastic bag in her hand tightly, she asked, "Honestly?"

"Of course," he said, shrugging.

"No."

CHAPTER THREE

$\mathcal{N}$o?" Red repeated, still unable to believe his ears. He didn't know why he'd even asked her the question. He knew where she stood regarding children, but her answer still surprised the hell out of him. "Are you serious?"

Calisa fidgeted under his glare. "I know you don't understand this, but no. I probably wouldn't tell you."

Red was a damn good litigator and a professional negotiator. He'd successfully represented corporations and won multi-million dollar lawsuits. But, right then, standing there looking at the beautiful, brown-skinned woman who seemed to always keep him on his toes...he was speechless.

Of course, he knew that they had an informal arrangement between them. No expectations. No love. But never in a million years would he have imagined that she would be standing before him admitting that if she was pregnant with his child, she wouldn't tell him—especially since she knew about everything he'd been going through. And considering they were friends.

"Red?"

The sound of her voice snapped him out of his thoughts. Anger came next and he embraced it. "I guess I'm surprised." He drew in a steady, slow breath. "You're well aware of everything I'm going through trying to find my daughter, but you'd keep a pregnancy from me."

Not too long ago, a woman from his past had shown up on his doorstep to let him know that he'd fathered her six-year-old daughter. It wasn't the best news he'd ever received, but after the initial shock he'd agreed to a DNA test. Once the results were back he knew he was the father, but she was gone. Red had exhausted every lead, looked under every rock to find his little girl, to no avail. He'd been beside himself trying to find them because he couldn't conceive of having a child in the world and not knowing her.

He'd just come from a meeting with the private investigator he'd hired and was discouraged by the lack of information about his baby girl. His mood had gone from bad to worse earlier, when the PI had told him that it was possible they'd never find his little girl, Corrine. The conversation with Cali wasn't making it better.

Maybe it was unreasonable to be so irritated about a hypothetical scenario. It was obvious by the unopened box that Cali hadn't believed she was pregnant with his baby. But her cavalier attitude was getting to him more than anything, making his blood boil hotter by the minute. Sure, he knew her stance on children, but he'd thought they were better than that. He thought he deserved more from her.

"Red, I know what you've gone through to find Corrine. Believe me, I can see that it's taken a toll on you." She walked away from him, toward the living room.

"So why would you keep a pregnancy from me?" he asked, following her.

"It's not the same thing." She stopped and slowly turned to face him. "Being pregnant with your baby is not the same as me *having* your baby and disappearing without giving you a chance to know it. You know that." Turning on her heel, she headed toward the kitchen.

"I thought I knew you." Red grabbed her arm. "Stop walking away from me." He spun her around to face him.

"I said *I* wouldn't tell you," she said, her voice thick with... tears?

Hurt. He'd hurt her and the guilt threatened to replace the anger that was fueling him. Almost. Calisa wasn't the type to show vulnerability. And Red was an asshole on a good day. It worked for them because she wasn't the cry-at-the-drop-of-a-dime woman that he avoided at all costs. She could give as good as she got.

"That doesn't mean you wouldn't know," she continued. She took a deep breath. "Your sister is my best friend."

"Syd?" Red balled his hands into fists. He tried to reason with himself to let this go, but he couldn't help but take his sour mood out on her. He was frustrated with life, with her, with... everything. "You would tell my sister and not me. How the hell should I feel about that?"

"I guess this is the moment that I tell you that I don't give a damn how you feel. You asked me, and I told you." Cali seemed to suck up all the emotion that had bubbled to the surface a few moments earlier, which helped Red because he could continue to nurse his own anger. "Besides, why are we even talking about this? It's not even a possibility. Obviously, you're trying to pick a fight with me. I have no idea why, but you're getting on my nerves."

Red rolled his neck to relieve the tension that set into his shoulders. The silence seemed to stretch on. "I thought we were better than this." The fact that they weren't frustrated the hell out of him.

"Apparently not."

"What's wrong with you?" he roared, gripping her wrist. She yanked herself free and backed away. "Nothing."

"I'm not sure why you don't get how fucked it would've been if you were pregnant and didn't tell me."

"I'm not pregnant! I'm glad, too!" she yelled. "It would have saved me from the unfortunate position of telling you that I don't want your baby."

Once again she'd rendered him speechless, and it irritated him to no end. But he was also extremely attracted to her when she was angry. Torn between storming out and pinning her against the wall, he glared at her. The anger he'd felt earlier turned inward. Had he turned into *that* guy? He wondered why he could even look at her and feel the overwhelming attraction that he did. *Because I'm a punk?*

He stepped closer to her and she actually had the nerve to retreat until her back was pressed against the wall. Before he could say anything, she shoved the trash bag she'd had in her hands at his chest.

"Back up," she ordered. "The last time I checked, I'm not one of your little groupies so don't talk to me like you're crazy. Not that it matters, but being pregnant with your baby would have been a nightmare and I can't think of anything worse."

Grimacing, he told her, "Wow. Thanks for making me feel so good about my place in your life."

Two days earlier, they had made love in his hotel room. And he'd asked her to spend the night—again. She'd turned him down, left him there. He'd been upset until room service had arrived with dessert. It was then that he'd realized that she'd planned on staying, but something had happened to make her leave. He'd assumed it was a reflex, an urge to run that made her bolt out of his room that night. That small gesture on her part renewed his efforts to win her. But this? Now he was forced to consider that things might never progress between them.

She shook her head. "You know me better than anyone, Red. Even Syd. We're friends and we've always been honest with each other. Why should that change?"

Over the years, their friendship had transcended into

something that mattered to him. She'd become one of the most important people in his life.

"The fact is, I don't want kids," she added. "I never did. If you're expecting that to change, then we have a problem. I'm not Syd. I don't want the picket fence and the two-point-five kids playing in the back yard. That has never been me. I'm not sure what's really going on, but I sense that this argument is about something other than a hypothetical question about a baby that will never happen."

Sighing, she grabbed his hand and pulled him toward her sofa. She took a seat, tucking her legs underneath her. Patting the seat next to her, she turned to him once he sat down.

"From the beginning, we've always told each other the truth. When we started this, we wanted the same thing—no strings, no expectations, no commitment, no falling in love. Somewhere along the line, this has morphed into something else."

He opened his mouth to speak, but she placed her hand over it.

"Please, let me finish," she said. "And don't get me wrong, I'm not complaining. I enjoy spending time with you. I thought I made that very clear. But my goals, my ambition, my desires haven't changed. You found out you were a father. That changed you."

"Of course it did." How could it not? Finding out that he was someone's daddy forced him to view life in a new way. "I never thought it would, but it did," he confessed.

"It should. It really should, Red. Honestly, if it didn't, I'd be worried," she said. "Being a parent is life changing."

"You act like I had a say in that."

She shrugged. "I know you didn't, but it's a reality. Unfortunately, it's one that will break us," she added with a sad smile. "I'm starting to come into my own. I'm doing Cali right now. Being a mother isn't part of that."

The truth was cold and cut like a knife sometimes. He

swallowed hard. "You say you don't like kids, but I see how excited you are about being a godmother to Syd's baby."

"That's because it's Syd's baby, Red. I don't have to teach the baby anything. More importantly, I don't have to disappoint the child when I fall short. I'm a mess—too messed up to raise a child. "

"You'd be a good mother," he said, his voice gruff.

She froze. "Yeah I don't know about that," she grumbled, dropping her gaze. "I like living alone. I enjoy time to myself. You tell me all the time that I'm selfish and I don't like to share. That's true. What part of that would make me a good mother?"

He focused on the way her thumb absently brushed the lengths of his fingers. Cali was definitely not kid-friendly, which he'd been happy with when they'd first started seeing each other. She was the best of both worlds. Sexy, sassy, and determined. She wasn't likely to fake a pregnancy to keep him and she damn sure wasn't the type to give ultimatums that would have him running for the hills.

"I'm perfectly fine with the way I am," she said, squeezing his hand. "It's why I always have a back-up plan for protection. I don't want to take any chances with an unwanted pregnancy. But you? You'd be an awesome father. If that's what you want, I wish you the best. I'd hope we could remain friends because you're one of my closest friends. You're a keeper."

The unshed tears in her eyes told him she was sincere. Yet, as much as he knew it was right to end things while they were still friends, he couldn't bring himself to agree to it.

"It would be that easy for you?" He cleared his throat. "You'd be able to let me go have babies with some other woman?"

"I didn't say it would be easy," she murmured, slumping forward. "Don't put words into my mouth. It would be nice to live in this bubble with you, to have you with me when I wanted, to continue what we have going on for the foreseeable future. But I care about you enough to know that this won't end well if we start with the expectations, the promises that neither one of us can keep." She wrinkled her brow and bit her lip. "Honestly, it worries me because I think that one day you'll want more than I can give you."

I already do. "Are you saying you're ready to invoke that easy-out clause?"

Cali took a deep breath. "I'd love to tell your ass to get out, but no. It probably would be wise to terminate our agreement, stop seeing each other now, and take a step back. I'm not quite there yet, but if you are, all you need to do is say it. I don't want to keep you from living the life that you want. You don't owe me anything. That's what makes it fair."

The fact that she'd actually admitted that she wanted to keep seeing him was a step in the right direction. "I guess it would be good to break things off with no pressure, no need to get a restraining order...no stab wounds," he said, chuckling at the memory of a few less-than-ideal breakups he'd had.

She giggled and his heart seemed to open up a little more. Her smile was one for the record books with her deep dimples, but her laugh was like a song.

"You're crazy," she said, nudging his shoulder with hers. She picked up a cough drop that was on the table and popped it into her mouth. "I guess we've both had some crazy exes, huh?"

"Tell me about it," he agreed.

"Is that what you want to do?" she asked, her voice low, uncertain. "Are you ready to end this?"

The only sound in the room was the low hum of her ceiling fan. The logical, sane part of him wanted to end it right then, walk away and wish her luck. But the stupid, insane part wanted to continue the ride, as dangerous as it was. Red wasn't naïve at all. He was crazy about *his* Cali. And he wasn't ready to give her up yet.

He brought her hand up to his lips and kissed her palm

softly. "No," he told her. When she exhaled, he realized she'd been just as invested in his answer as he'd hoped she was. "I'm sorry about starting that fight. I've had a rough day. I'm just . . . going through the motions and you were the easy target. Part of me is wondering if I'll ever find Corrine."

Knowing someone had made decisions for him that would affect him forever made him lose sleep. Then to come and see Cali and find out that she wouldn't tell him if she was pregnant either . . . His daughter was out there somewhere, with a mother that was as crazy as she was beautiful.

Red ran a finger down Cali's cheek. He'd been so angry, he'd forgotten the real reason for his visit. Looking at her then—clad in his pajama bottoms and a messed-up ponytail, a balled up piece of tissue stuffed in the pocket of her robe—reminded him. He placed the back of his hand against her forehead, then her neck. She leaned into his hand and he wanted to invite her into his lap so he could hold her.

They'd promised no commitment, and he accepted that. But he'd realized a long time ago that his life was better with her in it. She was right; she'd never changed. Before Corrine, he'd felt theirs was supposed to be a match made in heaven. The perfect merger. Until it wasn't. He knew that she hadn't wanted to hurt him. After all, she couldn't help that he'd turned into a sappy punk.

"Glad your headache is gone," he said.

She held his hand against her face. "Me too. I still feel a little congested, as usual." Cali's migraines always came with sinus-like symptoms and cravings. They hit her often. Most of the time she could work through them, but there were other times where she was no good to anyone. During her worst headaches, she'd retreat to a dark room for hours.

"I like you in my clothes." He let his gaze wander over her short frame. Even with her puffy, swollen eyes, red nose, and the smell of Vicks VapoRub on her skin, he couldn't help his body's natural reaction to her. Seeing her in his pajama pants did something to him. All of his anger seemed to melt away and the urge to take care of her hit him like a bag of bricks.

"I know. I like them, too. That's why you'll never get them back," she teased.

He leaned in closer, their lips almost touching. He could smell the cough drop on her breath. He wanted to kiss her, wanted to feel her lips on his.

She pulled back and sneezed, covering her nose and mouth. "I'm sorry, Red," she whispered.

"It's okay," he said with a frown. He grabbed a bunch of Kleenex off the table and handed some to her. "I probably shouldn't have tried to kiss you."

She laughed—a light, airy sound—and he couldn't help but join her.

She twined her fingers with his. "I'm sorry."

"Don't apologize. It's me. Like I told you, today was pretty messed up. I heard from the PI. We thought we had a lead, which turned out to be nothing. And now I'm wondering, when should I call this quits?"

"Never," she said simply. "You never call it quits until you find her. I'm surprised you're even considering it. That's not like you. You will fight to the death for what you want. That's what makes you Red."

"Come here," he said, opening his arms and letting her climb into his lap. He brushed his lips against her forehead and she snuggled into him. "I brought you soup from your favorite deli and ginger ale."

She glanced up at him. "Vernors?"

"With a side of vanilla ice cream," he added. When she graced him with her beautiful smile, he knew he'd made her day.

"I love Vernors' floats. You are so good to me."

"I am pretty good," he agreed. "You could do a lot worse."

"Red?"

"Yeah?"

"Can you take me to bed?" she croaked.

Is this a trick question? He frowned. "You mean, tuck you in bed with a heating pad and an electric blanket? Or take you to *bed*?"

She brushed her full lips against his neck and tugged at his earlobe with her teeth. "You can tuck me in, but I'd like you under the electric blanket with me."

Chuckling, he whispered in her ear, "Is this your way of asking me to spend the night?"

She leaned back to meet his gaze. "Hell, no."

He barked out a laugh and she followed suit.

"Oh, I get it." He stood up with her in his arms. "You want me to take care of you and then bounce, huh?"

"You know the rules. No sleepovers."

Red wondered when he'd turned into the guy *trying* to stay over. Over the last few months, he'd been in the unlikely position of arguing the benefits of spending the night. And Cali had never budged. She was content with their arrangement and stubborn as the day was long, and he wouldn't have it any other way.

After she was finally tucked in with her float in hand, propped up on a mound of pillows, he gazed down at her. As tempted as he was, he couldn't hop into bed with her.

"You're leaving?" she asked.

"I have work to do. Besides, I like you, but I don't like you that much to be getting my ass out of bed and going back into this cold weather in the middle of the night. Good night." He kissed her forehead. That urge to take care of her reared its head, but it was pointless. She may have let him buy her a float and tuck her in, but she would never let him take care of her fully. And despite the fact that he wasn't ready to end things with her that night, he knew it would be time soon. "Call me if you need anything."

*C*HAPTER FOUR

*C*alisa had never been so happy to see the morning in her life. She woke up feeling ten times better and ready to catch up on lost time. When she stepped outside for the first time in days, she was met with frigid, below-zero temperatures. *Ugh*. Buttoning her coat and pulling her hat down over her ears, she rushed to her car.

Michigan winters were pretty unpredictable, but this one had been colder than usual, and no doubt had contributed to her headache. She hoped Sydney's flight wasn't delayed because they were expecting a huge snowstorm in the next few hours. She prayed it would hold off until her friend landed safely.

Red had called early and she'd insisted on driving to his place to pick him up. On the way to his house, she'd stopped at his favorite café and picked up a cup of coffee and a muffin for him. As she parked in front of his place, she thought back on the short conversation they'd had earlier. He'd sounded a little irritated with her on the phone and she hoped it wasn't because he was still salty over their tense conversation the night before. After all, he had a right to be upset.

In hindsight, she realized she could have handled the situation differently. She'd hurt him, which was the last thing she wanted to do. Maybe he thought she didn't want him? That was definitely not true.

For a minute, she'd thought he was going to break things off, but she was so glad he didn't. They probably should end things, but she would keep her mouth shut for a little while longer and enjoy being with him.

Calisa knocked on the door softly, shivering as she waited. He lived in downtown Ann Arbor, close to the University of Michigan campus. She loved the area because there was plenty to do and he lived only a few short blocks from Restaurant Row. Then there was the Art Fair in the summer; and the famous "Big House" U of M football stadium was right down the street. As alumni, they all had season tickets and loved to tailgate.

Red opened the door, his shirt open and his pants unbuttoned. He stepped back, allowing her to enter.

"I'm not ready yet," he said, taking the bag and the coffee away from her. "I had to take a call earlier."

Pulling her gloves off, she tossed them on the table next to the door. "No problem. I'm early."

"Thanks for the coffee." He took a sip from the paper cup.

"I bought you a muffin, too." She leaned against the door. The condo was a four-floor brownstone, in a community filled with beautifully landscaped courtyards and a nearby park. She and Syd had decorated his place when he moved in, choosing neutral grays and browns to complement the hardwood floors, granite countertops, and stainless steel appliances. She scanned the room, noting that it was immaculate as usual. Never even a pillow out of place.

He arched a brow. "You can come in further, you know? Or is that breaking the rules?"

Rolling her eyes, she followed him up the stairs to the

master bedroom. "Ha-ha. I wasn't sure you wanted me in your house. You were kind of short on the phone."

He paused, leaving his shirt half buttoned.

She approached him, closed her eyes to savor his smell. "Red, I don't want things to be awkward between us. If you are feeling some kind of way...or something, I'd like you to be honest with me."

Turning around, he squeezed her shoulders and brushed his lips over her brow. "I'm fine, Cali. Just a little preoccupied with work. We need to stop by Morgan's before we head to the airport. Syd's stuff was shipped ahead and I want to drop it off."

Cali was excited to have her friend back. Syd had decided to come home to have the baby. Morgan would follow eventually, but she wanted to be close to her family and friends. Red pulled a pair of socks out of his drawer while Cali took the opportunity to admire the perfect fit of his clothes. As he brushed his wavy hair and sprayed on his cologne, she wondered why he'd lied to her about being fine. She'd been around him enough to know when he was lying.

Deciding not to press him, she took a seat on the edge of the bed. "I'm excited for Syd to be back in town. I have all kinds of plans. We have to shop for baby stuff—and mommy stuff. I'm planning the baby shower to end all baby showers."

"That's right up her alley," he said, folding his collar. He glanced at her and her stomach did what she called the "Red flip." "You feeling better?"

She nodded. "Much. Why do I get the feeling that you're holding something back from me?"

"Really?" he asked, cocking a brow. "Why would you say that?"

"You were pretty stank this morning," she said. "And you have every right to be that way. I pretty much suck. But you knew that about me from the beginning. So I got to thinking…maybe you think I don't want to be with you and that's why you hightailed it out of my house last night."

Red stared at her. Right through her, actually. He stepped closer to her—so close she could feel his breath on her forehead. He placed a finger under her chin and tilted it up so their eyes could meet. "Who do you think I am?" His smooth voice was like warm coffee first thing in the morning. It seemed to open her up in all the right places, fill her with warmth.

She swallowed. "You're Red," she whispered. *Damn*. She hadn't meant for her words to come out sounding like she was a shy schoolgirl.

"Damn right. How long have we known each other?"

"A long time." Cali and Syd had been roommates their freshman year in college. They'd been in each other's lives for over ten years.

"You think I don't know you want me, Cali?" he asked.

Red pulled her hat off and dropped it on the bed. As if her body had its own mind, she leaned in so that they were touching.

"I watch you," he continued, his voice low and husky. Her heart seemed to beat uncontrollably and she felt her pulse in her throat. "I see how you respond to me. As angry as you get, you can't help the way your eyes glaze over and close when I smile at you or step closer." He traced an invisible line from her chin, down her neck, and then pushed her coat off. "Or the way you suck in a deep breath when I touch you, almost in anticipation. The way you lean in when I say your name." He bent down and brushed his lips against hers. "Or your soft, breathless moans when I kiss you."

One thing was for certain: Red was a cocky son of a bitch. And Cali couldn't get enough of him. She found herself wishing that he wanted to take it further. Hoping that he'd continue to take her clothes off and…

He smirked and she held her breath. Normally, she wouldn't have thought twice about making the next move.

Deciding to wait him out, she held back and prayed he'd get to his point soon—preferably before she melted from the heat that seemed to overtake her treacherous body.

They didn't move for what seemed like an eternity.

"I'm not some poor, hopeless punk in love with a woman who doesn't love me back." Red stepped back, putting distance between them. A distance that seemed to grow even as they were standing there. "Love has nothing to do with this. You want to know what's wrong with me?"

Jarred by his sudden change in demeanor, the hardness in his voice, she took a few deep breaths in an effort to get her brain to catch up. Clearing her throat, she walked to the other side of the bedroom. "Okay. What's wrong with you?"

"I don't have time to be sneaking out of your house in the middle of the night for appearances. I don't care who sees us together. I don't owe any explanations for my behavior or whatever this is we're doing. I'm too old to even be having this conversation. If I wanted to play games, I'd go get me a real girlfriend."

Ouch.

"I've been doing some thinking myself," he continued. "Mostly on that long drive home from your place last night. You want me to have all the duties of a boyfriend but none of the perks, and I don't appreciate it."

Calisa and Red had what she liked to call a "fireworks" relationship. The spark was definitely there. Like all different types of fireworks, they burned hot and exploded with lots of light and tons of excitement. But like all firecrackers, the spark never lasted long or sometimes didn't work at all; and the sound could definitely get on a nerve at the wrong time. Staring at him, she thought this was one of those times. The spark just wasn't working. It was a dud.

"Cali?!" he shouted, bringing her attention back to him. "Did you hear what I said?"

"I did," she said, shaking her mind clear of her firework analogy. She hoped he hadn't snuck something in before she zoned out. "And I can honestly say I don't know what the hell you're talking about. What do you mean, you have all the duties of a boyfriend and none of the perks?"

"You didn't hear me," he said, his voice flat. From the look on his face, he was obviously not amused.

Shit. "I did hear you," she lied.

"You call me over to your house when you want me to fix your computer, unclog a drain, take out your trash, or mop the floor, whatever," he explained. "I drove fifty miles to check on you yesterday because I knew you were sick. I did that to help you. What did you do? You asked me to jump in bed, but I couldn't spend the night. How ridiculous is that?" He threw his hands in the air in frustration. "Are we two adults who entered into a relationship of sorts, with full disclosure?"

"Yes, but—"

"If you want to be with me, then we're going to have to revisit this 'no sleepover' clause," he demanded. "It's stupid to me."

Normally, Cali would dig in her heels until he agreed that her way was best. But she had a feeling that what was bothering Red had nothing to do with an overnight visit. "That's not what you're mad about. You know that you're full of shit, right?"

"Don't tell me what I'm mad about," he barked. "You do realize that I'm a grown-ass man? You don't control me and you damn sure don't know what the hell I'm feeling. Even if you did, you wouldn't actually care about how I feel because you do what you want to do always."

"Hell yeah, I do," she said, matter-of-factly. "I do what I want. That's the whole point of growing up and getting my own shit. I don't want to be accountable to anyone else but

Cali." She scrubbed a hand over her face, hating that she'd flown off the handle like that. *This isn't helping, Cali*.

"Exactly," he said. "You don't give a damn so don't try to act like it now. And that's cool."

She was getting whiplash from Red's moods. "Is this about that whole baby thing?"

"You don't get it."

I give up. She rubbed her temples with her fingers and groaned out loud. "Red, what is really going on here?"

"We've been friends for a long time, and I think you take it for granted that I'm going to accept what you give me. I'm not asking you to run off and marry me. But I need you or anyone else I mess with to respect me."

"I do respect you, Red." She let out a shaky breath. "How can you even say I don't?"

"You're missing the point," he said, stalking across the room to his dresser then back. "I'm not sure you ever will."

Cali really was confused. Deciding it had to be that, she went with it. "You're ready to skewer me over hot coals for some reason. I feel like I'm behind the veil here because I'm not sure why. It's like I can't win with you."

"Once again, you don't get it," he repeated.

"Well, goddamn it, tell me what the hell is going on!" she shouted.

Being friends for so long, arguments were bound to happen. Both of them were opinionated, passionate people who loved the last word in any confrontation. Yet, even in the midst of a disagreement, they could always have fun with each other. One of the things she loved about Red was he was hilarious. He made her laugh. They cracked each other up. They didn't need anything to have a good time with each other. Most nights together consisted of a movie, a beer, and good food.

Over the last six months, though, things had become so

tense. She guessed it had something to do with their feelings for each other. It was hard being in a no-strings relationship with your best friend. But maybe it was time to get back to the basics?

"Better yet, don't," she announced, throwing her hands up in the air. "You don't owe me shit. That's the benefit of a no-strings relationship. If this is too complicated, or…I don't know. I do agree with you, though. I don't get it. But I am sorry that it's come to this."

"Don't apologize. We always promised to tell the truth, right?" She cringed at the sarcasm dripping from his words.

"Exactly," she snapped, folding her arms across her chest. Frustrated, she wrung her hands together and took a few deep breaths in an attempt to calm her frayed nerves. Tears welled up inside and threatened to spill out. *What the hell is up with these tears?* Since when did she break down crying at the drop of a hat?

He rubbed the back of his neck and let out a heavy sigh. "Can I ask you a question?" he asked finally.

She peered up at him, brought a shaking hand up to her forehead. "What?"

"We've been friends for a long-ass time. I thought we could talk about anything. But you've never told me why you don't want kids."

She stared at him, eyes wide. "What? Why do I have to tell you that?"

"I've shared with you things I've never told another living soul," he said. "And I feel like I barely know you sometimes. So how about you tell your 'friend' and not your 'friend-with-benefits'? Does that make it better for you to talk to me?"

She rolled her eyes and the tears finally escaped. Swiping her hands roughly across her cheeks, she grumbled, "Let it go, Red. Just stop."

Talking about her reasons never seemed like a viable

option for her. She didn't like to think about her childhood and everything she went through with her mother, let alone tell someone about her experiences. But as much as she hated to admit it, Red had a point. He did deserve more from her.

"Look, my mother sucked," she said finally. "I'm not making an excuse, but I didn't have a happy home. She didn't cook dinner and help me with homework. I didn't even have the luxury of your mother, with all her damn flaws." Her shoulders dropped, and she regretted the words as soon as they left her mouth. It was common knowledge that Syd didn't get along with their mother. The woman had always seemed to hate her and treated her accordingly. Red had never talked about it with Cali, but Syd had told her plenty for her to form her own opinion.

"When I saw my mother, she was high or talking to the voices in the walls," she continued. Unable to look at him, she turned around. "I could count on my hand the times that my mother told me she loved me. I had to look forward to days without seeing her and wondering if she was dead in an alley somewhere. Then, one day, she told me she was all better. She took me on a road trip and I was so happy. She was awesome. The bottom fell out soon after, and she left me. But not before she told me she didn't want me; that I was the mistake that destroyed her life. I never saw her again. I was alone—in a hotel room—for days. Finally, a hotel employee called the police and Uncle Cal came to get me. I'm so grateful to him. If it hadn't been for him, I don't . . ."

Cali almost choked on that memory. The smell of the hotel room and the desperate hunger and loneliness seemed always just beneath the surface. She hated it. Just like she hated her mother for putting her through everything she'd been through.

Actually, "grateful" was an understatement when she thought about her uncle. What do you call a man who had no

experience raising a child and took in his sister's scared kid
with no hesitation? Uncle Cal had always been in her life,
but he'd stepped up in a huge way when her mother disappeared, becoming the parent that she'd wished she'd had all
along. He took care of her, invested in her, and had her back
through everything. He continued to do so, even from his
home in Atlanta.

The emotional abuse she'd suffered at the hands of her
mother stayed with her, even with Uncle Cal's unwavering
and unconditional love. The damage had already been done.
As a teenager, she didn't have friends and she didn't date.
She'd made it a point not to let anyone else get close enough
to hurt her again—until Syd breezed into her life and opened
her eyes to true friendship. And with her she'd brought Red.
Slowly, Cali was able to open up and found that she could
love and be loved.

Syd was a hopeless romantic so they'd often talked about
finding their *one*. She'd tricked herself into believing that
there was a man out there that was perfect for her. After
countless duds, she thought she'd found him.

Opening her heart had its downsides, though. The first man
she'd thought she loved—as wonderful and charming and gen-
erous as he was—had lied to her every day of their relationship.
James had told her she was his one and only, but it turned out
he'd been married with kids the entire time they were together.
It nearly destroyed her and ruined her life. How could she trust
her instincts with men after that? After him, she'd sworn off
love and relationships. They weren't safe for her.

Hard as she tried to *not* be like her mother, she started to
notice little things, traits that reminded her of· "Momma,"
including her horrible taste in men. With every new relationship gone wrong, every new "uncle" who passed through
their doorway, her mother had seemed to get worse. Cali
couldn't take the chance of that happening to her.

Then Red passed the bar and she'd offered to cook him dinner to celebrate. She remembered the night like it was yesterday. A horror movie, a bowl of French vanilla ice cream, and a bet led to their first kiss.

With one kiss, Red had unleashed something in her that she'd never been able to shake. She found herself yearning for him when he wasn't there, needing him. Eventually, she let it propel her into his arms. He didn't press her to give him more than she wanted and that was the best part for her. *Until now.*

Everything was a jumbled mess. The last thing she wanted to do was talk about her mother, but he'd pressed her. Her stomach rolled and her pulse quickened. Closing her eyes, she took a deep breath and whirled around to face Red. "My mother was selfish and only concerned about herself. And you know what? I'm not trying to fuck up a kid the way my mother fucked me up. I thought you understood that. If you don't, get the fuck out of my life."

When he didn't move, didn't protest, she deflated. Letting out a tortured sob, she ran out of his bedroom. The faster she moved, the more pathetic she felt. *Did I really lay it all out there for him?* He quickly caught up to her and pulled her to him, wrapping his arms around her.

She struggled against him. "Let me go, Red."

"I won't," Red whispered against her ear. "You don't have to run out of here like this."

She jerked out of his hold. "Don't you get it? That's not what *this* is supposed to be about. You're my friend, but we're not supposed to be heavy or complicated. I need that from you. I can't…If you don't want me anymore, feel free to say it. But if you do want me, then take off your fuckin' pants and do me."

*C*HAPTER FIVE

*R*ed wondered what the appropriate emotional response would be to Calisa's ultimatum. She was nothing if not direct and she'd certainly laid it out for him to take it or leave it. Could he take it? The answer was...no.

When she'd arrived earlier, as irritated as he was with her he was happy to see her up and running. As free-spirited and busy as she was on any given day, seeing her sick didn't feel right.

Red contemplated her words. He hadn't expected this latest revelation. She kept a lot of her past under wraps, choosing to only share her deepest thoughts with Syd. The more he thought about it, the more he realized that he didn't really know much about her at all. It bothered him, and he'd stewed on it all night. As long as he'd known her, she'd never talked about her mother to him. He'd met the only person she'd considered family years ago—her uncle. She'd described outings to amusement parks, museums, and vacations at the beach with her uncle, but that had been about it.

Syd once told him that they'd bonded over their horrible mothers. Cali had alluded to Syd's complaints about their mother earlier. Red didn't have the same experience as Syd, but he'd seen the way his mother had treated her growing up. He definitely understood why his sister felt the way she did. He'd been completely on Syd's side when she decided to move to Virginia with their father after their parents split up. Hell, he'd wanted to go himself, but his guilt had kept him in Michigan.

Red took in Cali's defensive stance—eyes wild, chest heaving, fists clenched. Somehow, he wasn't sure Syd even knew everything she'd gone through. He made a mental note to ask her when she got back to town.

Stepping closer to Cali, he ran a thumb down her cheek and hooked his hand around her neck. Slowly, he brushed his lips over hers. Spurred on by her soft moan, he pulled her deeper into the kiss. His desire was to comfort her, to bring her peace. He couldn't take her like she hadn't just bared her soul to him, shared her deepest secret. He wanted to help her.

Pulling away, he looked down at her, then leaned his forehead against hers. "Can we start over?" he asked softly.

She frowned. "How is that even possible? I've told you something that I swore I would never tell another living person. I can't forget that. How can you?"

"I don't know," he answered. He'd picked a fight with her two days in a row for reasons that were unclear to him. When he'd left her house last night, he wanted to be okay with it. But he was admittedly salty about the stupid rules in place. He'd wanted to hurt her when she showed up like nothing had happened. There were words spoken that couldn't be taken back. In that moment, though, Red wanted her in his life any way he could get her. "I just know I don't want to ever hurt you. You know that, don't you?"

She nodded. "Red, I don't want to hurt *you*. I'm sorry. I shouldn't have gone off like that. I get a little crazy when I'm talking about my mother. There's so much—"

"It's okay," he assured her as he pulled her into a tight hug. "You don't have to say anything else. I'm just glad you told me what you did. I'm so sorry you had to go through that. No child deserves to be mistreated or made to feel unwanted."

"Red?" She pulled away from him and glanced up at him.

He waited for her to speak.

"Thank you. For everything. You said you never wanted to be a person that would hurt me, and I appreciate it. I want you to know I feel the same way about you. I don't want this to change us, and I'm worried it will."

"Don't worry about that." He sighed, tucked a strand of her hair behind her ear. "I'm always going to be here for you."

She bit down on her bottom lip. "Promise?"

He opened his mouth to speak, but the words wouldn't come. There was something in her voice, the way she looked at him. A vulnerability he'd yet to see from her. Ever. She was looking to him to tell her everything was going to be all right. Only he couldn't be sure.

Swallowing, he squeezed her chin gently between his forefinger and his thumb and smiled at her. "I promise," he told her finally, even though there was no way to know how this would turn out. But one thing was certain: if they didn't end up together, neither of them would be left unscathed.

He noticed the tears standing in her eyes and guessed she'd realized the same thing. He kissed her eyelids softly. "Can you promise to always be honest with me?"

Being honest with him was what had gotten them in trouble in the first place. Yet he wouldn't have it any other way.

"I'll try. It's very hard to talk about my past. And it's not that I don't trust you because I do, Red. We're friends first. That's why this is good. I need you to understand where I'm coming from."

"As long as you understand where I am." If only *he* knew where he was.

"I'm sorry," she whispered. "I'm sorry for everything."

The sincerity in her eyes hit him right in the gut. He couldn't resist placing a tender kiss to her lips. "Me too," he murmured against her mouth.

"I guess we both have asshole tendencies, huh?" she quipped with a soft giggle.

"Pretty much," he agreed.

"Well, next time you drive out to my house to take care of me, you can stay the night."

He barked out a laugh. Smacking her lightly on her thigh, he said, "You're full of shit. Come on, we have to get to the airport."

* * *

Traffic was heavy as they headed toward the Detroit Metropolitan Airport. Red had muttered a string of curse words as he tried to maneuver between cars. At one point, he flicked off a truck driver as he cut in front of him. Calisa gripped her seatbelt as he weaved between the lanes.

She wasn't worried that they'd get in an accident. Red was an excellent driver. Her concern was the fact that she'd blurted out details of her past. Things that she'd never intended telling him. Then he'd turned down her invitation for sex, which was so unlike him. Although, in his defense, she had practically demanded he ignore her tears and her heartfelt confession to fuck her. *I can't believe I did that.* If it had been any other man, that entire scene might have played out in another way, but Red would never take advantage of her, even if she was begging him. Glancing at him out of the corner of her eye, she wondered what he was thinking, if he'd look at her differently.

"Fuckin' asshole," he blared with his hand on the horn.

Rolling her eyes, she stared out the window. Interstate 94 traffic was a beast during rush hour, but she couldn't figure out why it was so packed in the middle of the day on a Friday. Sydney had timed her flight perfectly, hoping to avoid any traffic jams. She swiped her phone and pulled up her traffic app.

"Construction on Wayne Road, Red," she said softly. "Maybe you can hop off and take the street."

He flicked on his blinker without a word and took the next exit. From there, it seemed the coast was clear and she relaxed a bit.

"Red?" she asked, turning to face him.

"Her flight is probably pulling in right now," he said, as if she hadn't called his name. "I hope they stall her on board for a minute. We have another ten, fifteen minutes."

"Red?" she repeated.

"Yes," he grumbled under his breath.

"I want to talk to you about earlier." She wished she could leave it alone. They'd seemed to come to an understanding, but it was still bothering her.

"What about earlier?"

"I didn't mean to... I guess I didn't think... About my mother... I've never told anyone much about her."

"Except Syd?" he asked.

She shook her head. "Some things, but others I haven't even told her. I don't want you to think that I'm this selfish person. I really—"

"I don't. No worries. And what you say to me stays between us."

"I never told Syd about the hotel room," she admitted, swallowing hard. "I was too ashamed."

"Why would you be ashamed?" he asked, a deep frown on his face. "You didn't do anything wrong."

She shrugged. "I don't know. I struggled with it for a long

time. I hate her, though. I still hate her for leaving me alone for so long, for telling me I was a mistake, for never being a mother to me."

It wasn't just that her mother had abandoned her all those years ago. There was more to her mother's story: a history of psychiatric hospital stays, wayward men, and a long rap sheet. By now, Cali figured she was dead. At least that's what she told herself so that she could feel better about the fact that her mother had never tried to contact her, never even came for a visit.

"My uncle told me she had a mental illness, but...it doesn't matter." Cali had asked her uncle what was really wrong with her mother right around her sixteenth birthday. *Schizophrenia.*

"We don't have to talk about his, Cali," Red said.

She knew that. But for some reason, she needed to say this to him. "The thought of me turning into that scares me every day."

Cali had read countless articles, talked to numerous mental health professionals. All in an attempt to reassure herself that she wouldn't become her mother, that she wouldn't make the same mistakes her mother did. And she damn sure didn't want to take the chance of continuing the cycle with a child of her own.

"I don't think you could ever turn into that," he assured her. "But I get it. No need to explain. That's why we're us, right?"

Is that sarcasm? If it was she wouldn't address it. He wouldn't be Red if he wasn't a sarcastic asshole at times—no matter what his promises were earlier.

Finally, they parked at the airport and walked into the area designated to meet passengers. Cali took a deep breath and waited. She pulled her gloves off and dropped her cell phone into her purse. Unable to put a word to what she was feeling, she scanned the area around them, smiling when a little girl threw herself into a man's arms, screaming "Daddy!" and hugging his neck. To her left, a couple embraced and held on to each other for what seemed like forever. And behind her, she could hear a woman screaming at her toddler to stay close to her and not step away "or else."

Taking long, deep breaths, she willed herself to calm down. Syd was bound to notice that something wasn't right if she kept it up. She'd never been able to hide much from her friend. Syd had a way of reading her like a good book.

Red was to her right, speaking with a man in an expensive suit. It seemed he knew someone everywhere they went. Whether they were in Burger King or Kroger, he always ran into a friend or a colleague. She watched as he slipped the man his business card and invited him out to shoot some pool while he was in town. They shook hands, with the man promising to give him a call, before the businessman jetted off toward a limo.

Red joined her after a few minutes. "I haven't seen him in a long time," he said, glancing at the business card in his hand before he tucked it into his pocket. "We went to high school together. He's visiting family this weekend. I have to tell Morgan and Kent I ran into him."

Shrugging, she wondered why Red felt the need to explain to her who the guy was. Sure, she was curious, but she'd never ask him. "That's cool. Are you going to hang out while he's here?"

"Maybe," he answered. "Syd should be walking down any minute." He tilted his head to the side, raised his eyebrows. "Are you okay?"

She nodded and adjusted the strap of her purse on her shoulder. Sighing, she tapped her foot on the floor and shifted. "I'm fine. Just ready to see Syd. I hope she's okay. I can just picture her waddling with her big 'cankles' and a huge carry-on. Maybe she needs help. You should…"

She smiled when she spotted Syd, riding on one of those golf-cart-like things. She was seated in the front, next to a fine man with long dreadlocks and a body built like a football player. Her friend was munching on a sub.

"Syd!" Red called, waving his hand high to get her attention.

Syd scanned the area and smiled when she saw them. "There they are." She pointed at them. "Hey!" she squealed.

Red barreled toward the cart and practically lifted his sister out. Syd embraced him tightly, her sub clasped firmly in her hand. When he finally let go of her, she motioned to Cali. "Girl, get your ass over here!"

Cali hugged her friend. "You're here. Finally."

"Yes, I am," Syd said, stuffing some cash into the driver's hand. Red had already grabbed her carry-on and Syd handed Cali her purse. "I think I stuffed too much in my purse last night. It is heavy. The seats were horrible. Luckily, I was able to upgrade to first class. I don't think I've ever been so miserable. Yuck." She rambled on about the horrible turbulence, the woman sitting next to her who talked about her ugly mother-in-law for the entire flight, and the lack of honey-roasted peanuts. "But this sandwich is so good. Want some?" She held it out to Cali.

Cali giggled. "You're a trip. No. I don't want your sandwich."

"Great because it's too good to share." She patted Red's shoulder. "Hope you're parked close because these ankles... Morgan's going to call and ask you if I'm swollen and I'd appreciate it if you lied. It was hard enough convincing him that I was okay to travel alone. Okay?"

"I'm not going to lie to my best friend," Red told her. "But how about we get you off your feet so that when he calls, your ankles won't be big as a log."

She smacked him playfully. "I'm your sister. You're supposed to be on my side."

"Well, Morgan isn't going to come to town and try to beat me down for lying about your health," Red retorted.

Cali hooked an arm inside Syd's. "Let's get you to the car. You did know we were supposed to head to Gabriel's on the way home. You're not going to be hungry."

"Yes, I will," Syd said, taking another bite of her sandwich. "I'm always hungry." She burped, then gasped. "Oh shit!"

"What?" Cali and Red said in unison.

"I forgot my cookies." She pouted.

Cali groaned. "Come on, girlfriend. I'll bake you some cookies myself."

"Um...I'm trying to enjoy cookies," Syd said, skeptically. "Last time you made me cookies, you burned them. For someone who can cook her ass off, you sure don't know cookies. Maybe Allina can bake me some? Where is she? Is she back in town?"

Cali cringed. She'd managed to avoid the topic of Allina for a while. Syd had asked about Allina often, but Cali always changed the subject. She knew it wouldn't be long before Syd would demand to know where their other friend was.

The answer was simple enough, though. Their friend finally snagged her a man, and decided to devote all of her time to him. A few months ago, she'd followed him to Cleveland, Ohio. Syd knew all of that, but what she didn't know was Allina had turned down an offer to take over the bridal shop where she worked and decided to stay in Ohio. It was an unfortunate turn of events for Cali because she and Allina had been finalizing plans to go into business together. Allina was a talented wedding gown designer. They'd decided to combine resources and start a one-stop-bridal-shop. With Allina making the decision to move, their business partnership was essentially done. In business, Cali knew there were no guarantees, even with a contract signed; only recourse. Allina was one of her dearest friends. As hurt as she was that their dream was placed on an indefinite hold, she couldn't begrudge her for following her heart.

Cali had implored Allina to tell Syd about her move, but obviously that hadn't happened yet. It seemed as if there was something more to the entire move. Nevertheless, she didn't want to broach the subject until later.

"We'll talk to her soon," Red said with a big smile.

Syd was satisfied with that answer because her focus was back on the sub. Cali mouthed "thank you" to Red as they headed toward the car.

Red ushered Syd to his car and helped her sink into the front seat, while Cali climbed in the back. She glanced at Red as he jogged around the car and hopped into the driver's seat. Things still didn't seem right between them. Honestly, she wasn't sure what could be done about it. The damage, it seemed, had already been done—by her.

Pulling her cell phone out of her bag, she scrolled through her e-mails. No fires to put out. *Yes.* Potential new clients. *Even better.* E-mail from her ex. *Delete.* Except... the e-mail said something different than the normal "I want you back, you're the only one for me, I'm sorry" drivel. This time he'd called her a slew of names because she'd dared to not return his multiple calls and e-mails. Rolling her eyes, she wondered if he'd forgotten that he'd lied about having a wife and two small children. This time he would get a response, but it wouldn't be the one he hoped for. Smiling at the sight of an e-mail from her uncle, she tapped the open button. She frowned as she read.

He's coming?

"Cali?" Red asked, peering at her through the rearview mirror. "Did you hear me?"

"Um, I don't... what did you say?" she stammered.

"Syd wants you to cook a big dinner tonight. Is that okay with you?"

With her mind still on the e-mail, she nodded and looked at Syd, who was eyeing her skeptically. "Sure. I figured you'd ask so I brought my clothes to spend the night at Morgan's."

Syd grinned. "You're awesome! A peach cobbler?"

"Girl, you are going to be big as a house!" She told her friend with a laugh. "Slow down, honey."

Syd's mouth fell open. "Hey! I still do yoga and I walk every day. I'm just hungry, eating for two. I'm not big as a house, right, Red?"

He scratched his head. "So did you want to go to the mall first or straight to Morgan's?"

"Red! I'm not big as a house." She punched his shoulder. "Stop."

Deciding to save Red, Cali chimed in, "Well, in my defense I said you're *going* to be big as a house. Not that you *are* big as a house. And I was joking anyway. You're beautiful, Syd."

Obviously satisfied, her friend finished off the rest of her sub and took a big gulp of her water. "Morgan insisted I make an appointment with my doctor as soon as I get here. It's at 3 o'clock. Do you mind driving me to the hospital later, Red?"

"That actually works out because I can stop by my office while you're there."

"I want to stop by the bar, too," Syd added. Since she'd moved to Baltimore with Morgan, Red and Kent had been left in charge of their joint business. Their bar, The Ice Box, had been launched successfully and had brought in a steady stream of business. "Oh, Morgan's house is too manly. I want to get started on the nursery in the next couple of days."

Cali smirked. Her best friend's mind was like a machine. It never stopped running, jumping from one subject to the next. What Syd didn't know was that Morgan had already called ahead a few weeks earlier and put her and Red in charge of clearing out a room for the nursery. He'd hired contractors and everything. The only thing left to do was pick out the furniture. She couldn't wait to see Syd's face.

Syd pulled out her planner and jotted some things on the page. Guess it was time to handle business. She had helped run the bar from hundreds of miles away and didn't miss a beat.

"I want to meet the couple who rented out my condo," Syd said. "How are they working out, Red?"

Red gave her the 411 on the newlyweds who'd recently leased Syd's condo. When Syd abruptly moved to Baltimore with Morgan, she'd asked Red to find her nice, working renters. Cali had considered moving in herself, but decided not to leave her beloved townhome, although it would have been nice to live closer to . . . Syd.

As Syd quizzed Red on details about the bar and the condo, Cali opened up the e-mail from her uncle again. He'd be in town in a few days, which was not like him. She'd usually have to pull a leg to get him on a plane to visit her and he'd booked on his own without telling her and attached his itinerary. She said a silent prayer that her only living family member was okay. Closing her eyes, she sighed and wondered what she would do if he wasn't.

CHAPTER SIX

Later in the day, Cali waited in the examination room with Syd, who was yapping on the phone with Morgan. She was happy for her friend. Really. But there were only so many sweet declarations of love she could take. How many times could a person say "I miss you" before it got to be too much?

Syd hung up and turned to her. "What's going on?"

"What?" Cali asked. "What are you talking about?"

"Something's...off," Syd observed, eyeing her. "Everything okay?"

She smiled at the way Syd always seemed to know when there was something wrong. And she also knew when to ask and when not to ask. It was a gift.

"I got an e-mail from Uncle Cal," Cali said. "He's coming to town."

Syd's eyes widened. "Really? Is he okay?"

She tapped a foot against the floor softly. "I don't know." Biting her lip, her mind raced with possible reasons for her uncle's impromptu visit. "The only thing he said was that. And he attached his itinerary. I can't help it; I'm concerned."

"Me too," Syd said, pinching the skin at her throat. "He hates flying."

Cali nodded. Uncle Cal was old school. He felt that if he couldn't get there by car, he didn't need to go. "I wanted to ask Red if he knew anything, but..." Red had done some legal work for her uncle at her recommendation. She hesitated to ask him about it because he took the term "attorney-client privilege" seriously, which was one of the things she...liked about him.

"Well, we all know that Red won't tell you what they talk about." Syd rubbed her legs. "Try not to think about the visit in a negative way. It could be that he misses you and wants to spend time with you. You're the only child he's ever had."

"True. I won't worry about it." Cali chewed on her thumbnail. "I'm going to focus on seeing him and getting the chance to take care of him for a change."

Syd squeezed her hand and pulled her in for a hug. Cali allowed herself to be soothed by her for a few minutes, before she pulled back.

"What about you and Red?" Syd asked. "Things seem different on that front, too."

"He's mad at me," Cali confessed. "He says he's not, but he is. We got into a discussion about pregnancy because he saw a pregnancy test on my bathroom sink. Long story, short...I told him that I wouldn't tell him if I was pregnant with his baby." When Syd gasped, she rushed on to explain, "But I let him know that I would tell you because I know you wouldn't keep that type of thing from him. He blew up, accused me of not respecting him. But then I thought we'd gotten past it. I think he's still upset."

Cali didn't want to get into the other part of their discussion—about her mother. It was too much, especially with her worries about Uncle Cal's visit.

"Can you blame him?" Syd asked.

Cali shook her head. "Not really. Anyway, I can tell it's still bothering him, but I don't know how to fix it. I mean, he didn't even bite when I practically begged him to do—"

Syd scrunched her nose. "Ew, please don't talk about your sex life with my brother. I get it."

"Then, like I told you, he wants me to spend the night. Or he wants to be able to spend the night with me. I'm not at that place. I didn't think he'd be so upset. I keep thinking it's time to end it before one of us gets hurt, but I can't. I want him. I don't want to, but I do."

"Have you ever considered telling him that?" Syd asked.

"No," Cali replied. "We all know what happened the last time I did the whole relationship thing."

If Cali were to tell Red that she had strong feelings that went outside of the no-strings agreement, there would be no turning back. Red would probably ask her to be his girlfriend, want to move in. Then they'd get engaged and eventually find themselves back in the same predicament they did the day before, when he brought up kids again.

"How can you ever move forward when you're so stuck in the past, Cali?" Syd asked. "Red is not married with two kids and making promises that he knows he can't keep."

"I just can't, Syd." Cali rubbed her wrist. "I'm not like you. I'm a mess."

Syd laughed. "And I'm not? Hey, I slept with my ex-fiancé's brother."

It was a running joke between them. Who was the biggest mess? Syd's affair with Morgan had put her on top for a while, but the novelty was wearing out. Syd and Morgan were together and deliriously happy. That wasn't messy.

"After he cheated on you multiple times," Cali said.

"Still." Syd opened her purse and pulled out a candy bar. "That was a hot-ass mess."

"But you're happy now." Cali broke off a chunk of Syd's candy bar and popped it into her mouth.

"You could be, too," her friend said softly.

Cali wasn't so sure. "Syd, it's not like we're actually a couple."

"Do you want to be a couple?"

Cali opened her mouth to respond, but a soft knock on the door made her pause. When the doctor stepped in, she figured it was a sign to keep her mouth shut on that subject. Judging by the discreet, sideways glance Syd shot her way, though, she knew her friend would not make it that easy for her.

"Hi!" Syd beamed at the doctor. Cali didn't recognize her, but it was obvious Syd knew her well. "I'm so glad I got you."

The perky doctor smiled at Syd. "Hi! I guess it worked out, huh? I wasn't supposed to be assigned here today. I'm filling in for a colleague. I saw your name and figured I'd come in and start the appointment. It's been a while. Tell me what's going on." After the professional assembled the traveling laptop, she turned to Cali. "Hi. I'm Dr. Lovely Washington," she said, extending her hand to Cali's.

"I'm Cali," she said, shaking the doctor's hand. "Sydney's best friend."

"Oh, you're Cali. Syd's talked about you. Good to meet you." Dr. Washington said, pulling out her pen.

Syd explained that she had met Dr. Love before she moved to Baltimore. She had been a resident physician at the time, working under Syd's regular obstetrician. The two had hit it off, and kept in touch while Syd was away.

Cali sized the doctor up while she set up her computer. Dr. Washington was one of those women who was beautiful without really trying. Her dark brown skin was flawless and her natural hair was styled into a twisted up-do.

Syd and Dr. Washington chatted a bit about the baby and moving back to Michigan, while Cali checked her voicemail. Red hadn't called and she wondered when he'd actually show up.

"Dr. Washington, can I ask you a question?" Cali asked, butting into the conversation.

"Sure." The petite doctor smiled at her. "And please call me Love."

Love? *Who the hell calls someone Love?* "Okay, I've noticed that Syd's ankles are swollen. Is this something we should be worried about?"

"It's normal in the later months of pregnancy," Dr. Love explained. "But we'll certainly keep an eye on the swelling. For now, we're going to send you out for some lab work. Your doctor in Baltimore sent over your records and I've gone over her notes. She did mention that you've gained a few more pounds than they wanted. I want to repeat the glucose test to be sure you're not developing gestational diabetes."

Syd nodded. "Okay. But I think I've gained weight because I've been eating. A lot. My cravings have been all over the place, but I do manage to get workouts in three to four times a week." Syd elbowed Cali. Hard. "My friend is overly concerned because she's not used to seeing me like this."

Cali rubbed her sore arm. "No, I'm concerned because your ankles are swollen. And, I can't be sure, but I think that's a bad thing."

"It's not necessarily a bad thing," Dr. Love said. "But it can be a sign of preeclampsia, which can be very dangerous. Or it can simply be a sign of water retention, to which I'd say Sydney needs to make sure she's off of her feet as much as possible. Is Morgan coming soon?"

"Yes," Syd answered, patting her belly. "He'll be here in a few weeks."

"Good." The doctor grabbed one of those oversized hospital gowns from a drawer and handed it to Syd. "I'm going to have you change into this so we can examine you. I'll step out."

When Dr. Love excused herself, Syd turned around to face Cali. Judging by the sour expression on her friend's face, she was in trouble.

"What?" Cali said, crossing her legs. "I wanted to be sure you're okay. I mean, it's not like I'd be able to deal if something happened to you, Syd. I thought we already established I'm a mess."

"You didn't have to point out my cankles to my doctor." Syd gingerly stood up and quickly undressed. She tugged on the flimsy gown. "Ugh. Way to make me feel like Ms. Piggy."

"Far from it, babe," Cali assured her friend. "But Morgan would kill me if I didn't take very good care of you. And so would your brother."

"Are you decent?" Red asked, poking his head in the door.

"If I wasn't, you would've seen all my goods." Syd pulled her gown closed. "Can you knock next time? Sure, we were in the womb together, but this is pretty awkward."

Red stepped into the room. "I'm sorry. I thought I missed something. Roc has already called me twice to ask what happened at the doctor. Maybe you should give him a call."

"Roc" was Morgan's nickname. His brothers and Red couldn't let the childhood name go.

Red helped Syd onto the examination table and sat down in the empty seat next to Cali. "Is there going to be an ultrasound or something?" he asked. "Why did you have to change? I thought you were here to discuss care going forward."

"Because we're at the doctor's office and I'm pregnant and your *boo* told her she was worried about my fat ankles," Syd told her brother. "Did you leave your brain in the office?"

Cali closed her eyes when a whiff of Red's cologne reached her nose and she instinctively leaned forward. The hint of lavender and orange, mixed with a refreshing lemony flavor, made her heart shift. When she opened them, Syd was looking at her. Cali straightened her back and cleared her throat, cursing inwardly that she had been caught by her all-too-observant friend.

A short, soft knock sounded and Dr. Love called from the other side of the door. Syd announced she was ready and the doctor entered, pushing an ultrasound cart.

"Okay, Sydney, I want to take some pictures of the baby." Love sat down on a stool and turned on the monitor. As she prepared the ultrasound wand, she said, "I read that you wanted to keep the sex a secret. Is that still the case?"

"I think so . . . yes," Syd replied. "I can change my mind at any time, right? Do you know what it is?"

"Not yet. But I will soon. And I'll hold on to the information." The doctor looked up for the first time and her eyes widened. "Oh, I'm sorry. I didn't know there was someone else here." She reached out with her free hand and shook Red's hand. "I'm Dr. Lovely Washington. And you are?"

Red stood up, practically knocking his chair over. "I'm Jared, Syd's brother."

Love smiled widely. "Oh, I see the resemblance. Good to finally put a face to the name."

The room was silent for a few seconds and Calisa narrowed her eyes on Red, who seemed to be smitten with the love doctor.

"Um, Jared?" Love said.

"Yes," he said. "Everyone pretty much calls me Red."

"Oh. Red? Can I have my hand back?" Dr. Love asked.

Red snatched his hand away and scratched the back of his neck. "Sorry," he said. "Are you from the area? You look familiar."

"No, I'm from Las Vegas," Love said. "But I've been here for a few years. Maybe I've seen you around."

Cali uncrossed her legs and muttered a curse.

"It's possible," Red said in the low, sexy voice that she thought was reserved for her. Well, maybe not reserved entirely and exclusively for her, but still... Even so, he wasn't supposed to use it with other women while she was in the room. She made a mental note to tell him about himself when they were alone again.

Dr. Love washed her hands and pulled a paper towel from the dispenser on the wall to dry them off, before tossing it in the trashcan. "Well, Red, I have to do a pelvic exam and—"

"Whoa," Red bellowed. With hands up, he backed toward the door. "No need to explain. I'm going to step out while you do that."

"Great," the doctor chirped. "Once I'm done, you can come back in and observe the ultrasound."

Cali watched as Red walked out without another word and wished she could kick him in his shin. Rolling her eyes, she observed the doctor position herself to do the exam.

More than a few minutes later, Red was allowed back in the room and the lights were dimmed. Dr. Love warned Syd about the cold gel before she touched the wand to her belly. Syd gasped when the monitor lit up and Baby Smith was wiggling around on the monitor.

"Aw, she's getting so big." Syd cooed. "I can't believe it."

"How do you know it's a girl?" Red said, his eyes glued to the monitor.

"I have a feeling," Syd said. "Love, you can tell me if I'm hot or cold."

"Are you sure you want to know the answer?" Dr. Love asked.

"No," Cali answered for her friend. "I'm here to be her conscience. She can't know unless Morgan is here." She squinted at the small screen and tried to make out the image. Unable to help herself, she smiled at her future godchild as the doctor pointed out little details and took measurements.

They all laughed when the doctor tried to take face measurements and the baby covered its face.

"This baby might be a little ornery," Dr. Love mused.

"I wonder where it got that from," Red grumbled.

"Shut up," Syd ordered.

Once the doctor completed her task, she wiped the gel off Syd's stomach with a white washcloth. Red helped his sister sit up before he stepped out of the room—with the doctor—so that Syd could get dressed.

The rest of the appointment flew by after that. Syd was told to go get some labs drawn and head home to prop her feet up until her swelling subsided. Between baby talk and Red flirting with Love, Cali was too through with the day. She was ready to down a couple of glasses of wine and eat a big bowl of ice cream.

After Red left them to go get the car, Syd hooked her arm into Cali's as they walked toward the door. "I think someone's jealous," Syd sang in that annoying tone she got when she thought she was right about something.

"Oh, be quiet." Cali refused to give Red the satisfaction of even admitting out loud that she was anything close to being jealous. Of course, she was probably a bite-sized amount of jealous, but that information would go with her to her grave. "I don't want to talk about it."

"You don't have to," her friend teased. "I see it all in your face. And it's okay. We've all been there."

"If you weren't pregnant, I'd push you down."

Syd laughed. "My poor friend. You really have it bad."

"Shush," Cali said. "Or you will not be getting a home-cooked meal."

The threat seemed to serve its purpose because Syd quickly changed the subject to baby showers. As they approached Red's car, Cali wondered why seeing Red flirt with the sweet doctor had made her blood boil. When did the very thought of him seeing another woman make her flip out?

CHAPTER SEVEN

Red was in a foul mood and he knew why. Who knew that one petite beauty with big, beautiful, expressive brown eyes would be his downfall?

Cali had opted to stay the night with Syd after dinner—a dinner she'd slaved over for hours, one so delicious he wanted to throw her over the kitchen counter and thank her all night. She was an excellent cook, having learned everything from her uncle, who taught culinary arts at a university.

After dinner, she'd offered him a private treat in Morgan's bathroom, sucking him off so long and so hard he'd thought he saw stars. Then, when he was standing with his pants pooled around his ankles, still hard for her, she'd turned around and left him standing there.

He'd tried to catch up to her, but by the time he'd gotten his pants up and fastened, she had locked herself in Morgan's spare bedroom. To make matters worse, she told him from the other side of the door to "keep hope alive." It took a few minutes, and a hint from Syd, to figure out why Cali had been irritated with him. Guess she hadn't appreciated how interested he was in the beautiful doctor. Over the years they'd dated other people, but had agreed to never sleep with anyone else while they were sleeping with each other. He didn't see what the big deal was, but apparently, Cali thought differently. That was fine with him.

After a restless night, he woke up, headed to the gym, and beat the shit out of a 100-pound punching bag. Even after his workout, he was still pissed. There was no way he would let that woman leave him panting after her like a lovesick fool anymore. He wanted to throttle her. But more than that, he wanted to...

He glanced at the almost empty bottle of beer on his coffee table and the empty one sitting next to it. The little minx had driven him to drink at ten o'clock in the morning. Pretty soon, he'd be a card carrying member of Alcoholics Anonymous. He wasn't sure when it had happened or why, but he felt it bubbling up inside him: resentment. He'd really tried to understand where she was coming from, but how had she consistently misunderstood him and his intentions? Normally, he wouldn't care what any woman thought. Then again, she wasn't just any woman.

"Why are you drinking so early?" Syd asked from the doorway. "Planning a stint in rehab for the new year?"

"Should I take my key back?" he asked, unable to hide his irritation.

"Hey! Turnabout is fair play," she said. "I seem to remember you constantly letting yourself into my place and eating all of my food."

Syd wobbled over to his loveseat and slowly sat down. She immediately pulled the lever and propped her feet up. "What's going on with you? I figured you could take me to breakfast."

"I'm not hungry," he grumbled.

"But I am. And that's what's important."

He laughed at his twin. He'd missed her, but he had to

admit, he was a little concerned about her health. He'd done a little research about pregnancy and swollen ankles and the results gave him pause. "You need to ease up on the food, Syd. Or at least eat some fruit and vegetables."

"I eat plenty of fruit and veggies," she insisted. "I want an omelet right now. Did Morgan call you?"

"No," he replied. "Was he supposed to?"

She shrugged. "I don't know. He said something about thanking you and Cali for helping get the nursery together. I don't know if I've thanked you enough for that. Thank you so much! You saved me a ton of time."

Red smiled, remembering Syd's scream of delight when she saw the newly decorated nursery for the first time. Morgan had turned into "Daddy Smith" overnight, it seemed. Instead of drinking cognac and shooting pool, now the highlight of his day was giving Syd foot massages and cuddling on the couch.

"You're welcome, sis," he said. "Besides, you know I'll do anything for you."

That was the understatement of the decade. Although they'd chosen to split up as children when their parents divorced, he was extremely overprotective of his sister. He'd move Heaven and Earth for her and he knew she felt the same. He glanced out the window and noticed that snow had started to fall.

"Cali went to work," Syd announced. "In case you were wondering."

"I wasn't," he said, his voice flat.

"Okay." She gave him a knowing smirk. "Are you all right? You seem preoccupied."

"A lot on my mind," he said. "Have you talked to Mom yet?" He knew changing the subject to their mother would keep Syd from focusing on him and Cali.

She turned her nose up. "Yeah. She called me this

morning to cuss me out for not visiting first thing yesterday."
His sister sighed heavily. "I can't understand, for the life of
me, why she cares. She's never seemed to care before."

"Well, maybe she's seen the error of her ways." *Yeah,
right.* His mother was nothing if not consistent. She'd consistently been a bitter woman who cared more about herself
than her daughter. And Red resented her for it, even though
he rarely talked about it with Syd. For the most part, he'd
played peacemaker between the two, choosing not to take
sides. Only he knew he was firmly on Team Syd, had always
been. Sure, he'd figured out the "whys" a long time ago, but
it still didn't make it right.

Young Syd had inadvertently walked in on their mother
with her lover, and told their father about it, effectively ending the marriage. His father had filed for divorce immediately, and because of his mother's infidelity, she didn't get
a dime. For some inexplicable and irrational reason, she'd
blamed Syd but fought for custody anyway. Red suspected
she knew she'd get a hefty amount of child support if she
had custody of both of them. The divorce proceedings had
dragged out over months and Syd grew tired of being treated
like she was the enemy. Eventually, the Court interviewed
them, and Syd proclaimed that she'd be happier residing
with their father, which infuriated their mother even more.
She'd accused the tween of betrayal, but Syd didn't care.
She'd moved away, and he stayed.

"I don't want to talk about her anymore, Red. I decided
not to bring this into motherhood with me. If she can't love
me unconditionally, that's her loss. What the hell was I supposed to do? I was a child."

"I know, Syd." Red didn't want Syd to get worked up. It
was still a sore subject, obviously. And stress wasn't good
for the baby. "Let's drop it, okay? Where do you want to
go eat?"

She smiled brightly. It seemed as though food was able to cheer her up quicker than anything. He chuckled when she named a slew of restaurants in the area. "Ooh, let's eat at Cracker Barrel."

He stood up. "Okay. Let me get dressed. Call Kent. He wanted to see you. Maybe he'll meet us for breakfast."

As he walked into his bedroom, he thought about Cali and how she'd described her childhood with her mother—and without her. But he could have sworn he'd seen her light up during Syd's ultrasound. He remembered the gleam in her eyes as the doctor described the baby's different little body parts.

He heard Sydney squeal when she reached Kent on the phone. He chuckled, amused at the way his sister gushed to their friend about pancakes and the different ways to eat them. Scowling, he shook his head to get the image of pancakes and peanut butter out of his head. She took weird cravings to another level.

Syd peeked into his room. "Kent wants to know if you canceled the staff meeting today."

Red cursed under his breath. "No," he grumbled. "I forgot. I'll take care of that."

"Why are you canceling it?" Syd asked with the phone still glued to her ear. Red heard Kent's voice over the receiver explaining the reasons. "Well, I'm here," she said. "I can do the meeting as planned if you have something else to do."

"It's better if we postpone," Red groaned. "We have a party scheduled tonight and the planner wants to get in early to set up. We need all staff on deck for that. Moving the meeting to next Saturday won't hurt."

Over the last few months, they'd received countless requests to rent out space at The Ice Box for banquets. After a few meetings and conference calls, they'd decided to rent out one side of the bar for certain events.

"Fine," she said, pouting. "We can move the meeting, but I want to get back in the swing of things."

"You need to sit your ass down somewhere," Red told her. "Right, Kent?" He shouted so that his friend was sure to hear him.

"Bye, Kent," Syd said, more than likely preventing him from responding in a way she didn't like. "I'll see you in a bit." She ended her call and tossed her phone in her purse. "Way to gang up on your sister."

"Seriously, Syd?" He glanced at his sister. He loved her so much and he worried about her. "You have to take it easy. Dr. Love said you needed to be off your feet as much as possible."

"Speaking of Love, you like her?" Syd asked, changing the subject.

Glaring at his grinning sister, he shook his head and walked past her out of the room.

"Wait; don't walk out. I wanted to talk to you about this last night, but . . . I fell asleep." She followed him into the living room. "You were flirting with her."

"She's nice," he said simply. "And you know how complicated things are right now."

"With you and Cali?" she pressed.

"I'm not talking about this with you, Syd. There is no me and Cali. As far as she's concerned, I can see whoever I want. No strings, remember?" Normally, right around this time, he'd shove her away from him—playfully, of course— but he didn't want to take a chance that she'd fall. "Let's go. You're hungry, right?"

Apparently, food was the only thing he could use to shut his sister up because she immediately started talking fruit toppings and pickles. Disgusted, he followed her out of his apartment.

At the restaurant, Red sat across from Syd, nursing a cup

of coffee. She was focused on the menu, naming everything that looked good to her.

"I can't wait to see the bar," she said. "I've missed it. I never really had a chance to enjoy it like I always dreamed I would." Grinning, she closed the menu and set it on the table. "But you and Kent have done a wonderful job with it."

"Did you say my name?" Kent stepped into the dining room.

"Kent!" Syd stood up gingerly and hugged Kent.

"Look at you," Kent said, smoothing a hand over her stomach. "You are big as hell."

"Hey!" she said, smiling wide. "Men aren't supposed to say that about pregnant women. What's up with that?"

"I mean it in the best way possible," Kent said. "You still look good. Besides, you have my niece or nephew in there. I missed you, baby. What's up, Red?"

"Shit." Red gave Kent some dap. Kent was Morgan's brother, but he was also one of Red's closest friends. They all grew up together, went to the same high school. "Took you long enough to get here. You only live right around the corner."

Kent smirked. "Well, you know, I had company I had to get rid of."

"Oh Lord," Syd said, returning to her seat. "I don't want to hear about your exploits, Kent."

Kent sat next to her and wrapped an arm around her neck. "Morgan called me this morning and asked if I'd seen you yet. He's pitiful."

"I know," Red agreed. His sister had successfully tamed his friend and it was funny as hell to him. "I don't think I've ever talked to him so much on the phone."

"Leave my man alone," Syd said. "He misses us."

"He misses *you*," Red countered.

"I miss him, too." The waitress came over and took their

orders and refilled Red's mug. "So, fellas, I'm ready to get back to work," Syd said once the waitress walked away. "You know I'm not content to sit around."

"We know," Kent gulped down his water. "But I need you to relax. You flew in and went straight to the doctor. Can you chill out for a few days before you jump back into bar business?"

"That was your brother," she told Kent. "He was concerned about the flight and everything. It was the only way I could get him to agree to let me fly by myself."

"Still." Kent waved the waitress over. "I changed my mind, I'll have a cup of coffee," he told the woman. Once the young lady filled his mug, he prepared it with two sugars and two creamers. "There is plenty of time for the bar, Syd. Take care of the house and stuff. We got this."

"I know," she conceded. "I will never regret asking you all to jump in with me. It has been such a great experience. Oh, Kent, what's going on with Allina? I've asked Cali and Red, but they keep beating around the bush. I've been trying to call her. She hasn't answered."

Red sighed. Cali had convinced him that telling Syd that Allina had picked up and moved to Ohio should wait a couple of days. At the time, he felt her reasoning was valid, but he wasn't so sure anymore. Of course, he'd failed to tell Kent to keep quiet.

"She left." Kent said, tossing an empty creamer into a bowl. "She's not coming back to Michigan."

"What do you mean?" Syd asked, a frown on her face. "She was just supposed to be down there for a visit. What about her business?"

Kent hunched his shoulders and twisted a straw wrapper between his fingers. "What about it? She doesn't have a business. She turned down the offer to take over and decided to stay in Ohio—with the preacher man. Or for the preacher man, since they don't live together and all."

"Are you sure?" Syd questioned. "I talked to her last month and she said she and Cali were finalizing the details for their business venture. She never mentioned moving to Ohio permanently."

"Well, she did," Kent snapped.

Red was tempted to interject, but decided to let Kent handle it. He knew that Kent was having a hard time with Allina's decision, especially since they'd been circling each other for years. Unfortunately, Kent and Red had a lot in common—happily single, stubborn as the day is long, and extremely attracted to one of Syd's friends. The only difference was that Kent had never been with Allina. She wasn't as open-minded as Cali when it came to sex and relationships.

"I can't believe she wouldn't tell me." Syd shook her head. "She'd move to another state without saying something to me? That's not like her."

"It's that guy, Syd," Red added. "He's very controlling. When you left, Allina didn't even come around. She stopped calling Kent all together. I don't even think she told her boyfriend that Kent existed at all. I wanted to tell you but I didn't want you to worry."

It was no secret that Syd was a worrywart. She worried over everyone else and little about herself.

"I'm going to call her." She picked up her phone and dialed. When her friend obviously didn't answer, Syd tapped the screen of her phone furiously and Red assumed she was sending her friend a text message. "Of course she doesn't answer," she mumbled. "But I will get to the bottom of this. Next time, don't hide shit from me. I'm not some fragile doll. I'm pregnant. Women get pregnant every day of the week, every hour of the day. It's not new science. I have to pee." With that she slid out of the chair and disappeared around the corner.

"She was pissed," Kent mused.

"I guess we should've told her sooner."

"It's cool." Kent leaned back when the waitress arrived with the food and set it in front of them. "Nothing she could do about it all the way in Baltimore."

"It doesn't matter." Red didn't like keeping things from his sister. Even if it hurt her, he always told her the truth. When she'd told him she wanted to marry Caden, he'd told her she would regret it. Although they didn't end up getting married, he was sure she regretted even saying yes to the proposal. "I knew she'd want to know. And, once again, I listened to Cali's ass and not my own gut."

Just like that, his foul mood returned with a vengeance. And along with it, the realization that he couldn't do this anymore.

Syd stalked back into the dining room, grabbed her bag. "I need this. When we're done here, I think I do want to go home and lay down for a bit. I'm sleepy and irritated." She headed toward the bathroom again.

Kent looked at Red again and shrugged.

"Just for that…" Red stabbed at his eggs with his fork. "You're going to help her put that damn Christmas tree up. And I'll be sure to explain to Morgan that you were the cause of her mood."

CHAPTER EIGHT

*R*ed shifted in his seat and grumbled at the cold cup of coffee in his hand. They were halfway home when Syd got a call from a nurse who informed her they needed to run another test because the first one was inconclusive. Cursing, he tossed the useless cup into the trash and opened his laptop.

Unable to concentrate, he scanned the hospital lobby. A few people were sitting near him, engrossed in magazines or tapping furiously on their tablet of choice. He could hear the faint sound of a piano in the background. Next to him, an older couple was chatting about a visit from their grandchildren. Red wondered if he'd ever know a grandchild.

As much as he tried not to think negatively, a part of him resigned himself to never knowing Corrine. All because of her trifling mother. He'd worked in family law for a couple of years and hated it. Custody hearings, parenting time disputes, child support battles . . . not his idea of fun.

"Mr. Williams?"

Red turned and smiled when Dr. Love approached him. "It's Red," he corrected as he stood up. "How are you?"

"I'm okay. What are you doing here?"

"We got a call from the lab," he explained. "I guess Syd needed to repeat a test. I'm waiting for her."

She nodded and glanced at his laptop. "Getting a little work done, I see."

"Not really. More like pretending. Are you on a break?" he asked. "Want to walk with me to get a cup of what you're drinking?"

Her mouth curved into a smile and her deep dimples caught him off guard. "Sure. I have some time."

He packed up his laptop and they set off at a leisurely pace. "So, you're from Las Vegas?" he asked, remembering their conversation in the exam room.

"Born and raised," she told him.

"I don't think I've ever met anyone from Las Vegas," he admitted.

"Really? I loved growing up there. Have you visited?"

"I love Vegas." Red and the fellas planned a yearly excursion to Sin City. "I try to get out there once a year."

"Gamble?" she asked.

"Definitely. And I never lose," he boasted.

She waved at a woman who walked past. "Game of choice?"

"Blackjack," he answered.

"My favorite, too. I guess we have something in common." She took a sip of her coffee. "Where did you grow up?"

"Here." It used to bother Red that he'd never left his hometown. He'd had great plans to escape after graduation, but one of the local firms had made him an offer he couldn't refuse. "I did undergrad and law school here at the 'U' and never left." In their area, The University of Michigan was affectionately called the "U" by students and alumni. "I love it here, though. Can't complain."

She finished her coffee and tossed it in a nearby bin. "It is

nice here, but sometimes I wonder if I made the right decision by moving here."

Maybe it was in his nature to be curious, but he was
intrigued by Dr. Love. She was beautiful, but she had a way
about her, a calming effect. There was an openness about
her, but there was an innocence there as well. "Why *did* you
move to Michigan?"

"It's one of the best programs in the country. And my
father is chief of surgery here," she told him. "The problem
with that is everything I get, I have to fight tooth and nail for
because of him. You'd think it wouldn't be so hard."

"I get it. They make it harder on the boss' kid. But something tells me you rise to the challenge every time."

She shrugged. "I try."

As they neared the cafeteria, he watched as the beautiful doctor greeted almost everyone with a warm smile and
still managed to pay attention to him as he went on about
the benefits of living in the Ann Arbor area. She told him
she had considered buying the house she was renting, but
wanted to keep her options open in case she decided to move
when her residency was finished the next year. He learned
that she loved sports, collected art, spoke fluent Spanish, and
had a desire to open a clinic for women and children in an
urban area. Talking with someone who was willing to share
parts of herself was refreshing. Cali was so closed off, so
determined to be in control, he feared there was a part of
her he'd never know. It not only made him sad, but he wondered why he'd spent so much time waiting for her to open
up to him.

Love was passionate about her work and it showed in the
way her eyes sparkled when she talked about her patients
and the advances in medicine that would make it so much
easier to care for them. He could admit it; he wanted to know
more.

After he paid for his coffee they wandered back toward the waiting room, chatting about Michigan football. She was easy to talk to and he appreciated that. It was like a burst of fresh air.

Syd was sitting in the waiting room with a frown on her face when they approached her.

"Hey Syd!" he called.

Syd turned to him, her eyes widening when she noticed Love standing next to him. "Hi. I wondered where you went. For a minute, I thought I went to the wrong area. Then I figured I'd better sit my ass down and let you find me. Hi, Dr. Love."

"Hello." Love gave Syd a brief hug. "How is everything?"

"Good," Syd told her. "Just tired. Ready for a nap."

"Well, you better get her home," Love told Red. "I'll see you soon, Syd. Good talking to you, Red."

"You too," he said. "Maybe we could talk more over lunch?"

Syd gasped and Red shot her a look. Love glanced at Syd then back at Red. "Sure." She pulled out a business card and placed it in his hand. "Give me a call. Bye, Sydney."

He watched as she walked off, noting the easy sway of her hips. The sting of a smack on his shoulder snapped him out of his thoughts. "What the hell are you doing?" he hissed. "Why did you hit me?"

"Because." Syd pointed her finger in his face. "Don't do that to Cali."

"Let's go." He grabbed her hand and pulled her toward the parking garage.

"I mean it, Red. You can't do that."

"Listen, I can do whatever the hell I please," he said. "Cali is not my girlfriend."

She stopped suddenly.

Sighing, he turned to her. "What? It's not a crime to meet someone and want to get to know them better."

She nibbled on her bottom lip. "It's just...I always thought you and Cali would get your shit together and move in next to me and Morgan."

He snorted. "Yeah, right. Cali is not trying to move in with anyone. She can't even bring herself to let me spend the night."

"That upsets you?"

"Can we please talk about this in the car?" he pleaded.

Syd started walking again. When they finally got to the car—after a stop at the restroom and the little booth near the elevators so she could get a muffin—she turned to him. "Do you really like her?"

"Who? Cali?" he asked.

"No, Dr. Washington." She thumped his shoulder.

"I don't know her, Syd."

"But you want to know her?" she prodded.

She is relentless. He thought about Syd's question. The easy way they'd talked and seemed to click told him yes. Then there was Cali, who wasn't budging on anything. No matter how hard he tried, he couldn't seem to move past the resentment he felt. Was the fight to be more in Cali's life worth it to him to keep trying? Red knew they could be happy together, but the back and forth with her was starting to take its toll on him. Why not try to see what was up with the lovely doctor? "I guess so," he admitted to his curious twin sister. "Is that a bad thing?"

She picked at a piece of thread on her coat. "No," she mumbled. "It's not. Correct me if I'm wrong, though—but don't you love Cali?"

He inadvertently pressed down on the brakes. When Syd lurched forward, he reached out and extended his hand in front of her in an effort to protect her from hitting the dashboard. Although, she was not even close.

"Are you okay?" he asked.

"I'm fine," she said, munching on the muffin. "That was a parent move, Red. I remember Dad used to do that in the car when we were young."

"You are pregnant with a big belly. It was instinctive."

"Glad you're on your toes. So, answer the question."

"Was that even a question?" He glanced at her out of the corner of his eye. "Sounded more like an accusation."

"I can see it all in your face when Cali is in the room. You watch her when she walks. You find any excuse to be in the same room with her. You always manage to end up seated next to her when we're in a group. Reminds me of...me— and Morgan. No matter what was going on, we needed to be close to one another. It's the way it is."

Man, she had him down. Unable to form a response, he grunted and decided to remain silent.

"It's okay, ya know?" she continued. "Love is strange business. You can't help when it happens. Then you try to control it and it never works. But if you love Cali, why not try with her?"

He rubbed his face. "Shit, you know Cali. There's no *trying* with her."

"I think you owe it to yourself and her to be honest about how you really feel."

"Syd, I'm tired." The more he thought about it, the more it irked him because it seemed to be a foregone conclusion that a relationship between him and Cali would never work. "Maybe it's time to cut our losses. I've been thinking about this a lot." He gripped the steering wheel. "Everything was fine when there were no responsibilities and we didn't have to answer to each other. Somehow, as much as we tried not to, we started having expectations. I know I did. And because of that, she always falls short. It's not because she isn't a beautiful person, inside and out. Cali is...she's everything."

No matter how infuriating she could be, Red still wanted to be with her. Through all her faults, she was still the person he wanted to spend his days and nights with. But he needed her to realize they were better together. "I'm not the same person I was when I came up with the 'easy-out clause,'" he continued. "I want more. And she won't—or can't—give me what I want."

"I think she's confused about why you're mad. Why are you mad at her?" she asked. "Is it because she doesn't want kids?"

He shook his head. "No. She thinks I'm talking about that. I'd be okay if Cali didn't have my child. I just want her to have my back. I want her to need me. Most of all, I need her to respect me. She says she does, but I'm not sure I believe her."

"Okay." Syd stretched and rubbed a hand over her belly. "I get it. So why not end it?"

That was the question of the year. Why *not* end it? "I don't know." He shrugged. "Maybe it's about that time, though."

C HAPTER NINE

$\mathcal{A}$fter Red dropped Syd off, he picked up dinner and headed home. Cali was waiting for him when he got there.

"Hi," she said. "I was in the area, figured I'd stop by." She held up an identical bag from the same restaurant he'd just left. "I brought dinner, but I guess you beat me to the punch."

It was the little things, the ways that Cali knew him, that made him want to keep trying. "Great minds," he murmured. Once he unlocked the door, he waited for her to go inside before he entered. "I'll grab some plates and we can eat."

She took off her coat and set it on the back of a chair. As he set up the food on the kitchen table, she walked up behind him and kissed him on his neck. "You'll have plenty for lunch tomorrow," she said, stroking his arm.

His fingers ached with a need to touch her, but he focused on the task at hand. "You know how I love leftovers."

They sat down to eat. Regular conversation between Cali and Red was never strained. Usually, she'd start by telling him about her day and he'd finish with tales about work or other employees at the firm. But tonight they pretty much ate in silence. She picked at her food, while he focused on her;

the way she hummed when she ate or glanced at her phone periodically to check her e-mail. He could tell she had something on her mind, and he wanted to ask her what was going on, but he had his own thoughts to contend with.

Syd had issued a challenge to him earlier. Could he tell Cali how he felt? *What do I feel?* "Cali?"

She peered up at him. "Huh?"

"Everything okay?" Yep, he was a punk.

She nodded. "Yeah. Are you okay?"

"I'm fine." He faked a smile.

"I feel like you're lying," she said. Before he could respond, she rushed on, "But it's okay. Sometimes it's better to be quiet, to keep things to yourself."

His sister had made many valid points when she suggested he be honest about his feelings for Cali. But Cali was right, too. Sometimes it was better to shut up. It didn't feel like the right time to talk about how he felt. He needed some time to think.

Cali leaned back in her chair and observed him. "Red, do you...I...miss you."

A flush of adrenaline shot through his body at her admission. Then he asked, "Why? I saw you last night, and you left me hanging."

She stood up and approached him slowly. "I'm sorry about that. I was...there's really no good excuse so I won't even try to make one up. I was wrong. This may sound totally selfish, and very inappropriate, considering our last few conversations were heavy and emotional and...I don't know, crazy. But I want you."

He wanted to tell her he didn't give a damn what she wanted, thank her for dinner, and show her to the door. But his body had already responded to the bait. When she reached out to touch his face, he gripped her wrist. "What makes you think I want you?" he managed to say.

She gave him a lopsided grin. "Do you?"

Yes. Without another word, he stood up and pulled her into a kiss. It started out slow, but slow wasn't really their thing. It quickly turned to desperate as they clawed at each other, tugging at clothes.

She finally pushed his shirt off and unbuttoned his jeans, letting them fall to the floor. His brain screamed at him to stop and end this once and for all, but he could never resist being with her.

"I hate you," he murmured against her skin with a chuckle.

She giggled. "Shut up and let's get this party started."

Pulling away, he assessed her. What a difference a few minutes and several well-placed kisses made. She was a vision—cheeks flushed, eyes closed.

"Take off your clothes," he ordered softly.

Her eyes opened. "You're not going to do me the honors?" she asked saucily.

"Take your clothes off," he repeated.

As she pulled her sweater over her head, he bit the inside of his cheek. Her eyes were on his as she pushed her jeans down to the floor and he groaned at the sight of her red lace underwear and black, suede ankle boots.

"Go to my room," he commanded. When she opened her mouth to speak, he ran a finger over her plump lips. "No words. Just go."

If she was apprehensive, she didn't show it. Instead, she followed his command and walked toward his bedroom.

"Walk slow," he told her when she picked up her pace.

She stopped and turned to him before continuing down the hallway leading toward his room. He followed, appreciating the exaggerated sway of her hips. Once she reached the entrance to his room, she bent down to remove her boots. He closed the gap between them, pressing himself against her butt.

Placing his hands on her hips, he murmured, "Leave them on."

She straightened and grinded into his erection, pulling a soft moan from him before she turned to face him. She smirked as she walked backward into the room.

Red couldn't help but smile when she reached behind her and unhooked her bra. The word "shy" was not in her vocabulary. He never had to keep her from covering herself up after they made love. She was as comfortable in her skin as he was in his. And he loved it.

The strap of her bra dangled from her index finger and she dropped it on the floor and brought her hands up to her ample breasts slowly. She pinched her own nipples until they were pert and ready for his attention, and slid a hand down over her stomach to the top of her boy shorts, which were his favorite.

She moved a finger under the line slowly.

"Stop," he told her. "Did I tell you to take your underwear off? But you can't resist teasing me."

"I'm not teasing you," she said with a smirk. "I just thought I'd help you out."

"You know I don't need any help." He circled her like a lion would his prey. When she reached out to touch him, he dodged her, chuckling at the frustrated groan that escaped. "Is it so hard to give me control, Cali?" he said against her left ear.

Silence.

"No words?" he teased against her right ear.

"Red," she whispered.

"Shhh. Lie down."

She lay back on the bed as she was told.

"Open your legs."

Her thighs parted on his command. He dropped to his knees in front of her and pulled off her boots. As he slid his hands up her legs, he kissed her all the way up to her inner thighs. She gasped when he nipped at her sensitive skin. Spreading her legs even more, he gently moved the thin fabric from her and ran his thumb over her tiny bundle of nerves. Her hips rose from the bed and she ran her fingers through his hair.

"Red," she panted.

"Quiet. Or I'll stop. You don't want me to stop, do you?"

She didn't answer, but her fingers dug into his scalp.

He pulled off her panties, taking in her sweet scent. Tracing her folds with his thumb, he opened her to him. When his tongue touched her skin, she moaned softly. Urged on by her soft pleas, he tickled her clit with his tongue. Her knees closed in on him as her hips continued to rise off the mattress. But he didn't stop. He couldn't even if he tried. She never lasted long, though. He braced a hand on her stomach to hold her down as she grinded her hips against his mouth.

"Please," she begged.

"Come for me, then," he said.

When she screamed out his name, shaking wildly, he kissed his way up her body to her mouth and kissed her deeply. As their tongues dueled, she pushed his boxers down with her feet and wrapped her legs around his waist.

She bit his neck as he fumbled in the drawer on the nightstand next to the bed. "Shit, Cali," he hissed. "Condom."

"Hurry," she told him, nipping at his chin.

He yanked the drawer out of the nightstand and tossed all the contents onto the bed next to them. When his fingers ran across the edge of a plastic wrapper, he picked it up and shoved the drawer and everything else off the side of the bed.

She snatched the condom from him, ripped it open and put it on. When it was secure, he pushed into her slowly, grinding his teeth as she enveloped him.

"I want you, Red," she whispered as she raked her teeth over his earlobe. "Don't stop."

He closed his eyes as she continued to whisper what she wanted him to do to her. He began to move inside her, pumping in and out slowly. Rubbing his nose under her chin, he hooked his hands under her knees. He bent down and pulled one of her breasts into his mouth until she groaned in pleasure.

"Faster," she ordered breathlessly. "I need you. Now."

"Shut up. I got this." He bit down on his cheek. She always felt so good and he wanted to relish the time they spent like this—when she was all his. But his need for completion urged him on. As he picked up the pace, she met his thrusts until they settled into their own rhythm.

Grabbing her hands, he lifted them above her head and pushed into her deeper. When she opened her eyes, he smiled down at her. Cali never closed her eyes. Unlike other women, she wanted to watch and he loved that about her. It saved him the trouble of telling her to open her eyes. They kept their eyes trained on each other as they made love. Scraping his teeth against her ear, he gripped her bottom and tilted it up. She fell apart immediately, and he followed, sinking his teeth into her shoulder.

Collapsing onto her, he struggled to catch his breath. She ran her fingers through his hair.

"Damn," he said. "That was..."

"I know." She brushed her lips against his brow, then his nose, and finally his lips. She burrowed in to his side. "Did I tell you Uncle Cal was coming next week?"

"No." She hadn't told him, but he knew. Uncle Cal had contacted him about setting up a meeting, but didn't go into much detail. He swept his hand up her back. "Is everything okay?"

She shrugged. "He sent an e-mail with his itinerary, said he couldn't wait to see me, and that was it."

He gazed down at her. Her gaze flitted across the room, never making eye contact with him. "You're worried."

"I don't know. I guess. It is kind of odd."

It was odd, considering the older man hated planes. "Well, maybe he misses you."

"Maybe," she said softly.

No words were spoken for a while. They stayed like that, her nestled in his arms. Making love to Cali felt right—and wrong—because he knew it wouldn't last.

It didn't happen right away, but eventually, she made up an excuse to leave. And he let her.

CHAPTER TEN

Cali waited for Uncle Cal in her car, nibbling on her thumbnail and watching the various people stuffing suitcases in their trunks and giving each other long hugs. She was torn between being ecstatic at the arrival of her beloved uncle and nervous because she didn't know why he was coming. He hadn't answered her calls when she'd phoned him numerous times over the past week. He'd only texted back to say he'd be there and they could talk then.

He wasn't the only one avoiding her, either. Red had been suspiciously absent since she'd paid him a visit at his house a week earlier. He hadn't called or stopped by to visit. Hoping to force his hand, she'd texted him a scandalous pic of her in her new leopard print boy shorts—and nothing else. His response? "Nice." One word? Usually, something like that was enough to bring him straight to her door. She'd finally broken down and phoned him, but he gave her some flimsy excuse about work and other obligations. He obviously needed space, so she'd given it to him. Even if space between them was the last thing *she* wanted.

Meanwhile, she'd spent her days helping Syd get ready

for her new arrival. Cali had never seen so many onesies and booties. She'd spent hours washing and folding brand-new baby clothes. Unisex, of course, because her friend had refused to make her life easier and find out the sex of the baby.

To make matters worse, Syd was a Christmas freak. It was her favorite holiday, and this was the first time she was in charge of decorating Morgan's house. She went crazy with the lights and the little manger scene on the mantel. And they'd finally finished decorating the Christmas tree after countless runs to the store to buy more ornaments and a brand-new tree skirt. Everything had to be perfect.

Cali couldn't bring herself to get that excited. Although she believed in the reason for the season, she didn't need all the hoopla surrounding the holiday. Send her to the nearest Christmas Eve service and she was good.

Event planning excited Cali, though, and she'd recently finalized the baby shower. She enjoyed the details, the little things that no one else paid attention to but made the shower that much more memorable. Since Syd was her best friend Cali went all out, complete with the theme "Hot Mama." Guests would be treated to a festive occasion, with good food and lots of laughter and sexy Syd in her best attire, because there was no way her friend would not be fierce—pregnant and all.

Smiling, she let herself imagine the looks on the guests' faces as they admired her work. She wasn't cocky, just confident. She tapped her thumb on the steering wheel and frowned, praying quickly that Syd didn't go into labor before the shower. She'd tried to convince her stubborn friend to schedule the event before Christmas but Syd had insisted on a January date. They were cutting it close because she was due the first of February.

When she saw her uncle emerge from the airport, she

hopped out of the car and ran straight into his arms. As usual, he lifted her small frame into his big arms and squeezed tightly.

"Baby girl," he said, planting a kiss on her forehead.

She peered up at her strong uncle. When she was a kid, she'd thought he was invincible. He was all hard lines and muscles. She'd known he'd be able to beat up anyone who dared to mess with her. And he did, she thought with a smirk. Her ex could vouch for that.

"I'm so glad you're here," she breathed, swallowing past a lump that had formed in her throat. He looked good. His wavy ebony hair had streaks of gray, which normally would make her think of an old man. Instead, it made him look distinguished. She studied him as he lifted up his suitcase and placed it in her backseat. He seemed to move a little more slowly than usual. He'd always been quick as a whip, but not this time. He tried to disguise it, but she could hear him wheeze and see the way he paused at times to rest.

An uneasy feeling washed over her, confirming that this was not a random visit. Uncle Cal had something to tell her and it wasn't going to be good.

Once they were buckled in and on the road, she asked him, "Are you okay, Uncle Cal? You normally don't visit in the winter."

He patted her on the knee like he had when she was little. "Well, I figured time with my favorite girl was long overdue. I missed you."

"I miss you, too. Did you want to go eat?"

"Actually, I was wondering if you could drive me over to see Red," he said. "I wanted to take care of some business with him. Do you think he has time to see me?"

She rolled her eyes. Red and her uncle had hit it off from the moment they met. Used to her Uncle Cal's undivided attention, she found their relationship hard to deal with because they talked about everything she hated—politics, basketball, and boxing.

"He should be available," she said. "I have to call him. Syd's here. I'm sure she'd love to see you. We can head over there and get something to eat. Maybe Red can stop by and you can talk to him then."

"Sounds good. I'd love to see Syd. She's been a good friend to you."

Nodding, she prodded, "So, are you going to answer my question, Uncle Cal? What brings you here? The truth, please."

He sighed heavily and she glanced at him out of the corner of her eye before putting her attention back on the road. "We'll talk later, baby," he promised. "They've certainly built the area up. I was just here summer before last and they didn't have all those hotels at the airport."

Born and raised on the west side of Detroit, Cali loved Michigan life. Her uncle had moved her to the suburb of Southfield when he became her legal guardian. He'd grown up on the streets, hustling to make ends meet, but when she came into his life he wanted to change for her. So he signed up to take classes at a local community college and, eventually, went on to a four-year university. From there, he made a name for himself as a chef and was asked to conduct a class on basic cooking skills by one of the churches. He found that he loved teaching and ended up making a good living doing it. She couldn't be more proud of him. If only her mother had had that same drive.

"Yeah, they are building everywhere," she agreed. "You should see some of the neighborhoods. I've actually been thinking about moving to Ypsilanti or Canton. I like the area and I want to be closer to my friends."

"Closer to your friends, or closer to Red?"

Am I that obvious? "Don't start. You know I wouldn't move anywhere to be closer to a man. That's what you taught me." He'd told her to never go anywhere without a knife, to make sure she always had a stash of cash, and always pay herself first. Paying herself first was the reason she'd been able to remain debt free.

Growing up, she had been the only girl in an extended family of boys. They taught her everything *they* felt she should know about men. Her uncle told her to never be dependent on a man and she held on to that piece of advice.

"Well, everybody needs someone, baby girl," he said. "You can't live life alone. If I could do it over, maybe I'd find me a wife and have a few kids. Sure, I did all right. I had you, but it gets lonely in my old age."

"You're not old, Uncle Cal. You have plenty of friends and I know you see lots of women." Her uncle was a player by nature. He always had a woman on the side.

"Actually, I did meet someone that I liked. We had fun together, travelled."

"Really? That's ... different."

They'd never had a problem communicating with each other. Uncle Cal had encouraged her to come to him about anything—even sex and boys. She wasn't a shy person and would often render him speechless with the things she told him, but he never judged her. He always listened and offered advice when she asked for it.

"It didn't last, though. I like my space." It was no wonder she'd turned out the way she was. Between a mother who had an array of men in and out of their apartment and an uncle who valued his freedom from commitment above all else, she was doomed to have a messed up view of love and relationships. "We were seeing each other for about six months, maybe seven," he continued. "But she started getting too clingy, wanted to move in."

Cali burst out in a fit of giggles and he followed suit. "You never change."

The car ride descended into silence as she drove toward Ypsilanti. The snow had let up and the roads were clear, so she had no trouble weaving through traffic. Still nervous about the nature of his visit, she decided to just enjoy her time with him. They rarely spent time with each other and she was grateful for the opportunity. "I meant what I said, Cali," he said finally. "Red...he's a good guy with a good job and a good head on his shoulders. That's all I've ever wanted for you."

Grumbling, she pushed down on the gas. "I know Red is a good guy, but we're not like that. We're friends." *Lies.*

"Friends with certain benefits," he added.

"What? W-what are you talking about?" she stuttered.

"Who do you think you're fooling?" Uncle Cal asked. "I know you. I raised you. You can't hide anything from me."

"I'm not trying to hide anything from you," she insisted. "But you're making it more than what it is."

"I see the way he looks at you." His voice was soft, tender. "Looks like love to me."

"Obviously, you don't know Red like you think you do."

Of course, Red didn't love her. Sure, he *loved* her as a friend, but...No.

"We'll see," Uncle Cal said, interrupting her thoughts. "Anyway, just don't close yourself off. You'll end up alone with a cat."

"Whoa, never a cat." She giggled. Uncle Cal hated cats. And any woman who had one was an automatic no.

He mussed her hair. "Just think about it. By the way, I was thinking I should rent a car."

"You don't have to do that," she said. "I can take you where you need to go. I have some vacation time coming up."

"I know you can, but I want to take care of some things,

see a few friends. I don't want to drag you along with me all over the place. Besides, I'm sure you have business to take care of."

"Okay," she said. The more he talked, she was sure he had something to hide. And she would get to the bottom of it. "I have a friend I can call to take care of a rental for you."

"Good." He pulled out his inhaler and puffed the medicine into his mouth. "What's the plan for Christmas?"

"We're spending the day with Syd and the crew." She blew her horn at the slow poke riding in the fast lane. "You know how she is about Christmas."

He chuckled. "That girl never grew out of that, huh? Do you think she'd mind if I cooked dinner for everyone?"

Of course Syd wouldn't mind, especially the way she'd been eating. "Unc, she's pregnant. All you have to say is 'peach cobbler' and she'll give you the world."

They both shared a laugh at Syd's expense. She couldn't wait for him to see her. Uncle Cal and Syd had a weird relationship. He picked with her all the time and she him, but they both secretly enjoyed trading barbs.

"I still can't believe she's pregnant with Morgan's baby," he said "What happened to Den?"

"Long story. I'll let her tell you the details."

"I'm sure she'll fill me in." He squeezed her hand. "Cali?"

Swallowing, she answered, "Yes?"

"I love you."

"I love you, too," she told him. Turning on the radio to his favorite oldies-but-goodies station, her heart seemed to slow as apprehension consumed her. Definitely not good.

* * *

Later on, Cali sat at the kitchen table with Uncle Cal, Red, and Syd. When Red had walked into the room earlier, she let out a sigh of relief. She'd missed him—more than she'd ever thought possible. He hadn't really paid attention to her, though, and spent most of the evening discussing basketball with her uncle.

Her uncle was firmly on #AnyTeamDetroit, while Red was pissed off that the hometown team had failed to snag the player he felt was most worthy to wear the red and blue uniform. They bickered back and forth on the merits of the team captain while drinking beer and munching on dessert. Uncle Cal had rocked Syd's world by whipping up a banana pudding, and Red was ecstatic because it just so happened to be his favorite dessert as well.

Cali was bored as hell. Even Syd was too busy, yapping with Morgan on the phone in the other room. Standing, she began clearing dishes from the table. She wished her uncle would put a sock in it so she could talk to Red. After her Uncle Cal's sudden declaration of love in the car ride over, she'd been a nervous wreck, imagining all sorts of illnesses and dire prognoses.

Uncle Cal's phone vibrated and he stood. "I'm going to go take this in the other room."

Finally. Once he was out of earshot, she turned to Red. "What the hell is going on?"

"What are you talking about?" Red asked, frowning.

Uh oh. "You're a jerk," she hissed, throwing her hands up in frustration at him. But she couldn't very well tell him that she'd missed him and wanted him to pay attention to her and not her uncle, so she improvised. "You know I hate basketball talk. You also know what's going on with my uncle but you're not telling me."

"I don't know what you're talking about." He shrugged. "Paranoid much?"

Huffing, she crossed her arms and plopped down in the chair next to him.

"I suggest you get that attitude under control," Red ordered with a smirk.

"I suggest *you* go to hell."

"Want a spanking?" he offered.

"Want your ass beat?" she countered, tapping the table with her fingers. "Stop playing with me and tell me what is going on."

"Cali, I don't know anything," he said, raising his voice.

"He told me he needed to talk to you about some business. What is it?"

"I haven't talked to him about it yet." Red scooped another spoonful of banana pudding onto his plate. "We're set to meet up Monday afternoon, if that's okay with you. Furthermore, once I do meet with him, I'm his lawyer and I'm not telling you shit."

Cali reeled back in her seat, screaming when the chair fell back too far. Red was quick and grabbed the rolling chair before it toppled over. She jumped up and smoothed her hair back. "Fine. You don't want to tell me, I'll figure it out myself."

"You know I can't tell you anything your uncle tells me in confidence," he said. "But I'm sure it's just routine."

"There's something wrong," she growled between clenched teeth. "He's not the same. I noticed he has a wheeze that's not going away even after he uses his inhaler. He's moving slow. He hardly touched his dinner. He seems weak. And I'm worried."

Red's eyes softened and he picked up her hand and squeezed. "I'm sure he's fine. He'd tell you if something was wrong. You have to know that."

"Not if he was worried that I wouldn't be able to handle the news. There's something wrong," she repeated. "I need to know."

"Instead of sitting here worrying, why don't you just ask him?"

It sounded so simple, but Red didn't know her uncle like she did. Uncle Cal was a manly man. He wasn't the type of person who talked about his ailments, especially to her. He only told her what he thought she needed to hear. Nothing more, nothing less. "How about you just let me know what you talk about with him?"

He sighed, shaking his head in exasperation.

Shoving him, she paced the floor, mumbling to herself and cursing Red. Logically, she knew it wasn't his fault, but she needed him to break the rules this time. For her. Actually, she just needed him. She couldn't admit it, though.

All week, she'd been forced to really consider a life without Red, since he hadn't been talking to her. She didn't like it. When her mind went into numerous scenarios regarding her uncle's visit, she wished Red was there to calm her nerves. He was *her* safe place and he made everything better. Instead of telling him that, she always reverted to starting arguments, saying things she shouldn't, hurling insults, getting mad for stupid reasons.

She whirled around to face him. "Please?" she whimpered, surprised by the desperation in her tone.

Apparently, he was surprised, too, because he stared at her with his mouth wide open. He approached her. Tipping her chin up, he whispered, "I'll talk to him. But..."

"But what?" Her voice sounded frantic to her own ears.

"If something *is* wrong, he'll need you to hold it together. Can you do that?"

"Yes." She nodded, unsure she'd be able to pull that off but not willing to admit it to him. "Yes, I can. I just want to know. I don't want to be blindsided by anything. But I know him. Something's off."

"Just make—"

Cali jumped when Red's phone tweeted. He glanced at the screen and flipped it over without responding. A random person, or someone who didn't know Red and his ticks would have probably missed it. But she hadn't. She'd noticed the way his mouth hitched up in a small smirk when he read the text. Red didn't smirk at text messages unless...

A muscle in her jaw twitched. "Who is that?" she demanded.

"A friend," he said simply.

"Really?" She folded her arms over her chest and glared at him. "I'm talking to you about something important and you're texting a friend?"

"I didn't text anyone," he reminded her.

"What kind of friend? Who was it?" she asked again.

"It was Love."

She stilled. "Syd's doctor?" *What the hell?* Her chest burned as she considered the fact that Red had obviously been texting someone else. And that *someone else* made him smile. "You exchanged numbers with her?"

"You just said it. She's Syd's doctor. She texted me to answer a question," he said. "Syd called her from my phone and she— Wait a minute, why am I even explaining this to you?" he said. "We're not talking about this. As I was saying, just make sure you don't spend too much time worrying before you have something to worry about."

Glancing up at the ceiling, she willed herself to let this text with Dr. Love go. It really didn't matter anyway. Her focus should be on Uncle Cal, not on who Red was texting. She squeezed her eyes shut.

"Cali?" Red called softly.

"Do you want her?" she blurted out before she could stop herself. Once the words left her mouth, she wished she could take them back. *What if he says yes?*

He threw his hands up and groaned. "Cali, stop," he warned. "Let's not go there."

But Cali couldn't let it go. "I just need to know why you're talking to her."

"I don't have to let you know who I talk to at any time, or why," he snapped. "You're not my woman."

Hurt at his tone and his words, she retreated a step. "That's true, Red. I'm not your woman. And you're not my man."

"Exactly. That's the way you want it."

"That's the way we both wanted it," she corrected. "Don't try to put this on me."

"I'm not even going to argue with you about this. What's the point?" He stuffed a carryout plate that he'd prepared earlier into a plastic bag.

"I'm not arguing with you. I just asked you a simple question."

"Why do you always do this?" he asked, his voice low and controlled. "Every time we get to a point where you're finally letting me in, finally opening up, you find a way to sabotage the moment. What does a text have to do with anything? I didn't answer it for a reason. I'm here with you. I'm concerned about *you*. You can't even receive that. You're so focused on something that doesn't even matter. And I can't do this anymore."

"What are you saying?" she asked, holding her stomach.

"I'm saying . . . this isn't working anymore, Cali."

Her mouth opened, but she couldn't speak. She pressed a hand against her throat and swallowed hard.

"I can't do this anymore," he said, his gaze fixed on hers. "There's too much that's been said and done. I keep asking myself the same question—what the hell *are* we doing? I want to feel needed, I'm ready to be with someone who wants everything I have to offer. Obviously, we both want different things. Pretending otherwise is only making this more complicated than it needs to be."

"Is this because of the good doctor?" she croaked. Cali hated feeling the way she did. Jealousy and a tinge of envy were not feelings she was accustomed to.

"Hell no. It's because of you, Cali." He let out a heavy sigh. "You can't let go of control. I don't want to stay on this ride with you anymore. One minute, you're here with me. The next, you're gone. I don't know Dr. Love like that for this to be about her. But I'd be lying if I told you that I wasn't intrigued."

"That much was obvious," she mumbled.

"Look, I'm not doing this right now." He broke eye contact. "You do you, okay. I'm going to do me."

"You mean, you're going to do Dr. Love," she sneered.

His expression hardened. "Maybe I will," he snapped. "Who knows?"

She flinched as if he'd attempted to smack her. *Ouch*. No matter how clear the writing was on the wall, she hadn't expected him to be so blunt with it. It shouldn't have surprised her, though, because Red was always truthful, even if it hurt.

"What's going on?" Syd asked, walking into the kitchen, rubbing her stomach. She opened the fridge and pulled out a bottle of water. She stretched. "Are you arguing?"

"She's arguing. I'm leaving." Red picked up his suit coat and put it on. He placed a kiss on Syd's forehead. "I'll talk to you tomorrow."

"Wait," Syd called. "You two have to stop this. I know you think you know what you're doing, but you don't. Cali, tell Red how you really feel about him. And Red, say something to Cali."

"Syd, don't," Cali commanded, pissed that her friend would put it out there like that.

"That's right," Red growled. "Don't. There's nothing to say. Even if I did feel something for her, she'd just stomp all over it. No sense in even going there."

"You don't know anything!" Cali shouted.

"Damn it, Cali, what the hell do you want from me?" He took a few swift steps to the other side of the room and back.

"Calm down, Red," Syd said. "Why are you so upset? What happened?"

"He's flirting with your doctor," Cali said. "She's sending him texts and he's all smiling. Then he got defensive when I asked him who he was talking to. We were in the middle of an important discussion. That's all." Okay, so maybe she'd downplayed it a little. A lot.

The truth was it had hurt her that she was ready to open up to him, about to tell him how she felt about him, when he got the text. It hurt her that it was from another woman. But what could she say? The rules were clear. They were allowed to date other people. It wasn't *supposed* to be a love thing. And that text confirmed it.

"Then, he goes on this rampage about how he doesn't owe me an explanation," she continued.

"I don't!" he roared, letting out a string of curses as he continued to pace the kitchen.

"Well, Cali, he doesn't owe you an explanation," Syd said. "You've been very clear that this thing between you has no strings."

She had to pick this moment to throw my words back at me. "We've been very clear," Cali said, motioning between herself and Red. "Both of us entered into this willingly."

"Whatever. It doesn't matter. I'm done," he said.

Cali scowled at him.

"Stop," Syd said, slicing a hand through the air. "Look, either make this right or leave each other alone. I'm tired of seeing both of you go through these motions. Obviously, neither one of you is willing to make the first move. So don't. Let go. And go on about your business. I'd hate for you to not be able to be friends because of this. That's supposed to come first, right?"

Syd was right. That was the one caveat they'd both insisted on. When things got too complicated, they'd agreed to end it.

Preserving their friendship was important to both of them. The sad part? She didn't know if she could be friends with him. There was too much water under the bridge to go back.

"She's right," Red murmured. "Cali, we didn't want this. This was supposed to be fun, a light thing. Companionship. But we're friends first. I'm not prepared to lose that. Maybe it's best that we end this, invoke the easy-out clause and keep it moving."

Cali's heart fell in her chest like a heavy paperweight. "Okay," she whispered. "You're right. Let's just...okay." Unable to find the words, she sucked in a deep breath and wrapped her arms around his waist. When he hugged her back, she closed her eyes and took in his smell one last time.

It was hard as hell, but letting him go was probably for the best, she thought. He deserved a woman who wasn't as jaded as she was, a woman who'd be able to give him what he wanted; someone who wasn't scared to love him. *How do I let him walk away?* She clenched his shirt in her hands, afraid to let go. She choked back a sob as her heart raced. *Say something, Cali.*

After a few seconds, she pulled back and forced a smile before turning away from him. "I have to check on Uncle Cal." She walked toward the living room and paused at the door. "Drive safe, Red," she said, glancing back at him over her shoulder. "I'll call you? About what we talked about earlier."

"Sure," he said, the tick in his jaw visible. "We'll talk."

Then she left him—and Syd—in the kitchen. She was such a coward. She wanted to cry. Hell, she needed to cry. But she wouldn't. After all, this was what she'd wanted. No strings. Right?

When Cali entered the kitchen a short while later, Syd was sitting at the table nursing a cup of hot chocolate.

"Thanks for letting us stay here tonight. I didn't want to

have to drive all the way home. Uncle Cal is in bed watching an old Western."

"What's really going on with you?" Syd asked.

"Nothing," she lied, unable to meet her friend's questioning gaze.

"I saw what happened," Syd said. "I mean, you two argue all the time, about stupid stuff, but this was different."

"Can you believe he's actually talking to your doctor?" The idea of him talking to the gorgeous doctor still infuriated her. "If you would've seen his face—"

"Girlfriend, Red has a right to flirt with anyone he chooses."

"True. But don't you think that's inappropriate?" Cali asked. "She's your doctor. It's a conflict of interest. What if something goes . . . ? Forget it. I just don't understand why he picked *her*. Isn't it awkward?" Awkward, only for her. Syd was going to be pregnant for a while longer and Cali would have to see Dr. Love—and Red. Maybe she'd see them together? Visions of Red flirting shamelessly with the doctor in front of her made her sick to her stomach.

"How so? If he sees someone that he finds attractive and they hit it off, why shouldn't he go for it?"

It was just like Syd to be calm and right. There was no good reason why Red shouldn't go for it with Dr. Love. For all she knew, the doctor was willing to be in an open, committed relationship with Red. With her luck, Dr. Love probably wanted a bunch of kids and a dog.

"Love is a beautiful woman and very nice," Syd continued. "I've gotten to know her over this pregnancy. She's on the ball, almost done with her residency. You have to admit that she's a good catch."

I don't have to admit shit. "I don't know her well enough to say she's a good catch. But I will say that, from what I've seen, she's a beautiful person. It kind of shines on her like a halo," she muttered, rolling her eyes.

Syd chuckled and took a sip of her drink. Tracing the rim of her cup with her finger, she sighed. "And she wants the same things Red wants."

"You knew he was talking to her?" Cali asked, shocked that her friend would keep something like that from her.

"I saw them at the hospital last week," her friend admitted. "They seem to have a lot in common. Why wouldn't you want that for him? Unless..."

Cali held up a hand. "Shut up."

"What?" Syd asked, frowning.

"Shut up. I know what you're doing. It's not going to work. If Red wants to be with *Dr. Love*, then let him be with her."

"You're so wrong, Cali," Syd scolded. "It's not even funny. You've been wrong. I love you, so I have to tell you the truth. You keep him at arm's length and then when it appears that he may be interested in someone else, you get all crazy. But when he confronts you on it, you retreat. You'd rather him walk away and be with someone else than admit that you want him for more than just a booty call."

Wow. She read her. "It's complicated," she mumbled, not even believing her own sorry explanation. "You should know all about complicated relationships." Closing her eyes, Cali cursed herself. That was a low blow.

"Ouch. The claws are out, huh?" Good thing Syd didn't seem too fazed by it. "Yeah, and I recall *you* calling me out then, too. You told me I needed to make up my mind. I'm returning the favor. Make up your damn mind. Either you want to be with him or you don't."

Damn. "I think he just made that decision for me. So this is a moot point right now."

With her head tilted to the side, Syd asked, "Do you really think he wouldn't change his tune if you told him you wanted to be with him?"

"I'll never know," Cali replied. "Besides, who says I want

to be with him? I mean, he's good in bed and everything—excellent, but...I'm good." *And if I say it enough...*

"Stop lying," her friend said, calling her on her bullshit. "You want him and you're too damn stubborn to admit it to him."

Cali didn't just *want* Red. She needed him. If she thought she could make it work, she'd be on his doorstep in a minute. When they were together, even in the midst of an argument, everything was all right. Ultimately, though, he was right. They wanted different things. He wanted trust, respect, and forever. She couldn't trust forever. She couldn't even trust herself. What if she ended up like her mother? Then Red would wind up a casualty of her emotional health.

"I do." Cali swallowed past a lump that had formed in her throat. "I do want him. I just...He was right, Syd. We don't want the same things in life. I really don't want kids and he loves kids. He wants a family. He dreams about the moment he finds his daughter and can be a father to her—as he should. I can envision a life with him—a home—and see myself happy. At the same time, I see him resenting me a few years down the line because I didn't give him what he wanted. And I don't want to apologize for not wanting it."

"I'm not telling you to apologize for anything." Syd waited until Cali met her gaze before she said, "I know how you feel about kids. Red knows how you feel and he hung in there. I think there's a gap in communication. You're assuming you not wanting kids is a deal breaker for him."

"Well, he does want kids," Cali said. "You know that."

"No, he wants *his* kid. He has a living daughter that he's never seen before. He wants to be in her life, but he's not putting some sort of stipulation on you to have his kids. And you would know that if you actually talked to him. He's been searching for Corrine for a long time. Do you even ask him how the search is going?"

Syd was right. And Cali felt like an ass. Red had never told her he wanted her to have his kids. He'd never even hinted at it with her. She just assumed he did because he was so adamant about finding his daughter and so angry with her after that baby talk.

"It's really taking a toll on him, and he wants to be able to share it with you," Syd continued. "What he wants is a relationship, a commitment. He wants to be able to know that you're working toward something together, that you respect him enough to tell him *if* you thought you could be pregnant. He always treats you with respect, even when he's being an ass. I know that because I know him. But his problem is you don't return the favor. That's all he wants. And he doesn't want to have to get up and go home in the middle of the night."

"Is that what he told you?"

"Yes. And knowing Red, he probably told you the same thing. You just didn't hear it."

Boy, I'm an idiot. "I guess not."

"I love you, Cali." Syd hugged her, smoothed a hand over her back. "You are my best friend, my sister from another mother. It hurts to see you like this. I want to see you happy, with Red. Because I know you would be. But you have to deal with your past. Some people run from it, like me. You, on the other hand, wear yours like a badge of dishonor. It's like you have this need to constantly remind yourself that you're going to end up like your mother." Her friend leaned back and looked at her. "From everything you've told me, you're nothing like her. You're not mentally unstable. You've never abused drugs. Cali, you're beautiful, intelligent, giving, and sweet. Nothing like your mother."

Cali's eyes filled with tears. "Well, my mother wasn't like that, either, until she had me."

From all accounts, Carmen Harper had been a gifted

artist with a great future ahead of her until she'd had Cali. Shortly after, she was diagnosed with post-partum depression and eventually schizophrenia. That's when everything went downhill. She descended into a vicious cycle of drugs, men, and madness. And although there was only a slight chance Cali would follow in her mother's footsteps, it was too big a chance to take. She'd never subject another child to that reality.

"It's not your fault," Syd said. "Your mom did the things she did and that's on her. Not you. In the end, you proved her wrong. You have a career, friends who are more like family, and an uncle who's been a Godsend in your life. He loves you so much."

"I know," Cali whispered, her chin quivering. "I'm worried about him. He still hasn't said why he's here."

"Well, I'm praying he's here just to see you."

"Me too," Cali agreed.

Syd pulled Cali into another hug. "Aw, it's going to be okay." She gasped and stepped back. "Did you feel the baby kick?" She grabbed one of Cali's hands and pressed it against her stomach. Cali felt the tiny movement against her palm. "I think he or she likes his Auntie Cali."

Cali giggled. "That's a good thing, considering I'm the godmother and I give the best gifts."

"See? You love kids," Syd said, squeezing her hand.

"I love other people's kids," Cali retorted.

"Oh, I get it."

"Finally." Cali grinned when Syd shot her a wary look.

"Well, I'll be sure to send the little one over periodically to keep you on your toes," Syd promised. "I think I want more banana pudding."

"You are so greedy," Cali told her friend.

"Hey! I'm eating for two." She dipped a spoon in the bowl.

"Yeah, two. Not three."

"Oh my God," Syd shrieked. "You just called me fat."

Cali barked out a laugh. "No I didn't."

"Yes you did. Just for that, I'm not going to tell you about the trip to the jewelry store with Morgan to look at rings."

"What?" Cali asked, gaping at her friend. "Get out. Ring shopping? And you held out on me? If you weren't pregnant, I'd kick you in the ass. I need full disclosure."

"It's not a big deal." Syd scooped a mound of banana pudding out of the dish and dropped it on her plate. "We just went to the store so I could show him what type of ring I would want if he proposed, which he hasn't. We're not ready for marriage yet."

"Well, you did pick up and move hundreds of miles away for him."

"We haven't even been together for a year." She licked the spoon in her mouth and groaned happily. "That would be so stupid to just up and get married like that. So, anyway, we went to the store and I was trying on rings. Girl, my fingers are like little miniature logs. They are so fat I couldn't get any ring on."

Cali laughed at her friend and thanked God for placing her in her life. She'd never know how much she truly meant to her. But she told her often. *Maybe it's time to tell Red?*

CHAPTER ELEVEN

Cali had made such a mess of things. Syd fell asleep after putting her best effort toward staying up to keep her company. Her Uncle Cal had been sleeping for hours. Normally about this time, she'd be calling Red and having phone sex with him.

Syd had given her a lot to think about, but Cali still had doubts. That's why she was sitting at a corner booth inside The Ice Box, nursing a healthy glass of cognac. It was Red's favorite liquor and he'd turned her on to it some time ago. She gulped the contents of the glass down and grimaced at the initial burn in her throat. Leaning her head back against the back of the booth, she sighed.

When a tear dropped on her cheek, she wiped it away with her palm. "What the hell am I supposed to do now?" she grumbled to herself, dropping her head onto the hard table.

"Is it that bad?"

Her eyes popped open. She recognized the voice immediately. Lifting up her head, she frowned at her ex, James. "What the hell do you want?"

"You look like you could use a friend."

"Definitely not you."

He slid into the booth as if he didn't even care that she was less than thrilled to see him. She'd met the much older James when he was teaching her Economics class her senior year in college. They'd had what she'd thought was a once-in-a-lifetime love affair—until his wife busted in one night and threatened to kill them both for the betrayal. That was enough for Cali to throw up the deuces and leave him the hell alone, and vow to never put herself in the same situation again.

Of course, he didn't take the hint. He'd insisted that he and his wife were on their way to divorce court and that he wanted to be with Cali, but she wasn't hearing any of it. She was many things, but home wrecker wasn't one of them. Eight years later he was still trying to get her attention.

"What do you want, James? I'm not in the mood."

He motioned to a waitress as she walked by and ordered a martini, dry. *Some things never change.* "I heard your friend Sydney owns this place. I come here often. I must admit, I always hope to run into you. Guess it's my lucky night."

Cali sized him up. She'd joked with him numerous times about his rigid posture. That hadn't changed. His salt-and-pepper beard was clean shaven and his shirt was buttoned up to the top. Still uptight. Still fine. "You didn't answer my question. What do you want?"

"I've been calling you." He paused when the waitress came back with his drink. After she left, he took a sip. "I wanted to talk to you. How are you?"

"I'm fine," she lied. "Just tired."

"I don't think I've ever seen you cry before."

"That's because you didn't see me when our relationship ended. And, excuse me, but I make it a point to never make the same mistake twice."

"Still a fireball, huh? And even more beautiful."

"Just go, James." From his e-mails, she knew James had

been trying to get in touch with her, claiming he wanted to apologize for everything he'd put her through.

"You're obviously not okay."

Even after all the time that had passed, she could still get lost in James's dark brown eyes. Rolling her eyes, she filled her glass again. "You're right; I'm not. And I was trying to deal with it—alone." Cali noted his ringless left hand. "Where's your ring?"

He snickered. "Put up in my safe. I've been divorced for almost six years. My children are grown and in college."

Her eyes started to glaze over and she pushed the bottle away.

As he lowered his head, he peered up at her. "I've wanted to see you for so long, to apologize for everything," he said softly. "All the lies. I've realized that not fighting for you was my biggest mistake."

James seemed sincere enough. But he always had. And she couldn't trust it. Not that it mattered anyway. She could never forget.

He picked up her hand and squeezed, leaning closer. "I just want a chance to make this right with you."

She slowly pulled her hand from his. "You're years too late. I'm not the same person I was back then."

"Neither am I. Let me buy you dinner."

She let out a heavy sigh and glanced at her watch. "It's eleven o'clock. It's too late for dinner."

"Dessert, then?"

Boy, he doesn't give up easily. "Fine."

"Still like cheesecake with caramel topping? I think I saw something like that on the menu."

"Yes."

He waved the waitress over and placed the order for the piece of cheesecake. They chatted about meaningless things—the weather, Detroit, and food. He was a foodie, so he spent a lot of time trying out different cuisines. That was one of the things she'd loved most about him. He wasn't afraid to try new things.

He shared with her travel stories about Paris and Milan, places they'd talked about going to together.

"Somehow we've managed to only talk about me," he said. "You've managed to evade all of my questions about you."

Tapping her fingers on the table, she thought about how she'd rather be at home in her bed. Finally, she said, "There's really nothing to tell. I've been working."

"Are you seeing someone?" he asked.

She thought about that for a minute, before shaking her head. "No. I mean, I was. But not anymore."

"Well, at least I'm not the only fool in town. Whoever it was should have never let you go."

Cali shuddered with his words, felt a flutter in her stomach. James always did make her feel good about herself. The thought of feeling anything but dread appealed to her on so many levels.

He grinned widely and a smile tugged at her lips. With his pretty white teeth, James's smile was just as contagious as it always had been. She used to muse that it was because he didn't do it often, preferring to maintain a serious persona. Yet, when he chose to grace anyone with a genuine smile, it was a beautiful sight.

The room seemed to spike in temperature. The bar wasn't that crowded, but Cali kept glancing around, checking out the customers. Anything to avoid the warm feeling in her gut. She folded her straw wrapper. "How do you do that?"

"Do what?" he asked innocently.

She peered up at him. "Look at me like you—"

"Still love you?" he asked.

"No. Like this isn't the first time I've seen you in years." Cali narrowed her eyes on him, glad that the warm feeling she'd had a few minutes earlier was gone. "I get that you're trying to make up for the past, but that's impossible. One drink and dessert is not enough to make me open up to you about my life or let you back in."

He picked up his glass and finished his drink. "We have to start somewhere."

"No, we don't. You fucked up. I've moved on. There's no going back for me, especially with a man who broke my heart. You can apologize all you want, but no apology will ever change what happened." Sighing, she clenched her fists together. "Look, this was fun, but..." She frowned when she noticed he wasn't paying her any attention. Instead, he was focused on something behind her. She turned around to see who he was looking at so intently.

Kent was standing there, arms folded across his chest. *Damn.*

"What's up?" Kent asked, approaching the table. "When did you start talking to this asshole again?"

"Wow?" James mumbled.

Cali sighed. It was just like Kent to put it all out there like that. "James was getting ready to leave," Cali told Kent without looking at him.

"You heard her," Kent said. "Get up."

James sighed dejectedly and rose from his seat. He opened his mouth to speak, but then snapped it shut. "Bye," he said before he turned and walked away.

"Wow, Kent. You do know I can take care of myself."

"Yeah, but I couldn't help myself." Kent called the waitress over and ordered a drink. "Besides, it was better me than Red."

She scanned the bar, wondering if Red was there.

"He's in the back," Kent confessed. "We walked in together, but after he saw you with the nutty professor, he went and made up something to do."

Cali took a sip of her drink, studied Kent over the rim of her glass. He was attractive, from his bald head to his groomed beard and goatee, to the pressed button-down shirt and khaki pants. "Did I ever tell you the nerd look was out?"

Kent chuckled. "Right around the time I told you raccoon eyes were last year."

Cali's mouth fell wide open, but she laughed. Kent's dry sense of humor always made him stand out from the crowd. During college, everyone had gone to Kent when they needed a good laugh. He had a knack for making even the most solemn moment a happy one. "You suck."

She picked up her phone and pushed the mirror app to check out her face. He was right, though. All that crying had messed up her normally flawless and supposedly waterproof eye makeup. Closing the app, she set the phone back on the table face down.

"Cali, Cali…" He paused when the waitress came back with his drink. After she left, he took a sip. "Are you okay?"

"What do you think? Me and Red…done. Not that we were ever officially anything. And Uncle Cal is here. I think he may be sick."

He leaned back and observed her. "Wow. That's a lot. I'm sure you and Red aren't done. And I'm sorry about Uncle Cal. I know how much you care for him. But from what you just said, you don't know for sure that he's sick, so don't worry about that until you have something to worry about."

Red had told her the same thing. Nodding, she said, "I know. I'm stressed right now."

"Hopefully when Red gets over here, you guys can talk."

She twisted in her seat and noticed Red heading toward them. Her heart raced as he neared them.

"What's up?" Kent asked. "Did you get your work done?"

Red stared at her, a deep frown on his face. "Not really," he told Kent, his gaze still fixed on Cali.

She couldn't bring herself to turn away from Red's penetrating stare—or was that a glare? The tiny muscle on the side of his cheek twitched.

"Join us," Kent said.

"Nah, I'm going to head over to the bar. I came over to let you know I was done." Then Red was gone, before she could say anything. Panic welled up in Cali, but she couldn't bring herself to get up.

Kent shook his head. "Are you going to go after him?" he asked.

Taking a deep breath, she jumped up and followed him. "Red, wait." She grabbed his arm. "Don't walk away like that."

He stopped in his tracks. His eyes bored into her and his mouth was set in a hard line.

"I want to talk to you," she told him.

"Cali. I came here to get a drink with my boy. I don't really feel like going round and round in circles with you again."

She shuddered at his tone. She couldn't believe he'd given her "the voice": the one he reserved for clients he knew were scum and people he couldn't care less about. It hurt.

"Maybe you can catch James. I'm sure he'd be happy," he sneered.

"Will you at least let me explain?"

He pulled out a bar stool. "No need. You're a grown woman. You can talk to anyone you want. None of my business, Cali."

"That's all we were doing," she explained.

She glanced at Kent, who'd appeared next to them and made himself comfortable in the seat next to Red. "Can you give us a minute, Kent?"

"Hell no," Kent said. "I came over here to tell you that y'all need to go to the back. No more scenes in the bar."

It wasn't that long ago that Syd's drama had spilled over into the bar, specifically on opening night, when Caden had blasted Morgan and Sydney for sneaking around behind his back.

Groaning, she asked, "Can we go talk, Red?"

Red turned to the bartender and ordered a drink before following Cali to one of the back offices.

CHAPTER TWELVE

Closing the door behind them, he sat on the edge of the desk.

"I'm sorry," she said before she could stop herself. "I handled everything between us the wrong way. But nothing is going on between me and James."

"Is there a point to this conversation?" he asked, his voice cold and detached.

Flinching, she blinked. She couldn't believe he was talking to her this way. "Red, don't be like that."

"Like what?"

"So cold," she said. She rubbed her trembling hands against her pants.

"Cali, what part of 'you do you' is up for interpretation?" he asked, a hard edge to his voice. "You don't owe me any explanations. I'm not sure why you feel the need to explain."

"Please, stop." Her stomach rolled and she wanted to leave, but she wouldn't.

"You're so much better than him," he hissed.

She'd seen him angry, downright belligerent at times. But she couldn't think of a time when she felt like he couldn't stand the sight of her—until now. "Obviously, you're mad at me."

"You know what? You're right. I'm mad as hell," he admitted, fury in his eyes. "I can't pretend that seeing you with him doesn't make me feel like my head is going to explode." He clenched his hands into fists, then released them. "The fact that you even gave that asshole the time of day after what he did to you irritates the shit out of me. He freakin' lied to you about a wife and kids—for years. More importantly, he broke you. He literally broke your ass down, almost caused you to drop out of school because he wouldn't leave you alone."

The downside of sleeping with friends was that they knew almost everything—good and bad. Red had been there when the fallout with James happened, how she was ostracized when students and faculty alike found out about the affair, and how she'd had to fight to prove she hadn't received any preferential treatment.

"As far as I'm concerned," he continued, "he doesn't deserve anything from you, not even an innocent drink."

"Red?" She cleared her throat and ran a shaky hand through her hair.

He shook his head. "I'm supposed to pretend I don't want you in public, but you have drinks with the married professor who broke your heart? Maybe it shouldn't matter to me anymore who you spend time with, but it does. That shit matters, Cali. And it hurts like hell."

She hadn't wanted to hurt him. Everything she'd done up until that point was to protect *both* of them from being hurt. She'd thought that keeping things between them casual would keep the emotions in check. Somewhere along the way, they'd crossed a line.

Cali knew she'd been acting crazy and wishy-washy. In hindsight, she realized her behavior had changed right around the time she realized her feelings for Red weren't *casual*. She thought she could keep her friendship separate from their sexual relationship, but whoever coined the term *friends with benefits* must not have taken into account the *friend* part of the term. It had been foolish on her part to think that the already existing feelings for her *friend* wouldn't change once they got to know each other on a more intimate level. "I'm sorry," she repeated.

The apology sounded hollow, even to her own ears. There was nothing she could say that would make this better. They'd gone into the whole no-stings-good-sex thing with their eyes wide open, but they didn't take into account their hearts.

Standing there, their gazes fixed on each other, she wondered what she could say to ease the pain that seemed to take root. He stepped closer to her, so close their bodies were touching.

His breath fanned across her lips and she felt it all the way to her toes. Her stomach tightened as she shifted. "Maybe we should…" She moistened her lips. *Maybe they should what?* She couldn't seem to concentrate when he was looking at her like she was his favorite dish ready to be served.

"Red?" she whispered.

Then he kissed her. She flung her arms around his neck and kissed him back. The intensity and desperation in that kiss seemed to take all of her breath away and she had to pull back to breathe. But he wouldn't be deterred. He pulled her back in for more, his lips pressing against hers hard. Grabbing a fistful of her hair, he nipped at her bottom lip before soothing it with his tongue.

She was in trouble. All she could feel was him—his scent, his lips, his tongue, his hands, his body. She thought her knees were going to give out on her so she clung to him like a lifeline, gripping the fabric of his shirt in her fists. He lifted her up and perched her on the edge of the desk, breaking the kiss and blazing a trail from her chin to her earlobe.

Biting her gently, he whispered, "I want you, baby. Now."

Yes, *yes*, and *yes* were the only words that came to mind.

He was pulling her back in, filling her with emotions she knew would overtake any shred of common sense she had left. But it was okay with her in that moment because she couldn't get enough of him. She wanted him too—more than anyone in her life. Ever.

She whispered his name against his neck before she sank her teeth into his skin. When he hissed, she grabbed the back of his head and kissed him hard. She needed a release, and damn it, he was going to give her one.

"Now, Red. Take it," she commanded breathlessly.

Moving his hands up her legs, he lifted up her skirt. "Only if you tell me it's mine to take."

He arched a brow at her, daring her to make the next move.

"Please, Red. You know I want you." She kissed his chin.

Slowly, he edged her panties off and rubbed her. "Seems like you're ready. Say it, Cali."

Unbuttoning his shirt, she kissed his chest while she pulled off his belt. She pushed his jeans off, and when she hooked her fingers under the waistband of his underwear, he grabbed her wrist. "No. Not until you say it."

"It's yours to take," she breathed finally.

He lowered his mouth to her nipple and she gasped loudly. Placing a finger over her lips, he shook his head. "Quiet, baby." Then he continued sucking and nipping each of her hardened buds. She rocked her hips against him, urging him to continue with soft pleas.

She closed her eyes when he slipped inside her, moaning with pleasure. If she could freeze this moment, she would. This was where they were always in sync, always in tune to each other's needs. He rested his forehead against hers and brushed his lips against hers before pulling out almost completely, and pushing back in harder. She let him determine the pace, take the lead, pulling him closer and kissing him deeply.

He planted one hand on the desk behind her head as she

leaned back and the other under her butt. The pace quickened as they moved in sync. Soon, her control unraveled and she felt herself barreling toward completion.

"Go harder," she whispered. "Don't stop."

He bit into her neck as he pounded into her, murmuring against her skin how good she felt. She gritted her teeth together as her stomach clenched and she came long and hard, her orgasm squeezing out his.

She struggled to catch her breath and he collapsed on her. They remained in that spot for a few minutes. It was her turn, her moment to tell him everything she wanted. But he pulled away from her—physically and emotionally. He wouldn't even look at her as he dressed quickly. She immediately missed the connection. She tugged down her skirt and watched as he buttoned his shirt.

When his clothes were righted, he peered at her for a second before looking away.

She bit down on her bottom lip until it stung. She was willing to do anything to make this right, but she feared it was too late. Still, she had to try. "Red, I—"

"We better get out of here," he said.

"Don't you think we should talk about this?" she asked, her voice frantic.

"There's nothing to talk about." He tugged on his shirt. "It doesn't change anything. We still don't work."

Hugging herself, she held back a sob. "I guess you're right." She brushed past him and walked out of the office, angry at him for hurting her, but more upset with herself for letting him.

* * *

Damn it. Red pounded his fists on the desk and grumbled a curse. He'd hurt her. No matter how much he'd tried to play it cool, keep his head, he'd let his desire for her win. It seemed nearly impossible to not be with her when every part of him was screaming to take her.

He could admit that he was fucked up by taking her on top of the desk. Seeing her with that guy had made him see red. He needed to know that he was the man that she couldn't get enough of, that he was who she wanted in her bed and in her heart.

Red wasn't sure when she'd clawed her way into his. He figured it was around the time he'd made seeing her a priority in his life. Other women had tried, but failed. He'd let *her* in. He'd never pretended to be a saint. Everyone knew he was an asshole, but Cali seemed to like that about him. Even though she pretended she didn't.

After a stop in the bathroom to splash some water on his face, Red slid up to the bar next to Kent.

"Everything all right?" Kent asked after they'd sat there for a few minutes in silence. "Cali bulldozed through here after she smacked me on the shoulder. What did you do?"

"I hurt her, after I . . ." He closed his eyes when he thought back to their lovemaking in the office.

"Um, that's nasty," Kent said with a grimace. "I will definitely have the cleaning crew clean up that office. Which one did you go in?"

"Yours," Red joked.

"I'll beat the shit out of you, Red," Kent threatened.

"Just kidding. I'll handle the cleaning."

"So how long are you going to continue to play this game with her?"

He contemplated Kent's question. How long did he expect to keep this up? He'd left Morgan's house with every intention to be done with her and their farce of a relationship, but he couldn't seem to help himself. He missed her already. He needed her. He had her.

It was always like this for them. The need was so strong they could never deny it. He understood Cali, knew what made her tick. That's what made them work, what kept him coming back for more. He knew any woman after her would not even be a close second. And he didn't want anyone else.

But it frustrated him that she couldn't see what was in front of her, that she didn't understand him. That's what it all boiled down to. She didn't get it. And that bruised him more than anything else could.

"I don't know," Red mumbled. He finished off his drink and motioned the bartender over for a refill.

Kent twirled his beer bottle between his hands. "Why don't you just admit you want to be with her and be with her?"

Red hunched his shoulders. "Because it won't change anything. Cali is dead set in her ways."

"So are you."

"Kent, man, I was. But I was actually ready to admit that I wanted her for keeps. I tried to meet her where she was, though. She fought me at every turn. The woman even admitted to me that she wouldn't tell me if she was pregnant with my child."

"What the hell? Wait. When did she think she was pregnant?"

"She didn't. We were having a conversation and I asked her a hypothetical question. Her answer told me what I needed to know. I'd already been feeling some type of way about our arrangement, but when she said that…it shed a harsh light on who I was to her."

"I wouldn't take it that far," Kent said. "You know Cali. She's not about that kid life."

Chuckling at his friend's dry attempt at humor, he shook his head in amusement. "But that's beside the point. I don't want her to be someone she's not. I like her for who she is."

"Don't you mean *love* her for who she is?" his friend asked.

Red sighed. "This is about respect. Baby thing aside, we've been kicking for years, lying to everyone—"

"Badly," Kent added.

Shaking his head, Red continued, "I even lied to my own sister."

"Syd knew before anyone," Kent said. "She's observant like that."

"We spent time together," Red went on. "Movies, late dinners, weekends away. I joined her on jobs and she went to conferences with me. But when things get heavy, she folds, reverts back to this 'me against the world' mentality. I'd hate to think what would happen if I was able to find Corrine. She'd be gone so fast, I wouldn't be able to catch her."

"Well, she's had a tough life. You know how that is." Kent finished his drink and pushed the glass away from him. "Look at Roc. It took him years to open up after his parents were arrested and he came to live with us. Shit, he still has trust issues, but he's living with Syd, about to be a father. Every now and then he'll share, but mostly it's an everyday choice to be happy. Cali hasn't figured that out yet. She's determined to maintain control, and we all know that love is not controllable."

"We're not talking about love here," Red said. "I told you, this is a respect issue."

"You keep telling yourself that. Maybe you'll believe it one day."

"Shut the fuck up," Red said, annoyed at his friend. "You have no room to say anything to me. You let the one woman *you* can't live without follow a fucking nerd down to Ohio."

"Hey, we're not talking about me." Kent waved at the bartender, who walked over and refilled his glass. "Allina is not the *one* woman I can't live without. She's my friend. You and Syd need to cut that shit out."

"Yeah right," Red grumbled.

"Seriously? I've never even kissed Lina, let alone take her into an office in the back of the bar."

Red barked out a laugh. "You're an asshole."

"The truth hurts, right?"

"You *wanted* to take Allina into a back office," Red grumbled. "You were just too chicken to do it."

Kent snorted. "I've never been scared of that. If I wanted to be with Allina, I would've been with her."

Allina's crush on Kent was as known as Cali and Red's *secret* fling, but Kent pretty much pretended not to know, choosing to take the strictly friends-and-nothing-else stance. But when Allina had announced her plans to marry a minister that she'd only known for a few months, Kent lost it—and her in the process.

"Well, wise one…you know everything. What do you do when the woman you love walks out of your life?" Red asked.

"Fuck you, man," Kent growled. "You're full of shit. But if you're asking me seriously that would mean you're admitting that you love Cali."

"I'm not admitting a goddamn thing, brother."

"For argument's sake, though," Kent continued, eyeing Red skeptically. "I guess you wish her well, and keep your memories close." He patted Red's back and asked the bartender to bring a full fifth of cognac. "But since this isn't about love, we don't have to worry about all that, right?"

"Enough about me." Red slung back the rest of his drink. "Let me take your money on that pool table."

CHAPTER THIRTEEN

The next morning, Cali snuck into Morgan's house like a wayward teenager and tiptoed toward the guest room Syd had designated as hers. After she'd left the bar, she'd driven home. She needed some time to herself, to sleep in her own bed.

"Where the hell have you been?"

Cali yelped and tripped, falling smack on her back. "Ouch!" she cried, wincing in pain.

When she opened her eyes, Syd was standing over her. "Where the hell have you been?" her friend repeated.

Syd extended a hand to help her up, but she waved her off and struggled to her feet. Brushing off her clothes, she said, "What are you doing up this early?"

"I've been up all night, worried about you. Red called. He was wondering if you were okay. Did something happen?"

Cali rubbed her lower back and rolled her neck. Her back was on fire and her leg was throbbing. Limping over to the table, she sat down gingerly. "I'm fine. I went home after I left The Ice Box. I needed some time."

Syd sat across from her. "You look like hell."

"Thanks."

"Red told me you and he had an... encounter."

"We've been having encounters for years, Syd," Cali said sarcastically. "What else is new?"

"How about the fact that you two had just invoked the 'easy out' clause? And I heard you were having drinks with James. What the hell is up with that?"

"It was no big deal," Cali said, throwing her hands up in the air. "I told Red that. Can we drop it?"

Syd held her hands up. "Okay," she said. "We'll drop it. What else is going on?"

"It wasn't enough that your brother humiliated me last night." Cali tilted her head. "But look what he left me with."

Syd's mouth hung open. "Oh my God. Is that a hickey?" She leaned closer and examined it, running her finger over it. "It is! Red lost so many cool points for this one. Who the hell does that anymore?"

"I know, right? I don't think he realized he did it, though. I didn't even notice until I woke up this morning."

"I want to take a picture and send it to Morgan and Kent so they can blaze him." Syd held her sides as she laughed.

"How do you even get rid of these things? Aren't there some home remedies for them?"

She picked up her phone. "I'm going to Google it."

Cali tried to remember what they did back in the day, thinking it had something to do with cold or ice.

"Got it!" Syd shouted, hurrying to a kitchen drawer. She pulled out a spoon and put it in the freezer. Then she grabbed an ice pack and joined Cali at the table. "Here, put this on it and hold it there for a few minutes."

Frowning, Cali held the ice pack up to her neck, shivering as the cold plastic met her skin. "I thought a lot about what you said."

Her friend rested her chin in her hand. "Did you get a chance to tell Red how you felt?"

"No. He didn't give me a chance. He told me it didn't

change anything." And that hurt like hell. She'd cried most of the night, but oddly, she wasn't mad *at* Red. No, her anger was directed at herself. It was her inability to let go of her past that led to her heartache. And she had to deal with the consequences. "I think it's too late."

"I don't agree. You two couldn't even go an entire day. That doesn't sound like a hopeless situation to me."

After a few minutes, Cali put the ice pack down. "There has got to be something else we can do. It's too cold."

"Oh. Hold on." Her friend read whatever website she'd been searching on and jumped up, heading toward the hallway leading to the bedrooms. Cali wondered if she was supposed to follow, but Syd soon reappeared with a toothbrush and a tube of toothpaste.

"I know you don't expect me to brush my neck with that toothbrush?" Cali asked dryly.

"Apparently, you can rub the toothpaste on your neck and let it sit for about fifteen minutes," Syd explained. "Then, rub it off with a warm cloth and, voilà, no hickey within twenty-four hours."

"Straight up?" As if the last twenty-four hours hadn't sucked enough.

"Okay, let's try this then." She stood up and tipped her head to the side. "Pull your skin flat," she instructed.

Cali did as she was told and screamed bloody murder when Syd scraped the area with a...coin? Grabbing her wrist, she yelled, "Girl, stop! That shit hurts."

"Do you want it gone?"

"It's already irritated, Syd," she shouted. "Forget it. I'll wear a turtleneck or a scarf. I'm hungry. What's for breakfast? Is Uncle Cal up?"

"He got up with the roosters and left, said he had to make a few stops. He asked where you were, but I covered and told him you had an early meeting."

Cali wondered where her uncle had gone. She hadn't expected him to be out when she got there. She was hoping to take him to breakfast so they could talk. If she'd known he had plans, she would have gone to work.

"I called Allina," Syd admitted softly.

Cali waited for her to finish, but when her friend didn't say anything else, she asked, "And?"

"She apologized for not telling me what was going on. But she said she'd be back for the baby shower. I don't know what to think. We're supposed to be best friends and she didn't even tell me she got engaged or moved. I'm trying not to be hurt by it, but I am."

"Well, you haven't exactly been available," Cali said. "There's a lot going on. You're pregnant and you moved."

"I'm always available for my friends, even from Baltimore. Last time I talked to Allina, she barely mentioned the preacher. Now they're getting married? Plus, you know how she feels about Kent. It just doesn't seem like she's thinking rationally. I don't know... Then, her business. She had an awesome opportunity to expand her brand by taking over the shop. What about you and her?"

Cali shrugged. "It stung at first, but hey... Allina has to do what she feels is right. I can't begrudge that. She's always wanted to live her life a certain way, married with two-point-five kids and a happy home."

Allina was one of Cali's best friends, but she was closer to Syd because they were more alike. Allina was a prude, for lack of a better term. She always seemed to disapprove of Cali and her choices. They'd gotten into it a few times over the years, but Cali had decided to just let her be who she was. She was a sweet, giving person, albeit a little judgmental. Syd had a different relationship with her, though. They had a bond that Cali couldn't quite understand, but she was cool with it. And when it counted, Allina had been there for her more times than not. That meant something to her.

Cali jolted up when she felt something cold on her neck. "Shit, Syd. Warn me next time," she said, snatching the cold spoon from her grinning friend. Standing up, she glared at her. "I'm going to get a shower." She placed the spoon back on her neck. "If this doesn't work, it'll be fine."

Syd laughed. "I'll make you some breakfast. It's the least I can do. You've had a rough night."

"Thank you. Can you make bacon? I have a taste for it."

"I was thinking Fruit Loops. Just kidding. Go wash your ass. I got—" Syd cursed.

"Everything okay?" she asked, rushing toward Syd, who was leaning over the table, holding her belly. "What's going on? Are you in pain?"

Syd breathed deep. "Oh no. I think that was a contraction."

"What?" Cali screeched, panic welling up in her. "Oh my God. It's not time. What do I do? Should we go to the hospital?"

Syd waved her off. "I'm sure it's nothing. I think it's normal, but I'm going to call my doctor. Hurry up and take your shower in case I have to go to the hospital."

"Are you sure? Maybe I can drive you to the ER right now."

Syd shook her head. "I'm fine. Just go. By the time you get out of the shower, I'll have heard from the doctor and know what I need to do."

Cali wasn't sure she should leave her friend in pain like that, even for a quick shower. Instinct was telling her to stay and insist on driving her to the hospital. She'd heard of early deliveries, but that usually meant something was wrong.

"Go, Cali!" Syd shouted, snapping her out of her thoughts.

Turning, she ran to the guest room. Working quickly to set out her clothes for the day, she hurried to the shower and turned it on. It didn't take long to get the water hot enough and she jumped in, praying the entire time that Syd was okay.

CHAPTER FOURTEEN

$\mathcal{A}$fter taking the quickest shower ever, Cali got dressed, put a comb through her hair, and put on a base foundation and some lip gloss. The hickey was still there, red and ugly as ever, and she scowled at the reflection in the mirror.

"Syd?" she called when she entered the kitchen. "Syd? Where are you?"

Syd didn't answer and all Cali felt in that moment was dread. She walked through the house, calling her name. She heard a faint moan in the master bedroom and pushed the door open. Syd was lying on the bed in a fetal position.

She rushed over to her. "Syd?" She climbed in the bed next to her. "Did you call the doctor?"

"Yes. They said it was normal," she groaned. "Braxton-Hicks contractions."

"This doesn't seem normal to me. Did you tell them how much it hurt?"

Syd moaned in pain. "I..." She screamed and squeezed Cali's hand so tight she thought she broke it.

Gritting her teeth through the pain, Cali announced, "I'm calling the ambulance."

"No," Syd said. "Just...take me to the hospital."

"Can you even walk? It seems like these pains are coming consistently."

Syd tried to sit up, but fell back on the bed.

"Syd?" she shouted. "Damn it. Don't do this to me. You're supposed to be in the hospital when the baby comes, not sitting here in your bedroom with me."

"I can't have this baby right now," Syd breathed. "It's too soon."

Syd screamed and Cali prayed for an intervention. She grabbed the landline next to the bed and punched in 9-1-1. When the operator answered, Cali shouted, "My friend is pregnant, due February 1st and she's in a lot of pain and clenching her stomach. I need an ambulance." She screamed when Syd squeezed her hand again. "I can't do this. Get someone here right now."

The operator explained that she'd send someone over right away and told Cali to try to encourage her to walk. She asked her a few more questions, which Cali answered right away. Hanging up finally, she turned to Syd. "You have to get up and walk."

"I don't want to walk." She rolled onto her back, rubbing her stomach. "This hurts like hell."

Cali clenched her hand to try to get some feeling back into her fingers. "You have to. The operator said it can help."

Syd held out her hand and Cali helped her to her feet. Screaming louder this time, Syd leaned against the bed. "Shit! This can't be happening. Something's wrong. I have to go."

"The ambulance is coming, babe. Hang tight. Walk in the bathroom."

Syd managed to shuffle to the bathroom.

"Now, come back," Cali told her.

She slowly made her way back over to her.

"Go back to the bathroom," Cali ordered.

"What...I'm not walking back to the bathroom. Let's go to the kitchen."

But then Syd doubled over in pain, screaming again and holding on to Cali's sweater. Cali screamed, too. Syd moaned. Cali moaned, too.

"Stop," Syd barked. "You're making it worse."

"Shit, I don't know what to do. I was trying to show some solidarity."

"Just...walk with me into the kitchen and grab that bag over there by the dresser. It's my hospital bag."

"Oh Lord. Oh my God. I'm calling Morgan."

"Don't you dare," Syd hissed. "I will call him if I have to, but not right now. Not until we figure out what's going on."

Cali knew that was a bad idea. Morgan wouldn't kill Syd if she didn't tell him, he'd kill her. *What about Red?* She picked up her phone and Syd snatched it away.

"Promise me. Don't call Morgan unless I tell you to."

Against her better judgment, she agreed and led Syd toward the kitchen.

A loud knock followed by the doorbell sounded and she breathed a sigh of relief. Opening the door, she stepped back as the paramedics rushed in and got to work on Syd. Her poor friend was poked, prodded, hooked up to an IV and some sort of monitor, and finally placed on the gurney. The paramedics asked questions along the way and Cali tried to answer them, thankful that Syd had talked about her birth plan with her. Cali requested they take her to University hospital, where Syd's doctor worked. Normally they would've taken her to the nearest hospital, but Morgan lived in a central location so that helped. As they wheeled her out of the house, Syd was barking orders at Cali between grunts and moans of pain. Cali grabbed the small bag, both of their purses, and the keys off the kitchen counter. Locking the door, she rushed over to the ambulance and hopped in.

Once they were secured in the ambulance, Syd turned to Cali, tears streaming from her eyes. "I'm scared," she cried. "The baby's not ready. What if..."

Cali shushed her. "Don't say it. The baby is going to be okay. There are so many advances in medicine now, they can stop it if it's labor. You know that show with the lady and the nineteen kids...she had one baby months ahead of time and that baby is like four years old now. It's going to be okay."

"Promise?"

"Yes."

Embracing Syd, Cali prayed that this was one promise she could keep.

A short while later, Cali followed the paramedics as they wheeled Syd into the maternity emergency room. Syd had cried the whole ride over, and she couldn't take it. Other people might look at their friendship and wonder why they clicked the way they did, but she knew why. It was Syd. Since she'd known her, Syd had embraced her like they were real sisters.

Syd was emotional and cried at the drop of a hat, but she was one of the strongest women Cali knew, beating the odds in everything. And Cali admired that in her friend. What would she do if something happened to her?

She tried dialing Red again. He hadn't answered the last ten times she'd tried him. *Where the hell is he?*

Scrolling through her contacts, she found the name she was looking for. She bit down on her lip. Hard decisions. Impossible decisions. She let out a deep breath and pushed the call button.

"What's up, Cali?" Morgan asked.

Her stomach churned and her mouth went dry. "Hey," she croaked. "I...um...I need to tell you something."

"What is it?" He already sounded irritated. One thing about Morgan, he was no-nonsense. He was a straight shooter, always in control, didn't beat around the bush. That's why it was so surprising that he and Syd had ended up together. The entire debacle between him, his brother, and Syd had been out of control.

"It's Syd."

"What about Syd?" he asked.

"So . . . Syd is in the hospital and—"

"What?" he shouted.

"Can you keep calm and not yell in my ear? It's not dire," she lied. Well, for all she knew it seemed pretty dire, but she didn't want him to flip out.

"What about the baby?" he asked. "Is the baby okay?"

"As far as I know. They just wheeled her back to a room. I'm going to go check on her as soon as I get off the phone with you."

"What happened?"

"She was having contractions. On the way over in the ambulance, I—"

"The ambulance!" he blared. "Cali, what the hell aren't you telling me?"

"I'm trying to tell you everything I know but you keep interrupting me." She took a deep breath and started again. "Anyway, the paramedics think she may be dehydrated which kind of caused her to start contracting."

"Do they think she's in active labor?"

"I don't know yet. I told you, I have to go check on her. We were at your house when she keeled over in pain. She told me not to call you because, you know, she didn't want you to worry. I just kind of thought . . . hmmm, maybe I should call Morgan," she babbled. "Can you call her? And don't tell her I told you. Act normal, like you're calling out the blue to check on her. Make it good. Don't tell her I called you because I promised. If you feel the urge to say something to her about this, tell her Red told you. I have no problem with throwing him under the bus." She tapped her chin with her finger. "Wait, that's not going to work. I don't know when she'll be able to talk on the phone. Plus, she's in a lot of pain and—"

"Cali!" Morgan blared, startling her. "Stop talking. Don't say another word, just listen." She clamped her mouth shut. "Go in the back and ask the doctor for an update and call me back. I'm going to get on the next flight out there, okay?"

"Okay. Oh, I forgot to say this... They did mention that her swollen ankles and wrists were cause for concern." Cali realized she was babbling a few seconds earlier, but she couldn't stop. She hated hospitals and she was terrified of something happening to her best friend or the baby. If she kept talking, maybe she wouldn't have to think about everything that could go wrong. "I thought it was because she was eating too much. She told me her doctor said she needed to slow down and watch her weight, but I wasn't supposed to repeat that to anyone ever. Damn. Yeah, so..."

Way to mess that up. "Anyway, I don't think you should come or anything," she told him. "Syd said they'll probably send her home and tell her to kick her feet up. I'll tell her to call you, or I'll give you the all clear to call her when she can talk. We don't want to make her more upset than she already is. She's a little scared, ya know? Well, she's not really that scared. I'm scared because I'm the only one here. Did I mention I can't get a hold of Red? And he's been flirting with Syd's doctor Love?"

"Cali, please," Morgan groaned. "You're making me tired. You're nervous and I understand why, but this isn't helping. I'm coming. Tell her or don't, but I'll be there as soon as I can."

Before she could say anything else, she heard the chirp that signaled he'd ended the call. *Great. Way to go, Cali.*

Cali stepped into Syd's hospital room. She was lying there, hooked up to all the monitors. The nurses were running around, barking orders at the techs. Cali couldn't imagine being pregnant, let alone being pregnant and scared for the baby's life.

Syd turned her head. "Did you reach Red?"

"I can't get him. I'm not sure where he is."

"Cali, I can't do this. I can't have this baby this early and without Morgan. Plus, it just hit me . . . we're not married. We should be married."

Cali scrunched her nose. "I think it's a little late for that."

"I want to marry him. I want to be with him forever. We have to make this official."

"I'm sure you will soon, Syd," Cali assured her friend. She wondered what it would be like to be so in love with someone that she couldn't go another day without being his wife.

"No, I want to get married right now."

Frowning, Cali asked, "Did they give you some pain medicine or something?"

"No!" Syd cried. "You have to plan us a wedding. I'm going to propose to him as soon as I get out of here. Cali, please."

Cali pulled some tissue from a bedside table and dabbed her eyes with it. "Come on, Syd. You have to calm down. I don't want your blood pressure to go up or anything."

"Not until you tell me you're going to plan my wedding."

"You know I'm going to plan your wedding." She grabbed Syd's hand and squeezed. "We can set it for July when you can fit into the dress of your dreams."

"But I don't want the baby to be born out of wedlock," Syd said, her eyes wild and wide. "What would my pastor say?"

Cali glanced at the bag of fluids hanging nearby. *Is that saline or morphine?* It wasn't like her friend to be so crazed. Well, not really. Even when she'd have her crazy moments, she was lucid. This Syd wasn't the occasionally whacky Syd she knew and loved. Thinking of something to say to appease her was harder than she thought. She drew a blank.

She'd heard all the weird stories of women in labor and the off the wall things they said, but she couldn't recall any tips on how to actually handle women going through it. The experience was definitely making her glad she'd never have to go through it herself. "Um, well, I think we should wait until you lose all the baby weight before we plan your wedding. Only because you'll regret the baby bump in the pictures. Then we won't be able to drink or do any shots at the wedding. Plus, your ankles are so swollen, you won't be able to dance."

"What if there's something wrong with the baby?"

"Nothing is wrong with the baby." At least she hoped there wasn't. She didn't know how her friend would get through it if something happened. She didn't know how anyone would get through it.

Syd sobbed loudly. "I'm scared."

"Me too. I'm terrified, but we're going to get through this. I promise."

She pulled Syd into her arms and let her cry it out, rubbing her back the entire time and whispering words of comfort as Syd grunted in pain. *Lord, please let someone else come here.*

A nurse pulled the curtain back. "Are you family?" she asked Cali.

"Yes," she replied. "What's going on?"

"We're going to move her into a bigger room. They're getting it ready as we speak." The kind woman smiled down at Syd. "Do you think you can give me a urine sample?"

"I think so." The nurse helped Syd stand up.

"What is that for?" Cali asked, knowing she probably sounded like an idiot to the nurse.

"They want to make sure she doesn't have preeclampsia," the nurse told her.

"Oh, okay," Cali said, trying not to let on that she had no idea what that even was.

Once the nurse had escorted Syd out of the room, Cali pulled out her phone. She signed into the hospital Wi-Fi and Googled preeclampsia. As she skimmed the causes, treatments, and complications, her stomach rolled with worry.

She paced back and forth, wringing her hands together. God, she wished they were home talking about hickeys and not at the hospital trying to figure out what was wrong with her best friend and her godchild. She called Red again. No answer. *Where the hell is he?*

CHAPTER FIFTEEN

$\mathcal{R}$ed knew he should have taken his ass home, but he figured he could use a distraction. He'd just left Uncle Cal. The older man had called him earlier in the morning to speak with him about legal business. He almost wished he hadn't answered the phone. Uncle Cal was dying, and he planned on telling Cali very soon.

It tore him up inside that he couldn't go to her, let her know that he was there for her. He couldn't even tell her that he knew anything. Finding out that her uncle—the only family she had left—was dying was going to be devastating. Now, she had to deal with another person leaving her life, never to return.

"Hey you," Dr. Love said with a wide grin. Instead of scrubs, she was wearing a pantsuit under her white coat. Her hair was pulled back into a tight bun. "I'm glad you called. What brings you here?"

Calling Love had been a huge step for Red. After he left Uncle Cal he tried to concentrate on work, to no avail. His thoughts were running a mile a minute and most of them were about Cali—their failed attempt at breaking things off, his need to constantly be in her presence, and now Uncle Cal's health. He figured spending time with someone who wasn't connected to him or his life would be a welcome reprieve.

"I figured I'd take my chances, ask you to have lunch with me?" he asked. The hospital was buzzing with activity as usual. Love glanced around as if looking for someone. "Or do you have plans?"

"No plans. I was looking for my friend. But he's late and I'm starved, so let's go."

They strolled at a leisurely pace to the cafeteria. Once he finally narrowed down his top three choices on the menu, he ordered and waited. Red wondered why he was there. He liked Love, and that's why he should have stayed far away from her. It wasn't fair to act like he was available when, in his heart, he wasn't.

"Red?" Love asked, tilting her head to the side. "Are you okay?"

"I'm fine." The cafeteria worker handed him his burger and fries and they went to the register to pay.

Out in the huge, open eating area, they found an isolated booth and sat down. They ate in silence for a few minutes. Red tried to come up with a witty question or joke, but he kept coming up empty.

"You know what?" She pointed her fork at him. "You're quiet today. I never pegged you to be a quiet person. Is there something wrong?"

"I'm good." Except for the fact that he was blowing it. He was with a beautiful, intelligent woman. He would be an idiot to not go for it with her. In theory, Dr. Love was perfect. But she wasn't Cali.

"I'm a good listener. Maybe I can help," she offered. "And I won't spill your secrets."

He smirked. "I won't bore you with my stuff. How are you?" he asked, plastering a smile on his face.

"I'm fine. Coming off a twenty-four hour rotation," she told him. "Any minute I'm going to pass out from exhaustion. But other than that, I'm good. It would be nice to get out of this cold weather, though."

"Yeah, a vacation would be nice right about now. I could use an all-inclusive beach resort and a few drinks."

She raised a brow. "Is it work?" she asked.

"No. It's . . . I made a mistake and I'm trying to figure out how to not make that same mistake again. But at the same time, I want to. You see the dilemma?"

"Not really. If you don't want to make the mistake, don't do it."

Makes sense, he thought. "But sometimes the things that don't make sense are very tempting."

She laughed. "You have a point. I guess I'm more of the mind frame that if it doesn't make sense, run far away . . . Just don't do it. It's not even worth it. God gave us common sense for a reason." She paused for a second. "Does this have to do with a woman?"

Direct, and straight to the point. "Wow, you came right out with it," he told her. "Why would you think that?"

"Well, for one thing, my best friend is a man," she said, wiping her mouth with her napkin. "I have an idea of what a man with woman problems looks like. It's all over your face."

"You don't miss anything, do you?" He was impressed. Another reason why he should be happy he was free to pursue something with her.

"Actually, I miss a lot," she admitted. "I tend to have my nose buried in patient files too much to notice much. But since we're sitting here having lunch and everything, I have some time to study you."

"Oh, you're studying me, huh?"

"Something like that." She squinted her eyes at him, arched a brow. "So who is she?"

"Um, I'm trying to work up to you accepting my dinner invitation," he said. "Why would I tell you about another woman?"

"Because. You're cute and all, but..." The corners of her mouth quirked up and she leaned in closer to him. "I can't date you so I figure we can be good friends."

He met her grin with one of his own. "Really? My game must be whack."

"No, you're quite charming, but I'm not looking for a 'boo.' I have too much going on right now, with boards coming soon and figuring out whether I want to apply for this fellowship." She tapped a finger on the table. "So who is Calisa to you?"

"Wha—what do you mean?" he stuttered. "We're friends."

"What kind of friends?" she questioned. "And I think I hit the nail on the head judging by your reaction."

"Why?"

"Well, she's standing over there mean mugging me." She pointed to his left.

Red whirled around and noticed Cali standing a few feet away. She had a tray in her hand. Her eyes were puffy and swollen.

"She looks upset," Love said. "Maybe you should go talk to her."

Red agreed, but he didn't have to go talk to her because she stomped over to the table and slammed her tray down.

"Red, I've been trying to reach you for the past hour," she hissed.

Frowning, he picked up his cell phone and browsed the call history. "Oh, I had it on silent, Cali. What's going on?"

"It's Syd," she cried. "She's here."

He jumped up. "What? Why?"

"Earlier today, she had some severe pains and I had to call the ambulance," she explained, her voice thick with tears.

Red took off, racing toward wherever Syd was before he realized he didn't know which way to go. *Guess I should have asked where.* Love was right behind him, though, giving him directions to the maternity emergency area. His legs were burning and his heart was beating hard in his chest when he eventually passed a giant Big Bird sculpture in the hallway. Love got ahead of him and grabbed hold of his arm, turning him toward a short hallway and the staff elevators. She pushed the button frantically and he bent down to catch his breath.

He glanced up. Cali had kept up, too, and was standing in front of him holding a sandwich. Tears were streaming down her cheeks and he fought the urge to go to her. He hated to see her hurt or in pain—no matter what she did, he always wanted to be her comforter. But he knew that if he continued to make himself available to her he'd never be able to move on, and riding to her rescue would probably be his downfall. Besides, right now, Syd was more important. The elevator doors slid open and they rushed in. Love punched the floor number and they ascended.

When the doors opened, he burst through them and ran to the information desk. "Sydney Williams?" he said to the worker. Red struggled to breathe—he should've had his ass at the gym.

"Red? She's down that hall," Cali pointed left.

"Let me check her chart," Love said, rounding the desk. She typed something into the keyboard there. "I'll be right down. It's room A4."

He bolted down the hall, looking at the room numbers along the way. The door to A4 was cracked open a little bit and he could hear voices. He knocked, but entered before anyone inside gave him the okay.

"Red?" Syd croaked, her voice raspy with tears.

"Syd," he said, rushing to her side. "I'm here."

"I had labor pains."

He gave his sister the once-over, noting all the machines and the big belt-like thing around her stomach. "It's early. Is it actual labor?"

Love entered the room. "You are in labor. I have a call in to the attending physician." She patted Syd's hand. "It's going to be okay. We're going to do everything we have to to keep this baby in there for a while longer."

"Thank you, Love," Syd cried. "Are you on call?"

"I'm actually off the clock, but I'll be in the hospital for a little while longer," Love assured Syd.

Red waited until Love met his gaze and mouthed "thank you" to her. She smiled and walked out of the room with a nurse.

Turning to Syd, he asked, "Did you call Morgan?"

"I did," Cali announced.

"I told you not to call him," Syd said to Cali. "I don't want him to worry."

Red ran a hand over Syd's hair. "He deserves to know."

"He's coming," Cali added, taking a bite of her sandwich.

"How can you eat right now?" Red asked her incredulously.

"I've been here for a while, Red," Cali said. "They had to run some tests, so I decided to go to the cafeteria. Luckily I did because I ended up finding you and the doctor eating."

Syd moaned as she struggled to sit up in the bed. "Ouch. What? You were having lunch with Love?"

Red sighed. "Yes." He hooked a hand under her armpit and helped her get comfortable. "It was no big deal. Just lunch." He eyed Cali across the room. She was staring down at her feet, the sandwich in her hand forgotten. Turning to Syd, he adjusted her pillow. "I think you're doing too much, Syd. Maybe you should stay in the bed."

"I have no choice," Syd said. "I heard the doctor whisper 'bed rest' earlier. That's going to suck."

"At least Morgan will be here to wait on you hand and foot," Cali pointed out.

"You have a big mouth," Syd hissed. "He's probably blowing everyone's head off trying to get here. I can see it now."

Red snickered. "Yeah, I'm sure someone has gotten cussed out."

Syd let out a series of short breaths and groaned. "This shit hurts. If it wasn't so early, I'd demand an epidural or a C-section. Oh God, make it stop."

"You want me to call Love back in here. She's probably still close by?" he asked.

"I'll just get a nurse," Cali offered in a flat, monotone voice. She wrapped the sandwich up and tossed it in the trash.

"You're not going to finish that, Cali?" Syd asked, concern in her eyes. "What's going on between you two? Cali, why are you so quiet?"

"I'm not hungry anymore, Syd. Can't focus on food when you're in pain." Cali glanced at Red before averting her gaze.

Syd grimaced. "My back is hurting. Can you rub my back, Red?"

He sat down on her hospital bed and began massaging Syd's back gently.

Things had never been so strained between them. Cali tried to hide it, but he knew she was bothered by his lunch date with Love.

There was a knock on the door and Love poked her head back in. "Hi." She brought in a laptop and set it up on a small desk in the corner. "So I've talked to the attending, and this is what we're going to do." She explained that Syd was dehydrated, which had caused the premature labor. They were going to push IV fluids and start her on a magnesium drip to stop the contractions. She had to stay overnight so they could monitor her. "Any questions?" Love asked after she went over everything.

"No," Syd told her. "Thanks for everything. I'm so glad you're here."

"But you should probably go home and get some sleep," Red told Love. "You've been here a long time."

"I'm going to head over to the lounge and take a quick nap," Love said. "I said I'd be around and I will. At least until we get these contractions under control."

Syd yawned. "You're awesome."

Love stood up. "Try and get some rest, okay?"

Syd nodded and turned onto her side. "I'm going to try."

"I'll make sure of it," Red said. "No worries. I'll walk you out, Love."

Red followed Love out of the room. "I'm sorry about lunch. I owe you one," he said.

She patted him on the arm. "It's okay. Everything worked out. I wouldn't have been here if we hadn't stopped for lunch."

They walked slowly down the hall. "So is she really going to be okay?" he asked.

"I'm going to do my best to make sure she is," she assured him. "Don't worry. I know it's hard, but we see this often."

He nodded, grateful for Dr. Love. He needed her calming presence in that moment. "Thanks again."

"Is Cali upset with you?" she asked, changing the subject.

He shrugged. "She's always upset about something."

"You can answer my question at any time, ya know?" she pressed.

Stuffing his hands into his pockets, he asked, "What question?"

"About the type of friends you and Calisa are."

"Oh, that question." He knew what she was getting at, but

he wasn't sure he wanted to tell her. Although the thought of talking to someone impartial sounded good. "Let's just say we're the type of friends that don't belong together."

"But you want it to be different?"

"You should have gone to law school," he told her. "I object. You're badgering the witness."

She giggled. "That's not an answer."

Figuring this conversation was going to keep going around in circles, he finally told her, "Maybe."

"Is that your final answer?"

"Yes. I wanted it to be different." His answer shocked even him. He'd just met Dr. Love and was already telling her his secrets.

"I'm sorry," she said, her eyes sad—for him.

"Don't do that." He waved her off. The last thing he needed was pity.

"What?" she asked innocently.

"Look at me like I'm a sorry sucka."

She laughed again, nudging him with her shoulder. "I meant that I'm sorry you can't have the woman you want. Everyone deserves a little happiness."

"Cali doesn't want the same things I do," he explained. "She wants her career, she wants to be free, not tied down."

"What do you want?" she asked.

"Truthfully, I don't know anymore." He hunched his shoulders. "I thought I knew, but lately I've realized that I want more than my career, a nice ride, and a luxury condo. At the end of the day, I go home alone."

"Yeah," she agreed. "I like alone, though."

"You say that now, but one day some man is going to change that."

"Like Cali changed that in you?"

"Not just Cali." He heard the sound of a machine in the near distance. "I have a daughter. And I have no idea where she is. Her mother disappeared into thin air, and I've been trying to find her. Finding out I'm a father did change my view on a lot of things, especially relationships."

"Wow, I'm sorry. I pray you find your daughter soon."

"Me too."

They reached the lounge and she turned to him. "Maybe your problems with Cali aren't insurmountable. Sometimes a sincere and honest conversation will make the difference. Think about it," she said, giving him a quick hug. "And go in there and hold your sister's hand."

He heard a crash in the hallway and turned toward the noise, scanning the area, but when he didn't see anything he headed back toward Syd's room.

CHAPTER SIXTEEN

Cali let out a deep breath when Red walked by without seeing her. Damn, she'd been reduced to following him around the hospital. *What the hell is wrong with me?*

Unable to help herself, she'd followed when they left the room, keeping a safe distance. The doctor had answered all of their questions. What could they possibly have to talk about other than Syd? She hadn't forgotten that she'd caught him eating with her in the cafeteria—before he even knew Syd was in the hospital. Frustrated, she considered bursting into the doctor's lounge to let *Dr. Love* know that Red was off limits. But then she'd look like the fool she felt like in that moment, cowering behind potted plants and rolling carts to watch him. He'd smiled at the doctor like he genuinely enjoyed her company, like he used to smile at her.

Cali stared at a passing happy couple, parents-to-be, walking the halls. The husband rubbed his wife's back gently and they shared a laugh and a hug. That was going to be Syd and Morgan pretty soon. She'd tried to convince herself that she didn't want or need something like that, but she did.

When Red touched her, when he smiled at her, when he

made love to her... everything about him made her want to take a chance. But then she'd let that fear, that need to be in control prevent anything meaningful from happening. She'd kept him at arm's length for so long now that she had no idea how to pull him back. Or if she even wanted to. For all she knew, what she was feeling could stem from him breaking things off with her, or her need to "win." *Somehow I doubt it.*

Cali looked up. *Shit.* She'd been so engrossed in her own thoughts she'd walked straight into another wing of the hospital. The Taubman Center was always busy, it seemed. Spotting a bench, she took a seat. Deciding to take care of some work, she pulled out her cell phone and checked her e-mails.

She deleted a message from her ex and marked his e-mail address as spam. *That'll teach him.* There was a small fire with a vendor which she happily put out. Feeling like she'd accomplished something worthwhile, she closed the app, but her phone slipped out of her hand and fell on the floor.

Bending down, she picked it up. She was dusting it off, making a mental note to get a screen cleanser, when a familiar laugh sounded in the hall. Too familiar. She glanced down the hallway and her heart dropped. She stood up and headed toward the unsuspecting man—Uncle Cal.

As she got closer she heard him tell the tech, "Thanks. I think I can find my way from here. I'll be sure to—"

"Uncle Cal?" she asked when she reached him.

He turned his attention to her, closing his eyes with a sigh. "Cali? What are you doing here?"

"I should be asking you the same question. I thought you were going to see your friends."

"I did."

"Why are you lying to me? What's going on?"

He grabbed her hand. "We should talk, baby."

Cali let him lead her toward a bench. Once they sat down,

he wrapped an arm around her. "Remember you always used to ask me to stop smoking?"

Her heart seemed to slow as apprehension consumed her. "You're sick." It wasn't a question because in her heart she already knew the answer. She'd known since he'd texted her and told her he was coming. "Is it your COPD?" Cali knew her uncle had Chronic Obstructive Pulmonary Disease, but as far as she knew it was a mild case and very treatable with lifestyle changes.

He sighed heavily. "No, it's my heart. It's gotten worse over the past year."

"But you had bypass surgery already. Then angioplasty last year. I thought everything was going to be okay after that."

"Normally it would be okay, but it's not. They're calling it end-stage advanced heart failure."

She gasped. Closing her eyes, she took a minute to process the news. Most people lived with heart failure for a long time, but hearing "end stage" and "advanced" threw her. She needed all the facts. She needed to talk to his doctor. They'd get another opinion.

Her chin quivered and tears sprang to her eyes. *End stage.* She choked back a sob. Her uncle needed her to be strong. And she would be—for him.

"There have been so many advances in medicine, especially here," he told her. "That's why I came here. I wanted a second opinion."

She could hear him talking but the words weren't registering anymore. *End stage.* Visions of the one man who'd always loved her unconditionally—dying—flashed across her mind on endless replay. Suddenly, she was transported back to that hotel room, small and hungry and alone—until he'd saved her. He made her life bearable. She didn't know how she would have made it without him.

"Right now, we're talking about a transplant or even a mechanical heart. But you know how the waiting for the heart is the worst part." He held her chin in his hands like he had when she was a child. "I'm not giving up, Cali. I did feel like I needed to see you, spend some time with you. Tell you what I need you to know in case."

Taking long, slow breaths, she willed herself to keep calm. *Advanced.* "What's next then?" she managed to get out.

"They want to run some additional tests. I have another appointment at the end of the week. I'll know the plan of action then."

Cali flung her arms around her uncle and held on tight. He embraced her as she cried softly.

"It's okay," he told her, his own voice thick with tears. She'd only seen her uncle cry a few times and it broke her heart every time because he was such a strong man.

"I don't want anything to happen to you, Uncle Cal," she whimpered.

"It's going to be okay. But it's important for us to discuss some things."

She jerked back. "No." Shaking her head frantically, she hopped up. "I'm not discussing *things* with you." Whenever sick people wanted to discuss *things* it meant funerals and burials. She wasn't prepared to think about that.

"Cali, wait—"

"No. I can't do this right now. My best friend is in the hospital in premature labor. And now I find out my uncle's heart is failing. There is only so much I can handle right now. I don't want to talk about you dying."

"You're being unreasonable. It's important to talk about my affairs, Cali. You're my family, my daughter, the only one I have to discuss this with. I want to make sure you have what you need to take care of everything."

As much as she hated to admit it, he was right. They did

need to have a conversation. But it wouldn't be then, and certainly not in the hospital. She swallowed and exhaled slowly. "Fine. We'll talk about it. Just not today. Why don't I come with you to your appointment so I can hear what your doctor says? We can go to lunch or dinner afterward to talk."

He stood up and pulled her into another strong hug. Cali peered up at the ceiling, angry that her life was spiraling out of control with every passing minute.

"Where is Syd?" he asked.

"Oh my God. She's probably wondering where I am." She grabbed his hand and took off toward the elevators.

* * *

Red rolled his neck and stretched his arms above his head. Syd had finally fallen asleep. He gently pulled the blanket over her shoulder. It had taken a minute for her to calm down. She'd been talking a mile a minute, worrying over everything.

Morgan had called—his flight would arrive in a couple of hours and he planned to head straight to the hospital. Red had offered to pick him up, but Morgan told him not to leave Syd. Red didn't want to leave her either.

From the moment Red had learned to say her name correctly, he'd appointed himself Syd's protector. Even as kids, he'd threatened other boys on the playground for pulling her hair or teasing her. Living apart all those years, he'd wondered if the bond would diminish, but he knew it was as strong as ever. He'd been ecstatic when she announced she was moving back to Michigan to attend college with him.

By the time she arrived on campus, he'd already warned the fellas on his hall that she was off limits, promising a beat down if anyone dared to challenge him. Syd was furious when she found out, because no one would go near her for the first few months. She couldn't buy a date. Eventually, he'd let up on the reins and she went out with a few guys—until she was brutally attacked one night.

His sister had been through so much, so he'd been happy when she fell in love with Morgan. Red had expected to feel rage that his best friend had bedded his sister, but he'd surprised himself when he gave them his full blessing. He'd even encouraged Morgan to make the move, to admit he loved her. Looking at her now, he knew it had been the best move for her. Morgan made her happy and that was all he could ask for. And because happiness looked good on her, he wanted some for himself.

A soft knock on the door snapped Red out of his thoughts. He set his laptop down on the window ledge and said, "Come in."

Cali stepped into the room with Uncle Cal on her heels. Things were tense between them, but he couldn't deny he was happy to see her. Even when he wanted to throttle her, the sight of her face gave him peace, made him feel complete. "Look who I ran into," she said.

Syd's eyes opened, and she gave them a wobbly grin. "Uncle Cal? What are you doing here?" Uncle Cal placed a kiss on Syd's forehead. "I'm here to see you. How are you? I heard you had a scare."

"I did," she said. "But the medicine worked. Contractions stopped."

"Really?" Cali smiled and thanked God. "That's so good, Syd. I'm so happy."

"I'm so tired. It's been a long day." Syd closed her eyes and soon her light snore filled the room.

Cali's smile faded. "Is that normal?" she asked.

Red, assuming she was talking to him even though she'd yet to look him in the eye, answered. "The doctors gave her something to help her relax. She needs sleep. They're going to keep her overnight and she should be able to go home in the morning. Morgan will be here soon."

"Do you need a break?" Cali moved Syd's hair off her face. "Maybe I should put this in a ponytail for her? I can sit here with her if you need a break."

"No, I'm fine. I'm going to wait for Morgan to get here. But you look tired," he said, taking in her dark, swollen eyes. "Maybe you should go home and get some rest."

Rubbing her eyes, she nodded. "You're probably right. I'm thinking I should go home and grab some clothes and come back. I want to stay close. What do you think, Uncle Cal?"

Uncle Cal was still standing next Syd's bed, his eyes trained on her intently.

"Uncle Cal?" Cali repeated softly.

"Yes?" Uncle Cal finally said.

"What do you think about going to my place with me so I can get a change of clothes?" Cali explained. "I want to stay close to Syd, so I'm going to get a hotel room in town."

Swallowing visibly, Uncle Cal nodded. "Sure. I'll ride with you. Let me make a quick call and we can go."

Cali's gaze followed Uncle Cal as he left the room, worry lining her features. She stared at the door a minute before turning back to Syd.

She gave Red a slight smile. "She looks so peaceful," she mumbled, pushing another piece of hair out of Syd's face.

"Are you okay?" he asked. Her eyes were glassy, like she'd been crying. He got up and rubbed the skin under her eyes with his thumb. She closed her eyes and took a shaky breath. "You've been crying?"

Averting her gaze, she busied herself with straightening up the bedside table and tossing empty cups into the bin. "Would you believe me if I said no?"

"Probably not." He tilted his head to meet her gaze. "Well?"

She picked at her fingernails. He gently took her hand in

his and squeezed. Sighing, she peered up at him. "I don't know. I have a lot on my mind. Besides, I didn't think you cared."

"You know I care. Cali, breaking things off was supposed to preserve our friendship. No matter what happens between us on that front, I hope you know you can always talk to me."

Red watched her eyes dart around the room and wondered which door she'd walk through—the door of truth or the door of holding back the truth. He wouldn't push her.

"How are you?" she asked softly. "I know you're scared."

It was one thing he knew they had in common. Cali loved Syd almost as much as he did. "I'm better, now that I know she's going to be okay."

"Can I ask *you* a question?" she asked.

"What?"

"Do you like her? Dr. Love?"

Red resisted the urge to say something he'd regret later. At the same time, he wanted to be honest, if only a little evasive. "I do like her. Talking to her is refreshing. She listens to me, doesn't pull away when we're with each other. That's . . . nice."

"I don't know what to say to that. I guess . . . be happy."

That response was not what he'd expected. He'd put out the bait and she'd completely missed it. *What else is new?*

He inched closer to her. "Is that what you really want, Cali?"

The sight of a tear falling from her eye told him she was struggling with something. His heart skipped a beat at the mere thought of the struggle being about him and their relationship. But more than likely, he guessed she was thinking about Uncle Cal. The older man had called him earlier with the news on his health. He could only assume he'd just broken the news to Cali.

With her head held high, she sniffed. "If you're asking

me if I truly want you to be happy, yes." Her voice cracked
with emotion. "You know that I'd never wish anything less
for you."

Her eyes gleamed, her lips parted. Everything about her
called to him, and he wanted to touch her.

"I do," he whispered, now standing so close to her that he
could feel the heat coming from her body. Sliding his fingers
into her hair, he pulled her to him in an intense kiss.

She clung to him as he feasted on her lips, her arms wrapping tightly around his neck. He ran his tongue over her bottom lip and she opened for him. The sound of the machines,
Syd's light snore... all of it faded away as they kissed. It had
only been a day since he'd held her in his arms, but it had
been too long. Their tongues dueled with each other and he
wanted nothing more than to pin her up against the wall and
make love to her right there.

Cooler heads prevailed, though, and he reluctantly pulled
back. Leaning his forehead against hers, he said, "I shouldn't
have done that. I guess it's a habit that's hard to break."

"I understand the impulse," she breathed. "I feel it, too."

He ran his fingers down the side of her face. "What do we
do with this?"

"We can't avoid each other."

"So how do we do this?"

She backed away toward the far end of the room. "Keep a
safe distance? Avoid being alone? That's all I got."

"It's a start."

Uncle Cal peeked into the room. "Ready to go, baby girl?"

Cali rubbed the back of her neck. "Yes, we can go." She
brushed past Red and rubbed Syd's leg. Glancing back at
him over her shoulder, she said, "Please let me know if anything changes. I'll stop back by here once we check into a
hotel."

"Will do," Red said. "Talk to you soon. Bye, Uncle Cal."

Uncle Cal waved at him, planted another kiss on Syd's forehead, and ushered Cali out of the room.

"Why didn't you tell her you love her and want to be with her?" Syd slurred.

"Go back to sleep," he ordered.

"I don't get it," she mumbled.

"You don't have to."

"You don't get it, either."

Red groaned. Syd knew him like no other and wasn't afraid to call him out when he needed it. "You just worry about you and my niece or nephew. Take your ass back to sleep."

Soon she was snoring again, and he was left with the irritating feeling that she was right.

C HAPTER SEVENTEEN

$\mathcal{R}$ ed couldn't get Cali off of his mind. Something was off, but they weren't exactly in the best place to discuss it. Work forgotten, he closed his laptop and stuffed it into his bag. He stared at his phone, tempted to call her and check on her.

He heard a knock on the door and Morgan walked in, spotting him right away. "What's up, Red? How is she?"

They greeted each other with a handshake and a hug, before Red gave him the latest update. Syd was doing very well and the doctors expected her to be able to go home in the morning. Morgan breathed a sigh of relief and rubbed Syd's forehead with his thumb.

She opened one eye and smiled. "Baby, you're here," she grumbled.

Morgan dropped to his knees and kissed her. Although he was tempted to leave them alone, Red waited while they exchanged declarations of love and whispered "I miss you" more times than he could count.

"Sit down," Syd told Morgan. "Stay a while."

Red laughed at his sister's attempt at humor and understood why. Judging by his friend's swollen and bloodshot eyes,

Morgan looked like he was going to dissolve into tears any minute. Red couldn't say he blamed him. He couldn't imagine being hundreds of miles away from the woman he loved, not knowing what would happen next with her or their baby.

Instead of letting Morgan pull up a chair, Syd scooted over and Morgan climbed onto the bed with her, wrapping his arms around her.

"Now that you're here, Roc, I'm going to go on home." Red announced. He pulled his phone charger out of the outlet and tossed it into his briefcase.

"You don't have to go," Syd said.

"She's right. You have to tell me about the doctor you've been flirting with." Morgan said with a snicker.

Red groaned. "What the... Cali. She told you, huh?"

"Sure did, but Syd had already told me about Dr. Love. In Cali's defense, though, she was scared and babbling."

Unbelievable. "I'm not flirting with Love, Syd. You and Cali need to quit with that shit."

"Obviously she's upset about it," Morgan added. "It had to be on her mind if she mentioned it to *me*. If I wasn't so worried about Syd, it would have been funny."

Syd popped Morgan. "Stop. That's my friend you're talking about."

"Think about it," Morgan continued. "She's so used to having control over a situation and there she was, losing it. I don't think I've ever heard her like that before."

"Hey, she had a rough day," Syd said, defending her friend. "She was with me when I went into labor this morning. Then, yesterday she and Red broke things off and—"

"Wait," Morgan turned to Red. "You broke things off with Cali? What's that about?"

Shrugging, Red took his seat again. "It's about knowing when enough is enough. It's about accepting that me and Cali... we don't work as anything more than what we are."

"What are you talking about?" Syd asked.

Red glanced at Morgan, who was watching him pensively. "You know how we are, Syd. We argue, we misunderstand each other...basically, we're doomed. Which is fine because we weren't supposed to be more. We went into this knowing what we wanted from each other. We never made promises, we were always free to see whoever we wanted—and we did. Now, it's done."

"Because you broke the rules," Morgan added.

"I didn't break any rules."

"Bullshit. You wanted more. Let's call it what it is." His best friend certainly didn't beat around the bush. "You want Cali, and your arrangement doesn't work with your feelings for her. And you're mad at her because she doesn't get it."

Morgan grinned and Red wanted to kick the shit out of him. "Whatever," Red grumbled. "You just got here after being gone for months. You don't know what the hell you're talking about."

"I know you're a punk," Morgan said. "And trust me, I've been waiting to be able to say that to you for months. Turnabout is fair play."

Red sighed. It wasn't that long ago that he'd accused Morgan of being a punk because he'd chosen to move away when he should have been fighting for Syd. Morgan hadn't taken too kindly to being called a punk and made it known.

Morgan shrugged. "Look, if you want Cali, go get her. Otherwise, you're going to end up meeting some unsuspecting woman who will fail to measure up to her. How fair is that?"

"That's a good point," Syd agreed. "And I don't want Love to be that woman. She's too good for that."

Red didn't need to be told that. He knew Dr. Love was a good woman, even though he'd only known her for a short time. But Love had already made it clear that they were strictly on the friend train, so that was a moot point.

"For your information, sis," Red said, "Love and I are not even a consideration. She's cool. I like hanging out with her, talking to her. But that's all."

"I was just making sure," Syd said. Morgan whispered something in Syd's ear and she giggled before burrowing into his side. "I think what you and Cali need is a conversation. A real, honest talk about what is really going on."

That was all fine and dandy, but Red knew that it was hard to talk to someone who didn't want to listen. "Cali has already made up her mind about what *I* want. She refuses to hear anything else."

"It's about the baby issue?" Morgan asked. "Syd told me what happened and I'd have to agree with you . . . to a certain extent. I can see why you feel like she doesn't respect you, but it's more than that. Cali is content with the status quo. She wants the friendship, the benefits of companionship, without the long-term commitment."

"Exactly." Red slapped his legs, relieved that someone understood where he was coming from. "That's it right there. She knows I never wanted to change her. But *I* changed when I found out about Corrine. I want to be a father to her. She's mine."

"You don't have to tell me how things change when you realize you're going to be a father," Morgan said. He smoothed a hand over Syd's stomach. "Having a child was the last thing on my mind, especially with Syd."

"Hey," she said, feigning offense.

"That's not what I meant." Morgan kissed her forehead. "I just meant with everything that happened between us, a baby was the last thing on my mind. I knew your past, you knew mine. Kids weren't necessarily in the cards for us."

When Syd was attacked her freshman year, the doctors had told her she'd never be able to carry a child to term. A positive pregnancy test was a shock to everyone. But Syd had always wanted to be a mother. And despite the drama in her life at the time, it was a welcome surprise.

"Kids aside," Syd added. "If you want to be with Cali, why not go for it? She's being stubborn right now. One thing I know about her is she is more apt to deny feelings than embrace them. Don't assume she doesn't feel the same way about you."

Red peered up at the ceiling. Sighing heavily, he said, "I'm not blind; I know she feels something for me. I can see it in her eyes; I can feel it when I'm with her."

"She's scared," Syd said, shifting in the bed.

"Are you okay?" Morgan asked, concerned. "You want me to get up?"

Shaking her head, she intertwined her fingers with Morgan's. "Just getting comfortable. Anyway, Red, you know that it's not that easy for her. When I see her and hear the way she talks about you, I know she wants to be with you, but something always stops her from exploring it. I think it has a lot to do with her mother."

"I don't doubt that, Syd." Frustrated, he raked his hand through his hair. "She's talked to me about her mother. I know it hasn't been easy for her."

"Don't give up on her, then," Syd said.

Red thought about what his sister said. He and Cali had spent so much time acting one way, trying to be hard or tough. Now he was ready for something different. Was it fair to push her away because she wasn't there yet?

Red cleared his throat. He noted the tender way Morgan rubbed his sister's stomach and the way her eyes lit up when he said something to her only she could hear. He'd never been the type of man who needed that, but watching his sister happy and in love . . . Could he and Cali have that?

"Well, I'm going to head home. You need some rest." Rubbing his sister's hair back, he pressed a kiss against her cheek. "I'll talk to you tomorrow, okay?"

"All right, bruh," Morgan said, clasping his hand in their signature handshake. "I'll let you know if something changes overnight."

"Okay. My cell phone is on."

Red walked to the door. Turning back, he smiled as Morgan turned off the lights and pulled the blanket over Syd. *Time to have a talk with Cali.*

* * *

Three o'clock in the morning. Red kicked the comforter off and groaned. He couldn't sleep. And sleep was one of his favorite things to do, coming in at a close second to…never mind. No sense in thinking about sex because thoughts of sex always included Cali.

Even the mere thought of her was enough to make him want to call her and tell her to get her fine ass over here, but that wouldn't help. The problems they had would be there in the morning.

His cell phone buzzed on the nightstand. Picking it up, he couldn't help but grin at Cali's picture.

"Hey," he answered.

"Red? I'm sorry. Did I wake you?"

"Yeah," he lied. "What's up? Is Syd okay?"

"She's fine," Cali assured him. "Haven't heard from her. I…can we talk?"

"It's late."

"I'm outside," she said.

He held his breath, wondered if this was a trick—or Providence. Cali loved sleep almost as much as he did. For her to venture out into the cold to come to him…

When he opened the door, she was standing there head down. "Cali? What's going on?" He pulled her into the house and rubbed her shoulders. She fell into his arms, held him tightly. She was rarely like this with him or anyone. It made him happy to have her so close, so open for him.

"Red, just hold me." She looked up at him, tears standing in her eyes. "Please?"

Red unbuttoned her coat and let it fall to the floor, then pulled off her hat and gloves. Without another word, he lifted her up and carried her into his bedroom. He gently placed her on his bed and climbed in next to her, pulling his heavy comforter over her. They lay like that, in silence, for well over an hour. The only sound in the dark room was her muffled crying.

Finally he asked her, "Do you need anything?"

"No," she said, her voice low and raspy. "Just sleep. I can't seem to fall asleep."

"What's going on?" He brushed his lips over her forehead. "What's happened?"

"Uncle Cal is sick. That's why he's here. I don't know what I'm going to do without him," she cried. "What am I going to do? He's the only family I have left."

Red swallowed. "What did he say?"

"Don't you already know?" she asked.

Deciding the truth was better, he answered, "Yeah, he told me earlier."

"Why didn't you tell me?"

"It wasn't my place, Cali. He needed to be the one to tell you."

Her chin quivered and another tear escaped. "I keep thinking about how he saved me." She squeezed his hand tightly. "I should've gone to see him more. I could've told him I loved him more. I needed to do better. But now it feels hollow, like if I do all those things now, it will be because he's dying. And he's so much more than that."

"Cali, he loves you. You're his daughter in every sense of the word. And he's still here. He hasn't died. You still have time with him. Make the best of it."

Burrowing into his side, she let out a deep, heart-wrenching sob. Her despair seemed to fill the air around them, seep into his soul. He felt the sting of her tears against his chest and an overwhelming urge to make it all better took him by surprise.

He brushed his lips over her eyes, then her nose, and finally her lips. Pulling back, he swept a thumb under her eye and down her cheek. "Tell me what you need, and I'll do it."

"I need this," she breathed. "I need you."

Cali coming to *him*, confiding in *him*, made him feel good. Over the past few weeks, with everything going on between them, he'd missed the part of their friendship that was easy. It strengthened his resolve to talk to her. He needed to make sure she understood what was at stake if they truly ended things between them, what they'd stand to lose.

Every hard conversation, every misunderstanding, was worth this moment. She was in his arms, she wanted to spend the night. And he didn't plan on letting her go—ever.

"Red?" she whispered.

"Yes," he replied, pulling her into his arms.

"Thanks for letting me stay here tonight and for not turning me away after everything that's happened between us."

"You don't have to—"

"I do. I don't know how to tell you…" She propped herself up on her elbow. "A thank you just doesn't seem like it's enough and it kind of cheapens the moment. I want you to know how important you are to me. How important you've always been to me."

Her admission touched him. He knew that he was important to her, but he'd been waiting to hear her say it for so long.

"When Uncle Cal told me about his illness, there was never a question," she continued. "I knew where I wanted to be and who I wanted to be with." She looked him in his eyes and offered him a small smile. "I missed you."

She knew *where* she wanted to be, and *who* she wanted to be with. He couldn't believe it.

"I missed you, too," he admitted. She rested against him again and he squeezed her tightly. Maybe there was hope for them after all? He kissed the top of her head. "And you never have to thank me for being there for you." *That's a given.* "Now, get some sleep. I'll be here when you wake up."

CHAPTER EIGHTEEN

Cali awoke to the smell of bacon. Opening one eye, she glanced at the clock on the nightstand and groaned. She'd slept longer than she'd planned. She'd promised her uncle that they'd go to breakfast before she met with a client. But she hadn't been able to sleep, tossing and turning for hours until she decided to drive to Red's house. Glancing around his bedroom, she sighed.

She'd often dreamed of waking up in Red's bed, but even in her wildest dreams she'd never imagined it would be like this. There was a lightness in her chest, a warmth she hadn't felt before now. As tired as she still was, she wasn't exhausted. She was content, satisfied. Spending the night with Red, waking up in his arms, was amazing.

"Hungry?" Red asked with a smile. He was carrying a tray of food.

She sat up in bed and took the tray he offered. "Um, smells good. Thanks for this."

As she ate, he moved around the room. Noting his wet, wavy locks and the smell of cologne, she guessed he'd already showered. There was so much she wanted to say, so much that needed to be said, but she figured it could wait. Obviously, he had somewhere to be.

Looking at him, she wondered if he regretted letting her spend the night. She toyed with a lock of her hair. "I'll be out of your hair in a few." She took a sip of orange juice.

"You can stay as long as you need. I have an early deposition, but you don't have to rush."

"Thanks for breakfast. I'm starving."

He glanced at her. "No need to thank me. I'd do anything for you."

Their gazes held for a moment before she turned away. She bit into a piece of thick-cut bacon. "Well, I figure all those dinners I cooked for you must be rubbing off. You seem to have a way with bacon."

He sat next to her on the bed, rubbed her chin with his thumb, and placed a tender kiss to her mouth. "It's okay, you know?"

Shifting over to give him more room, she asked, "What is okay?"

"To need someone. I'm just glad I was here for you."

She exhaled as his words washed over her. "I'm glad you were, too."

"And you look good in my bed." He treated her to his dimpled smile.

She smacked him lightly on his arm. "Stop."

"I'm serious. Damn good." His gaze dropped to her mouth. A charge shot through her body and settled in her stomach.

"Red, I—"

His phone buzzed on the nightstand. "Hold that thought," he said, looking at his phone. "It's work. I have to get this."

Grabbing the phone, he took it into the bathroom. She heard him tell the person on the other end that he'd be there in thirty minutes. She watched as he rushed back into the bedroom and finished getting dressed.

"Cali, I have to go. It can't be helped."

She slid the tray over and got out of the bed. Straightening his tie, she smoothed a hand down the lapel of his tailor-made suit. It was something she'd always done, but somehow this morning it seemed more intimate. "It's okay. I get it; you have to work."

"Can you meet for dinner later?" He brushed his lips over her forehead and pulled her into a tight hug.

They rocked back and forth to a tune only they could hear. "I promised Uncle Cal I'd hang out with him tonight," she said.

"That's cool. We'll talk soon."

"Definitely. I plan to stop by to see Syd later on."

"Maybe I'll see you there." He gave her a quick kiss. "Stay as long as you need. I'll leave a spare key on the kitchen table."

"Red?" she called as he turned to leave. Suddenly, she was nervous. She wanted to tell him that waking up in his home felt right to her, that she wanted to rethink their entire agreement, that she hoped it wasn't too late. But as much as she'd enjoyed their night together, wanted to see where they could go, she didn't think right then was the appropriate time to bring it up. They needed to talk, work some things out. Their problems wouldn't disappear because she'd spent the night.

"Yeah?" he asked.

"Never mind." She smiled at him. "Have a good day at work."

He smiled and walked out. A few minutes later, she heard the front door close. Falling back on his bed, she stared at the ceiling. *Damn.*

* * *

Red slammed the phone down and scribbled a few lines on his notepad. Most days he loved his job, but today wasn't one of them—especially when one of his clients was facing fraud charges after Red's attempts to get a plea bargain had failed.

His assistant had graciously offered to grab him some lunch when she heard his stomach grumbling loudly. He was expecting her any minute. When he heard a knock on the door, he called for her to come in. "Thanks, Charlotte. Just set the food on the table over there," he instructed without looking up. "I appreciate you running out for me."

"Your assistant wasn't out there."

Red peered up, surprised to see Uncle Cal standing in his doorway. "Uncle Cal? I wasn't expecting you until later."

"I know. I was already in the area, so I figured I'd drop by."

Red motioned to the chair in front of his desk and Uncle Cal took a seat. "You're good."

Uncle Cal had approached Red when he'd decided to leave town, and hired him to oversee some business he had locally. Over the years, Red had acted on his behalf in many actions—most recently, finalizing his will.

"After our conversation, I realized I hadn't disclosed a few important details."

"Okay." Red pulled out a new legal pad. He walked over to his file cabinet and located Uncle Cal's file. When he was seated, he waited for the older man to spell out what he needed.

"Before we get started, I'd like to ask you to do something for me."

"Anything I can do to help, Uncle Cal. Cali told me you finally shared with her what's been going on with your health."

"I did. However, I just left the hospital and the news wasn't what I hoped. I'm not an option for a pacemaker or a heart transplant because of my age, my smoking history, and the COPD."

"I'm sorry to hear that. Was she with you when you visited the doctor?"

Red couldn't help but pick up his phone, checking to see if he'd missed a call from Cali. He'd been tied up all morning and wanted to make sure she hadn't been trying to reach him.

"No," Cal said, his breaths coming out in short spurts as if he was struggling to breathe. "She wasn't with me this morning. I didn't tell her that I was going to the doctor today. We'll meet with them together tomorrow and I've given them free rein to discuss my prognosis in front of her. They're going to try to use medication to control this, but..." The older man pulled out his inhaler and took in the medicine. "But she's going to need you."

When Uncle Cal started coughing, Red grabbed a bottle of water from a small refrigerator he kept under his desk and handed it to him. "Uncle Cal, you know that Cali and I are..." Despite waking up with her that morning, he wasn't going to jump to the conclusion that she wanted more than his comfort. They still had a lot to work through.

"I know. She's told me that you two have not really been getting along. But she wasn't in the hotel room this morning. I assumed she was with you."

Red nodded, unwilling to go into any detail.

"I see it in your eyes." Uncle Cal took a sip from the bottle of water with trembling hands. "You care about her. I know whatever's been going on with you two for the past couple of years has turned into something that neither of you are ready to say out loud. But I need you to be there for her."

"Of course I'll be there for her," he assured Uncle Cal. "We're friends first."

"I don't know how much longer I have," Uncle Cal admitted. "Honestly, I knew all along what the doctors would say. I told Cali that the doctors were hopeful, but my doctors at home...They already told me that my heart wouldn't last much longer. I wanted to come up and see her, spend time with her so that she knows how much I love her."

Red thought about Cali. Her instincts had told her all along that something wasn't right with Uncle Cal. "She knows. And she loves you, too."

"So promise me?" Uncle Cal asked.

As far as Red was concerned, that was a given. He didn't need to make a promise to be there for Cali because it was a guarantee. "I'll be there for her."

Clearing his throat, Uncle Cal sighed. "There's something else."

"What is it?" Red asked, noting the look on Uncle Cal's face. Whatever it was couldn't be good.

"Cali's mother...she's alive."

Red stared at the older man, his mouth open in shock as he processed those words. "What? You've been in contact with her?" From what Cali had told him, he'd assumed her mother had never made contact with either of them after she'd left.

"I've known where she is for a while now," the older man confessed.

"Uncle Cal, I—"

"Hear me out," Uncle Cal said, holding a hand up. "Cali doesn't remember a lot about her mother because she was a child. I told her that her mother had some issues with drugs and mental illness. That part is true. Cali's mother, my sister Carmen, is a paranoid schizophrenic. I remember the night I got Cali from her like it was yesterday. She'd called me from her hotel room, scared and hungry."

Red listened as Uncle Cal recounted what had happened in the hotel room that night all those years ago. He explained that Cali did call him from the hotel room that night, but his sister didn't stay away. After a few weeks she'd tried to come back to get Cali, but Uncle Cal had refused to let her see her.

"Carmen wasn't stable. She had so many problems, and I couldn't very well subject Cali to that pain anymore," Uncle Cal said. "A few years after that, I got a call from the hospital. Carmen had been beaten to within an inch of her life. She'd sustained multiple injuries, including a blow to the head. She was in a coma for weeks, suffered a stroke which left her paralyzed on her right side."

It wasn't often that Red was rendered speechless, but Uncle Cal had managed to do just that. "So, she's not dead?" he asked finally. "I think Cali thinks she is."

"She's alive, but her quality of life is such that she needs constant care." Uncle Cal continued the story, explaining that Carmen's condition was controlled with meds, and that she didn't remember anything about the beating.

"Why not tell Cali that her mother's alive?" Red asked. And how was he supposed to keep that from her?

Uncle Cal leaned forward, resting his elbows on his knees. "My poor baby girl was hiding in a closet, crying her eyes out because her mother left her alone. And she didn't just leave her; she told her she didn't want her, that she wasn't good enough to be her daughter." His eyes glistened with unshed tears. "My main concern was taking care of Cali. I brought her to my house and tried to give her a normal life. One day she told me she thought her mother was dead and I let her continue to think that. I told her about Carmen's mental illness because I figured maybe she wouldn't hate her so much if she thought of her mother as unable to help her actions."

"Well, I don't know how that worked out." Red crossed his arms. "She pretty much hates her mother."

"And she fears ending up like her," Uncle Cal said with a nod.

Red had to know. "Where is she?" he asked.

"Carmen is in a nursing home facility. I've been taking care of her, paying all of her bills. I need you to make sure she's taken care of when I"—Uncle Cal finished off his bottle of water—"When I'm not here to do it."

"I hope you're going to tell Cali all of this," Red said. He didn't want the older man to die without telling Cali something so important.

"You have to understand where I'm coming from," Uncle Cal said. "It's not that easy. Cali wondered why her mother left her, why she never even called to check on her. When she finds out that her mother *did* come for her and I turned her away, that her mother is alive and I've known about it all this time… This may sound selfish, but I don't want her to hate me."

"You did what you thought was best at the time. She'll understand that."

"Would you?" Uncle Cal pulled out his inhaler and used it again.

Red thought about that for a minute. He probably wouldn't understand it. But knowing Cali and how much she loved her uncle, he hoped she'd take his actions for what they had been—him protecting her. Plain and simple. "I don't want to have to lie to her."

"I get that, but I can't tell her yet. Hold on to it for a little while longer."

"When? Until you die?" Red wanted to take his words back immediately. "I'm sorry. I didn't mean to say that. You know I can't say anything, and I won't. But I'd hope that you wouldn't put me in the position to have to tell her something after you're gone—at a will reading or something. She needs to know her mother is alive. She deserves to know that you've been taking care of her all these years."

"She probably does. But what is knowing going to do?"

Uncle Cal asked. "I'd never ask her to take care of her. I want to set up a trust for Carmen, so that she would be taken care of. I need all of her expenses covered until she dies. It's only going to hurt Cali more if she knows."

"What's hurting her is thinking her mother deserted her in a cold, dark hotel room," he said, trying to keep his voice even. "That she left her and possibly died before she got a chance to confront her, to tell her how she felt. What is going to hurt her even more is the fact that the person she trusted above anyone else has lied to her for years."

The older man sighed heavily. "You don't understand. When I came to get Cali...if you would've seen the look on her face...I don't think I could take seeing that same look again—disappointment, fear, and anger."

"I get it. I do. I'm sorry, but...Cali is a grown woman now," Red added. "She's able to handle many things. I know she'd rather hear it from you."

Uncle Cal stood up. "I can't tell her, Jared. Not now."

"I don't want to have to tell her this if something happens to you." It would only cause more problems between them.

"She'll understand that you were doing your job," Uncle Cal insisted. "She's a professional woman."

"No she won't. She's not going to understand that I knew this and didn't tell her," Red argued. Hell, he wouldn't if the shoe was on the other foot. Their relationship was already delicate. He didn't see it surviving a secret of that magnitude and he resented Uncle Cal for putting him in this situation in the first place. "You want me to take care of her? Do the right thing and tell her the truth so that I can do that."

Dropping his head, Uncle Cal nodded. "Okay. I'll tell her. Just take care of the arrangements." He laid a folder on the desk in front of Red. "This is the information needed for you to set up a trust. I want to make sure everything is all set."

"I'll take care of this for you. But can you take care of

something for me?" The older man gestured for him to continue, his eyes tired. "Keep me posted on your appointment tomorrow and let me know when you've told her the truth about her mother." He got up and walked around to the front of his desk until he was standing in front of Uncle Cal. "Please let me know if I can do anything else for you. Cali is important to me. If it makes you feel better, I'm ready to say how I feel about her."

Uncle Cal gave Red a fatherly pat on the back and squeezed his shoulder. "I always knew you'd be the one to take the plunge first. Red, I know you'll take care of my Cali. You're a stand-up guy—honest, discreet when you need to be, loyal, and fiercely protective of those you love. If you and Cali get your asses in gear and try to make a go of it, I know you'll do everything in your power to make her happy. That makes me happy."

Before Red could respond, Uncle Cal pulled him into a brief but strong hug. Words escaped him yet again as he watched him shuffle out of the room slowly. Red hoped that the progress he'd made with Cali in the morning wouldn't be destroyed once the revelations he'd just heard came out. He knew too well the effect of secrets and lies on a relationship.

CHAPTER NINETEEN

It had been a week since Cali had stayed the night at Red's house. Syd had been released from the hospital with strict instructions to stay in bed. They'd successfully stopped her labor and it was important to give the baby more time in the womb.

Red had been preoccupied with an important case. He'd called to check on Cali every day, and she'd seen him at Morgan's place a few times, but they hadn't been able to talk about their relationship because they were both focused on Syd.

It turned out to be just as well because Cali wasn't in any shape to deal with anything other than her uncle's illness and Syd's upcoming baby. After crying herself to sleep several nights in a row, she'd resigned herself to her bad luck and tried to prepare herself for life without her uncle. He needed her to be strong for him and she'd do that.

They'd met with his doctors and she'd heard the devastating news—her uncle's heart wasn't strong enough to work properly and he wouldn't be able to get a new heart or even a pacemaker. She'd left the office in a huff, with her mind made up to find a doctor who would tell her something different. But Uncle Cal had stopped her and told her that he was ready to...Cali swallowed, still refusing to even think the word.

She'd arranged to take a leave of absence from work. But Uncle Cal had ordered her to go back after she'd stayed in bed for a day with a box of Kleenex.

It was Christmas Eve, and the gang was gathered around the massive Christmas tree at Morgan's house. Syd had been like a Christmas-tree-zilla. Her tree had to be perfect and, since she'd been ordered to stay off her feet for the remainder of her pregnancy, she'd spent hours barking at Cali about last-minute ornament changes and extra lights. As she stood before the completely transformed tree in front of her, Cali couldn't say she blamed her.

"What are you thinking about?" Red whispered in her ear.

"I have to say, your sister is bossy but her tree is gorgeous."

He chuckled. "So are you."

Turning to face him, she grinned at the silly hat he was wearing. She squeezed the furry ball on the tip. "I guess you've been designated 'Santa' for tonight?"

"Well, someone had to do it. And since she is posted on the couch, and Morgan said 'hell no,' I'm it. Do you want to see what Santa got you for Christmas?"

He planted a soft, wet kiss on her neck. "Red, you know we haven't had a chance to talk since I spent the night at your place. I think we probably should do that before we exchange any gifts."

The tension between them had faded since she'd slept over at his place. When she'd seen him walk in tonight, for the first time since she'd resolved herself to Uncle Cal's fate she'd felt at peace. And with the smoldering looks he'd been giving her all night, her desire for him was palpable.

"You're right. It has been pretty hectic. Uncle Cal seems to be doing okay. He's got the house smelling like heaven."

Uncle Cal had insisted on cooking a six-course dinner for the evening, complete with five different types of dessert—for Syd, of course.

"It does smell good in here," she agreed. "I think Syd is already in heaven. I saw her with a big piece of chocolate cake."

"Correction. She had a big piece of cake until Morgan took it from her."

Cali laughed, remembering how Syd had called her screaming because Morgan was monitoring her food intake like a hawk. She'd demanded that Cali sneak her some chocolate chip cookies. "She can't be too happy about that. I'm going to go check on her." She ran a finger down his chest. "Maybe Santa can schedule some time for me later? It's long overdue."

An hour after dinner, the gang was still on ten, telling stories and cracking jokes with each other. Cali had missed getting together with everyone. When Syd and Morgan had moved, gatherings with the crew became few and far between. They were seated around the huge sectional as Syd started to tell everyone about how Morgan had tried to beat down the phlebotomist at the hospital because he dared to give her more than a passing glance.

"That wasn't it," Morgan insisted. "The fool was so nervous, he could've nicked something. His hands were shaking and everything. I mean, I know my woman is fine, but…"

"I thought the man was going to pee his pants," Syd explained. "Morgan shouted at him to leave everything where it was, get the hell out, and send someone else that could do the job without slobbering all over himself."

"Damn, bruh," Kent said, laughing. "You flipped the fuck out."

"That's what I'm talking about," Uncle Cal said, giving Morgan some dap. "That's how you protect your woman."

"Don't encourage him, Uncle Cal," Syd said, kissing Morgan.

Cali stood from her comfortable position on the couch, needing to walk off that enormous dinner. Across the room, Red's eyes devoured her as she sauntered toward the kitchen. During dinner, they'd sat on opposite sides of the table. Every moment, every laugh, every trip to the counter to retrieve more food, he watched her. He always seemed to know where she was and what she was doing. She wouldn't have it any other way. And judging by the look in his eyes, he wouldn't either.

She purposely brushed past him as she headed toward the hallway leading to the bathroom. Boisterous laughter echoed in her ears as she glanced back at him and smirked.

Entering the bathroom, all the confidence she'd had seemed to drain from her and she was left with a bundle of nerves. This wasn't her. And this definitely wasn't her with Red. They'd never had a problem being alone. Things were very different, though.

She glanced at her reflection in the mirror and it seemed to mock her. Who did she think she was? On the verge of trying to change everything about them? *What the hell is my problem?* Even as she asked herself that question, she knew the answer. He was her problem, like a drug habit she couldn't kick. No matter how many men she'd dated, how many times she'd told herself it was nothing more than two friends helping each other out from time to time, she always ended up at his doorstep.

She heard the click of the door. "It's about time."

He stepped up behind her. Her heart pounded in anticipation as his eyes locked on hers in the mirror. As his breath fanned across her ear, her eyes fluttered closed. "Santa is ready to put you over my knee."

She opened her eyes and grinned. "As much as I would

love for Santa to give me a special treat, I think we need to talk."

"How about we talk later? I can't think of anything else but being inside you. Right now."

She felt a blush spread across her cheeks and she turned to face him. Sliding her hands up his arms, she whispered, "I think it's important that we talk now."

He leaned against the vanity. "Okay. Let's talk."

"I spent the night—at your house."

"Yeah, I remember. Is this going to be another conversation about how that can't happen again? Because I don't want to hear it."

"No. I . . ." She sighed, frustrated that she couldn't find the right words. "Well, I thought it was nice, waking up to you making breakfast." *Oh God, this isn't coming out right.*

He grabbed her hand. "Cali, you don't have to thank me again. You know that, right?"

"I know. I wasn't going to thank you." She wrung her hands together. "I can't seem to find the words when I'm trying to be open and honest with you about how I feel."

"You told me a long time ago that you didn't do anything you didn't want to do."

"Neither do you," she countered.

"That's right," he agreed. "I don't do anything I don't want to do."

Cali thought about what she'd wanted to say to him over the past few weeks. Seeing him with Dr. Love had sucked and she hated knowing that he was technically a single guy. Even though she was scared of life with him, life without him would be worse. After she slept over, she'd realized that she wanted to spend more nights with him, wake up every night with him if she could. She loved him. She knew the words wouldn't fix everything, but she wanted him to know it, to feel it.

Taking a deep breath, she said, "There has to be a reason why we keep doing each other." *Oh no.* "I mean, not like that. But I...oh boy." She ran a shaky hand through her hair. "I run a business. I talk to important people every day—politicians, CEOs, doctors. I'm never nervous, especially around you, but today...phew. I don't know what it is. But you're standing there, looking so good. All I can think about is being with you, but I feel like we need to have a conversation—if I can ever get it out."

His mouth curved into a smile. "I think I can help you with that."

"Really?" Exasperated, she blew a piece of hair out of her eyes. "Because I could sure use the help."

He traced his finger down her cheek. "I think what you're trying to say is you want to take me off the market." His eyes gleamed in the soft lighting of the bathroom. "You want to be my girl."

Covering her mouth with her hand, she laughed. "You're a cocky son of a bitch."

"But you want me to be *your* cocky son of a bitch," he teased with a wink.

She dropped her head onto his chest and beamed when she felt him press his lips to the back of her head. "I'm sorry," she whispered.

"What? An apology, too?"

Peering up at him, she nodded. "I'm so sorry, Red. I didn't hear you. I was so dead set on what I wanted that I couldn't hear you. Syd tried to tell me and I didn't even hear her. Then seeing you with Dr. Love...The thought of losing you scared the shit out of me." She placed her hand over his heart. "I love you...I want strings. I don't want to just be your friend anymore. I want more. I wanted to tell you how I felt. Then things happened that seemed to shine a light on everything that could break us before we ever started and it scared me. But I'm ready to take the leap—if you are?" Tears sprang up in her eyes and she sucked in a deep breath. *No tears today.*

"I could've said something, too," he told her, tucking her hair behind her ear. "I guess we screwed this up, huh?"

"I guess so," she said.

"Can you...repeat what you said?" he asked. "I don't think I heard it."

"You heard me," she said, giggling. "You just want me to say it again."

"Please...say it again," he whispered, his voice thick with emotion.

"I love you," she said, her voice strong and clear. "You're the only man I want. Everything that is good about us is worth the ride to me. I can't take all the words back, but I do respect you. How can I not? You've never tried to change me, no matter what I've said or done. I know I can count on you to be there in anything. When I came to you that night, you could have turned me away. In fact, you had every right. I didn't make it easy."

Cali wasn't naïve. Admitting that she loved Red was big. But learning to trust herself to take the chance and not let her fears dictate her actions was huge. There was still his daughter and her unresolved issues with her mother to contend with. Relationships were hard work, but she was willing to give it a try.

"I could never turn you away," he said.

"I still don't want to have kids, but if you're willing to accept that—"

He placed a finger over her mouth. "Let's not go there. I know that. I've always known that. It's not a deal breaker for me. Never was."

She opened her mouth to speak, but his lips were on hers, his tongue tracing the corners of her mouth, begging for entrance. He kissed her with a hunger and desperation that took her breath away. Her body trembled with the intensity and she groaned, sliding her tongue against his as he slowly backed her up. She fumbled with the buttons on his shirt as he backed her into the open, standing shower.

She'd truly missed him—everything about him. When she was enveloped in his arms, she felt safe, like nothing could hurt her.

Finally breaking the kiss to breathe, she pushed his shirt off of him. She gasped when he yanked her body forward and kissed her again. He tugged her sweater over her head and unhooked her bra. Dropping to his knees, he slipped his hands under her skirt. Slowly, he pulled her panties down. Her head fell back against the tile as he kissed her knees, her thighs and then...She trembled when his tongue touched her core, circling her clit with his tongue before suckling it into his mouth. Raking her hands through his hair, she ground her hips in time with his tongue. She could feel herself unraveling as she sped toward orgasm. When she felt his teeth dig into the inner part of her thigh, she was done and she climaxed with a low, long moan as pleasure washed over her.

"Maybe we shouldn't do this here?" she said breathlessly. "Morgan's going to kill us."

"Fuck Morgan," he growled.

Before she could say anything else he kissed her again, then turned her around and inched her skirt up again.

He nipped at the back of her neck and her shoulder, blazing a trail with his tongue back up to her earlobe. "Cali," he whispered against her ear.

Bracing her hands against the tile, she breathed, "Yes."

"I love you, too."

When he entered her from behind, she closed her eyes and moaned. If there was one word to describe him and this moment, it was "perfect." He was perfect for her and they were perfect together.

"I didn't think it would feel this good to hear that." She craned her head around and kissed him with everything she had as he moved inside her. He cupped her breasts in his hands and increased his pace. She met him with the same intensity as he gripped her hips, digging his fingers into her flesh.

He made love to her against the shower wall like they hadn't a care in the world, let alone a house full of people in the den.

"Damn, you feel so good," he murmured, biting down into her shoulder.

She shuddered as he slid in and out of her, winding her up like a doll on a string and holding her like that until he was ready to release her. He had all the control in that moment and she wouldn't have it any other way.

Smoothing a hand down over her stomach, he found her clit and pinched it, kissing her to muffle her moans. Pounding into her once...twice...a few more times before she came, shaking uncontrollably in his arms. He followed her with a low groan.

He braced one arm against the shower wall while his other was wrapped around her waist. When Cali was able to catch her breath, she turned around and slid down to the floor. He sat down next to her and they both laughed.

Wrapping her arms around him, she buried her face in his neck.

A knock at the door startled them and Cali's eyes widened. "Oh shit. They heard us."

He put a finger over his mouth, signaling for her to be quiet. "What?" he shouted.

"Red? What the hell are you doing in my bathroom?" Morgan called through the door.

"Don't worry about what I'm doing. I'll be out in a few minutes."

"You know we heard you, right?" Morgan shouted.

Her mouth fell open and he pinched her lips closed. *How embarrassing.* More like mortified. If Morgan had heard them, Uncle Cal had too. *Oh my God!*

"Roc, just go," Red demanded. "I'll be right out."

"Okay, fine. But I'm warning you . . . you two are going to get blazed on." Morgan laughed.

When his laughter tapered off, Cali jumped up. "Oh my God, Red. My uncle is out there. He probably heard me— you— Oh my God."

Red pulled up his pants, leaving them unbuttoned. "It's cool. I doubt they heard us. Roc is messing with you. Every room in his place is soundproof and he did that for a reason. It's fine. Don't worry about it."

"You better be right because I'm blaming everything on you if you're not."

"Good luck with that," he grumbled, tossing her a clean washcloth from one of the drawers. "Why don't you just take a deep breath and let me clean you up a little."

Smirking, she wondered when they'd ever get out of the bathroom. But that was okay, too.

CHAPTER TWENTY

 $\mathcal{R}$ ed watched Cali sleep and wondered why it had taken them so long to get here. After they'd left Morgan's house the night before, they'd dropped Uncle Cal off at the hotel and had come back to his place. Waking up with her nuzzled up against him was as close to perfection as he could ever hope to touch.

He couldn't get enough of her and he'd proven that multiple times, even waking her in the middle of the night to make love again. As he took in her plentiful curves, her pouty mouth swollen from his kisses, her hair fanned out against his pillow, the smell of her skin, he thought he was the luckiest man in the world.

When she'd finally admitted that she loved him, it had felt surreal. He'd known that she loved him, but neither of them had gone into this expecting to leave their hearts with the other. Her eyes opened and he brushed his thumb over her cheek. "Good morning." He kissed her.

She covered her face as a blush crept up the back of her neck. "Oh my God, did this really happen?"

He lay back, peering up at the ceiling, and pulled her into his side. "Yes it did. Any regrets?"

She grinned up at him. "Not a one—right now anyway. You know me."

He smacked her butt playfully. "Stop. We are really doing this."

They settled into a comfortable silence, his fingers intertwined with hers, their breathing in tune with each other's. He ran his thumb over her palm and brought it up to his mouth and kissed it.

"Truthfully, I can't even believe I'm here," she said softly. "Over the past few weeks we were on different pages. I don't know how you put up with me."

He laughed quietly. "Lots of patience."

She gaped at him, feigning offense. "Be quiet."

"It's okay, though, because there are a lot of things that impress me about you. Everything evens out."

With eyebrows raised, she asked, "What impresses you?"

"I think I'll keep that to myself." He smoothed a hand up and down her back. "Don't want you to let it go to your head."

"You know you're wrong, right?" She draped her leg over him snuggled closer.

"I can only be me."

Casting a glance at him, she bit her bottom lip. "So I'm not sure what happens next. I haven't been in a real relationship in years."

"That one doesn't count, because he was more of an asshole than I could ever be," Red said frankly. "Liars who hide the fact that they're married with children cannot be included in your relationship history, so let's scratch that one off the books."

"I guess that means crazy bitches who try to kill you don't count either?" she countered, with a wink and a wide grin. Her body quaked with laughter.

"Ouch." He barked out a laugh. He'd missed their back

and forth banter. Not too many people could deliver a zinger like Cali. "Good one. But Nia was never my girlfriend, so I'd agree with you that she doesn't count. How about we nix this entire conversation and say that this is a first for both of us?"

"Agreed." She rested her head on his chest, her fingers flitting over his skin. "I don't mean to sound all sappy, but last night was everything—like a dream come true."

"And to think it wasn't even a hard dream to attain," he quipped.

She pinched his nipple and he winced in pain. "I'm serious."

"I'm serious, too," he told her, tilting her chin up to meet her gaze. "Seems to me that an actual conversation was all we needed to get it together. History has proven that communication is the key. If we do anything, I think we should promise to always listen to each other."

"Deal." She pressed her lips against his. Drumming her fingers over his chest, she pulled back. "I think I want to get in the shower. Better yet, a soak in the tub since my body is so sore."

He smacked her ass softly. "Okay. I have some bath gel under the sink."

She sat up and smirked at him over her shoulder. "I'm going to run the water. I expect your ass in there within the next five minutes."

"No doubt." His phone buzzed on the table next to the bed. He rolled over and picked it up. "Jared Williams," he answered.

"Red?"

Red sat up, recognizing the voice immediately. "Nia. Where the hell are you?" he roared. He opened the drawer and felt around for a pen.

"I need your help," she said. "We need to talk."

"If you're not calling to tell me where my fucking daughter is, you don't have anything to say that I want to hear."

"Your daughter is *safe* and that's all that matters," she snapped.

Furious, he slammed the drawer. "Like hell," he growled. "Where the hell do you get off asking me for anything? You told me that I had a daughter and vanished before I even met her. Your crazy ass is really on one if you think I'm going to help you do anything."

"Listen, I'm in trouble. I need some money."

"You're serious?" he asked incredulously. "Where are you?"

"I'm in jail," she replied.

"What?" he shouted. "Where is Corrine?"

His mind immediately raced with all the possibilities. His daughter could be anywhere. Was she scared? Alone? He wanted to throttle Nia. He bit the inside of his check in an effort to calm his nerves.

"She's with a friend," Nia said.

"Nia, don't play with me," he warned. "What the hell did you do?"

"Don't worry about that. Pay my bail and I'll make sure you see Corrine."

Red contemplated her request. Nia had always been nuts, from the moment he laid eyes on her. Syd and everyone had warned him about her from the beginning. It wasn't until she tried to stab him with a fork—and ended up stabbing Morgan instead—that he'd actually started listening. Syd had hauled off and clocked her, which ended the farce of a relationship.

Ending their *fling* wasn't as easy as he thought, though. She hadn't gone away as quickly as he'd hoped and eventually she'd tried to run him off the road. Then there was the time she'd slashed all of his tires and tried to bash him in the head with a bat. He'd had to take out a Personal Protection Order. He'd thought he was in the clear when she up and left town out of the blue.

She didn't show up until years later, when she tried to insert herself back into his life by revealing that they had a child.

"Red?" she called, snapping him out of his thoughts. "Answer me. Are you going to help me or not?"

"Nia, where is my daughter?" He heard the water turn on in the bathroom. "You tell me that and maybe I'll help you."

"I'm not stupid, Red," she said. "I'm not going to tell you where she is so you can come and take her from me. I don't have anyone else to call. I know you want Corrine to be safe. If I'm not with her, how can I guarantee that?"

"It's not going to take me long to figure out what jail you're in." He tapped the tip of his pen on his knee. "Your best bet is to just tell me where she is."

"Why are you so cold to me?" she whined in her grating voice. "We had a relationship. I loved you."

As with every conversation with Nia, Red felt like he had whiplash. How did the conversation go from "help bail me out" to "I loved you"? She was incapable of forming linear thoughts. Her mind constantly jumped from one thing to the next, very rarely making sense. He wondered what had possessed him to do anything with her.

"You should have thought about that before you took my daughter away from me, sweetheart," he said sarcastically, running a hand over his face and massaging his temple. "That's neither here nor there, anyway. You know we never had anything more than sex."

"You're going to regret this," she threatened, once again switching gears. If she wasn't a mental case, he didn't know who was. "I'll make you pay."

"The only person with regrets will be your ass when I

find you and make sure whatever charges they have on you stick," he sneered. "The simple fact that you called *me* to ask me to help you proves that your ass is crazy. You have no business raising any child, let alone mine."

The next sound was the click of her hanging up. For an instant, Red wished he hadn't let his temper get the best of him. He should have played her game and told her what she wanted to hear. But he was done playing with her. Red pounded a fist onto the night table. Punching in the number to a friend in the police department who had been doing some investigative work for him as a favor, he waited. When the officer picked up, he told him everything.

After he ended the phone call, he walked into the bathroom. The phone call from Nia was still running through his mind. He was still angry, and wondered if he should wait until he calmed down to talk to Cali about it. At the same time he was concerned that telling her would somehow stop what was happening between them.

The sight of her soaking in the oversized tub immediately put him at ease. Bubbles covered her body, and her eyes were closed. Soft jazz played on the stereo dock on the sink. The urge to be with her seemed to take over.

She opened one eye. "I was wondering when you were going to join me."

Dropping his pants, he climbed into the tub behind her and she leaned back into him. He ran his hands over her knees. He traced her ear with his tongue, enjoying her quick intake of breath. The feel of her body against his calmed him and he wanted to revel in that peace for a minute. She ran her fingernails through the hair on his legs.

"Something wrong?" she asked eventually.

He swirled a finger around one of her nipples until it hardened into a stiff peak. Then he dipped his other hand into the water and cupped her, moving one finger over her slit. Tilting her head up to his, he kissed her deeply, running his tongue over hers. He continued to ply her with his fingers until she screamed out his name.

With hooded eyes, she peered at him. "That feels good," she whispered with a hint of a smile.

Looking into her eyes, seeing her feelings shining back at him, made him want to share everything with her—even if it made him vulnerable. "I have something I want to tell you."

Her body went stiff in his arms. "Is everything okay?" She shifted so she could face him, concern shining in her brown eyes. "What's wrong?"

"Nia called me."

She frowned. "Today?"

"I just got off the phone with her," he said. After the night and morning they'd had, he hated to throw a damper on their time together. But if they were going to be together, Cali had to know.

"What did she want?" she asked.

"To ask me to bail her out of jail."

Her eyes widened. "Seriously?" she asked. "Where's… where's Corrine?"

He shrugged. "I have no idea. I called my friend at the police department and he's going to search the Vinelink database to see if he can get some arrest information. In the meantime, she called me from a restricted phone number, but it's possible he can get the call information from my provider."

"Wow. She's… I can't even believe she's playing these games," she said, her nostrils flaring. "Why wouldn't she just tell you where she was?"

Red, surprised at Cali's reaction, answered her, "I asked multiple times, but she refused. Then I threatened her."

"I would've threatened her, too." She shook her fist into the air.

It felt good to know that she had his back. Not that he thought she wouldn't. But as he listened to her swear under her breath and call Nia a few choice words, his heart swelled. "I swear, Cali. I have to check myself every time I think about her. Part of me wants to..."

"Don't say it," she said, holding her hand against his mouth. "You're not even that type of man. But believe me, if I ever see her, I'll take care of that for you."

Red smiled at his feisty Cali. While Syd wasn't the type to beat someone down, Cali wasn't afraid of a fight. She'd had more than a few scrapes growing up with her uncle and even during their time in college. He'd never want to put her in that position, though. Nia was a nut on her best day and he'd never want Cali in harm's way.

"Do you think she's in the state?" she asked.

"I'm not sure." He knew she had family in Ohio and Mississippi. He'd been checking with contacts in both of those states for a while now. "Every time I get a lead, the trail turns cold. It seems she's always one step ahead of me. My gut is telling me that she's close, though."

"Actually, I agree with you," she said, relaxing her back against him again. "It would be just like her to hide in some small town where you'll least expect her to go. Somewhere like Hell or even Boyne Mountains."

He snickered and rubbed his thumb over her belly button. "That would be a stupid move on her part. But it makes sense to me. Hopefully, he can find something. This has gone on for far too long."

"I hope you get some answers," she said. "I feel for that little girl. She doesn't deserve to be used as a pawn. It's not fair to her." The water sloshed as she turned around and wrapped her legs around his waist. "Or you. I'm so sorry, Red."

Their lips met again in a passionate kiss. Wrapping his arms around her, he held her to him. Her concern for him—and Corrine—made him feel like they'd get through anything together.

"Baby, I could definitely get used to this." He took one of her nipples into his mouth and suckled on it before kissing his way to the other one and giving it the same attention.

"Oh," she moaned, "me too."

Grabbing her hips and moving her over his hardening erection, he asked, "Why don't you hop on that and fuck me like you mean it?"

The corners of her mouth turned upward in a grin. "It would be my pleasure."

*C*HAPTER TWENTY-ONE

*C*ali basked in Red's love for the rest of the week. They'd eaten breakfast together every morning and spent every evening together watching movies, eating out, or just playing video games. Cali was partial to the fighting game where she could turn into a big fat giant and stomp on Red's character. Uncle Cal joined them most evenings, but she made it a point to spend alone time with him. She'd taken him to the mall to spend his Macy's gift card on a new suit and for pedicures, which he fought her on until he realized how good it made him feel. It was heaven spending time with her two favorite men and she didn't want it to end. When Morgan called with an invitation to a private dinner at the bar on New Year's Eve, she was tempted to turn it down for some alone time with Red, but he'd insisted, so they all planned to meet up around eight o'clock.

Rummaging through her suitcase, she groaned at her lack of forethought when it came to packing. She hated living out of a suitcase, but felt better being closer to the hospital. She pulled out a pair of tights and held them in the air. Black or Blue?

"Black?" Red said from his position on the chair in the corner of the room.

She hadn't realized she'd spoken out loud. "Thanks. This is for the birds. I'm thinking I should finally try and find a place closer to..." *Him?*

"I've been telling you for years to move closer. It's definitely not a bad idea. Why don't you and Uncle Cal stay with me? I have an extra bedroom for him and you..." His gaze traveled over her body like a caress. "You can sleep with me."

"Are you serious? I don't want to put you out."

"I don't mind."

She sat down on his lap and wrapped her arms around his neck. "It would definitely be better than this hotel. It would only be for a little while."

"Stay as long as you need."

"Do you think this is moving too fast?"

"Really, Cali?" The sarcasm in his tone wasn't lost on her. "I've known you for a decade. I've seen all your goods, multiple times. I'm in love with you. How is offering you and your uncle a place to stay in town moving too fast?"

She dropped her head on his shoulder. "Okay. You do have a point. I just don't want to jinx this."

"I don't believe in that. You know that."

Red had always been practical; he didn't subscribe to notions of luck and certainly didn't think anything could be "jinxed." He worked hard, plain and simple. Hard work had gotten him everything he had, from his scholarship to college to his entrance to law school to junior partner at his law firm. He'd been the youngest and only African American male to make partner at that particular firm. His ambition was one of the things that attracted her to him, made her want to be a part of his magic. It had reminded her of . . . *her*.

"If we're going to make it," he continued, brushing his

lips over the delicate skin at the base of her neck, "it's going to be because we worked at it. Relationships are work."

She caressed his face and kissed him gently. "God, I love you, Red."

"You can keep saying that all night."

"Um, not with my Uncle Cal in the other room."

"Maybe I need to pay for Uncle Cal to spend another night in the hotel. It is New Year's Eve," he said before he barked out a laugh.

"Ooh, I'm going to tell on you." She hopped off his lap. "First, I should probably pack everything up."

"I'll go talk to Uncle Cal for you." He left the room, leaving her alone with her thoughts. Sighing, she picked at her fingernails. As much as she wanted to move forward with Red, embrace the idea of a full and fulfilling relationship with him, she couldn't help the feeling of dread that seemed to lodge itself in her stomach.

Everything seemed to be perfect between them since they'd confessed their love for each other, but…could it be too good to be true? Or was she worrying about it too much? There was no doubt that there were other things going on with both of them, outside of *them*. Uncle Cal was extremely ill and dying right before her eyes, Syd was high risk, and the hot mess that was Nia threatened to ruin everything wonderful that had happened between them. Each one of those three things had the potential to destroy her newfound happiness.

Although she tried to focus on the present, she couldn't deny how worried she was about her uncle. They'd had a few conversations about his plans and he'd insisted on going over his last wishes with her. That had been the hardest day of her life—taking notes on what type of funeral he wanted, what he wanted to wear, and how he wanted his life eulogized. Others would probably say it was better to know ahead of time than to be called in the middle of the night and blindsided by his death, but Cali knew better. Every day, watching the only father she'd ever known slip away, was torture. In the mornings, after she'd had breakfast with Red, she'd head to the hotel and let herself into his hotel room with trepidation, praying that she didn't find him dead. She'd wake him up, ask what he wanted for breakfast, and leave his room within a few minutes. Then, she'd go back into her room, pull the latch, crawl into bed, and cry. Every single morning it had been the same routine. Each day, she grieved for a man that was still there; and it chipped away at her sanity a little bit at a time.

Red had been her saving grace. He'd kept her busy, checking in on her throughout the day, bringing up stupid reality shows that she knew he didn't watch and offering to beat up every client that pissed her off. If she hadn't already known that she loved him, that alone would have sealed the deal for her. Their not-so-clandestine meeting in Morgan's bathroom was long overdue.

"So, Uncle Cal is fine with staying with me," Red said, entering her room. "He wants to stop at the grocery store so that he can cook."

She smiled at him. "Well, okay then. I guess we better check out."

He massaged her shoulders, kissing her temple. "I was thinking…maybe we could keep this room in case we need to slip away."

"Boy," she said, pulling away from him. "You're trippin'." She threw a stray bra at him. "Help me finish packing. The sooner you help me, the sooner we can discuss *slipping away*."

Red picked up a mound of clothes and stuffed them into a duffle bag.

"Wait—" she said.

He swept her perfume and makeup into a grocery bag.

"Red, that doesn't go in there. Wait—"

He picked up a pair of flip-flops and stuffed them into a garment bag.

"Hold on!" she shouted, pinching him playfully. She yanked the garment bag from him and pulled the shoes out, setting them on the bed. "You're messing up my system. My shoes do not go in this bag."

"Oh, well, I was only hurrying up like you said." He shot her a dimpled grin. "We have to discuss how we're going to *slip away*. I have some ideas."

"You are a mess." She hit him with a nightgown. "Let's start over, shall we? Shoes are too important to just stuff in anything."

They finished packing, between stolen kisses and one extremely satisfying liaison against the full mirror. And for a minute, Cali let herself forget about everything that could go wrong and focused on what was right.

* * *

"Why is it so damn hard to find one woman? It's not like she has any money, any connections. She's crazy as hell." Red paused, phone to his ear, and jotted a few notes down on his legal pad. "I don't care what you have to do, just find my daughter. Call me back when you have something." Red slammed the phone down on his desk, muttering a curse.

"Everything okay?" Uncle Cal asked, entering Red's home office. "Tense conversation."

Leaning back in his chair, Red crossed his arms. "I'm frustrated, Uncle Cal. Nothing for you to be concerned about."

"Cali told me about your daughter. Any leads?"

"My ex called me from jail," Red explained.

Cali had successfully managed to distract him in the tub that day, but once they were out of the bathroom, his mind wandered back to his conversation with Nia.

"I'm trying to figure out where she is so I can find my daughter," Red continued. "There's no telling where she is or who has her. She's a six-year-old little girl, probably wondering where the hell her mother is, terrified."

Uncle Cal sat down on the couch and crossed his legs. "I'm praying this can be resolved quickly."

"If I had just kept my cool talking to her on the phone...I lost it. I never lose it."

"This is your daughter, Jared," Uncle Cal said. "Your emotions were running high. It happens."

"It was the wrong time to lose it." Red tried not to focus on how he'd ruined any chance of getting Nia to cooperate. He prided himself on maintaining control in all situations.

Lately, it seemed that he was dangling on the string of his life, waiting for the next shoe to drop. It seemed to finally be working out with Cali, but they had a long road ahead. Corrine was his daughter, his flesh. He'd already made it up in his mind to move Heaven and Earth to make sure Nia lost custody. After this stunt, he was sure he'd have no problem with the court. Finding her was the problem.

"Did you tell Cali your truth yet?" Red asked, needing a change in subject.

"I haven't," Uncle Cal admitted.

"Why?" The last thing Red needed was an angry Cali on his hands. Learning that her mother was alive and being taken care of by her uncle for years was bound to set her off. He was sure that he would bear the brunt of her anger.

"It's not the right time."

"When is the right time?" Red gritted his teeth. "Listen, you're putting me in a bad position. We've just turned a corner in our relationship. With Corrine and this...I can't help but think we're doomed before we start."

"Cali will be angry with me. Not you." Uncle Cal muttered. "She loves you. From what I can see, you two have finally pulled your heads out of your asses and are ready to make a real go of things. If you set up the trust, once I die, she never has to know."

"But *I* know!" Red paced the room in an attempt to burn off the anger building up. "I love Cali. I'm in love with her. I wouldn't understand if she knew where Corrine was and didn't tell me, regardless of whether it was her job or not. I don't expect her to *understand* that I knew her mother was alive and didn't tell her."

"Put yourself in my shoes. Cali is the only daughter I have, my only child. I'm dying." Uncle Cal pulled out his inhaler and sprayed the medicine into his mouth, taking a few breaths. "I don't want to spend the last few weeks, or even days, of my life, wondering if she hates me. Forgive me, but I'm a coward like that."

Shaking his head, Red peered up at the ceiling. How could he deny this dying man the right to live out his life in peace?

"But you're right, Jared," Uncle Cal continued. "I'm sorry I put you right in the middle of this. You're right. I should tell her. I will. After New Year's."

"What's going on in here?" Cali asked, stepping into the room, a deep frown on her face. "Is everything all right?"

"Yes," Red lied. "I was giving Uncle Cal an earful about my issues."

"Are you sure?" She leaned against the desk. "I heard shouting."

"We're good," Uncle Cal said with a smile. "I'm going to get ready for dinner."

Once Uncle Cal was gone, she turned to Red. "Baby, is everything okay? Really? You can tell me if it's not."

Wrapping his arms around Cali, he took in her scent—flowers and fruit—sensual. "It's fine. I'm a little irritated with myself."

She pulled back, concern on her face. "Why?"

"I lost it—on the phone with Nia." He lowered his gaze, hated that he had to lie to her. "That's all."

"It's going to be okay," she told him. "You're going to find her. You will."

Hopefully it would all be over soon, he thought. "Thanks, baby," he said, kissing her. "For now, you better go get dressed for dinner."

"Okay," she groaned. "Syd needs to be at home in the bed, not having dinners."

As much as he loved his sister, he couldn't agree more with Cali. "According to Morgan, he got doctor approval for this dinner so it must be important."

"Hmm, must be." She walked to the door. Glancing at him over her shoulder, she smirked. "Want to help me get dressed?"

"You know I do," he said. "Just give me a second."

As he watched her leave, he thought back to his conversation with Uncle Cal. He knew the older man was simply afraid of losing Cali. He definitely understood that because he felt the same way.

* * *

Cali glanced at her reflection in the mirror. She'd purchased a new winter white pantsuit earlier in the day and had decided to wear it to dinner. It was a simple yet sexy choice and she knew that Red would love it.

The sound of the shower running drew her attention away from the mirror toward the partially open door. Red was moving around in the master bathroom, his boxers hanging low on his waist, giving her an appreciative view of his lean waist and six-pack stomach.

As usual, they'd been sidetracked by a burning need to be with each other and were now rushing to get ready for dinner. As steam filled the bathroom, he closed the door and she turned back to the mirror.

Even though Red had tried to give her his undivided attention, she sensed something was bothering him. Every time she asked, he'd say he was thinking about his daughter, but she couldn't help but think it was more than that. The talk she'd interrupted between Red and Uncle Cal had seemed intense, and Red seemed almost angry with her uncle.

"Babe!" Red shouted from the bathroom.

"Yes?" she called.

"Can you bring me another towel?" he asked.

"Yes!" She hurried to the linen closet and pulled out a fresh towel. Pushing the door open, she walked into the bathroom. "Here?" She hung the towel up on the hook next to the shower door.

"Thanks," he said.

"What do you think this dinner is about?" she asked, rubbing the skin under her eyes and checking herself out in the mirror again.

"I think Morgan is about to propose."

"Aw, that's so sweet." After the wedding ring story Syd told her, she hoped the ring fit. Giggling to herself, she said, "She'll be happy. She told me she's ready to get married."

"Really?" He seemed genuinely surprised by that revelation.

"Yeah. She was drugged up, though." She relayed the conversation she'd had with Syd in the hospital. "She seemed sincere. I can't wait to plan that wedding. I've already started inspiration boards for that event."

"You're silly." He chuckled. "Don't you think that's jumping the gun a little? You know Syd has definite ideas about her wedding."

"Syd trusts me. And I know her. This baby has changed my friend. I'll bet you one hundred dollars that she'll just tell me to plan it."

"I'll take that bet. I know my sister, too," he said. "She's as anal as ever and she'll want to plan everything."

"Watch. She's already let me loose on the baby shower, with little push back on my plans. So, I can see her letting me run the wedding."

"We'll see." He sighed and turned off the shower. Stepping out, he tugged the towel off the hook and dried off.

She leaned against the door and watched him dry off. "What were you really talking to my Uncle Cal about earlier?"

He stopped and dropped the wet towel on the floor. "I told you . . . we were talking about Corrine."

"Would you tell me if you were talking about something else?"

Shrugging, he slipped on a new pair of boxers, avoiding eye contact. "What else would we be talking about?"

"Him? His illness," she answered. "That fact that he's . . . dying."

"Cali, your uncle has said some things to me that have to do with his business. Things I can't really discuss. You understand that, don't you?"

She thought about it for a minute. "Honestly?"

"Is there any other way?" he asked.

"I do understand the attorney-client privilege," she said. "But he's my uncle. I'd want to know if he's told you some timeline or something like that."

He put on his deodorant. "What are you talking about? A timeline on . . . ?"

"His life." One thing she knew about her uncle was he was

very private. He'd probably told the doctors not to mention certain things, especially if he thought it would hurt her.

"And you think he told me?" he asked.

She shrugged. "I don't know. But if he did, I'd want to know."

"What if I couldn't tell you?" He eyed her in the mirror. "Would you hate me for it?"

The question threw her for a loop. *Would I hate him for it?* "I don't know. Logically, I'd know that I shouldn't, but I'm not sure how I'd feel if you knew something about my uncle that could change my life and didn't tell me."

"That's honest." He put lotion on his body before he went into the bedroom. She followed him, waiting on him to say something else.

"Is that it?" she asked finally.

He raised his hands at his sides. "I don't know; is it? Cali, I'm your uncle's lawyer. Whatever he's said to me is protected. I can't confirm or deny anything."

"So he did say something?" she pressed. "And you can't tell me?"

"I will tell you this . . . you know that heart failure at this stage is serious. The doctors have told him that he's not going to get better. Those are things you know. Please don't start expecting death because it will prevent you from enjoying whatever life he has." He squeezed her hand and pulled her into his embrace. "He's still here, babe," he murmured in her ear. "Love on him while he's here. He loves you. And he's here to spend time with you."

Cali eyes filled with tears. Nodding, she pulled back. "You're right. I can't control this. I just have to live through it."

He smoothed a hand over her hair and kissed her forehead, then her nose, and finally her mouth. "I'll be here right with you."

"I know." She dabbed her eyes with a tissue. "But you

better hurry up and get dressed. I'm going to go check on Uncle Cal."

Cali picked up her clutch from the bed and walked toward Uncle Cal's room. As she neared his door, she called out, "Uncle Cal? You ready?"

There was no answer. Knocking on the door, she called out again. "Uncle Cal? Are you ready?"

When he didn't answer again, she tried the knob. It was open, so she slowly pushed the door open. "I hope you're decent in here."

She scanned the room for Uncle Cal. "Uncle Cal?"

Figuring he was in the bathroom, she walked down the hallway toward the second bathroom. She placed her ear against the door when she heard what sounded like running water. "Uncle Cal? What are you doing?"

Closing her eyes, she said a prayer before she opened the door. "Unc— Oh my God." Uncle Cal was lying on the floor, unconscious, inhaler in one hand. She dropped down on the floor next to him. Placing two fingers under his ear, she exhaled when she felt a faint pulse. "Uncle Cal!" She examined him, noting a knot on the top of his head. "Oh my God! Red!" Tilting his chin up, she blew into his mouth, and began performing CPR on him. "Uncle Cal!" she shouted, frantically counting the number of compressions as she pushed against his chest. She smacked his cheek lightly, trying to jar him awake. "Oh my God. Please! Don't let him die. Red! Red!!! Oh my God! Uncle Cal," she sobbed. "Don't die on me. Please don't die on me."

*C*HAPTER TWENTY-TWO

*S*ometimes life seemed to take a turn for the worst so quickly there was no way to brace for the trauma. Instead of toasting the New Year with friends, Cali sat in the emergency room waiting area; legs shaking, palms sweating, stomach in knots. Every time she closed her eyes she saw her uncle lying on the bathroom floor near death. She vaguely remembered Red running into the room, jumping into action by phoning the ambulance. She'd struggled with him, smacking him in the arm when he tried to pull her away from her uncle when the ambulance finally arrived. She'd screamed when they'd grabbed those damn paddles and shocked Uncle Cal, begging them to save him. She recalled threatening the paramedics with bodily harm and ordering them to be gentle when they placed him on the gurney. When they'd pushed him toward the waiting ambulance, her heart seemed to fall in her chest and her knees gave out. She didn't hit the floor, though, because Red had been there to catch her.

Even now, his hand was on her knee, the other squeezing her hand. His strong presence seemed to be her only lifeline as people came and went through the ER doors.

Families were cracking jokes and munching on chips. An older man was lying on a chair with his feet propped up. A teenager was checking her social media account on the public computers.

Cali was freaking out. They'd rushed him to the back so fast. She'd tried to follow him, but the nurses told her she would have to wait. The doctors should have come to get her, but so far...nothing.

"Why haven't they come back out?" she asked. "What's taking them so long?"

She felt his lips against her temple, his warm breath against her skin. "Baby, they're probably doing everything they can for him. They'll come out and update us soon."

She rested her head against his. "Did you call Syd?"

"I did. She actually tried to come."

Cali imagined the argument between Syd and Morgan when she'd informed him that she was going to the hospital. "I'm guessing Morgan wasn't having that."

"You know it," he confirmed.

Morgan was right, though. Syd didn't need to be there, even though Cali needed her best friend.

"He'll be here, though," Red said. "Since she couldn't come, she's sending him."

Nodding, she covered her face with her hand. "What if he doesn't make it, Red? What am I going to do without him?"

"Baby, don't focus on that."

"I can't get that image out of my head," she cried. "Seeing him like that..."

"Shhh." He brushed his lips over her cheek and pulled her closer.

Morgan rushed into the emergency room a bit later, followed by Kent. Cali lifted her head off of Red's shoulder as they approached her. "Hi," she said, forcing a wobbly smile.

"Hey," Morgan said, squeezing her shoulder and shaking

Red's hand at the same time. "We came as soon as we could. Syd sends her love. She wishes she could be here."

"I know. I wish she could be here, too," she said. "You should be ringing in the New Year with my friend."

"We're fine," Morgan said. "She wouldn't have it any other way. Mama is over at the house with her."

Kent gave her a tight hug and greeted Red with some dap. "Any news?"

Shaking her head, she shrugged. "No. Red just asked the front desk for an update. They are supposedly checking as we speak."

Both men took a seat across from them and Cali was grateful for their support. "I'm sorry about dinner, Morgan," she said.

He waved her off. "Please don't. This is more important. We can reschedule at a later time."

"Tell me," Red said. "What was the dinner all about, anyway? Are you proposing to my sister?"

Morgan snickered. "I've been trying to do that for days, but your sister isn't cooperating."

Cali grinned, content that her friend's dreams were finally coming true. "What has she been doing?"

"Initially, I'd planned to propose after Thanksgiving," Morgan told them. "I even took her to look at rings. Once she tried on the ring and realized that her finger was swollen, she bolted out of the store."

The group laughed at Syd's antics while Cali remembered a slightly different version of the ring store debacle.

"I already have her ring," Morgan confessed. "I just took her to the store so that I could do the whole surprise proposal there. I mean, it was perfect. We spent Thanksgiving in New York and I planned this elaborate trip to Tiffany's, like in the movie that you two watch constantly."

"*Sweet Home Alabama*?" Cali and Syd had watched the

proposal scene back to back. There was nothing like spending time with her best friend, watching cheesy chick flicks. "Ah, we love that movie."

"I know," Morgan said. "Don't ask me why your friend is so weird."

"Well, you love her," Kent added with a snort, covering his smirk when Morgan glared at him.

"Is that the only time you tried?" Red asked, rubbing his thumb over Cali's hand.

"I tried again one night at home." Morgan clasped his hands together and leaned forward. "I had decided that elaborate measures with a pregnant Syd weren't going to work, so I came home from work early and cooked dinner. We sat down in front of the fireplace, cozied up to watch a movie. The ring was under the pillow. She fell asleep."

Cali's mouth fell open and Kent leaned back in his chair, laughing loudly.

Red shook his head. "Wow. I can't even offer anything to that. Maybe you should wait until after the baby is born for the proposal."

"You're probably right," Morgan said.

"I think it's wonderful," Cali told Morgan. "You make her so happy. Her neurotic behavior seems to make you smile. And your jerk tendencies don't faze her. I'd say you're a match made in heaven. To think, you both were hell-bent on denying it for so long."

"Look who's talking," Kent said. "You and Red's ass... who sleeps with someone for years and pretends that they are just friends?"

"I don't know. Who lets a woman that he's obviously into leave town to marry a preacher man?" Red retorted.

Cali giggled. "That's right. You tell him, baby." They gave each other a high five. "The point is... we're not pretending now. That's all that matters."

Kent rolled his eyes. "For the last time, there's nothing going on with me and Allina."

"Whatever, Kent," Morgan said. "Keep telling yourself that. Maybe you'll start to believe it."

"Ms. Harper?" Cali turned toward the call, standing up when she realized it was the doctor.

"Yes." She glanced at the older man's name on his badge. "Is my uncle okay, Dr. Hessler?"

"He's stable for now." The doctor gestured toward an empty room in the hall. "I'd like to give you an update on what's going on. Do you mind following me to one of the family rooms so that we can have some privacy?"

Privacy. Pulling on her suit coat, she held her chin high as she followed the doctor. Turning to Red, she asked, "Can you go with me?"

He nodded. Cali pretended not to notice the looks passing between the three friends. They knew it was bad news, too.

Once they were in the small room, the doctor sat in a rolling chair. He motioned Cali and Red to have a seat on the couch in the room.

"What's going on, Dr. Hessler? Is he...?" She swallowed hard. "You said he was stable. What does that mean? Is he conscious?"

"Ms. Harper, we've done all we can do." The doctor opened his file. "Your uncle's heart is failing."

"I know his heart is failing," Cali said, frustrated at the doctor's condescending tone. "I've already talked to the cardiologist. But what is going on with him now?"

"Mr. Harper developed a blood clot at the stent site and as a result, suffered a heart attack," the doctor explained. "Thanks to your quick action in performing CPR and the prompt arrival of the paramedics, we were able to treat it in time with an aggressive course of medicine. However, the heart has suffered severe damage. His heart is enlarged. Surgery is an option, as you know, but with your uncle's history and the weakened state of his body, it's not recommended."

"I know all of this," Cali said. "What I'm not understanding is why you can't do another angioplasty or a different procedure? I've been reading up on it, and there are so many options."

Cali had heard what the doctors said a few weeks ago, but she'd researched heart failure and complications and there always seemed to be a treatment, a miracle. "We've already met with the doctors about his prognosis," she said. "I just... need to know why."

The doctor told her that each case was different. Uncle Cal had presented with multiple problems. Because his heart didn't work correctly, his other organs were affected, including his kidneys and his lungs.

Resting her elbows on her knees, she dropped her head and choked back a sob. "Will he be able to leave here? Is he conscious?"

"He's in and out of consciousness—and asking for you," the doctor said. "I must warn you; he's very weak."

A few minutes later, Cali slipped into the dark hospital room, Red right behind her. After the doctor had left the small family room, she'd cried on Red's shoulder until she was drained. Heart failure was one horrible thing; now they were dealing with the effects of the heart attack among other things. She could read between the lines. Uncle Cal's organs were failing and medicine could only do so much.

With trepidation, she inched closer to the bed. He was lying so still, his chest rising and falling, and there was an oxygen tube coming out of his nose. "Uncle Cal?"

He opened his eyes. "Baby girl," he said, his voice raspy.

"Hi." It was the only word she could get out and it frustrated her to no end because more needed to be said.

He reached out to her and she placed her hand in his, careful not to disturb the tubes and lines and everything. "I love you, baby girl. So much. I need you to know that."

"I do. I love you, too," she told him. "But I'm mad at you."

He smiled. "I know."

"You scared the shit out of me," she continued. "You know I don't know anything about medicine. I had to do CPR. Can you believe that?"

"Maybe you should have listened in first aid class," he said with a low chuckle.

"You always told me you'd be here. But look at you... over there dying."

He started to laugh but coughed instead. She pulled a few pieces of tissue from the bedside table and held them up to his mouth. He took it from her, spitting out phlegm. "Listen to you, taking a page from my book, huh? Finding humor in everything. The doctor talked to you?"

She nodded. "He did."

"I don't want any extraordinary measures."

Peering up at the ceiling, she sniffed. "I know."

"I just want to be with my girl, for however long I have."

She took another Kleenex and dabbed his eyes. "I'll be here."

"You've made me so proud," Uncle Cal said, his voice thick. "I'm so grateful that I had a chance to raise you."

"No, I'm the one that's grateful. My life could have turned out so different if you hadn't saved me from that hotel room, from my... mother."

Uncle Cal glanced behind her shoulder. "Red, thanks for being here with her."

"I'm going to be—" The buzz of his cell phone sounded in the room. He glanced at the screen and turned to them. "I have to take this."

She nodded and watched as he exited the room.

"He loves you, Cali," her uncle said.

"I know." She smoothed a hand over the hair on his arm. As a child, she'd always complained that he was too hairy and he'd always tell her she'd like "hairy" one day. Smiling at the memory, she had half a mind to tell him that she never did like men with lots of hair.

"Good. I'm glad you two got it together. Always keep an open mind when it comes to relationships. Be willing to bend."

"This coming from a man who once told me that love was for wimps."

"That was because I didn't want you to date. See, I had a reason for everything I did. Always for your protection."

"Well, I won't go into you threatening all my dates with sewing their lips shut if they dared to kiss me. I will say that I'm so glad that you had my back. I don't know who my real father was, but it never mattered to me. You've been the only father . . . the best father I could have."

"Cali," he said, his voice full of emotion. "I need to tell you something."

"What is it?" she asked. Uncle Cal had an urgency in his voice that concerned her.

There was a soft knock on the door, and Red stepped in.

"Is everything okay?" she asked.

"Can I talk to you outside for a second?"

"Sure." She turned her attention back to Uncle Cal. "Hold that thought. I'll be right back."

Following Red outside the room, she leaned against the wall. "Are you okay? Is it Syd?"

"No. It's Nia."

"What about her?"

"My contact at the police department . . . he found her."

She paused as his words registered. "That's . . . great. Do you know where Corrine is?"

"Not yet. But I will."

"Where is she?" Cali asked.

"It's just like you thought." He stuffed his hands in his pockets. "She's been staying in Niles." Niles was a small town on the western side of the state. No one would ever guess she'd go there, especially since she had no family in the area. "But arrested in Benton Harbor, Berrien County."

"That's not far," she said. "You should go."

"I hate to leave you," he admitted.

"You have to go see about your daughter, Red," she insisted. "I have support here. I'll be fine."

He rubbed her hair. "You'll call me if anything changes?" When she nodded, he told her, "I'll be right back here."

"Baby, just go. If I need a break, I'll head over to see Syd."

He pulled his keys out of his pocket and unhooked a key. Holding it up to her, he said, "Here's my house key. I'll text you my alarm code so you have it."

"Are you going by yourself?" she asked.

"Kent is going to ride with me. Morgan needs to be close."

"Of course." She gave him a watery smile. "I'm glad he's going with you."

He pressed his mouth to her forehead, then her lips. "I love you. I'll call to check on you."

She swallowed, biting back the urge to beg him not to leave her. "I love you, too. Drive safe. Let me know when you get there."

He glanced at his watch. "Happy New Year," he whispered against her lips.

"Happy New Year to you, too," she murmured.

Cali didn't know how long she stood there after Red raced out of there. She couldn't bring herself to go back into the hospital room, to sit there and stare at her uncle's dying face. A kind nurse stopped to ask her if she needed anything. She told the woman that she could sure use a stiff shot of tequila, to which the nurse giggled, then offered her a cold apple juice and a warm blanket instead. As the nurse hurried off to get those things for her, Cali closed her eyes. *I got this.* Psyching herself out was never her strong suit. But it was the only way she was going to be able to face this head on. Turning on her heels, she walked back into the room.

CHAPTER TWENTY-THREE

Red spent two long hours in the car as he sped toward the Berrien County jail. Even though he'd tried, Kent had been unsuccessful at keeping Red's mind off of his troubles. He was worried, both about Cali and his daughter. It seemed as though he'd searched everywhere for Corrine, questioned every member of Nia's family, every ex-boyfriend she'd told him about. No luck. Now, he could very well be meeting his daughter within the next day. He should be happy, ecstatic even. But it was bittersweet. He was on the verge of getting everything he'd worked for and Cali was preparing for a huge loss.

"Morgan just sent me a text. He's leaving the hospital, heading home to check on Syd. But he'll go back up there in a few."

"Okay."

Red had met Morgan in high school when they were both starting for the basketball team. The two soon became tight as thieves, more like brothers than friends. They had similar goals in life and worked hard to achieve them. They played even harder, but that was a story for another day. With

Morgan came Kent, and unfortunately, Caden—the ass-hole who'd hurt Syd time and time again. He couldn't stand Caden, but he appreciated Kent in his life. They'd become good friends, family. Bottom line, Red was fortunate to have people in his life that would be there, no matter what. Since he couldn't be there with Cali, he knew Morgan would step in.

"Thanks for riding with me, man," Red said after a few minutes of silence.

"Man, you know I'm not doing shit anyway."

Red gripped the steering wheel when he spotted the exit number ahead. "Well, you could *not be doing shit* at home, but you came with me. I appreciate it."

"Someone needed to make sure your ass doesn't blow a gasket and end up in Berrien County yourself, with your license in jeopardy."

"Shut the hell up, man. I'm cool. I know what I have to lose. My main goal is to find out where Corrine is and see to it that Nia goes down for all the trouble she's caused."

"I'm down for that myself. I still never did get over that stabbing incident all those years ago. She could have killed Roc."

Kent had been furious when Nia stabbed Morgan all those years ago. He'd threatened to choke the life out of her and not even think twice about it. It had thrown them all for a loop because Kent was generally not a violent person. Snarky, sarcastic, and a bit of an ass, but definitely not violent—especially not toward women. Of course, he'd gotten into a few scrapes back in the day, but those had always been because his back was against the wall.

"Yeah, but Syd handled that. Talk about the date from hell."

"Tell me about it."

They pulled up at the police station. Approaching the

desk, Red asked to speak with the officer in charge of Nia's case. He'd spoken to the man over the phone on the way there. Nia had been arrested for assault with a deadly weapon and possession with intent to distribute. For someone who'd grown up in an upper middle class suburb of Columbus, Ohio, Red figured she'd sure turned out to be a menace. During his investigation, he'd found out that her parents refused to deal with her and no longer provided monetary support to her. They hadn't spoken to her in at least three years.

"Mr. Williams?" A portly man with a bald head and a huge bottle of water in his hands appeared in a nearby doorway.

"Yes." Red greeted him with a handshake.

"I'm Detective Powell."

"Good to meet you. This is my friend and business partner, Kent Smith."

Kent gave him a curt nod. Powell led them through the doors to his desk in the back. He explained that Nia was being held on a $50,000 bond. So far, she hadn't been able to come up with the bail money. They'd interrogated her but she had refused to tell them where Corrine was and who she was with. Fortunately, however, Nia wasn't as smart as she thought she was. She'd used the phone and her call had been recorded. The police had traced the number and a car was being sent to the source of the call's location as they spoke.

Normally, Red wouldn't be able to see Nia, but an old college buddy of his was a prosecuting attorney in Berrien County and had called in a favor for him. It definitely paid to have friends in high places.

Red waited, literally twiddling his thumbs. Kent had decided to grab a cup of coffee while Red talked to Nia. His friend also offered to check in on Cali and Syd for him. He took a look around the room, which had one metal table and two chairs. The door opened and an officer led Nia in toward the table. Years of hard living had obviously taken their toll on Nia: her hair was lifeless and her dark skin blotchy. She looked like she'd been in the fight of her life, judging from the scratches on her face. Her steps faltered when she noticed him.

"What are you doing here?" she asked.

He peered up at her. "Sit down."

She plopped down into the chair. "Are you here to bail me out?"

"Where is my daughter, Nia?"

She slumped back in her seat and shrugged. "She's *my* daughter, and you will never find her."

"Want to bet on that? I'm also willing to bet your stay in here is going to be longer than you think. Assault with a deadly weapon—again? Possession with intent to distribute?"

He'd been a lawyer long enough to know that a judge wouldn't have much sympathy for a woman who refused to cooperate with authorities trying to locate her young daughter. Gaining custody at this point would be easy for him.

"Just so that we're clear..." He narrowed his eyes on her. "Corrine better be safe and sound when I do find her, or you can add child abuse to those charges. After I'm done with you, there won't be a single judge in the state who will give you custody of Corrine ever again. That's if you get out of jail before she's eighteen."

He stood up slowly. "Remember what I said. Watch your back in here. You never know who I know."

She screamed at him as he walked out of the room. Of course, he didn't know any damn body in that jail, but he couldn't resist scaring the shit out of her. He checked his cell phone as he headed back toward the front, where Kent was waiting for him.

His steps slowed when he noticed a crowd near the front

reception area. He couldn't tell what was going on at first, but then he noticed a female officer bending down and smiling at a...child? He picked up his pace, passing the officer who was escorting him out of the holding area.

Red searched for Kent in the crowd, and saw him standing in front of the small girl with a smile on his face. An armed guard stopped Red to check him before he walked out into the public area, but once he'd passed through the security check, he raced toward the little girl. He stopped when she turned and looked at him. Her hair was piled into a ponytail on her little head, her light skin matched his and her eyes...she had bright hazel eyes—like his.

He swallowed at the emotion that rushed through his body. Was this...?

Kent motioned for him to come closer and the female officer stood to her full height. He glanced at Kent who gave him a slight nod, letting him know the girl was in fact Corrine. Red approached his daughter slowly. She looked up at him and retreated behind the officer's leg.

He bent down to her level and tilted his head. "Hi, my name is Jared."

"Hi," she said, her tiny chin quivering. "My mommy said...my daddy's name is Jared."

He fought the urge to pull her into his arms and never let her go. Before he could say anything else, Powell appeared to his left.

"We found her in the house we raided this evening. The owner of the house had agreed to watch her for a few days. Had no idea what was going on."

"Thanks," Red told Powell. "I appreciate it."

"As part of procedure, we had to contact Children's Protective Services," Powell explained.

"I understand." Red turned his attention back to his daughter. "What's your name?"

"Corrine Niyah Williams."

Overwhelmed, Red ran a shaky hand over his face. He looked over at Kent, who was watching silently. Then the strangest thing happened: nothing. He was at a loss for words so he just stood there, staring at her.

"Um, Corrine?" the female officer said after a few moments passed. "How about I take you to get something to eat in the back?"

Corrine wiped her eyes. "I want my mommy."

"Aw, honey," the kind woman said, rubbing Corrine's back. "Let's go eat and we can talk about it some more."

That seemed to appease her, because she gripped the woman's hand and went toward the back, leaving Red kneeling in the small hallway.

Kent shoved him and he almost fell over. "What the hell are you doing? That's your daughter and you didn't say anything."

"Kent, what do I look like, just telling her I'm her daddy?" Red exclaimed. "She doesn't know me. You heard her; she wants her mother."

"She can't have her mother," Kent said. "But she has her father. You came all this way to get her."

Red shook his head, still unable to believe he'd actually found her. "She's so beautiful."

"Yeah, she's a beauty," Kent agreed. "Looking like Syd."

"I know." Red couldn't wait for the two to meet. Syd would definitely dote on her niece and he was sure Corrine would take to his sister.

"So snap out of it," Kent commanded. "Go in there and talk to her."

He knew his friend was right, but he didn't want to scare her. "This seems so awkward," he told Kent. "I want to know her, but . . . what if she's afraid of me?"

"Obviously, Nia told her about you. Tell her who you are."

Red glared at Kent and headed toward the small eating area where Corrine was seated with the officer, munching on some crackers. He took a seat across from her and asked the officer, "Do you mind giving me a minute?"

The officer seemed skeptical, but complied.

Once they were alone, he asked, "Do you like crackers?"

"Yes. I like Cheez-Its," she told him. "But they didn't have any."

"Well, I can buy you some Cheez-Its, if you want?" he said.

Her eyes widened. "Do you know where to buy Cheez-Its?"

"I sure do. I'll buy you some tonight." He tapped a finger on the table.

"Can we bring some to my mommy?" she asked.

He blinked, unsure how to respond to that. "What grade are you in, Corrine?"

"I'm in the first grade," she replied.

"Wow, the first grade?" he exclaimed. "You must be pretty smart."

She gave him a small smile. "I know how to read and I can count. Really high."

He chuckled. A daughter after his own heart. Smart and she knew it. "Good. Listen, remember when you told me your daddy's name was Jared, like mine?"

She nodded and bit into a cracker.

"Well, what would you say if I told you I *was* your daddy?"

Gasping, she dropped her cracker onto the table. Frowning, she said, "My mommy told me my daddy was never coming."

Red gritted his teeth together. If she was a little older, he would've told her about her stupid ass mother. *Calm down, Red.* He took a deep breath. "Your mommy got into some trouble and she needed me to come and take care of you," he lied. "Is that okay with you?"

Tilting her head, she peered at him, her matching eyes boring into his. "You're going to babysit me?" she asked finally.

"Sure," he told her. "But you have to come with me to my house."

After a few uncomfortable seconds, she asked skeptically, "And you're going to buy me Cheez-Its?"

"Yes." If a box of crackers would make her happy, he'd buy up the entire grocery store. "You can have as many as you want."

"Is my mommy going to pick me up from you?" she asked.

He grinned at his intelligent daughter. She was like him in the fact that she definitely stayed on the topic at hand. "I wish I could tell you that your mommy was coming to pick you up, but I can't promise you that, honey. Your mother has done something that got her into trouble and she has to take care of that before you can see her. Do you understand what I'm saying?"

Kidspeak obviously wasn't a bullet point on his résumé.

"I can promise that I'll take good care of you," he assured her. "I won't let anyone ever hurt you."

Tears gathered in her eyes. "I just want to be with my mom," she whimpered.

"I know." His eyes watered, too. "I'm sorry."

"You look like me," she said, changing the subject.

He chuckled. "I do, huh?"

"You have eyes like me."

"Yes, I do," he said, nodding. "You're going to meet my sister. She has eyes like you, too. You look just like her."

"I do?" She gave him a half-smile and his heart melted.

"Yes, she's very pretty, like you."

"Does she have Cheez-Its?" Corrine asked.

"If she doesn't, I'll make sure she gets some," he promised. His daughter certainly could badger a witness. He swelled with pride.

"Do you have a car?" When he nodded, she asked, "Can I sit in the front seat?"

Red chuckled. "I don't think you're big enough for that yet. Maybe soon. Why don't you finish eating your crackers and I'll go talk to these nice people and we can leave."

She stuffed one cracker into her mouth and nodded.

Powell and Kent were talking when Red rounded the corner. He explained his conversation with Corrine. Powell told him the next steps he had to take to retrieve his daughter. Red was quite aware of the differences between counties. Each county had its own procedures in place and he wanted to be sure he followed the law to the letter. Unfortunately, he discovered Corrine wouldn't be able to leave with him until the children's agency was able to interview her, since his name wasn't on her birth certificate. They also put a rush on an additional paternity test.

Corrine would have to go home with the female officer, who'd graciously agreed to "babysit" her for the night. But he made sure he let his child know that he was staying close at a nearby hotel. Only a few more steps, and he'd be able to take his daughter home.

Later on, Red lay scrawled across the hotel bed. As tired as he was and ready to put the long ass day behind him, he was wound up. He'd tried calling Cali but got no answer. He did reach Morgan, who told him that Uncle Cal had been sleeping off and on and Cali had been posted in his hospital room. Syd had tried to get her to leave and come stay with them, but she turned the offer down.

"Hello?" he said, picking up his buzzing phone.

"Red?" Cali's voice sounded raspy, as if she'd been crying.

He leaned against the headboard. "Baby, what's going on?"

"Everything is pretty much the same. I saw that you called me. I left my phone in the room when I went out to get some soup from the cafeteria. Uncle Cal is sleeping."

"Are you spending the night at the hospital?" he asked.

"I haven't decided. I just thought about something, I don't have my car. I rode in the ambulance."

Red had been talking to Syd and Morgan throughout the evening, getting updates on Uncle Cal's condition. "Call Morgan if you need a break. He said he'd come and get you."

"I'm okay. How are you? Did you talk to Nia?"

"I did. And I talked to Corrine," he told her.

"Really?" she exclaimed. "That's so good."

"She's beautiful," he told her before describing his daughter's plump cheeks and curly hair.

"Wow, she sounds gorgeous."

"She looks like Syd," he added.

"She'll be glad to hear it." Cali giggled then and Red smiled in response. "I know you're so happy the search is over."

"I am. But I'm worried about you," he confessed. "I wish I could be there."

"When will you be back?" she asked.

"I'm going to try for tomorrow. There are some loose ends to tie up before I can leave."

"Hopefully, sooner than later."

"I know. Did you get a chance to talk to Uncle Cal?"

He hated to ask, but with Uncle Cal's health taking a turn for the worse, he was nervous about how his secret would affect her. He wanted to be there and support her through everything.

"I talked to him for a little bit." She sighed. "But he's so tired. The doctors said it's normal. I wish they could do something for him. I hate seeing him like this."

"It's hard to see someone you love going through something you can't do anything about," he said.

"Yeah, it is." She sniffed. "So tell me more about Corrine."

"She loves Cheez-Its," he told her. "Just like someone else I know."

Cali was addicted to those nasty crackers. "Well, she has good taste."

"You sound so tired," he said, switching the phone to his other ear.

"I am." He heard her yawn through the receiver. "I'm going to curl up in this chair. It lets out into a little bed-type thingy. The nurse left another warm blanket. Hopefully, I'll be able to sleep."

"If you don't, when I get home, I'm putting you to bed," he promised.

"I'm looking forward to it. Oh, Red...I have to go. The nurse is here."

"Okay. I'll call you tomorrow."

"You better," she said. "Love you."

"Love you, too."

CHAPTER TWENTY-FOUR

Cali knocked on the door and pulled her coat closed. She'd spent the night pretending to be asleep for Uncle Cal's sake. That last thing he needed was to be worried about her, but she could tell he was when he kept rolling over, calling her name during the night. Eventually she stopped answering, hoping that it would give him a sense of peace that she'd finally fallen asleep. But then he'd started calling her mother's name. It was as if he couldn't rest, as if he was wrestling with something.

Morgan opened the door, a spatula in one hand and an oven mitt on the other. "Hey."

He motioned her into the house. "Come on in, I have some eggs on the stove."

As they neared the kitchen, she pulled off her gloves. "I'm sorry to stop by unannounced. I went to Red's this morning and everything was so quiet. I guess I just wanted to see my friend. Is she up?"

"Been up all morning. She had a rough night, pretty uncomfortable. Plus, she's worried about you. Coffee?"

"Yes. I don't want her worried. Then I'll worry about her. That baby needs to stay in there for a while longer."

He poured piping hot coffee into an empty mug and slid

it over to her. "Tell me about it," he agreed. "Something tells me that the baby will make a grand entrance when she's ready, and at the right time."

"She?" she asked.

"I think it's a girl." He set a bottle of creamer and a container filled with sugar in front of her. "I'm ready to find out for sure. Don't tell her I said that, though."

She watched as Morgan finished cooking. He'd been through a similar ordeal as a child, losing his biological parents to their bad choices. "How did you do it?" she asked.

He poured the scrambled eggs onto three plates and set the pan into the sink. "Do what?"

"Live without your parents."

He smoothed a long finger over his eyebrow. "I didn't. I had two awesome parents."

"I know that, but... you lost both of your biological parents, and your grandmother. How did you do it?"

"I don't think anyone ever has a set way they deal with things," he said. "I hated my father, so when he died I wasn't that hurt. My mother... she pretty much only lived for my father. It hurt when she died, but I'd already lived with the Smiths for years. I'd only talked to my mother a handful of times." He shrugged and picked up thick pieces of bacon from the skillet and placed them on each plate.

"My mother pretty much deserted me," she admitted. "The thing is I remember things about her; I remember being happy with her. But somewhere along the line, she morphed into this horrible person who made my life worse. She didn't give me any stability. I grew to this point where I was happy she was gone because at least I didn't have to tell her I hated her."

"If you remember good things, why would you hate her?" he asked.

"She told me she didn't want me." She finished her story as she fixed her coffee the way she liked it. "That was before she left me in a hotel room by myself. I think I was about sixteen when I realized that I liked life with Uncle Cal better than I ever did with my mother. He was there for me through everything. And the thought of not having him, not being able to call him..."

Morgan leaned against the counter. "I understand the feeling. When I lost my grandmother, I was inconsolable. I get it. Then when Papa Smith died, we all struggled without his presence. I think you always miss them, but you move on."

"Last night, in his sleep, Uncle Cal kept saying my mother's name. It was like he was trying to tell her something. Makes me wonder if he sees her or something. I've heard the stories about people near death seeing their loved ones. I want to be able to be okay with him moving on, but I'm not. Actually, I wanted to scream at him to stop saying her name."

"Can I ask you a question?" he asked.

She took a sip from her mug. "Yeah, if you hand me a plate of food."

Chuckling, he placed a full plate in front of her and scooped some grits into a bowl. "Salt and pepper? Or heaven forbid, sugar?"

She grinned. Sydney insisted on having her grits with a lot of butter and a heaping spoonful of sugar. "Salt and pepper for me. I never did understand why Syd liked sugar on her grits. Makes me think of oatmeal."

"Thank you," he said. "She and Red are a trip with that."

"Red eats his either way."

He nodded. "True. Anyway, do you think if your mother was still alive, you'd be able to forgive her?"

"No." Throughout her childhood, she'd tried to rationalize her mother's behavior. But, no matter how sick in the head she was, or how many drugs she took, there was just no excuse. "How could a mother treat her child like scum on the bottom of her shoe? When I think about how much I loved her and wanted her to love me back, I get angry all over again."

"I used to wonder how I'd react if my father ever came and apologized to me, for everything he put me and Den through, if I'd be able to forgive him. A couple months ago, I would have said a resounding hell no. And now...I can't muster up enough energy to hate him anymore."

She wondered if she'd ever feel that way about her mother. She guessed Morgan's about-face had something to do with the fact that he was going to be a father himself.

"He did give me life, no matter how fucked it was back then," Morgan continued. "At the end of the day, he was just him. I'm sure we'd never be cool if he was alive, but I can't deny that life with him taught me things I'd never have learned otherwise."

Cali stabbed at her eggs with her fork. Morgan and Den had grown up in the suburbs, but behind closed doors their parents had been straight criminals. Eventually, they were caught and arrested. As a result, Children's Protective Services were called in to take care of the boys. Kent had begged his parents to take them in and the rest was history.

"Your mother, she wasn't a drug-dealing pimp," he said. "She had problems, from what Syd told me. Those problems were in her mind. She used drugs to cover it up. Either way, her problems aren't yours. It took me a long time to know that about my parents. It's not easy, though."

"I don't even want to talk about her anymore," Cali grumbled. "Didn't mean for this conversation to go in that direction. I just wanted to know how to deal with my uncle's death."

"He's not dead yet," Morgan said.

She smiled, her mind drifting to a similar conversation she'd had with Red. "True."

"Stop focusing on the 'when.' Enjoy him while he's here. Ask him all the questions you need to know the answers to." Morgan topped off her mug with more coffee. "Know, at the end of the day, you had a great father. He loves you and he's always done anything in his power to protect you. Come on... let me take your friend her plate before she starts calling me."

She picked up her food and her mug and followed Morgan through his house, down the hallway leading to his bedroom.

When they walked into the bedroom, Syd's eyes lit up. "Cali?"

"Hey, girlfriend."

Morgan grabbed a tray and set the plate on top of it. "Eat," he ordered. "I'm going to try and get some work done."

"Thanks, babe." Syd said, taking a bite of her bacon. When he leaned down to her face, she gave him a quick peck. "Love you."

"Love you, too," he said. "Let me know if you need anything else, ladies."

Once he left, Cali climbed into bed next to Syd. "You are so spoiled. Morgan did his thing on this breakfast, though."

"Breakfast *is* his specialty. But truthfully, I would have rather fixed my own breakfast. Bed rest is not what's up."

They giggled and Cali bit into her crescent roll. "I know you're going stir crazy."

"Yes, I am. I should be at the bar handling business, but no... I'm stuck here all day. There's only so much TV a person can watch."

"Girl, there is never enough Investigation Discovery Channel," Cali said.

"I thought the same thing—until I sat here and watched it all day." Syd laughed. "Anyway, how's Uncle Cal?"

"He's...the same. He was sleeping when I left. I was talking to Morgan earlier about losing parents."

"Yeah, he's had a lot of loss."

"I know." Cali picked up her mug and cradled it in her hands. "But it turned into a conversation about my mother."

"Yikes. I know that wasn't something you were happy to revisit," Syd picked up another piece of bacon.

"I guess it's partly my fault, because I mentioned that Uncle Cal was calling for her."

Syd stopped chewing the bacon she'd plopped into her mouth.

"It threw me for a loop," Cali admitted. "Even made me a little angry."

Swallowing visibly, Syd guzzled the rest of the bottled water that had been sitting on her nightstand. "I can see how that would make you angry. It's kind of weird that he was calling her name."

"Go ahead and say it," Cali said, knowing what her friend was thinking.

"It's just that whenever I've heard of someone who's... near death calling someone who already died, it's not good."

"I know." Cali's appetite was suddenly gone and she slid her half-eaten breakfast on the tray next to Syd's. "Have you heard from Red?" she asked, changing the subject.

"He called Morgan last night, told him the good news about Corrine. They should be able to come home soon."

She hooked her arm in Syd's, who didn't let that stop her from finishing her food. "Girl, you are on a mission with that breakfast."

Syd barked out a laugh. "I'm eating for two now." She bumped her. "Seriously, though. This bacon is the truth." She held up a piece like a beacon in the sky before she popped it in her mouth.

"I'm so scared, Syd," Cali cried softly.

"Aw, babe." Syd pulled her closer and wrapped her arms around her. "I know. It can't be easy. I wish I could be there with you at the hospital."

"I wish you could, too." She rubbed her friend's round belly and leaned closer. "My little godchild needs to bake a little longer," she said to her stomach.

Syd gasped and grabbed her hand, planting it on the side

of her stomach. "Feel that. The baby kicked for you. That means you need to babysit."

Cali snatched her hand away. With a wide grin on her face, she chuckled. "Really Syd? What does that have to do with babysitting?"

"Well, you spoke to the baby and he likes your voice so he kicked."

"He?" Cali thought back to Morgan referring to the baby as a girl earlier. "I think maybe you and Morgan need to get on the same page with this baby. He thinks it's a girl."

"I know that," she said, waving her off. "It's probably a girl, but I want to give the baby love in case it's a boy."

"O...kay. I think the baby is going to be beautiful, whatever it is."

"Yep, and it's going to have a great babysitter."

Cali smacked Syd's hand lightly. "Stop. On another topic...Can you believe I miss Red already? He hasn't even been gone for a full day."

Syd squeezed her friend. "You are so gone. And I couldn't be happier to see you going through it for a change."

The girlfriends laughed and caught up for another hour before Cali yawned. Finally relaxed, Cali hugged one of Syd's pillows and drifted off to sleep.

A few hours later, Cali awoke with a start, jumping out of the bed. She glanced at the empty spot where Syd had been. *Where is she*? Picking up her phone, she checked for missed calls. Four missed calls from the hospital. *Shit*.

She tapped in the number to the nurse's station on Uncle Cal's floor. "Hello?" she said when a nurse answered. "This is Calisa Harper. My uncle is Calvin Harper. I'm returning someone's call."

"Ms. Harper, I'm glad you called. I'm Mr. Harper's nurse. The doctor asked me to call you. Are you close to the hospital?"

"Yes, I can be there within twenty minutes. Is he okay?"

"There was an episode earlier. Our nurse went to check on your uncle and he'd pulled his oxygen out and slipped into a semi-conscious state. We had to insert a nasotracheal tube to aid him in breathing."

Cali's stomach churned and she swallowed. "He's on a ventilator?"

"Yes."

"I'm on my way." Ending the call, she wiped her face and went off in search of Morgan and Syd. Nearing the kitchen, she heard their voices and walked in. Syd was sitting at the table with Morgan. Her legs were draped across his lap and he was massaging her feet.

"Hey guys," she said.

"Hi babe!" Syd said. "I figured I'd let you sleep some. You were exhausted."

"I have to go."

"What's wrong?" Syd asked, concern in her hazel eyes.

"The hospital called. They had to put him on a ventilator. I have to go."

Morgan stood up and grabbed his keys off the counter. "I'll drive you there."

"No, it's okay. I have my car."

"Maybe you shouldn't drive like this," Syd added.

"I'm fine," Cali insisted. "I'll call you when I get there."

She hugged Syd, then Morgan, and left.

CHAPTER TWENTY-FIVE

$\mathcal{R}$ed knocked on Morgan's front door. A friend of his who played golf with a judge in Berrien County had got him to sign an order giving Jared emergency custody. It took hours to get everything straight, including setting up future court dates, but he was back now, with his daughter.

He looked down at his baby girl, who had a pair of headphones on, listening to some CD Kent had suggested they buy at a local Walmart. Obviously, his friend knew what he was talking about because Corrine hadn't stopped singing since she got it.

Hours had passed since Morgan had called to let him know that Cali had rushed to the hospital because something had gone wrong with Uncle Cal. He'd tried to call her, but he couldn't get through.

He knocked again.

"Hold on," Morgan called from inside.

When the door swung open, Red grinned at his friend, who was frantically buttoning his shirt. "I thought Syd was supposed to be on bed rest, not doing it."

"Shut the hell..." Morgan didn't finish his sentence

because he looked down and spotted Corrine, who was hugging Red's leg and peering up at him. Morgan looked at Red, then back at Corrine. "Wow," his friend said. "She's . . . beautiful. Like a miniature Syd."

Red smiled and rubbed the top of Corrine's head. "Corrine, this is my best friend, Morgan."

Corrine reached out to shake Morgan's hand. "I'm Corrine," she said in a timid voice.

Instead of shaking her hand, Morgan bent down to talk to her eye to eye. "How about a high five?" He asked, one hand in the air.

Corrine grinned, then jumped up and smacked Morgan's hand. "You're tall," she said.

Morgan peered up at Red. "You're pretty tall yourself."

Red's daughter stood up on the tips of her toes. "I'm going to get bigger, too."

Morgan patted her head and straightened to his full height. "Come on in. Syd is going to love her."

Corrine stuck her hand in Red's and they walked through the house.

"Morgan?" he heard Syd call from the bedroom. "Who is it?"

"Want some company?" Red said, poking his head in the room after Morgan opened the door and went inside.

Syd's face lit up. "Red? You're here."

"Not by myself," Red said, ushering Corrine into the bedroom. "I wanted you to meet your niece."

Syd pushed herself up and straightened the covers. "Oh my God."

"Corrine, I want you to meet my sister," he said softly.

Syd gasped when Corrine peeked at her from behind Red's leg. "Oh, my . . . you're so pretty," she told her niece. "Hi! I'm your auntie Syd."

Corrine flashed her a shy smile. "You look like me."

Syd giggled, her eyes filling with tears. "I guess I do."

Red's heart swelled. He'd waited for this moment for months, waited for the opportunity to have his sister and his daughter meet each other for the first time. He fought back the tears and they sized each other up.

Corrine stepped closer to the bed and pointed at Syd's belly. "Are you going to have a baby?"

"Yes, I am." Syd grinned. "Want to feel the baby kick?"

Corrine nodded and Syd placed her tiny hand on top of her stomach. Corrine's eyes lit up and she squealed with glee after a few seconds. Red assumed the baby had finally kicked.

Syd wiped her eyes with her hand. "Did you feel that?" she asked, holding Corrine's hand in place.

"Am I going to see the baby?"

"You can even help me take care of the baby." Syd ran her hand through Corrine's unruly, dark curls. "Do you think I could have a hug?"

Without a word, Corrine wrapped her tiny hands around her and Syd closed her eyes, then peered up at Red. She mouthed, "She's beautiful."

He smiled at her through his own tears and whispered, "Like you."

Corrine looked at Morgan then. "Since she's my aunt, are you my uncle?"

Morgan barked out a laugh. "Sure am. You can call me Uncle Morgan."

"Are you famous?" she asked. "You have a big house."

They all laughed at Red's inquisitive daughter. She definitely had no filter, like him. If it was on her mind, she said it.

"Thank you," Morgan said. "But I'm not famous, just a hard worker."

"Do you have a swing set in your backyard? Me and my mommy used to go to the park."

"I don't have a swing set, but I know where a park is. Maybe we can go one day, when it's a little warmer. Are you hungry, Corrine?" Morgan asked.

"Do you have ice cream?"

"I think I do. Let me check on that. Want to come with me?"

Surprisingly, Corrine grabbed Morgan's hand and dragged him out of the room, asking all kinds of questions about food and parks and toys.

Red watched her leave the room and sat down on the bed next to his sister. "I can't believe she's finally here, with me." He pulled her into a hug.

"I'm so happy for you, Red." Syd wiped her eyes again. "You have a beautiful, intelligent daughter."

He filled Syd in on the details of his trip. He explained the next step with the court and told her all about Nia and her crimes. "My baby has been through so much. I hope I can be a good father to her."

"You will," Syd said. "You're great with kids."

"But I don't know anything about raising a little girl." He'd always wanted to find his daughter, but he never thought he'd end up having to take her in and raise her full-time. A weekend here or there; maybe a summer, but not her entire childhood.

He was now responsible for making sure that she was healthy, happy, and well taken care of. It was all on him to be the parent that she needed, to be there for her through anything. The situation actually mirrored the one with Uncle Cal and Cali. Red understood a little better the choices Uncle Cal had made. On the drive home, he wondered how he'd respond when Corrine started asking for her mother. Would he tell her the truth? Could he tell his daughter that her mother would probably be in jail for the foreseeable future?

"Have you heard from Cali?" he asked.

"She hasn't called since she left."

He wanted to go check on her but he didn't want to leave Corrine. Their relationship was so new he felt like he needed to keep her in his sight.

"What happened with Uncle Cal?" he asked, concerned that he hadn't heard from Cali.

"He's on a ventilator," she told him. "I'm a little concerned. I've been trying to not think about it, but..."

"I want to go see her, but..."

"Corrine will be fine with us." Syd squeezed his hand. "She seems to like Morgan. I can call Kent over since she's familiar with him. But you should go see Cali. She needs you. She's not doing too well."

He kissed Syd's palm and stood up. "I'll be back."

* * *

Red peeked through the window in the door to Uncle Cal's room. Cali was sitting bedside, her head down.

"Cali?" he called, his voice soft.

When her head whipped up, her eyes softened. She ran into his arms, hugging him tight. He wrapped a hand around her neck and held her to him, whispering random words of comfort to her. She fell apart in his arms, sobbing like it hurt too much to even bear. He eyed Uncle Cal. Holding her face in his hands, he pulled her into a tender kiss. She gripped his shoulders, digging her fingers into his muscles.

He leaned his forehead against hers. "I'm so sorry, Cali."

"He won't wake up," she sputtered.

Taking his thumbs, he rubbed the wet skin under her eyes and pulled her into his arms. The words seemed to die on his tongue because, really, there was nothing he could say to make this better for her.

He'd never seen her like this, but he guessed she deserved a moment to let it all out. And he was glad he was there for her.

"I wasn't here, Red."

"What do you mean?"

"I left. I took a break. While I was gone, he had some sort of attack. He was all alone and I was asleep on Syd's bed. I just couldn't sit in that chair anymore. I had to stretch my legs, get some fresh air. I should have stayed with him."

"What are the doctors saying?"

"They suggested a call to hospice. I can't... I can't bring myself to do it."

"You don't have to. I'll take care of it if that's what you choose to do."

She swept her hands under her eyes and returned to her seat. He scooted another chair next to hers. "Is this how a person is supposed to die? Not knowing if the people he loves are near him?"

"I'd like to think he knows."

She nodded and picked up Uncle Cal's hand. A tear fell onto her jeans. She wiped her eyes again with the back of her hand. Sniffing, she turned to him. "I'm a mess. I probably look crazy."

"Not even a little. You're beautiful." He took in her perfect fit, dark jeans and form-fitting sweater. Her hair was pulled back into a simple ponytail. The only sign of her distress was her red-rimmed, swollen eyes.

"The doctors did say he could wake up any moment... or not at all. I just want to hear his voice. I want to be able to tease him about the nurses seeing his goods, or fuss over how much he's eating. I want more dinner, more vacations... more time."

"Talk to him now. Like I said, I'm sure he can hear you. Imagine what he would say to you about those nurses."

Red stared at Uncle Cal and thought about the last conversation he'd had with him. He wasn't happy with the older man and had made it perfectly clear that he didn't appreciate what he'd done. Although he was serious, he still hoped that wouldn't be the last time he'd ever get a chance to speak to Cali's uncle. He'd been his lawyer for a while but he also considered him a friend, family.

"How did everything go?" Cali asked. "With Corrine?"

"She's here. I left her with Morgan, Syd, and Kent so that I could come and be with you for a while."

"I'm so happy you were able to bring her back. How is she? Has she asked about her mother and why she's with you?"

"Every half an hour or so. I hate lying to her about it, but I'm not sure what I'm supposed to say. Do I tell her the truth—her mother is in jail and she'll be living with me—or do I continue to protect the image she has of her mother?"

Red's words struck a chord with him. Glancing at Uncle Cal out of the corner of his eye, he could finally understand what the man was going through with Cali. The situations were different, but eerily similar. Cali and Corrine both had mothers who probably didn't deserve to have them and they both had male figures in their lives that would do anything to protect them—including lie.

"Well, I'm always on the truth bandwagon, no matter how much it hurts."

He knew Cali would say that. She was all straight talk, no chaser. He was usually the same way. It was one of the reasons they became good friends. Most of the women he knew couldn't handle the truth. Even Syd had to be handled with kid gloves in certain situations.

"I can't wait for you to meet her."

"I would love to meet her," she told him.

"Do you think we should have a conversation about how this may change things? I plan on keeping her here with me."

"I wouldn't expect anything less."

"What does this mean for us?"

She shrugged, rubbed her legs. "I'm not going to lie; it's pretty scary. She's going to need so much. You have to take the time to get to know her, get her settled into a routine. I don't want to intrude on that time with her. It's pretty important."

"But you're part of this. I don't want to make you do anything you're uncomfortable with. We went into this relationship never knowing if I'd ever find her."

"I think I've always known. Come on, Red. You would've never stopped looking. It wasn't a matter of if, more like when. You wouldn't be Red if you didn't give your all to her."

"Full disclosure?"

"Honestly, my mind is so clouded with Uncle Cal, I haven't had time to really think about it other than praying that you found her."

"That's honest. We'll have time to talk about it. For now, just know that I'm here for you."

"There was never a doubt." She leaned in and kissed him, sighing when he ran his tongue across her bottom lip.

An alarm on a machine went off and they jumped up. She raced out of the room, shouting at the nurses. Doctors and nurses swarmed in the room, pushing her back so they could work on Uncle Cal. Red held on to Cali while she begged the doctors and nurses to tell her anything. Eventually, they asked them to leave the room. In the hallway, Cali collapsed into his arms. He held on to her and would continue to do so as long as she needed him.

*C*HAPTER TWENTY-SIX

*C*ali jolted awake, struggling to breathe.

It had been a few days since the doctors rushed in and pushed her and Red out of the room. When they'd finally come out to talk to her, she'd braced herself for the bad news. It didn't come. It was just the opposite. Uncle Cal was breathing on his own again and conscious.

She'd been so relieved her knees had given out on her and she almost fell over. Red, of course, had been there to catch her before she hit the floor.

Closing her eyes, she exhaled slowly. Even though she'd received good news, she'd been plagued with nightmares the last couple of nights. *It was just a dream.* She'd decided to sleep at Red's house for the first time since he'd been home. But she was so exhausted she hadn't even made it up to his bedroom. She'd fallen asleep right on his couch, with one glove and one shoe still on.

When she opened her eyes again, a big-haired, beautiful little girl was staring at her quizzically. "Hi," Cali whispered and looked around the room for Red. "You must be Corrine."

"Who are you?" Corrine asked. She was holding a stuffed bear in her arms.

Clearing her throat, Cali tugged her shirt down. "I'm Cali."

"Do you live here?" the young girl asked.

Cali smoothed a hand over her head and swallowed. "No. I'm a friend of your dad's."

"His girlfriend?"

Boy, she's tough. Nodding, Cali answered her. "Yes."

The answer slid out of her mouth easier than she thought it would. She was indeed Red's girlfriend, which wasn't a problem—before he found Corrine. Cali couldn't help but wonder if the beautiful little girl in front of her would take to her.

"You're up?" Red asked as he walked into the room. "I wanted to let you sleep a little longer." He leaned down and gave her a kiss. "I see you two have met."

Cali wiped her mouth. "Yes, we have. Corrine asked me if I was your girlfriend."

He sat down on the couch next to her, squeezed her leg. "Do you have a problem with that, baby girl?" he asked.

Corrine's gaze darted back and forth between them and Cali wondered what the child was thinking. Finally she climbed up on the couch between them. "I guess it's okay." She looked up at Cali. "You're pretty. Do you like Cheez-Its?"

Red laughed and Cali let out a sigh of relief. She'd passed the test.

A few hours later, Cali smiled to herself as she walked through the hospital toward Uncle Cal's room. Corrine had talked her ear off before she'd left with Red to buy some essentials. They'd discussed hair, Cheez-Its, and the latest episode of her favorite Disney Channel show. Cali couldn't help but be impressed by her. She was definitely her father's child. She was intelligent and perceptive. Nothing got past her. Every time Red inched closer to Cali, Corrine inserted herself in the middle. That was something Cali used to do to Uncle Cal when he brought women over—which wasn't often, but still.

"Uncle Cal?" Cali said, entering the hospital room.

"Cali, you're here."

Dropping her purse in an empty chair, she unbuttoned her coat and shrugged out of it. Cali had been running around, trying to get things ready. Uncle Cal was being released. "You're up. I'm sorry I'm late. Did the nurse come in with your discharge papers?" she asked.

"Not yet."

"I wanted to talk with your doctors to make sure I have everything covered."

The low hum of the oxygen tank and the continuous beeping from his machines was a daily reminder that he was still very sick. But his condition had improved so much, the baffled doctors agreed that he was ready to be released. The only caveat was that he remain under the care of visiting nurses for a while.

Uncle Cal was chomping at the bit to be let out. He'd been calling her all morning, asking her when her estimated time of arrival was. Judging by the way he kept looking toward the door at every movement, she figured the moment he could leave wouldn't be soon enough.

It was hard to believe that a few days earlier she'd been thinking about funerals, not planning his discharge. Red had insisted they return to his home, which relieved her. Driving all the way to her own home wasn't going to work. She did wonder how they were going to swing living in the same house, since Corrine was there. Red wasn't worried, though. He'd cleared out his office for Corrine and moved in a hospital bed and other things for Uncle Cal.

The nurse arrived shortly with all the necessary paper-work and a new prescription for Uncle Cal. Cali scribbled notes in her planner while the nurse described the after-care plan. In the meantime, Uncle Cal flirted with an older nurse, flashing his signature smile multiple times during the conversation.

Later, Cali helped Uncle Cal into Red's house. He was moving slowly, holding himself up on the rolling oxygen tank. Red greeted them at the door, a dish towel in his hand, and helped the older man to the couch.

Uncle Cal sat down. "Smells good in here."

"Cali started a roast in the crockpot before she left," Red told him, taking his coat and his hat from him.

"I found a heart healthy recipe online," she added, noting the scowl on her uncle's face when she said "healthy."

"I don't really have an appetite, baby."

"It's fine if you don't. I bought a bunch of those protein shakes so you can have one of those if you're not in the mood to eat solid food."

Even though he was up and walking, she couldn't forget that his prognosis hadn't changed. But she'd purposed it in her mind to enjoy being with him.

"Thanks for making room for me, Jared." Uncle Cal said with a nod. "I appreciate it. You've definitely been a godsend to us."

"No problem. We're family. But we've already had this conversation."

"I hear you have another little house guest?"

"She's in her room. I told her to go comb her doll's hair. I wasn't sure how you'd be feeling when you got here."

"I'd like to meet her." Uncle Cal turned to Cali. "Don't you have work to do?"

That definitely wasn't the question she'd expected. "I do have some work I could be doing." Spending her days and nights at the hospital had put her behind. She'd pushed countless appointments back and even referred potential clients to other local event planners so that she could stay with him. It was time for her to get back into the swing of business, but she was nervous about leaving him for too long.

"I think you better get to it. I'm tired and could use a nap."

Corrine bounded into the room, jumping up on the couch. "Hi, Cali."

"Hey, Corrine. I want you to meet my uncle."

The little girl stared at Uncle Cal and reached out to touch his silver cane. "What is this?"

"A cane," he explained. "I use it to help me walk."

"Okay. I'm Corrine."

"Hi, Corrine." He took her extended hand and looked at her in awe as she shook his hand. "Whoa, that's a pretty good handshake you have there."

"My daddy said a firm handshake is impo-tent. We practiced this morning. Then Daddy yawned and then gave Cali a kiss and hit her on her butt."

Cali gaped at the little girl, and sputtered out, "Okay, let's help Uncle Cal to his bed." She'd told Red not to be overly affectionate on the first day. "You want to come with us, Corrine?"

"I saw the man bring a new bed," the spunky little girl continued. "I pushed the buttons for you already. It works."

"Well, thank you, young lady," Uncle Cal said. "I appreciate you testing the bed out for me. Let's go."

The walk to the bedroom took three times longer than normal, not because Uncle Cal was moving slowly but because Corrine had insisted on showing him everything she thought was awesome with Red's condo, like the blue nightlights in the hallway and the cool floor good for sliding on in her socks.

Once they got Uncle Cal all settled in his bed, Corrine

insisted on reading him a story because her mom read her a story one time when she was sick. Uncle Cal listened intently to Corrine reading *Green Eggs and Ham* with enthusiasm. At one point, he was even reading along with her, making funny voices with her.

"Okay, Uncle C—" Corrine kept forgetting his name. "It's time for you to take a nap. You look tired. I'll be back to check on you. Daddy put me in charge of bringing you water."

"Thanks, little one, for helping me today. I really appreciate it."

"You're welcome. Bye." Then she was gone, her little feet shuffling across the floor as she walked.

Cali turned to Uncle Cal. "She's something else, huh?"

"Reminds me of someone else."

Corrine did remind Cali of herself. They had so much in common—energetic, stubborn, smart. Cali knew that as time went on, Corrine would come to depend on her. That's what little kids did. They needed consistency and love. But could she be the person Corrine needed? Cali couldn't stop thinking about her own mother and how she was pretty normal— until she wasn't. If there was even the slightest possibility she'd end up like her mother, she'd leave Red. As much as it would hurt her, she wouldn't risk ruining their lives.

Speaking of my mother . . .

Turning her attention back to her uncle, she said, "I wanted to ask you something. One night, while you were in the hospital, you were calling my mother's name."

He lowered his gaze. "Did I? I don't remember that."

"Do you think about her a lot?"

"Sure I do. She's my sister."

"It's just that . . . it seemed odd."

"Cali, I want to talk to you about your mother." He shifted in the bed.

"Can we not?" she snapped. "I really have nothing to say about her."

"There are some things you don't know, baby," he insisted. "You need to know all the facts."

"Uncle Cal, stop." She threw her hands up in the air. "I understand what you're doing. But I can't do this right now. I need to be focused on you and Red and work."

"I think this is important, too."

"You're right, but not today important." She didn't want to spend another minute talking about her mother. "Maybe tomorrow important?"

He sighed heavily. "Fine. So tell me about you and Red and this instant family you got here."

Cali froze. "Instant family? That's not what this is."

Corrine was a wonderful girl, and Cali liked her a lot. But she wasn't ready to be a stand-in mother for her. The idea of getting close to her scared Cali. She didn't want to disappoint an innocent child—especially one who'd already had so much heartache.

"That little girl is adorable."

"She is, but she's not my daughter," Cali said in a firm voice.

"You're with her father, living with him."

"Temporarily," she added, tossing a piece of paper into the tiny recycle bin nearby.

"Cali, you can't stick your head in the sand and pretend that your whole relationship hasn't changed because of this," he said.

"Trust me. I know things are different. But I told Red that I'm in this with him," she said defensively. "I'm not trying to take Corrine's mother's place. But I'll be there for Red—and Corrine."

"Why are you refusing to see how serious this is?" He coughed a bit and adjusted the small tubes in his nose.

It was very serious. One false move, one bad decision, and Corrine would be...her. Every time Cali looked at the little girl, she saw herself.

"Uncle Cal, you should rest. I'll go ahead and bring you a glass of water so you can take your medicine." She headed to the door, stopping at the threshold and turning to look at her uncle. "Uncle Cal?"

He looked at her, his face solemn. "Yes?"

"I love you."

"I love you, too, baby girl."

* * *

It could be hormones, or just plain exhaustion, Cali thought as she stared at her computer screen. For the past hour, she'd attempted to focus on weddings and centerpieces. But she'd spent forty minutes of that hour crying silently. When *did* she become such a big baby?

She ran a shaky hand over her face and sighed, dropping her head on the keyboard. "Ugh, get it together, Cali," she grumbled to herself.

"Cali?"

She whipped her head up, startled by Corrine standing in the doorway. The teary-eyed girl was clutching a doll in her arms and rubbing her eyes.

"Hi," Cali said. She still hadn't figured out a nickname for the child, which made her feel like a mean old lady for some reason. "What's wrong? It's very late."

"I miss my mommy." Corrine twisted the hem of her nightshirt. "I want to know when she's coming to get me."

Aw. Cali patted her lap and opened her arms. "Come here." Corrine walked over to her and climbed onto her lap. Cali pushed her wild curls out of her face and kissed her forehead. "It's going to be okay, sweetie."

"I miss her."

"I know you do." Tears pricked Cali's eyes and she was transported to a time when she'd cried herself to sleep over her own mother. "I know exactly how you feel."

"You do?" she asked.

"When I was a kid, my mother left. But before that, she wasn't around very much."

"Daddy keeps telling me that Mommy is away. Where is she? Can I call her?"

Cali was still irritated with Red for not telling Corrine that her mother was in jail and not coming back anytime soon. They'd argued about it a few times, but Red thought he was doing what was best for her as her father. She didn't want to overstep, but sitting there with a hurt Corrine, she wasn't sure if she could hold it in much longer.

"Sweetie, sometimes people can't see a person they love."

"But why?" Corrine asked. "Mommy always told me she would call me. I think they have a phone where she is. Why can't I call her?"

Cali's heart broke for Corrine. She hadn't truly realized how much their situations mirrored each other. They were both blessed with good fathers, but cursed with crazy mothers. Cali remembered crying herself to sleep at night, wondering where her mother was and why she'd left her. Thinking back to that time, she wished someone would have told her the truth about her mother. Maybe she should do that for Corrine. "Actually, your mother may not be able to get to a phone."

"But why?" Corrine asked again.

Cali was at a loss for words. *Why?* It was a simple question with a not-so-simple answer. "Do you remember when we watched that movie and the woman that froze the whole town got locked away?"

"Yes, but she didn't do anything bad."

"I know, but she made a mistake and people got hurt," Cali explained, hoping the inquisitive girl would get it. "Sometimes that happens in real life. People make mistakes and other people get hurt. Your mommy made a mistake, Corrine. Now she has to go away for a while."

Corrine's eyes widened. "She's in jail?"

"Cali?" Red said, walking into the room, his lips pulled into a frown.

"Daddy, Cali was telling me a story about Mommy," Corrine said.

"I heard her," Red said, glaring at Cali. "Why are you up this late, baby doll?"

"I miss Mommy," the little one repeated.

Red lifted her into his arms. "I know. Maybe she'll call soon so you can talk to her."

Cali shook her head as Red left the room. Sighing, she unlocked her laptop and attempted to actually get some work done.

C HAPTER TWENTY-SEVEN

$\mathcal{W}$hat the hell were you doing?" Red asked, stomping into the room.

Cali looked up from her laptop, twisted her pen between her fingers. "I know you're upset, but she's upset, too. She's asking questions and she needs to know the truth."

"That's not your truth to tell, Cali," Red yelled. "Shit, she's a child."

"She's a child that got picked up from her babysitter's house and brought to a police station in the middle of the night!" she shouted. "Not telling her the truth is stupid at this point."

He shook his head, muttering a curse under his breath. "Don't do that."

"Red, think about it. She's six years old, not two," Cali said. "She knows what jail is and knows the concept of getting in trouble. You're not giving her enough credit. I'm sure she's heard people talk about jail in school before."

"Hearing people talk about jail and knowing that your mother is in jail are two separate things," he argued, pacing the room. "I've already uprooted her from her life and brought her to an unfamiliar place, around a bunch of new people. I just don't think she's ready to know that yet."

"But you're lying to her every day that she asks where her mother is. Kids know. Believe me, they pick up on all kinds of things." She closed her laptop and sighed. "You're not good at hiding it because you're not a fake person. You're angry with Nia and it shows. If she hasn't already, eventually, Corrine will catch on."

"I understand that your childhood was bad, but I don't want Corrine to have that same experience."

"I don't either," she said. She couldn't help but care about Corrine. The little girl was like a breath of fresh air in her life. Looking in her eyes, Cali could believe in the good in the world. She wanted it for her.

"I'm her father, Cali," Red said. "I don't want to see her hurt."

"Then don't hurt her!" she shouted, throwing her hands up in the air. "Lying to her is only going to hurt her. She thinks she's here because you're babysitting her. She's waiting for her mother to pick her up. Don't you think she needs, deserves, to know that her mother is not coming back to get her anytime soon—if ever?"

"Even so, *you* shouldn't have told her that."

"Fine." She crossed her arms. "It's not like I set out to tell her. She asked me could she call her mother. What was I supposed to say?"

"Tell your daddy," he said. "How about that?"

"Red, I don't want to have this conversation anymore." Cali was tired, irritated, sad, and angry all at once. "Corrine is your daughter and you do what you think is best. I'm telling you...the sooner you tell the truth, the sooner she'll be able to get this idea out of her head that her mother is going to be here. My Uncle Cal, he didn't tell me that my mother was dead. I just mentioned it to him one day and he cried."

Red averted his gaze, but not before she caught the look that passed over his face when she mentioned her mother and Uncle Cal. Frowning, she asked, "What was that look for?"

"What look?" he asked, avoiding eye contact. He gathered up some papers lying on the desk.

"When I mentioned my mother being dead, you looked like you—"

"I'm frustrated, okay?" He ran his fingers through his hair. "Nia is looking at a ten-year prison sentence, which means I have to be the person that Corrine can count on. That means making hard decisions."

"I know that, Red." She approached him, smoothing her hands over his broad shoulders. "I get it. I feel for that little girl." Hell, she *was* that little girl. Finding out her mother wasn't the woman she'd built up in her mind had been devastating. "It's so hard. Unfortunately, she's going to have to deal with it."

"You really haven't dealt with your mother, Cali," he said. "Your way of dealing is pretending that she doesn't mean anything to you and we both know that's not true."

"You don't know what you're talking about," she said. "My mother has been dead for years. I've had plenty of time to let that sink in."

"Really?" he asked, sarcasm bleeding through his tone.

"This isn't about me," she said. "I want you to help your daughter by telling her the truth."

"Let me handle it in my way, then."

Raising her hands, she took a step back. "Okay. That's your daughter. I won't say anything else." She sat down, opened her laptop, and pretended to not be hurt by Red's words. "I have work to do."

"Cali, I'm sorry."

"Okay. But I need to get this done," she told him, squinting at the screen. "So, if you don't mind…"

Red stalked out of the room, slamming the door behind

him. She took a sip from her warm glass of water and grumbled a curse.

The next morning, Cali checked on a sleeping Uncle Cal and headed to the kitchen. Red and Corrine were sitting at the breakfast bar, eating bowls of cereal.

"Good morning," she said. "Coffee?"

"Brewing now," he said, dipping his spoon into his bowl. He'd yet to meet her gaze since she walked in the kitchen. The tension didn't faze Corrine, though, because she was singing along with the commercials on the television.

"Cali?" Corrine said, her feet dangling over the side of the stool. "Why don't you eat cereal?"

"Because cereal is for kids." She grinned at Cali then scowled at Red, who set a spoonful of cereal into his bowl.

"Daddy eats cereal," Cali said, looking pointedly at Red's huge bowl of Apple Jacks.

"My point exactly," Cali murmured. Red glared at her and stabbed at his cereal with his spoon. "Did Syd call this morning?"

"Earlier. We're going to go over for the afternoon," he murmured.

Cali poured a cup of coffee into her favorite mug, followed by a healthy shot of hazelnut creamer. "I had planned to visit her as well. Her baby shower is fast approaching and we need to finalize the menu."

"Are you going to be able to focus on that with everything going on?" he asked.

"I have no choice," Cali said. "My work doesn't stop for holidays and illness."

"Are we going to keep doing this?"

"Doing what?" she asked innocently. She took a sip of her coffee and plopped two pieces of toast into the toaster.

He eyed her over the rim of his own coffee mug. "You didn't come to bed last night."

"I was working and fell asleep on the couch," she lied. She'd purposefully stayed away from Red, choosing to watch television until the wee hours of the morning instead of climbing into bed with him like nothing had happened.

"Whatever." He patted *his* daughter on the top of her head. "Corrine, you want to go get on your boots so we can go?"

"She can't go out like that," Cali said, taking in Corrine's mismatched clothes, unkempt hair, and milk mustache.

Red glanced at Corrine and then back at her. "What's the problem?"

"Her hair," she hissed. "Her clothes don't even match."

He shrugged. "She picked that outfit herself."

"I can tell," she said.

Cali had graciously offered to take Corrine shopping for new clothes, but Red insisted he knew what he was doing. If her ensemble for the day was any indication, she could safely say he was dead wrong and had no clue what he was doing.

"Maybe you should take her to get her hair braided or something," Cali suggested.

"Syd said she'd do it."

Cali covered her mouth, unable to hide her smile at Red's cluelessness. "Syd? She doesn't know how to do hair."

"Her hair looks fine," he said.

"Yeah, but…" Sighing, she placed a hand on Corrine's back. "Baby, why don't you run in the bathroom, get a comb and a brush, and hurry back out so I can do your hair."

"Yay!" Corrine cheered, jumping down from her chair and running out of the kitchen.

"Her hair was fine," Red repeated.

"I can't have that beautiful baby walking out of this house looking like that." Cali traced the rim of her mug with her finger. And she couldn't explain the need she had to protect Corrine.

"I thought about what you said," he admitted softly.

"Really?" she asked.

"You're right. I don't know what I was thinking. I hate lying, so I don't want to start that with Corrine. I plan to talk to her soon."

Pleased that he'd actually taken her thoughts into consideration, she walked up to him. "It's going to be okay." She wrapped her arms around him and kissed him. "I'll be here for you."

He squeezed her ass. "You know what else?"

"What?" she asked.

"I think it's long past time that we reconnect in other ways."

He was right. It had been days since they'd made love and it was starting to drive her crazy. Her life had turned into one big ball of uncertainty and she'd barely been able to keep her head above water. Then with Corrine in the house, toys scattered in every nook and cranny, and Uncle Cal, they'd barely had any time alone. She'd been exhausted every night, struggling to keep her eyes open when her head hit the pillow. Most of the time, they shared a simple kiss before she fell asleep. Sometimes she wondered how she'd gone from enjoying her single life to living in a house full of people.

"I agree." Her head fell back and his tongue swept down her neck. "That sounds good right about now."

"I say we take a little break for ourselves tonight."

"Aw man. I'm supposed to have a dinner meeting tonight with a bride."

He laughed. "We can figure something out for later."

"Cali, I can't find it!" Corrine screamed at the top of her lungs.

"I'm coming!" Cali shouted. "I better go see about that and get her hair combed before you leave." She kissed him. "Hook something up and I'll be there."

"I'll ask Syd to babysit."

"Syd can't even walk," she reminded him.

"True," he said. "How about we have a date here once she's asleep?"

"That's a great idea." There was no way Red could leave Corrine with just anyone. And she respected that about him. "I'm going to go check on her."

Cali left Red and went off in search of Corrine. She found her on her knees, her head in the cabinet. There were cleaning containers strewn across the floor. "Wait, baby." Cali rushed over to her. "You shouldn't be under here. It's dangerous." Replacing all the stuff in the cabinet, she smiled at Corrine, who was watching her intently. "See, here is the comb and brush," she said, pulling out a small drawer.

Pulling herself to her feet, she sat down on the toilet. "Turn around and we can get you all dolled up."

"Okay. Cali?"

"Yes, doll," she said.

"Daddy messed up my hair, didn't he?"

Cali laughed at the little doll's candor. "Yes he did. But don't worry because I'm going to fix it. Then I'm going to make you an appointment to get your hair braided."

"Yay!" Corrine clapped her little hands.

She went to work on Corrine's hair, parting it down the middle and starting a French braid. As she worked, Red stood in the doorway watching. "I didn't know you braided hair," he said.

"There's a lot about me you don't know." She grinned at him.

"I bet there is."

Once she finished the last braid, she picked up a small mirror and held it in front of Corrine. "You like it?"

"It's pretty," Corrine said, twirling a braid around her finger and examining her hair. "When I grow up, I want to be beautiful, just like you."

Cali's heart swelled. Who knew a little girl could bring her to tears with a compliment?

"Daddy says you're beautiful and it's true," Corrine continued.

"He did?" Her eyes met Red's and she smiled.

"Yep. Are you going to marry him?" Corrine asked. "Because if you are, I want to be a flower girl."

Cali cleared her throat. "Well, your daddy and I are pretty close." She pinched her throat. "But I'm not sure about marriage."

"You sleep in the same bed," Corrine pointed out. "My friend's parents are married and sleep in the same bed, so you and Daddy can get married. I saw him kiss you. People only kiss each other when it's true love."

Red laughed loudly.

Cali shook her head once again, wondering how such a little girl could often render her speechless. "Let's go get your boots on."

CHAPTER TWENTY-EIGHT

$\mathcal{H}$ey, Syd." Cali walked into Syd's bedroom and tossed her briefcase on the bed.

"Hi," Syd grumbled.

"What's wrong?" Cali asked. "Are you in pain or something?"

"I'm tired of being in the bed, Cali. I'm ready to get up and go outside and drive my own damn car. I haven't even had a chance to finish the baby's room."

"Well, unfortunately, I'm not willing to incur Morgan's wrath, but I'm here to keep your mind off of your troubles. Let's talk baby shower. Has Dr. *Love* given you the okay to go to your baby shower?"

Syd rolled her eyes. Hard. "Shut the hell up. I can go to the damn baby shower. But I have to keep my feet up and come right home."

"Okay. That's good."

"Whatever. I'm going stir crazy. Morgan and Red and Kent have been in here talking about the bar and everything. I want to go to the bar myself," she whined. "Then, I'm horny as hell and Morgan won't touch me."

"Aw, baby." She pulled Sydney into a hug, chuckling when she struggled to get out of her hold.

"Let me go," Syd warned. "I'm liable to punch you."

Cali released her and sat down on the edge of the bed. Pulling a folder out of her briefcase, she handed it to her furious friend. "You really should watch those frown lines. This is the menu. I need you to okay it."

Syd put on her glasses and studied the menu. "Can you add some cheesecake bites?"

"Syd, there's like eight different desserts on the menu."

"Just do it. They are not for me. Mama loves them."

"Fine." Cali scribbled a note to herself to call the caterer. "How is Mama Smith?"

"She's fine, excited about the baby and ready to spoil her."

Cali was glad to hear that. The Smith family had been dealt their fair share of heartache. She knew that Morgan's relationship with Caden was still strained, which was to be expected, but it did her heart good to know that Mama Smith supported Syd. "That's great. I can't wait for her to meet Corrine."

Syd observed her over the rim of her glasses. "Listen to you. If I didn't know you, I'd think you're loving being a mother figure."

"What is that supposed to mean? You're talking like you think I ain't shit."

"Ha! That's not what I meant. You're awesome, when you're not being annoying. But your eyes ... they lit up when you mentioned Corrine."

"She's adorable, that's all. And if I want to be with Red, she's part of the package."

"Is that it?"

"Yes." The words left her mouth, but Cali wasn't even sure if she believed them. "Anyway, let's finish this up. The favors arrived and the shower gifts are all wrapped and ready."

"Thank you."

A soft knock sounded and they turned to the door.

"Surprise." Allina walked into the room, a big smile on her face.

"Allina!" Syd shouted.

Cali jumped up and hugged her long lost friend first. They held on for a few seconds before they pulled apart. Allina made her way over to Syd.

"Look at you," Allina said, smoothing a hand over Syd's full belly. "You look like you're ready to pop."

"I am," Syd said. "I'm so glad you're here. I missed you."

"I missed you, too—both of you."

Cali pushed her briefcase onto the floor and climbed next to Syd. She patted an open spot. "Hop up. When did you get here?"

"This morning. I'm so sorry about Uncle Cal." Allina squeezed her hand. "I want to see him while I'm here."

"He'll be glad to see you. He's at Red's right now. We had to hire a nurse to come over and help."

"What is this I hear about you and Red?"

Cali's cheeks burned and she dropped her gaze to her hands. "Girl, please. Stop. And how do you know about us? I've been trying to call you for weeks. Where have you been?"

Allina swallowed, pulled her hand back and pushed her glasses up. "I've been busy, trying to find work in Ohio."

Syd rubbed her belly. "Is everything okay? Why did I have to hear about you moving from Kent? Excuse me, but I thought I was your best friend."

"You are. It happened so quickly. Isaac's father asked him to take over the youth ministry at their church. He was ready to move."

"What about your opportunity?" Cali asked, shocked that Allina was actually sitting there admitting that she'd relocated to another state for a man that wasn't her husband.

"There are plenty of opportunities in the Greater Cleveland area. Besides, my parents are close by."

Allina was born and raised in Akron, Ohio, which was about forty miles from Cleveland. Cali had only visited one time. Syd had dragged her down to keep Allina company while her parents were away one summer. The best thing about the visit was the Galley Boy burger and a refreshing drink called California from a place called Swensons.

"They're both getting older," Allina continued. "I don't mind being a short drive away from them. And there are a few premier bridal shops in Cleveland that might take me on."

"How is that better than taking over for Bessie here in an already established shop?" Cali knew she probably should shut up. But Allina had spent so many years living a life that was beneath her. It infuriated Cali that she would throw away an opportunity to be a business owner to chase after a man. "Allina, you're a talented seamstress and businesswoman. You can do something here."

"Cali, don't." Syd squeezed her arm. "Let's not talk about this right now. I want to catch up. Tell me about Isaac."

"There's time to talk about him. I want to hear about you two."

Cali and Syd exchanged glances and she knew her friend was thinking the same thing she was. Allina had moved away from everyone she cared about to be with the man of God and didn't want to talk about him. Sounded a little fishy.

"Are you sure you're okay, Lina?" Syd asked, rubbing her ever-growing stomach. "You look tired and stressed."

Syd was spot on. Allina *did* look tired. Allina was a fair-skinned person, but right now her skin was pale, almost colorless. Her normally smooth skin was blotchy. And she looked like she'd missed a few meals—or ten. In college, Allina never ate a lot, but Cali had never seen her friend so thin. Her clothes were hanging off of her.

Before Syd moved, though, Allina had seemed to go through a transformation. She wasn't the type of person to wear a lot of makeup but she'd started. She even straightened her long, natural curls and cut her hair into a short bob. In front of her was a woman who was anything but the friend she remembered. Her hair was still short, but it was flat and lifeless.

"I'm fine." Allina rubbed the back of her hair. "Just tired from the drive. But I wouldn't miss this occasion for anything."

"Allina, there's something you're not telling us," Syd said in her calm, comforting voice. "And you know you can tell us anything."

"I'm fine. You don't need to be focused on anything but your baby. And Cali, you have enough to worry about."

It was just like Allina to push herself and her needs aside. She'd always been that way. Syd had a different relationship with her than Cali did. Allina often confided in Syd things that she would probably never tell Cali. Then again, she'd confided in Syd herself and had sworn her to secrecy more times than she could count.

"Well, I can't promise that I won't worry about you, Lina," Syd told her. "I can look at you and see something's wrong."

Allina's eyes filled up with tears and she slid off the bed. "I told you I am good. Stressed about money, that's all. You know how I hate to ask anyone for help. But I'll find a job soon." She walked around the room, picked up a bottle of perfume on the dresser and sniffed it. "This smells good. Do you need any help with anything, Syd?"

Cali crossed her arms and stared at Allina. She couldn't fault her friend for choosing to suffer rather than ask for help. That was one thing they all had in common, because she'd done it plenty of times herself. And she knew Syd had, too. "I could use some help with the nursery," Syd said, elbowing Cali.

"Ouch," Cali growled, rubbing her arm. "Your elbows are like sharp darts," she whispered.

"Nursery?" Allina asked. "Where is it? I can help with that."

Syd scooted to the edge of the bed and Allina rushed up to her. "Should you be getting out of bed?"

"I can walk to the nursery. I just can't do anything once I get in there."

* * *

"There's something wrong with Allina." Cali rubbed lotion onto her palms and climbed into bed with Red.

"What do you mean?" Red asked, his nose buried in a pile of paperwork. "She seemed fine to me."

They'd spent the day at Morgan and Syd's, catching Allina up on their lives. Kent had stopped by for a few awkward minutes. It seemed as though he and Allina were still doing their little dance, walking around each other when they really wanted to walk into each other. Throughout the evening, the conversation would turn back to Allina and her life in Ohio. She always seemed to avoid the questions about her man, though, and that bothered Cali. That had always seemed to be the case with Allina: she'd expect everyone to tell her their business, but never shared hers with anyone else—except Syd, and only sometimes. Cali suspected Syd was in the dark just like she was in a lot of ways. It was hard to get close to someone who was content keeping everyone at arm's length.

If anyone could understand the propensity to handle people with a long-handled spoon, it was Cali. But even she had to admit that having a confidante was important. Holding things inside only served to destroy rather than build. She had been lucky to find Syd, but she'd already had an outlet in her Uncle. She wondered if Allina had ever had that. Unlike her and Syd, Allina had a seemingly great relationship with her mother, but looks could be deceiving.

"You would think that," she said. "You've never really paid that much attention to her."

He gaped at her in mock offense. "That's not true. I pay attention to her. She's family."

"Yeah, right. You didn't even realize she'd cut her hair until it had been like that for months."

He shrugged, closing a folder and dropping it on top of his briefcase. "Of course I didn't notice that. Allina is like my sister, always has been. I'm not supposed to notice stuff like that. Kent did, though."

"Don't you think their whole exchange was weird?"

"I think you're reading too much into this. Kent was fine when he came in."

Men. "You see what you want to see. I bet if Allina came in with a pan of her famous fried chicken you would've been all in."

He laughed. "It's food. Of course I'd pay attention. Her fried chicken is slamming."

It was a running joke among their group of friends that Red would eat all day if he could get away with it. Syd always teased that he had an *eat-a-lot* condition or something. Cali had quickly learned that she could pretty much get away with anything if she had the right food to dangle in his face.

"I thought you liked *my* fried chicken," she said with a pout.

"Oh, I like it." He pulled her close to him and kissed her. "I like your fried chicken and everything else you cook. But food is not the first thing I think of when I think of you."

"Oh really?" she asked, pulling his specs off and setting them on the bedside table.

He lifted her nightshirt off and cupped her breasts in his hands. "We have to be quiet."

"I'm quiet."

"Um hm." He tugged her underwear down and lowered himself on top of her. "Quiet as a freight train."

She smacked him and pulled him into a deep kiss. Her body needed a release. Pushing him on his back, she tugged his boxers off and straddled his waist. He sat upright, running a hand down her spine. "Damn, I've missed you," he murmured against her mouth, running his tongue across her bottom lip before he captured it with his own.

She dug her fingers into his scalp and lowered herself onto his erection, closing her eyes. He covered her neck with wet kisses. When his body went stiff, her eyes popped open. His gaze was on something behind her.

Slowly, she turned and gasped when she noticed a little girl with hazel eyes standing in the doorway, staring at them. Mortified, she pulled the sheet over her naked body and rolled off of Red.

"Oh my God," she said, scrambling for her nightshirt.

"Corrine, turn around, baby doll," Red grunted, struggling to put his underwear on. Once they were secured, he jumped out of bed and rushed over to Corrine, who was still staring at Cali. She hadn't been able to locate her nightshirt so she had no choice but to sit there looking, more than likely, like she'd got caught with her hand inside the cookie jar.

Red stood in front of his curious daughter, blocking Cali from her view. He leaned down. "Baby doll, aren't you supposed to be asleep?"

"What were you and Cali doing?" Corrine asked, looking back and forth between them.

"We were..." Red's cheeks turned a bright shade of crimson and Cali thought it was the cutest thing she'd ever seen. Syd blushed often, but she'd never seen Red that way. She'd be sure to tease him about it later. He cleared his throat. "We were...playing..."

"We were play wrestling," Cali said, putting Red out of his obvious misery. "And I beat your daddy."

"But he's strong," Corrine exclaimed in awe.

"I'm stronger," Cali whispered, grinning when Red gave her a *yeah, right* look.

"Why are you up, baby doll?" Red asked.

"I had a bad dream," the little girl whined.

Cali finally spotted her nightshirt peeking out from beneath the comforter. She quickly pulled it out and slipped it on. "What kind of dream?" she asked.

Red glanced over his shoulder at her and then led Corrine over to the bed.

She climbed in next to Cali. "About my mommy."

"What about her?" Red asked, laying on the other side of Corrine.

"That she was hurt," Corrine whimpered, cuddling into Cali.

Cali shared a glance with Red and he nodded. "Baby doll, I have to tell you something about your mother," he said.

Corrine turned to her father, eyes trained on him.

"Your mother got into some trouble," he continued. "Bad trouble. She hurt someone and the police don't like it when people hurt other people. So . . . your mother had to go to jail."

"Jail?" Corrine said, her eyes wide. "But my mommy is nice. Why did she have to go to jail? That's where bad people go."

"Sometimes good people do bad things," Cali explained. "Remember like in the movie we watched. The queen was good, but she did a bad thing."

"Is she going to be okay?" Corrine asked.

"I think so, sweetie," Cali assured her.

"Can I go see her in jail, Daddy?"

"I don't think that's a good idea, honey," he said. "Your mother wouldn't want you to see her like that."

"But I want to see my mommy!" Corrine shouted with a pout. "I want her."

"Corrine, it's going to be okay," Red told her.

"No, it's not!" Corrine kicked her feet in the air and crossed her little arms. Grumbling, she yelled, "I want my mommy."

"I'm here for you," he said, his eyes portraying his true emotions.

"I don't want you!" she yelled. "I want my mommy."

"Corrine," he said, rubbing her arms.

She jerked away from him and burrowed into Cali's side. "No! I want my mommy. I don't want you."

Tears pricked Cali's eyes as Red seemed to deflate right before her eyes. He slumped back against the headboard as Corrine sobbed hard in Cali's arms.

"Sweetie, it's okay to want your mother," Cali told her, kissing the top of her head. "But your father is here to help you. He loves you."

"Why can't he get my mommy out of jail then?" Corrine asked. "He's a lawyer."

"You're right," Cali said. "He's a lawyer and, normally, he could get someone out of jail. But your mother committed a crime, baby. She has to pay the price for that. You know how when you ate all the popsicles and told me you didn't? Then your dad had to take your dessert away?"

Corrine sniffled and nodded.

"That's called a punishment," Cali explained.

"Mommy used to punish me." Corrine wiped her eyes.

"I know. Parents have to punish their children so that they can grow up to be responsible."

Lifting her gaze, Corrine peered into Cali's eyes. "Are you susponsible?"

Cali giggled. "I try to be."

"I just miss my mommy," Corrine cried. "She was only mean sometimes."

Cali couldn't stand to look into her sad eyes anymore. The little doll had carved out her own space in Cali's heart. And it scared her. Pulling Corrine closer, she held her until she fell asleep.

C HAPTER TWENTY-NINE

$\mathcal{A}$ week later, the baby shower was in full swing. Cali made her rounds, greeting guests, giving hugs, and directing people to the radiant Syd, who was seated in a huge chair in the middle of the room. The doctor had given strict instructions for her not to walk around too much and to keep her feet propped up. Cali had refurbished an old foot rest, putting a layer of cushion on it that matched the theme of the baby shower.

Syd wore a beautiful, low-cut, quarter-sleeved, hot pink maxi dress that had a high slit. It fit her like a glove, accentuating all of her curves and especially her round belly. She capped off her look with a sleek matching fedora. Her best friend was so sexy that when the fellas saw her fully dressed, Morgan gaped at her like he was seeing her for the first time and Red threatened to throw his coat over her.

The hot pink and coffee brown color scheme was a hit with party guests and Cali couldn't be happier. She'd also set up a separate area for the men near the pool tables. While the women nibbled on cucumber sandwiches with the crusts cut off and sipped on Moscato and sparkling water, the men were treated to sweet and sour meatballs, chicken wings, and beer. As a result, Cali lined up at least three jobs from a few ladies who'd recently found out they were expecting and booked a wedding with a former coworker of Syd's.

Red had disappeared with Morgan and she began to wonder where they'd gone. Syd kept asking where they were and Cali had no idea. She'd tried calling Red a few times and even dialed Morgan, with no luck. She hoped everything was okay. That last thing they needed was drama. She'd already checked on Uncle Cal, who hadn't been feeling well earlier. The home health care aide she'd hired also sent her hourly texts with updates. He was doing okay. Corrine was running around the room with another little girl.

Dinner was served and Cali finally had a chance to sit down. She pulled up a chair next to Syd, who was shifting uncomfortably. "Are you okay, babe?" Cali asked.

"I can't seem to get comfortable. My back is hurting and I just feel icky."

"Was it something you ate?"

Syd shrugged, a deep frown on her round face. "I can't eat anything."

"Uh oh. You can't eat? Maybe we should call Dr. Love."

Cali had invited the doctor at Syd's request, but Love's schedule didn't allow her to attend. That was fine with Cali. Although she had nothing against the good doctor, she didn't want to be reminded that Red had been attracted to her. Yep, she was a bitch like that.

"Where's Morgan?" Syd grimaced and set her plate aside. "He still hasn't come back yet?"

Cali sighed when Morgan and Red chose that exact moment to reappear. Morgan winked at Syd and kissed her.

Red squeezed Cali's shoulder. "What did we miss?" He swiped a chicken wing from her plate. "Did Allina make this chicken?"

"Yes, I did," Allina announced from her seat nearby.

"I'm going to go ahead and get me some food." Red hurried over to the buffet line.

Morgan sat next to Syd. "You okay, baby?"

"I don't feel good," Syd told him.

"I told her we should call Dr. Love," Cali said. "But she said no."

Morgan nodded. "Is it your back?"

"That, and I can't get comfortable."

"Well, we only have a little bit to go. Can you hang on or do you want to go to the hospital?"

"No." Syd scrunched her nose. "No hospital. I should be okay."

"Cali, you think we could speed things up?" Morgan asked.

"Sure. All the games are done. We can start opening gifts right now."

Cali made an announcement, stating that Sydney wasn't feeling well so they were going to go ahead and open the gifts.

Once every gift was opened, Syd leaned back in the chair, discomfort on her face and a light sheen of sweat on her brow. Cali noticed a lone gift on the table that hadn't been there before. "Oh, Sydney, you have another gift." She picked it up and handed it to her. "Only one more," she assured her friend, who looked like she wanted to strangle her.

Sighing, Sydney tore open the beautiful light blue gift wrap. The Tiffany & Co. emblem was unmistakable and Cali gasped as Morgan dropped to one knee in front of a shocked Syd.

"Sydney," Morgan asked, his face serious. "I love you so much. You've made me so happy. I could think of no one else that I'd want to make my wife. Will you marry me?"

Cali glanced at Red, who was grinning.

The crowd giggled as Morgan pulled the gorgeous ring out of the box and slipped it on Syd's pinky finger. Cali cheered when Syd gasped, expecting her to shout "Yes!" at the top of her lungs.

"Shit," Syd exclaimed.

Everyone in the room was watching, confused by Syd's response. Cali wanted to say something, anything, to break the silence that descended upon the room.

"Oh shit," Syd repeated. "I think my water just broke."

Morgan jumped up and into action, running around the room like a chicken and barking orders at Red and Kent. Cali rushed up to Syd, who was breathing in short bursts. Allina helped her get Syd into a standing position.

"Oh my God, I ruined my dress," Syd yelled.

The room was buzzing with excitement as Morgan raced back into the room, picked Syd up, and ran out with her screaming orders at everyone around.

* * *

At approximately, 8:02 p.m. on January 12th, Syd gave birth to Red's first niece, Brynn Morgan Smith. She was healthy, even though she was born a little early, and arrived with a head full of hair.

Cali and Allina arrived shortly after 8:30 and were directed to the family waiting area where they were seated. Kent told the ladies the hilarious story of Syd in labor. Red had wanted to choke the doctor who'd gone in to examine Syd in the hospital room. He could hear her scream from outside the room and he hated to hear her in any pain, even the expected pain of childbirth.

Syd's labor was so quick, Dr. Love barely got into the room before she had to push. They weren't able to give her an epidural, which had sent Syd into a crazed panic. Despite

Red's insistence that he not be in the room with them, Syd demanded that he come hold her hand, which was why he was holding an ice pack to his knuckles. Fortunately for him, Morgan had pried her hand off of Red's and excused him from the room.

They were waiting for Syd and the baby to get cleaned up. Morgan promised he would come and get them as soon as the coast was clear.

Red checked his watch. Mama Smith had graciously offered to keep Corrine even though she wanted to be at the hospital to meet her new grandbaby.

"Hey," Morgan said, walking into the waiting room. He had on a pair of blue scrubs. "She's ready."

They followed Morgan to Syd's hospital room. Red clapped Morgan on his back. "I can't believe you're a father, man."

His friend grinned. "She's beautiful, Red."

"I bet. How's Syd?"

"Your sister, man." Morgan shook his head. "She cut the fool after you left the room. But she's good, just loving on the baby between naps."

"You don't have to tell me about my sister." Red laughed. "The drama queen."

"Stop talking about my friend," Cali said. "She had a baby. Geez. Give her a break."

"Look at your man's hand, Cali," Morgan said, staring pointedly at Red's swollen hand. "Your friend cut the fool," he repeated.

Cali laughed. "I'm glad I wasn't here." Red glared at her and she shrugged. "Sorry, babe."

Morgan knocked on a door at the far end of the hallway. When they stepped in, Red smiled at the sight of his sister holding his niece. Dr. Love was in the room also. He gave her a quick hug before turning to his sister and his niece.

"Hi," Syd said, her voice hoarse. "Come meet Brynn."

Red hesitated, only moving when Cali pulled him with her closer to the bed. As Cali cooed over the beautiful baby, he squeezed Syd's foot. "She's adorable," he said when Cali picked her up and brought her over to him.

"Isn't she?" Cali said, her voice soft. "She's gorgeous."

"I don't normally say this, but she is a doll," Dr. Love said. "Congratulations."

Cali smiled at Dr. Love. "Thanks. I'm a proud godparent." She wrinkled her nose and mumbled something in "baby."

"Thank you," he told Dr. Love before she walked out of the room.

Cali was beautiful holding the baby. There was no nervousness around the baby on her part, no fear. Holding little Brynn looked natural for her. Red thought about what it would be like to see her holding a child of her own.

Red ran a thumb over the baby's hand, marveling at how tiny she was. Her little hand was smaller than his thumb.

"Did she scratch herself?" Red asked, running the back of his finger over a red line on her plump cheek.

"Yes," Syd replied. "That's why we have those gloves on now. She's a feisty one."

"I'm not surprised," Red winked at Syd.

"Do you want to hold her?" Cali asked him, swaying back and forth.

He shook his head. "She's too small."

"I know, right?" Morgan said. "I get a little nervous holding her. The nurse said it helps if you sit down with a pillow on your lap and hold her that way."

Red shrugged, stuffing his hands into his pockets. "I'll wait until she's a little bigger."

"You're such a wimp," Cali teased.

"Fine, I'll hold her." When Cali placed the baby in his arms, he took in the baby smell and felt his heart open up a little more. His niece. *She's definitely going to be spoiled.* He gave her the once-over, pulling off her sock and counting her toes.

"Hi, Brynn," he said, tickling her stomach with his finger. "I'm your uncle." The baby frowned and started whining and Red looked at Cali for help.

Cali laughed. "She might be hungry." She took the beauty from his arms and walked her over to Syd. "I think she wants her mama."

"They're trying to get her to latch on, but I'm having some problems."

Latch on? After Red put two and two together, he backed away. "I think…" He pointed at the door. "I'm going to go on out."

"Yeah, I don't want to see that," Kent added, following Red out of the room.

* * *

The next morning during breakfast, Red and Cali told Uncle Cal about the baby and showed him all the pictures Red had taken on his cell phone. Red couldn't get enough of his little niece. Watching Syd and Morgan fawn all over the newborn made him think about all the time he'd missed with Corrine. Seemed like there was a ton of her life he hadn't been a part of. He vowed he'd never miss another important event in her life.

"She's a beauty," Uncle Cal said. "Looks like Syd."

"I think she looks like Morgan," Cali said. Corrine appeared with a handful of Cheez-Its and climbed onto her lap. She wrapped her arm around her and squeezed. Red smiled at his two favorite girls.

"Is that the baby again?" his daughter asked, with a mouth full of crackers.

Cali swiped one and popped it in her mouth. "Yes, it's her. Isn't she pretty?"

"Her nose is scrunched up."

Uncle Cal started to laugh, but ended up coughing. Red watched as he used a Kleenex to catch the phlegm.

"How are you feeling, Uncle Cal?" Cali asked.

"I'm tired."

"Well, how about we leave you to get some rest?" Red said.

"I'd like to talk to you for a minute, Red," Uncle Cal said, his eyes meeting Red's.

"What's going on, Uncle Cal?" Cali asked, worry lining her face.

"I wanted to go over some business with him. When he leaves, though, I'd like to talk to you."

Cali whispered something into Corrine's ear. When his bundle of energy hopped out of her lap and disappeared around the corner, Cali stood and followed without another word.

Sighing, he turned to Uncle Cal. "What's going on?"

"Have a seat."

Red had an idea what was going to come next, but he would let the older man lead the conversation. He'd promised himself he wouldn't pressure him anymore to tell Cali the truth. Every time he did, Uncle Cal's health seemed to take a turn.

Plopping down on the couch, he crossed his legs and waited.

"Jared, we've had a couple of conversations about my assets and what I want done when I . . . die."

"Yes. Everything is set; notarized copy is in my safe at the office."

"Thanks. I plan on telling Cali tonight."

Red knew this was for the best, but he couldn't help

feeling a little apprehensive. He wasn't sure how Cali would feel about this news. "What are you going to tell her exactly?"

"There's a lot to say. I want to start with what really happened the night I came to get her at that hotel."

"Do you need anything else from me?"

"I won't be here much longer."

Red stared at the older man, unsure how to respond. "What are you talking about? How would you know that?"

"I want to thank you, again, for opening your home to me and loving my daughter." Uncle Cal sucked in labored breath. "I'm tired."

Leaning forward, his elbows on his knees, Red dropped his head and took a deep breath. "Uncle Cal, you're still here. You've been fighting. Don't give up now."

"I'm tired," he repeated.

"I can't listen to you tell me that you're going to give up the fight. You've beaten the odds every time. The doctors didn't even think you'd leave the hospital, but you're here. You've been here. You can still get up and walk to the bathroom. You can eat your own food. Doctors don't know everything. They say terminal, but people live as long as God puts breath in their lungs and pumps blood through their heart."

"If I woke up tomorrow and ran a mile, it would definitely be a miracle," Uncle Cal said with a weak laugh. "But if I don't wake up tomorrow, I have to be okay with that, too. And I have to make sure that Cali is okay with that. She acts like she's tough."

"She is tough."

"She is. But her heart . . . if you get past that hard exterior, it's all mush. You know that by now. I need to know she's going to be okay."

"I'm not sure what you want me to say. Cali will be okay, but not for a while. Losing you won't be easy."

"I know, but I need you to do something for me."

"Anything you need."

"When I... when that time comes, please make sure she knows that I loved her more than anything." He coughed, covering his mouth with another tissue. "Tell her that I only did what I thought was best."

"She knows that."

"There's a good chance that she'll be angry with me, say things she may not mean. If I leave here, she'll feel guilty. Don't let her. Tell her about this conversation."

"I will."

"Can you go let her know that I'm ready?"

Red got up from the couch and hugged Uncle Cal. "Thanks for being there, Uncle Cal. You're family."

"You're family to me, like a son. When you propose to my Cali, know that you have my full blessing."

Proposing wasn't something Red had thought about, but if—or when—he ever got to that point, knowing that Uncle Cal gave his blessing would mean a lot to him. "Thanks. I'll go get Cali."

CHAPTER THIRTY

$\mathcal{I}$ brought you a protein shake," Cali said, walking into Uncle Cal's room. The aide had told her he'd barely eaten. "You need to try and drink it."

"Look at you," Uncle Cal whispered, his voice thick. "You're such a beautiful woman. It does my heart good to know that I played a part in that."

Cali sat down in the chair next to the bed. She picked up his hands, memorizing the feel of them in hers. Something told her this conversation was going to be important and she wanted to make sure she remembered everything about it. Uncle Cal wasn't a television watcher, so Red had put a stereo in his room instead. Smooth jazz played softly in the background, a song that she remembered listening to as a child riding in the car with her uncle.

Back then, he'd been like a giant to her. Still was. His appearance, though, was drastically different. He used to weigh a solid 225 pounds. Sickness had taken a toll on him, though, and now he was but a shell of the man that used to hold the neighborhood arm wrestling title. She knew how to win a few bucks hustling men in a game of pool because of him. She could change a tire without breaking a sweat because he'd taught her. Multiplication and division were a breeze to her in school because he'd made sure she practiced every day. She'd spent hours with him in the kitchen, taking in everything he knew about cooking and baking.

And as he lay there—struggling to breathe, his heart and every other organ failing him—she felt an overwhelming sadness. At times she thought it would suffocate her, but she managed to stay afloat.

"I wanted to talk to you about Carmen," he said.

The mention of her mother's name got her attention and she gripped the arms of the chair. "What about her?"

"There's a lot you don't know."

"I know enough. Please, Uncle Cal, let's not talk about her."

"Cali, listen to me," he told her in that voice that he reserved only for moments when she had been in trouble as a teenager.

"Is this really necessary? I'm not stupid, you know. I can see that you're not getting better. I don't want to waste any conversations on that woman."

"Your mother isn't dead."

Cali reeled back as if he'd slapped her. "What?" she gasped.

"Carmen is still alive."

Clutching her stomach, Cali tried to make sense of what he was telling her. If her mother was still alive, where was she? Why hadn't she come for her? Cali stood up, tipping the chair back.

"How do you . . . Why . . . ?" she stuttered, choking out the words. "Why didn't you tell me? I thought she was dead. She never came back."

It didn't make sense. Uncle Cal knew she thought her mother was dead. He'd never corrected that assumption. He didn't . . .

"You have to understand, baby girl. When I came to get

you in that hotel room, you were crying, scared. My heart broke for you. It took years for you to stop having nightmares about that time. I couldn't tell you she was alive. You were doing well thinking she was dead."

"Oh my God," she said as she struggled to recall specific details, grasping at fragments of memories long buried. He never *did* say she was dead. Cali gagged. She wanted to throw up. "That means she really didn't want me?" She didn't recognize her own voice. It was like she was that same scared, defeated little girl in the closet—alone.

She hadn't realized she was crying until he wiped her cheeks with a tissue.

"Baby, she did want you. She was just sick."

Cali held up a hand and backed away. "How could you do this?"

His eyes flooded with tears. "I wanted to protect you. That was my number one priority."

"Where is she?"

He shut his eyes. "She's not any better than she was all those years ago. Then, she was injured pretty badly. They thought she wouldn't survive, but the doctors were able to save her. She's had several strokes since then and she can't take care of herself. I've been taking care of her. She doesn't even talk anymore."

"You've been taking care of her!" she shouted. "This whole time…you let me believe she was dead and she's been alive?"

"I'm sorry, baby. Please…forgive me," he pleaded. "I did what I thought was best at the time."

"At the time?" She clenched her hands closed and her nails bit into her palms. "Were you ever going to tell me?"

"Honestly, no," he admitted softly. "I didn't think there was a reason to tell you."

"My mother is alive and you didn't feel like I had a right

to know?" she blared. Anger, blinding and hot, seemed to coat her insides. "How could you do this to me?"

"I love you, Cali. I had to protect you the best way I know how."

"And what about her? She just let you take care of me and never asked to see me? Never once demanded to see her own child?"

He let out a tortured breath. "Only once. But she wasn't in the right frame of mind. I couldn't trust her with you. So I turned her away." He closed his eyes and took a deep breath, adjusting his oxygen tubing. "When she got hurt, I wanted to take you to see her. She didn't want to see you, Cali. How was I supposed to tell you that?"

"I deserved to know. No wonder I'm so fucked up. I always knew my mother sucked. She was a selfish woman, only concerned with her drugs and her men."

"You know that's not completely true. Your mother had—"

"I know. No need to tell me again. She was a paranoid schizophrenic. As if that makes it all better. No matter how many times she let me down, I still loved her, even though she thought of me as nothing more than an inconvenience for her. But then she took me on that trip, told me we'd make a new start...I still remember the exact moment she changed. The way she glared at me, how she yelled at me. She told me I was nothing, that I was a horrible child. I had to live with the idea that she hated being my mother so much she was willing to leave me in a hotel room to starve to death. I have dreams, nightmares, about being in that hotel room..." She swallowed past a hard lump that had formed in her throat. "It was cold and dark and I was all alone. As strange as this sounds, I was okay thinking she was dead. I mean, she didn't want me anyway, right? And she would never hurt me again."

"Cali, please. I'm so sorry. Every tear you shed, every

scream in the middle of the night...I was there. I didn't want
to hurt you any more than you were already hurting. I felt
like I was doing the right thing. Then, when time passed,
and you seemed to be doing okay, I figured..." He shrugged.
"It was better that you never know."

"So why tell me now?"

"I'm going to die, Cali. Initially I wasn't going to tell you,
but it was only right to tell you."

"What am I supposed to do with that? I know you don't
expect me to take care of her."

"I'm not asking you to take care of her."

"So I'm assuming you've made arrangements to continue
her care?"

"I did."

Her eyes widened as realization dawned on her. "Red
knows, doesn't he?"

Uncle Cal sighed, his eyes tired. "I told him, yes, so that
he could set up a trust."

She squeezed her eyes shut. Cali felt like someone had
plunged a dagger in her heart. Uncle Cal had always told
her he had her back. And he'd lied to her for years. Red had
promised he wasn't like the other people in her life that
had disappointed her, but he was. Both men that she loved
had betrayed her, by keeping something so vital to her life
from her. But she should have known it wouldn't last. "How
long has he known?"

"I only told him when I got here. Don't be mad at him,
Cali. He wanted me to tell you the truth from the beginning."

"That's what you were arguing about that day in his
office." And Red had lied to her, to her face.

"Yes. Baby girl, don't do this...your life is still good.
Carmen being alive doesn't have to change that."

"It does, though. And there's nothing you can do to
change that now."

Letting out a whimper, she stomped out of the room, grabbing her coat and purse on her way to the front door. She muttered tearfully to herself as she darted through the house. Red was waiting near the front door. She couldn't look him. Everything was wrong. She had to get out of there.

"Cali, wait," Red called to her, grabbing her wrist as she tried to rush past him. "Don't walk out of here like this."

Stopping in her tracks, she snatched her arm from him and whirled around. "How could you not tell me?" she demanded, her finger in his face.

"I couldn't tell you, Cali," he insisted, his voice thick. "Your uncle is my client."

"I asked you." Her eyes narrowed on him. "I flat out asked you if you knew something that I didn't. You lied to me."

"I had no choice." He threw his hands up in the air. "You know that. This is my job. I can't go around telling my clients' business." He stepped closer to her, reached out to touch her, but then pulled back. "Cali, your uncle did what he thought was best for you at the time. It was a complicated situation, too complicated for a ten-year-old little girl."

Cali pursed her lips, hell-bent on keeping it together. *Damn it, don't cry.*

Red pulled her into his arms, held her tight. "He's not perfect," Red continued. "He's made mistakes, but he loves you. Don't walk out like this. He needs to know that you are okay."

Her head was pounding. She didn't know what to do. Her life was a lie. How could she trust him again? Drawing in a slow, steady breath, she dropped her head on Red's chest. As angry as she was with Uncle Cal, she didn't want to leave him. And Red...it hurt her that he didn't tell her. Logically, she knew why he'd kept quiet. It was his job. But didn't she mean more to him than his job?

"I'm so angry with him," she growled, pulling away from

him. "How could he keep this away from me? And I'm furious with you for lying to me, for not telling when you promised you'd always be honest."

"Ask yourself why knowing about it would have made it better?" he asked her, his gaze fixed on hers. "Bottom line is your mother was everything you ever thought she was. That hasn't changed. She left you alone in that hotel room like you remember. How does knowing she's alive change that?"

"I deserved to know the truth—from both of you, but mostly from him."

"Of course you did," he agreed. "There's no doubt about it. Now you know the truth. Put that in the place in your mind reserved for your mother and keep it moving."

"I hate you right now," she snapped.

His shoulders dropped as he lowered his gaze. "You can hate me all night if you want to, but go back in there and talk to your uncle. If you don't, you'll regret it. I promise you that." He took her coat and her purse and dropped it on the chair next to the front door. "Pull up those big girl panties, like Syd says, and go talk to him."

He was right. If she left and something happened to Uncle Cal, she wouldn't survive it. She sniffed. "Okay," was all she could say at that point.

"Do you want me to go with you?" he asked.

She nibbled on her thumb and shook her head. Taking a deep breath, she walked back to Uncle Cal's room.

"Uncle Cal?" she called softly.

He turned to her. "You came back."

As she neared the bed, she noticed the tears standing in his eyes. Deciding he needed more than her words right then, she hugged him. When his arms came up around her, she closed her eyes. They were like that for an eternity it seemed, her holding on to him for dear life and him whispering how sorry he was and how much he loved her.

That moment between them was everything. Despite what had happened, he was her only true parent and she loved him so much.

"Uncle Cal?" she said, finally pulling away. She wiped her eyes with the back of her hands. "I know you did what you had to do, in everything. There is no man like you and there never will be."

He closed his eyes, a smile spreading across his face. "I'm so happy to hear you say that," he told her, his voice low and gravelly.

It was true. He'd taken care of her when she needed him and never complained. "You're my father in every way that matters. I love you, Daddy," she told him, as tears streaked down her face.

Uncle Cal cried then, a gut-wrenching sob pulled from deep inside. Red was right. As hurt as she was, she couldn't let a night pass without telling her uncle—her father—that he was still her hero, that she loved him more than he probably would ever know.

* * *

Cali woke up feeling hungover. She'd stayed up with Uncle Cal for hours talking about old times and laughing. He'd laughed so hard it made everything they'd gone through worth it. It had been ages since she'd heard him laugh like that. It did her heart good.

Red had joined them for a little bit, taking in all the stories of Cali as a teenager. She was still mad at Red, although she knew it was irrational. By law, Red couldn't have told her what Uncle Cal had told him in confidence. But the fact that he'd kept that from her added to her still-present fears of being in a relationship with him. Her first reaction was to run for the hills, but she'd decided that Uncle Cal came first.

She needed to make whatever time he had left comfortable and peaceful.

Uncle Cal seemed to perk up, eating half of a sandwich and drinking an ice-cold Pepsi, his favorite. It was amazing.

She slid out of the bed and padded to the bathroom. The house was quiet, which was perfect. Red and Corrine had an appointment with the caseworker in Berrien County, so she didn't expect him for a while. Her plan was to spend some time with Uncle Cal and then take care of some business. The doorbell chimed and she frowned. Who the hell was ringing the doorbell so early in the morning? Lucky for whoever was on the other side, Corrine wasn't there to be awakened by the loud bell.

Pulling open the door, she grumbled, "I hope—" Her rant died on her lips at the sight of Allina. "Allina? What are you doing here this early? Is everything okay?"

"Sure." Her friend twisted the strap of her purse. "I wanted to talk to you."

"Come on in. I just got up, so there's no coffee yet and I can't be held responsible for my attitude. Do you want some hot tea?" Cali knew Allina didn't drink coffee, and she wished she could say the same. But it was her liquid drug and she couldn't function without a cup.

"Okay," Allina said. "I could use some tea. It's cold out there. Where's Red?"

"He and Corrine got up early and went to Benton Harbor. He's trying to finalize custody."

Allina followed her into the kitchen and took a seat at the breakfast bar while Cali threw a K-cup into the Keurig. If she could do a commercial for that machine, she would. It took the hassle out of making coffee.

"What's going on?" Cali asked after both were situated with their full mugs.

"I just dropped by to check on you. Syd told me that Uncle Cal wasn't doing too well. How is he?"

Cali blew on the coffee, then took a sip. "He's...hanging in there."

Allina's warm brown eyes met hers. "I just want you to know that I'm here for you. I can't even imagine what it would be like to watch my parents go through this. But I'm here for you, whatever you need. I can come sit with you, cook dinner for you all...anything."

Her friend was a sweetie. And she was glad she was there. She'd missed her. "I appreciate you. How are you? Are you happy?"

"I'm happy. I'm engaged to be married to a wonderful man. I'm closer to my parents. I'm good."

"I know that, but..." Cali picked up her ringless left hand. "You don't look happy. Most women would be shouting it from the rooftops, but you... You've barely said a word about him or the wedding."

Allina dropped her gaze. "There's a lot going on so I haven't had a chance to plan anything. We do know that we want to be married in his parents' church in Cleveland, probably sometime next year."

"Well, that's a start. As long as you're okay." Cali glanced at the microwave clock. "I need to go check on Uncle Cal and give him his medicine. I'll be right back."

Cali left Allina in the kitchen and walked into the Uncle Cal's bedroom, immediately opening the blinds because Uncle Cal preferred natural light in the mornings. She grabbed his medicine dispenser off the dresser. "Uncle Cal?" she called. "Wake up. You have to take your meds." She opened up the daily journal on the dresser and jotted down the date and time and what she planned to give him. The doctors had stressed keeping a log of what he ate every day and what medicine he took.

"Uncle Cal?" She turned around and immediately dropped the pills she was holding onto the floor. Her heart dropped and she rushed over to him. She shook him, called to him. *Oh God, no.* But he was too still. "Uncle Cal?" she cried. She touched his forehead and a shiver went through her body. *Please.*

She threw herself on him, rested her head over his heart. "No!" she screamed. "Don't leave me. Please. Don't go," she sobbed. "Please, I need you."

But he was already gone. Her Uncle Cal was dead.

CHAPTER THIRTY-ONE

Cal Harper was pronounced dead at 12:30 in the afternoon. Cali watched as the house swarmed with people. The hospice nurse had arrived, followed by the police. Allina stood to the side, speaking with the representative from the funeral home.

Cali had managed to pull herself together long enough to take care of the phone calls and make a few arrangements. But when the funeral home carried her uncle's lifeless body out of the house, she collapsed onto the floor.

Now, she sat nursing a beer in a private booth at the bar. She'd locked herself in Uncle Cal's room earlier, even while her concerned friends were in the house trying to help her. Syd had even come over although she'd just been released from the hospital, but Cali needed to be alone. She needed to process everything. So she snuck out.

She thought that a few drinks would numb the hurt. That didn't work out quite the way she'd planned. The feeling of emptiness had taken her by surprise. Logically, she'd known this day would come, but nothing had prepared her for that actual moment, the moment she knew that she'd never hear his voice again. Her uncle had died in the middle of the night, in the room right down the hall from where she'd been asleep. Her only family member had succumbed to an illness that took away his quality of life slowly, and there was nothing she could do about it. No money would bring him back—nothing.

She didn't want company. She didn't need to hear about how he was in a better place. All she wanted was to grieve for the one person in her family who'd never turned his back on her.

Sliding the bottle back and forth between her hands, she thought about the last thing he'd said to her. "Chin up, baby girl." At the time, she'd wondered why he said that, knowing she was just going to bed. Now she knew. It was his way of telling her to move on, to live even though he wasn't going to.

The bar was pretty empty, the lunch crowd long gone. She ordered a shot, but service was slow. Then there was a shot glass in front of her. She peered up through wet lashes. Red was standing before her with a fifth of Patrón in one hand and a bowl of tortilla chips in the other.

He didn't speak, though. He slid into the booth beside her and poured the liquor into her glass. Lifting the glass, he tipped it in her direction and downed the contents, slamming it back on the table when he was done. He filled the little glass again and slid it toward her.

She took the shot, enjoying the way the liquid burned her throat. Setting the glass back on the table, she waited while he poured her another. Wanting to avoid eye contact for fear that she'd break down yet again, she ran her thumbnail over a crack on the table, then traced it with her finger.

She hadn't expected him to be there. He was supposed to be on the other side of the state, but he'd shown up again— right when she needed him, even though she'd treated him like crap. All the anger and resentment she'd felt toward him melted away.

He placed a hand on top of hers and squeezed, bringing her palm up to his lips. "Cali," he said softly. "You don't have to talk. But I'm so sorry about Uncle Cal. I want to be here for you and give you whatever you need. If you want silence, then we won't talk. If you need me to hold your hand, I won't let go. The only thing I won't do is leave you while you're hurting so bad."

Cali met his gaze then, lacing her fingers with his.

They sat like that for a while—in silence, hand in hand. After a while, she took the shot and pounded the glass back on the table. He never let go of her other hand, he simply poured more.

"I miss him already," she murmured, rubbing her thumb over his knuckles. She cleared her throat. "He was an awesome father. I loved him so much." Despair threatened to choke her. "I've lost so much, Red. How am I supposed to get through this?"

He scooted closer and pulled her into a hug. She buried her face in his neck, taking in his masculine scent, letting it wrap around her.

"You don't go through this alone, baby," he whispered. He held her face in his hands. "We're all here for you. I'm here for you."

There were tears standing in his eyes. He'd been crying— for her. She rested her forehead against his, closing her eyes as he swept his thumbs across her cheeks. When his hands traveled to the back of her head, she sucked in a deep breath.

He stroked her back, holding on to her. She clung to him, grateful that he was there. "Where's Corrine?"

"At Syd's."

Cali knew she shouldn't have left the way she did. Her friends were probably worried sick. "I know everybody was trying to help but I couldn't be there, in the house where he…"

"They know. They're just worried about you."

Once again, he filled up her glass. This time, though, she pushed it toward him, motioning for him to take the shot. When he did, she smiled. "Thank you," she said.

"Never say thank you for this. There's nothing I wouldn't do for you, Cali." Their gazes met and locked. She moistened her lips, noting the way his gaze followed her motions. Smiling slightly, he gave her a sweet kiss—on her forehead.

Before he could pull away, she grabbed his face. "Do you mean that?"

"You know I don't say things I don't mean."

Tilting her head up, she kissed him. It wasn't intense, but it was persistent. "Red," she whispered against his mouth.

"Yes."

Touching her lips to his again, she pulled him into another kiss—deepening it almost immediately. She wanted to kiss him forever, forget about everything else but how he made her feel. Eventually, though, she realized she couldn't spend the day kissing Red in a public booth. She pulled back, holding his hand to her cheek.

"Cali, I'm—"

She placed her forefinger against his mouth. "Don't… don't say anything." She filled the shot glass. "Take another with me."

He obliged without another word. Reaching out, he ran his finger down her cheek and over her lips. She smiled.

"Uncle Cal told me I was the best thing in his life. I hope he realized that he was the best thing that could have ever happened to me."

"He knew you loved him, Cali."

"He tried to take care of me the best he knew how. I remember when he enrolled in school. He left a good job at the plant so that he could set an example for me. My mother hit me lots of times, but not Uncle Cal. He was patient, stern but kind. He never hit me, and the only time he threatened to whoop my ass was when I snuck to a concert and didn't come home until the next morning. He was waiting for me on the couch. I was grounded for weeks over that." She giggled softly.

"Sounds like he had you figured out."

She glanced at him. "I tested him, but besides that one time, I never gave him a reason—to whoop my ass. Even then, instead of yelling, he showed me pictures of every girl he could think of that got hurt after they snuck out without their parents' knowledge. He was there for every moment—high school graduation, college. What am I going to do without him?"

"Cali, your uncle loved you. And he'll live on." He placed a hand over her heart. "In you. Then one day you're going to wake up and feel grateful for his presence in your life. Then you'll be at peace because you did everything you could to show him that you loved him while he was alive to feel your love. Right now it hurts, but it won't hurt forever."

CHAPTER THIRTY-TWO

$\mathcal{U}$ncle Cal hadn't wanted a funeral. He thought they were too depressing. There would be no trips to the cemetery either. Cremation was his choice. Cali watched as the casket went through the fire, Red at one side and Syd on the other. She was all cried out. Even if she wanted to shed a tear, she didn't think it was possible. Over the past month, she'd been an emotional wreck, crying more than she had when she was a child. The well had dried up.

After the cremation, they gathered at Morgan and Syd's house. It wasn't a huge gathering, just a few of Uncle Cal's close friends and her family. She smiled as her eyes connected with those of each member of her "family." Syd had carted Brynn around in that baby carrier for days, running errands with her to get ready for everything. Cali wondered if her arm would fall off, but she never complained. Morgan managed everything else, with Kent's help. They hired cleaners to thoroughly clean out the room Uncle Cal had lived in and even hired painters to come in and give the room a fresh coat. When Red had to go back to Berrien County, Kent stayed on the couch. Allina took care of Cali's business, rescheduling appointments and handling small tasks. Cali couldn't deny she felt blessed.

Red held her against his heart every night. It was where she felt the safest, lying against him, feeling his heart beat beneath her. She didn't think it was possible to love him as much as she did. Uncle Cal had been right; love was worth it. Yet, she couldn't shake the feeling that *she* wasn't worth it. And despite Red's unwavering support of her, she didn't feel whole, complete. A feeling of emptiness had settled in her gut, threatening to pull her deep into an abyss from which she would never return.

Not only was her uncle dead, but now she had to decide whether to deal with her mother. A mother who'd been dead to her for many years. A mother who it seemed couldn't care for herself. Cali was faced with a dilemma. Could she take care of a woman who'd never bothered to take care of her?

Corrine ran up to her and flung her arms around her neck. "Cali!"

She hugged the little girl. Before Corrine, Cali had never considered the blessing that a child would be. She enjoyed getting to know her and it scared her. She hadn't changed her mind, she didn't want kids, but how could she deny a child love? No matter what Cali wanted, Corrine *needed* a mother figure in her life. She needed someone that she could count on, a woman. Could Cali be that woman for her? She didn't think so. She was still too messed up to even consider stepping in, not that Red had asked her. He'd never made her feel like she had to be a stand-in mother to Corrine.

As Corrine rambled on about the new doll Auntie Sydney had bought her, Cali realized that she needed time. She'd never really had time to process anything that had happened to her in her life. It was high time that she took the time needed to get herself together.

"Cali?" Corrine asked, a small frown on her doll face.

"Yes, sweetie."

"I'm sorry Uncle Cal died. He was nice to me. He gave me all of his crackers and his juice."

"He gave me all of his crackers and juice, too," she told Corrine.

Cali gently ran a hand over Corrine's hair. That little girl needed stability in her life. She deserved the best in life. Cali just couldn't be sure she was it. The more she watched Corrine, the more she fell in love with her. But now that Uncle Cal was gone, she couldn't stop thinking about her own mother, and how she'd fallen short.

"You look sad."

"I am sad. But I'll be okay."

"Do you want me to bring you a juice box?"

Chuckling, Cali shook her head, wiping an errant tear from her cheek. "I'm okay. I have a nice big bottle of water with me."

Without warning, Corrine threw her tiny arms around Cali's neck and gave her a little peck on her cheek. "I love you."

"I love you, too," Cali said, rubbing her little button nose with her own.

Corrine jumped off her lap and took off toward Syd and baby Brynn.

A few hours later, Cali stood in Uncle Cal's bedroom. The huge, clunky hospital bed was gone, replaced by the full-sized mattress that used to be in there. She ran her fingers over the oak dresser and picked up the journal that was on top of it. She flipped through the pages, noting her messy scribbles with medicines and times. Also in there were notes that Uncle Cal had written to her: simple instructions on which bills to pay, what he wanted from the store...why she shouldn't yell at Red in the middle of the night. Chuckling, she turned to the last page and gasped. Right there, in his impeccable handwriting, it read, "Everything I've ever done was for your protection. I can't stand to see you hurt. Take care of yourself. Don't kill Red. I love you more than the stars in the sky."

As tears filled her eyes again, she dropped to her knees and hugged the journal to her chest.

* * *

Red found her in the same spot an hour later. He nudged her gently, hating to disturb her sleep. She'd tossed and turned every night since Uncle Cal died. Last night, he'd found her sprawled out on the floor in the family room, her eyes wide open. She hadn't acknowledged his presence but when he got down on the floor with her she rolled over into his waiting arms. Eventually she fell asleep.

He could feel her pulling away, retreating into herself. He was worried. And he wasn't the only one. Syd called multiple times a day, asking for updates. Allina made up excuses to drop by, just to "look at her." Even Morgan was calling to check in. He'd claim he was calling for Syd, but Red knew the real reason.

Cali's eyes opened, then closed again. "What time is it?" she grumbled.

"It's six o'clock. Do you want to eat dinner or something?"

She lay flat on her back. "I don't know."

"You have to eat something. You didn't eat much at the..." He didn't want to keep hounding her but he needed to make sure she was taken care of. Her eyes, normally big and expressive, seemed small and dead. If he could take her pain away he would, but he knew it was a process. A long one.

"I'll eat. I need to pack."

"What? Where are you going?"

"I can't stay here forever, Red. Now that..." She swallowed and threaded a hand through her hair. "There's no need for me to stay anymore."

She tugged her shirt down and picked up a box that contained Uncle Cal's things. Something about this didn't feel right. "Where are you going, Cali?" he repeated.

"I need to leave. I bought a plane ticket. I have to go to Georgia. Uncle Cal's house needs to be packed up, I need to notify people. I— I have to leave."

She carried the box toward the living room and dropped a few more items into it. As she moved around the room, his mind raced back to something she'd said. *There's no need for me to stay anymore.*

Cali scanned a piece of paper and went to stuff it in her purse. He took it from her hand when he recognized the logo. He scanned the itinerary. Balling the paper up in his fist, he peered up at her. "This is a one-way ticket," he said.

Her shoulders slumped and she lowered her gaze, shifting nervously.

"Cali, this is a one-way ticket."

"Yes," she whispered, so softly he wasn't sure she'd said anything.

"What does this mean?" He tried to hold on to his temper. She was already in a fragile state and he didn't want to make it worse. But damn it... he needed to understand what it meant.

"I told you... I have to go to Georgia."

"I understand that, but usually when a person is visiting somewhere, they purchase a round-trip ticket."

"I'm not... I don't know when I'll be back—if ever."

* * *

Cali and Red stood there, staring at each other. She hated to hurt him. He didn't deserve it. But she had to go.

"Don't do this," he pleaded, a deep frown on his face. "Cali, don't do this. Why would you say that? You can't just leave."

"Red, I have to." She finally lifted sorrowful eyes to his. "I can't stay here. This isn't working for me, Red. I don't have it in me to give anything. I need to concentrate on me."

"What about us?"

"There is no us. I don't want it anymore."

"There will always be an us," he said, his tone heated. "Death doesn't change that. Leaving won't either."

"I think we're fooling ourselves. I could stay here, and live this life with you and Corrine, but I'd just be going through the motions. And you deserve better than that, better than me. Corrine deserves better than me." Her life was messed up. Everything she'd gone through had shaped her into the person she was. Corrine already had a rough road ahead of her and Cali would only make it worse. She couldn't stay there pretending to be part of a happy family when she didn't even feel like a whole person.

She hated her mother, more today than yesterday. When she wasn't hating her, she felt as if she was going to buckle from all the pain, the despair. It was so strong she thought it would destroy her. And she didn't want to bring him—or Corrine—down with her.

A tear fell onto her cheek and she wiped it off. She knew Red wouldn't let her go so easily, so she'd have to hurt him to get him to let go.

"I know what this is about, Cali. Fight, damn it!" He grabbed her arms and pulled her closer. "Fight for your life. Fight for me. Don't do this."

"There was nothing to fight for," she said, cringing at the pained expression on his face.

Cali had to face the fact that she could end up like her mother. Where would that leave Corrine? Where would that leave Red? She'd been thinking about it more and more, especially after she'd found out her mother was alive. She'd heard all those stories about how her mother had been a funny, happy child. Smart as a whip, a social butterfly. Then something had changed and she'd turned into a nightmare. Red once told her that she was nothing like her mother. She couldn't be sure. *Everything I am today is a direct result of what she did to me.*

"That's bullshit," he argued. "There is so much to fight for. You're not your mother. I know that's what this is about. And you're not her. Your mother doesn't get the credit for the woman you turned out to be. Uncle Cal made sure of that when he brought you into his home and raised you as his daughter. You've worked hard, you fought hard, you made the rules and everyone followed them, including me. You could have let what happened to you break you, but you used it as a stepping stool. Every time you took a step, you stepped on your mother for every bad thing she told you." He sighed heavily. "You're scared, and lost. I understand that. Uncle Cal was…he was a good father to you. He took care of you. Why won't you let me do the same? Why won't you let me be there to catch you when you fall?"

"Because it's not just me, Red. You have Corrine to think about. You're a father. You have to devote every bit of time that you have to make sure that Corrine doesn't buckle under her pressures. Corrine needs a mother figure. And that's not me. I told you…" she swallowed. Why couldn't he just let her go? She hated herself for what she was about to say. "I don't want to be a mother." Her head fell onto his chest and she clutched his shirt, letting out a low sob. "I have to go."

"Don't," Red murmured, holding her face in his hands. "I love you, Cali. Don't walk out on me."

Before she could pull away, he pressed his mouth to hers. She wanted to give in to him, feel his love, but she resisted. Until she couldn't anymore. She opened her mouth to him and fell into the kiss. She kissed him like her life depended on it, like her soul needed his mouth against hers for its survival.

Her heart tightened in her chest, and she pulled back reluctantly. "Bye, Red." She picked up her purse and set it inside the box. Turning on her heel, she swung the door open. "I love you," she cried, her back facing him. Then she left.

CHAPTER THIRTY-THREE

Cali, it's Allina. Please call me when you get this message."

"Hey Cali, it's me again. I miss you. Baby Brynn wants to see her godmother. More than that, I need to hear from my best friend. Call me."

"Hi, Cali. It's me, Corrine. Daddy told me I could call you. I miss you. My hair looks a mess."

"I'm not even sure why I'm calling you. Well, yes I am, Syd forced me to. But it's only because she loves you. You're her family. And I guess you're mine, too. You don't have to call me back. Just call someone. Later."

"Cali, if you don't bring your black ass back here, I'm going to fly down there and bring you back myself."

Cali chuckled at Kent's message. It had been a few weeks since she'd left Red and everyone else behind. She'd hopped on a late flight and arrived in Atlanta early the next morning. From there, an airport limousine drove her to Uncle Cal's midtown condo. She'd spent the first few days cleaning up, packing boxes, and donating clothes and furniture to Goodwill. It's what Uncle Cal would have wanted. He was a proud man, never forgot where he came from and never hesitated to help someone else in need.

She hadn't heard from Red except in a curt e-mail regarding Uncle Cal's affairs. She'd responded, asking how he and Corrine were, but he never replied. That last conversation haunted her. The look in his eyes, the desperation in his tone, cost her many hours of sleep.

In fact it seemed as though Red had taken up residence in her dreams. It was like he lived in there. Every time she closed her eyes she saw him—his dimpled smile, his hazel eyes, his lean figure. And it wasn't only in her dreams. She'd walk outside to have a glass of wine on the deck and swore she saw his face in the stars. She'd wake up in the morning, missing his arms around her and the way he kissed her awake.

Over the past few days she'd picked up the phone to call him more times than she could count. Something always stopped her. Even if she wanted to call him, she figured he probably wouldn't pick up, after the way she'd walked out on him. She'd hurt him, and he was the last person she wanted to hurt.

Sighing, she picked up a stack of mail held together by a thick rubber band. One return address read "Sunny Day Homes." She pulled the single envelope from the pile and opened it up, reading the small print. Her eyes zeroed in on the name there—Carmen Harper.

The paper slipped from her grasp, floating onto the carpet. It was a bill. Not only was her mother alive, but she lived in the area. *What now?* Pushing that stack aside, she picked up another stack of envelopes, all addressed to Uncle Cal in perfect handwriting. All were unopened except one—the first one. According to the postmark, it had been received seventeen years earlier.

Curious, she snatched the letter from the open envelope. Realizing who it was from, she read on.

Dear Cal,

I wanted to write to tell you how sorry I am. You didn't deserve the way I treated you when you came to visit me. You've never deserved anything I've ever done to you. I've put you in a bind all our lives. And now I've done the unthinkable. I've hurt my own child. Cali has always deserved a better mother than I could ever be. It's the reason why I'll never contact her. When you turned me away, I was angry. But I know now that you did the right thing. That's why I told you I didn't want to see her. It's best that she move on with her life. It's the only way she'll ever be free.

I wish I was strong enough to fight the demons inside of me, but I'm not. I'd only hurt her. I'm stuck, I can't walk, can barely talk, and I had to ask a nurse to write this letter for me. But it's what I deserve. Cali told me she hated me before I left her alone that night. Let her. It will propel her to do better with her life. Take care of her like you would your own. I know you will.

                                             Carmen

Cali folded up the letter and opened the next one. Before long, she'd finished all of them. Each of them said pretty much the same thing, some offering excuses and some not. As time passed, the letters became shorter, often only one or two sentences. She figured by now her mother wasn't communicating at all. Uncle Cal hadn't read any of them, and she wondered why. Before, she'd have taken the fact that her mother couldn't communicate as vindication, punishment for the way she'd been treated. Instead, she was just sad.

Forgiveness isn't for them. It's for you.

Uncle Cal's voice rang in her head. He'd told her that

one random night. They'd been sitting on the porch, drinking a glass of wine, and he'd just said it. She'd always wondered where those words came from, but it all made sense to her now.

Glancing at the roaring fire in front her, she tossed the pile of letters into the flames, watching as they engulfed the pieces of paper. She finished packing up the last of Uncle Cal's things and labeled the box for the Salvation Army. They were scheduled to arrive in the morning. She spun around the empty condo, surprised by the sense of accomplishment she felt. Uncle Cal had been all about getting a job done, and she'd done what he would want. She just had to do one more thing.

* * *

A few days later, Cali sat in a rental car staring at the building in front of her. She tapped the steering wheel with her thumbs and wondered if being there was the right thing to do. Scanning the grounds, she watched as women in scrubs pushed people in wheelchairs toward a beautiful park. It was a peaceful scene, one right out of a book.

Cali opened the car and walked into the building. She smiled at an elderly lady shuffling down the hall on a walker. The young receptionist greeted her and asked her who she was there to visit.

"Carmen Harper," Cali told the blonde.

The woman instructed Cali on the rules, pushing a clipboard toward her so that she could sign her name. Once she completed the visitor's form, the lady smiled. "Are you Carmen's daughter?"

Cali nodded. "I am."

"You look like her. I'm so sorry to hear about her brother passing. His attorney called and informed us of his death.

He was always so nice when he came to see her, such a wonderful man."

"He was a great guy, a great father to me."

"Carmen is at the park. Take the path down toward the pond. She likes to sit out and watch the ducks." Cali took a shaky breath. She was finally going to see her mother again after all these years. She wanted to see for herself the woman Carmen Harper really was.

"Thank you." Cali started to walk away, but turned back. "The attorney…Did he take care of the bill? I mean, does she have enough to take care of her daily needs?"

"I processed the paperwork myself. I'm actually one of the accounting reps for the facility, filling in at the front desk. The trust that was set up will ensure that she has a bed here for the rest of her life. However, it doesn't provide for the incidentals that may come up. I did tell Mr. Williams that over the phone and he told me he'd handle any extra expenses himself."

"There's no need. I'll take care of it. You can contact me from now on. The only thing I ask is that you don't tell…my mother anything about it."

"Honestly, I'm not sure she'd understand if I did. You're welcome to talk to her doctor if you want."

"No. I just want to make sure she's comfortable. And I'd also like to be notified if her health changes for the worse."

"I can definitely make a note in the file. Right now, everything is set up to flow to Mr. Williams, but I'll add you to the list."

"Thank you." She passed her business card over the counter.

The woman smiled kindly. "I'll be in touch."

Cali twisted the strap of her purse around her finger and pushed the door open, turning toward the pond. What a difference a state makes: instead of frigid temperatures and snow storms, the weather in Savannah was perfect—not too hot or cold.

She stepped across the grass, cursing when her heel sunk in as she walked. *What the hell was I thinking wearing my good pumps*? Deciding to chance it, she bent down and pulled off her shoes and continued down a hill. She stopped when she spotted a woman sitting quietly in a wheelchair. She had an empty feeling in the pit of her stomach. In a few minutes, she'd be face to face with her mother.

Cali tilted her head, trying to make out the features. The woman was brown-skinned; her graying hair was pulled back into a ponytail. She sat staring out at the water. Another woman, an aide or something, sat near her, reading a book.

"Carmen," she heard the aide say. "Are you getting cold?"

Holding her breath, she watched while the aide stood up and adjusted the blanket on her mother's lap. The years had been kind to Carmen Harper despite her many vices. She looked exactly like Cali remembered: beautiful.

The aide looked at her and smiled. "Hi. Are you here to see Carmen?"

Cali glanced at her mother, who didn't seem to be aware that a conversation was happening behind her. She continued to gaze at the water, not moving. If Cali hadn't seen the slow rise and fall of her chest, she'd think she was unconscious or something.

"Excuse me?" the aide asked. When Cali met her questioning eyes again, she pointed toward Carmen. "Are you here to see Ms. Harper?"

Cali couldn't take her eyes off of her mother's back, her slumped posture. Then her mother turned to face her, looked at her—or through her. Holding her breath, Cali waited. As she stared into her mother's eyes, she didn't feel any connection to the woman who'd given birth to her. Not love, not hate. Nothing.

Red was right. Cali was *not* Carmen. She'd spent so much time living behind her mother's crazy shadow and she didn't have to. Uncle Cal had made sure she had choices. Her life was better without her mother. She'd thought she would feel better if she could confront the woman before her, tell her how much she sucked. But what would that prove?

I don't need this. The realization struck her like a bolt of lightning and she stumbled back a few steps.

What she needed was Red. What she wanted was a life with Red. She wanted to be there for Corrine in a way her mother had never been there for her. When she thought about her future, she hoped she would be taking Corrine to dance class, helping her get ready for her first date... planning her wedding.

The aide started to stand and Cali held up hand, signaling that she was fine.

"Do you know Ms. Harper?" The aide asked.

Shaking her head, Cali cleared her throat. "No. No, I don't."

Without another word, Cali turned and tore across the lawn, running as fast as she could until she reached the car. And she didn't look back. She was done letting her past rule her future. She tossed her shoes onto the passenger seat and rested her head on the steering wheel. Taking a deep breath, she turned the key in the ignition and took off down the winding driveway. She was going home. And she prayed it wasn't too late.

*C*HAPTER THIRTY-FOUR

*S*now. Three to six inches, to be exact. It was enough to piss Cali off on a normal day. Except she couldn't even muster up the appropriate amount of disgust. She was home. And she couldn't be happier.

She got out of the car, her hat and her new suede boots on, and sniffed the cold air around her. Trudging up the unshoveled walkway, she thought about what she'd say, whether whatever she said would be enough. There were bound to be hurt feelings, anger. But she wasn't going to let that keep her from trying.

Knocking on the door, she stepped back and waited. Morgan pulled the door open, a burp cloth on his shoulder, a bottle in hand, and a pacifier in his mouth. His eyes widened when he saw her standing there.

"Cali?" he mumbled between his teeth. "You're back."

"Hi, Morgan. Can I come in?"

"Yeah, come on." He held the door open for her and she stepped inside.

Nervous, she tugged her gloves off and twisted them in her hands. "Is Syd here?"

"Yep. She's in the family room."

Cali followed him through the house. As they neared the family room, she could hear Syd singing, albeit off-key, "Twinkle Twinkle Little Star." As usual, she butchered the words in a way that was so Syd. Cali had definitely missed her BFF.

"Look who's here," Morgan announced.

Syd was on her knees, changing the baby's diaper and making funny faces at her. "Who is it?" She looked up with a smile that quickly disappeared. For a minute, Cali thought she'd misjudged her normally understanding friend—until Syd placed little Brynn into the little bouncy thingy, rushed over to her, and pulled her into a tight hug. "You're here!"

"Syd!" The girls hugged each other, rocking back and forth, both of them crying like babies. When they finally pulled apart, Cali snatched a Kleenex out of the box Morgan was holding out for her. "Thanks."

"I guess I should get another box. Looks like it's going to be a teary day."

Syd smacked Morgan on her arm. "Stop." She turned to her. "I'm so happy. We've been so worried about you."

"I know, Syd. I just had to deal with things on my own."

Morgan squeezed her arm. "I hope you found what you needed to find."

"I did. You were right; sometimes it's best to move on. Being so focused on the past...it can mess up your future."

"Exactly," he agreed with a quick nod.

"How's my godbaby?" she asked, walking around the couch to glance at the little one. "Oh my God! She's so beautiful, with all that hair. Just like her momma and her uncle." Kneeling down in front of her, she rubbed Brynn's tiny hands with her finger and placed a kiss on her forehead. "And she's quiet. Nothing like her momma and uncle." She laughed softly when she glanced up Syd, who crossed her arms and tapped her foot.

"Hey! I'm quiet."

"Wow," Morgan said. "That was a lie if I ever heard one."

"Oh, be quiet." Syd shoved Morgan playfully.

Brynn stared at Cali, cooing and moving around. She lifted her out of the seat and bounced her in her arms, the smell of baby powder and lotion wafting to her nose. She nuzzled her nose against the baby's soft skin. "Aw, I love her," Cali said.

Syd stood next to her, a gleam in her eyes as she squeezed the baby's foot. "I know. She's perfect, isn't she?"

"I'm so sorry I haven't been here for her."

"Cali, you had to do what was best for you."

"I hope everyone is as understanding as you and Morgan."

"I wouldn't count on it," Morgan grumbled.

Syd shushed him. "Don't listen to him. Everyone will understand."

"How is he?" Cali asked.

"He's good." Morgan put the pacifier in Brynn's mouth when she started getting fussy. "Nia's facing a sentence of no less than fifteen years. Trial is sometime in the summer."

"Good. She needs to be in prison. How's Corrine?"

"She asks about you all the time," Syd answered. "Keeps a full bag of Cheez-Its for you in the pantry."

Cali's stomach churned. She handed Brynn to Morgan. "I'll have to make a date with her to eat them and watch a movie, if he'll let me."

"You know he will," Syd assured her.

"I don't know, Syd. I hurt him pretty bad when I left."

"But you're back now. That's all that matters—unless you're going to leave again."

"I'm here for good. I realized…my life is here." Her gaze locked on Morgan's. "No more running, right?"

"Right," he said.

"Where's Kent's ass?" Cali asked. "And Allina?"

"Kent is working," Morgan said. "He's on a big project at work."

"Allina is still taking care of your business for you," Syd said.

"Aw, I told her she didn't have to. I was prepared to deal with a bunch of angry clients."

"Well, she figured you'd be back. And she needed something to do since she decided to come home."

Cali took a seat on the large sectional. "What else is new? Any thoughts about the wedding?"

"I wish," Morgan said.

"There you go." Syd stuck her tongue out at him. "I told you I wanted to wait for Cali to come back so she could plan."

"I can't wait," Cali said, wiggling her eyebrows. "Be prepared to spend some money, Morgan."

"Hey, I just want it done. I'll spend what I have to. I told her we should go to the courthouse."

"Hell no," Cali and Syd said simultaneously.

He rolled his eyes and walked out of the room, bouncing Brynn in his arms. When he was gone, Syd sat next to her. "Are you okay, babe?" she asked. "How did it go down south? Did you get everything done?"

"Yep. It was hard...saying good-bye. Sometimes I'd be in his room and I swear I could smell his cologne. Then there were the times when I thought I heard him calling my name. It sounded so clear. I found a bunch of books in a box. At first, I was going to throw them away, but I'm so glad I didn't. He'd written little messages in the margins. It was like he was talking to me."

"What else did you do?"

"Cried," she said with a humorless chuckle. "Sat on his deck. Everything and nothing, if that makes sense."

"It makes perfect sense."

"I think I'll always miss him. There's a void in my heart that can never be filled. But I'm extremely grateful for his life, for his love. I know he's in a better place. That makes it better."

Syd squeezed her hand and they leaned into each other, settling into a comfortable silence.

"I'm nervous," Cali admitted.

"You'll be fine. He's going to lash out, but you can't give up. That's what he'll expect."

* * *

"Corrine, don't run," Red warned. "You're going to slip on that ice and hurt yourself."

His big girl was alternating between hitting the snow-covered bushes with a stick and sliding down a hill of snow. When he and Syd were children, they'd make a snow slide and spend hours climbing up and sliding down. Somehow it was easier to make the snow hills back then. It had taken him an hour to get it just right. He smiled at the glee in Corrine's eyes as she slid down and landed on her butt in the yard. She fell back laughing and then flailed her arms and legs back and forth.

"Daddy, I'm making a snow angel."

"I see." He couldn't believe that two months ago he'd been a single man searching near and far for his daughter.

"Are you going to make one, too?"

"Not right now."

It was worth it, he thought. He couldn't imagine his life without her. They'd only been together for a short while, but he knew beyond a shadow of a doubt that his life was better with her in it. Being a father wasn't something he'd planned, but it was everything to him now.

After Cali walked out on him, she'd cried for her, which infuriated him. His little girl had already lost so much. He knew he couldn't protect her from ever getting hurt, but he'd vowed that he would try to minimize it. She deserved the best life he could give her.

"Daddy, I'm hungry."

"Okay, baby doll. Let's go make you a sandwich."

She put her hand in his and they headed off toward the entrance to his building. The community courtyard in his subdivision was a godsend for him. Corrine needed to be able to run around and burn off some of her energy. She talked a mile a minute and was constantly moving around, getting into things.

He pulled his keys out of his pocket as they rounded the corner of the building.

"Cali?" Corrine screamed, breaking free and racing toward the front door.

He looked up, surprised to see Cali standing out front. Corrine threw herself into Cali's arms. After she'd left him, he wondered when he'd ever see her again, what he would say when she saw her. Raking his eyes over her form, he couldn't help but feel relief that she was standing in front of him. She looked tired, but she looked... okay—good.

"Hi," Cali said to him as he drew closer.

"Hi," he said.

"Daddy, see!" Corrine cheered, jumping up and down. "Cali's here."

"I see her, baby doll."

"Are you coming to stay with us again?" Corrine asked. "I got a new Hello Kitty bedroom set."

"Oh, really?" Cali kneeled down and tugged on Corrine's ear. "I bet it's pretty."

"It is. You want to come see it?"

"Sure." She stood to her full height and asked, "Can we talk?"

He nodded and unlocked the door, waiting while she and Corrine entered. Once inside his place, he dropped his keys on a table near the door. Corrine made quick work of removing her hat, coat, and mittens.

Cali pulled her gloves off and scanned the room. "You're packing?" she asked when she noticed the numerous boxes scattered throughout the living room.

"We're moving by Auntie Syd and Uncle Morgan," Corrine said, clapping her hands. "Uncle Morgan said he'd build me a treehouse."

"That's nice of him," Cali said. She turned to Red. "You bought a house?"

"Yes, I did. Corrine needs space to run and play. One of Morgan's neighbors is moving out of state for his job. He was selling cheap. It was a good deal. I couldn't pass it up."

Corrine pulled on Cali's arm, excitement on her face. "Come on, Cali. You have to see my room. Daddy said I could paint my room in the new house any color I want. I chose pink."

"Pink is your color," Cali told her. "I like pink, too."

"Daddy says you like black."

"I like black *and* pink," she said, meeting Red's gaze. "But my favorite color is green."

Corrine scrunched up her nose. "Green? That's ugly. It's a boy color."

Cali grinned. "Wait until you see an emerald, sweetie. It won't be so ugly then."

"What is an emerald?"

"It's a pretty stone." Cali lifted her hair up and leaned close to his little girl. "See my earrings?"

Corrine examined the pair. "That's a green diamond."

Cali laughed, that same laugh that used to make Red want

to yank her into his arms and kiss her forever. Her smile was genuine, real. A great departure from the fake smiles she'd grown accustomed to giving after Uncle Cal died.

"You're staring," she said.

He snapped out of his thoughts. Clearing his throat, he shrugged. "Just looking at you. You look good."

She smiled shyly, tucking her hair behind her ears. *If I wasn't so angry with her, I'd . . .*

And he was angry. Furious. His thoughts kept going back to their last conversation. He'd begged her to stay and she left anyway. He knew why she'd left, what she had to do. He understood. But it still stung.

If it was just him, it would be one thing. But Corrine had been affected by Cali's absence and that wasn't acceptable.

"Cali, let's go." His daughter was persistent. Soon, Cali was being dragged off toward the bedroom.

Twenty minutes later, they appeared in the kitchen, where he was fixing Corrine's lunch. He'd given up trying to get his stubborn little girl to eat something else besides bologna and cheese sandwiches. He'd bought ham and turkey, Lunchables . . . but she loved that nasty shit.

Corrine climbed up on a stool and bit into her sandwich. He poured some baked chips on a napkin next to her plate and scooped some mandarin oranges into a bowl. She dipped her finger into the bowl and plopped one into her mouth, chewing happily.

"All set?" he asked, flicking on the TV. He'd learned about a week or so earlier that Corrine would sit still for more than thirty minutes during a silly television show about a dog and a blog. He never understood the fascination. But if she liked it, he loved it.

"Yep," she shouted, bobbing her head to her own beat.

"Okay. I'm going to go and talk to Cali for a second. Call me when you're done." Leaning down, she kissed him on his cheek and he kissed her back on her cheek. He'd recently enrolled her in school, so he looked forward to lazy Saturday afternoons with her.

Cali followed him into the home office. "She's doing so well," she said, closing the door behind her.

Turning to her, he folded his arms across his chest and asked, "What the hell are you doing here?"

* * *

Cali was taken aback at the cold fury in Red's voice. She'd known it would be an uphill battle but Syd's advice still rang in her ears.

"What—what do you mean?" she sputtered, digging her fingernails into her palms.

"What do you *think* I mean? You walked out of here like you were never coming back. Now, weeks later, here you are."

She swallowed, scratched the back of her neck. "I know. I just... I was in a..." She shrugged. "There really is no excuse."

His eyes widened, obviously surprised with her answer. "No excuse, huh?" he finally said after a few beats of silence. "What the hell am I supposed to say to that?"

Nothing. She hadn't come to make excuses. She just wanted to apologize for hurting him. "I'm sorry. I'm here to ask you to forgive me."

"You think it's that easy?" he asked, narrowing his eyes at her. Even knowing he was angry with her, she couldn't deny the flip her heart did when he looked at her. The light reflected in his eyes made her stomach flutter.

"I don't know. I would say no."

"Good. Because it's not that easy."

"I understand." Unable to look at him at that point, she focused on the Band-Aid on her pinky finger.

"I don't think you do." He took a step closer to her. "You left, after I begged you to stay. I begged you, Cali!" he shouted. "You still walked out that door like I wasn't shit."

"That's not true," she whispered.

"Really?"

"No. Red, please understand. I needed time. Losing Uncle Cal was so hard. Then I kept thinking about my mother and what happened in my childhood. I was scared."

"Are you still scared?" he asked, folding his arms over his chest.

"A little. I still have some issues to work through." She'd made an appointment with a therapist. She hoped it would help her get over her fears. "I'm willing to work on it. I don't want to let my past control me anymore."

He ran a hand through his hair. Grumbling, he pounded his fists into the table. "Shit, Cali. You can't do this. You can't come back in here and try to change up my routine. Corrine cried for you when you left."

Her heart broke at the admission. The last thing she'd ever wanted to do was hurt that sweet girl...her sweet girl. "I'm sorry," she whispered. "I never meant to hurt her."

"It's too late for that because you did hurt her," he snapped. "And she's already been through too much."

Her cheeks burned. Corrine didn't deserve what had happened to her, and Cali felt ashamed that she'd added to the poor doll's hurt. "I know."

"You know? Look, I'm glad your back. Syd really missed you—Allina, too."

"I missed them. But I missed you the most," she admitted. His eyes locked on hers.

"You and Corrine," she continued. "I love her, more than I ever thought I could. And I love you." She reached out to touch him, and he dodged her. "What do you want me to do?"

"Leave," he demanded.

"No."

His brows snapped together. "Get out of here," he growled. "I can't do this with you."

"No. I'm not leaving." She walked up to him, fists clenched. "You told me you wanted to be there to catch me when I fall. I want to do the same for you. I want to be with you, Red. I think we can make it work."

"I don't believe you," he said, his lips pressed into a fine line. "Why should I? The going got tough and Cali went running."

She winced at the barb. He wasn't going to make this easy for her. And she wouldn't stop trying. "I was wrong."

"That's not enough."

Ouch.

"You still haven't told me why I should believe you. Why is this Cali any different from the Cali that walked her ass out of my door?"

"She's gone." She'd left her at the nursing home with her mother. "This Cali," she said, pointing a thumb at her chest, "wants you."

"It's not just me."

"I know that. I want Corrine, too. I want her." She wanted to show her everything her Uncle Cal showed her, how to work hard and rise above her circumstances. "It's just... when Uncle Cal died, I was so lost. I couldn't see clearly and I didn't know how to deal with his death, or my mother. I thought that leaving before I could hurt you even worse was best for everyone. But something happened while I was away. I didn't shrivel up and die. I was able to take care of his house, like he would've wanted. Then I went to see my mother."

His eyes snapped to hers. "You did?" He leaned on the edge of his desk.

Peering up at the ceiling, she sighed. "Yes. I was there, ready to confront her, to...I don't even know what I was going to do." She told him about the letters, what her mother said in them. Reading those letters did something to her, changed her in a way she couldn't quite describe. "I was standing on that grass, right behind her. She was still as beautiful as I remembered, but still as distant as she's been my whole life. Her *death* didn't change that. Thinking she died, as bad as it sounds, was the best thing that happened to me."

Truth was, Carmen Harper had never been in her right mind to be Cali's mother. "She gave me up so that I could be with the person that would nurture and care for me like I deserved," Cali continued. "She wanted that for me, and I'm glad she did. I didn't need to confront her. I didn't need anything from her."

She took his right hand in hers. "I couldn't stop thinking about you. Being without you was a different kind of torture, self-inflicted of course. I would lay there at night, staring at the ceiling, wondering why I can't stop loving you." Stepping between his legs, she leaned in, rubbing her nose against his.

His face softened. "Did you want to?" he asked.

"Sometimes," she admitted "Only 'cause it hurt so much to be without you. With the way I left, I wasn't sure if you'd even talk to me."

"I understand the feeling. And you could've avoided that feeling if you had just stayed your ass here."

She reached out, traced his face with her finger, needing the contact. "You're right. Now that I'm here with you, I know I did the right thing coming home. Please...tell me that it isn't too late. Tell me that we still have a chance."

He swept his thumb under her chin and her eyes fluttered closed. He stood up, held her face between his hands. "No," he whispered. Hurt, she started to back away, but he held on to her. "It's not too late."

Then he pressed his lips to hers, kissing her deeply. He picked her up and perched her on the edge of the desk. Unzipping her top, he pulled it off slowly, baring her shoulders. "I missed you," he murmured against her skin.

"I missed you, too."

He placed a searing kiss on the skin above her bra, then lifted his head. "Cali, I meant what I said. If you're going to be here, be here. My house is not a revolving door. You can't walk in and out. I can't do that to my daughter. She needs stability."

She placed a finger over his mouth. "Nothing will ever keep me from my family again. Nothing. I love you, Red. I'm here for the duration."

"Does this mean you want to have my babies now?"

She grinned. "Don't push it."

He barked out a laugh. "I'm just kidding."

"Good, because I—"

"Quiet." He pinched her lips closed with his fingers. "Let's not rehash that conversation. I think there are more important things to discuss right now."

She pushed his fingers away. "Wait. You don't even know what I was going to say."

"I figured you were going to go into speech number 1,179 about how you don't want kids."

Laughing, she nudged him. "Stop. That wasn't what I was going to say. I was going to say that I want to make sure Corrine knows how much I love and care for *her*. I want her to know she can count on me, that I won't abandon her."

"You can tell her that now."

She whirled around, pulling her shirt closed. Corrine was standing at the door, a confused look on her face. Cali rushed up to her. "Hi, baby doll."

"Were you wrestling with Daddy again?"

Red laughed out loud and Cali's cheeks burned. "Um, well…"

"Yep," Red said.

"It looked like you were kissing to me," Corrine said.

Cali wrapped an arm around her and led her to the small sofa. "I'm glad you're here, though," She ran her fingers over the fresh braids in her hair. "I love your hair, by the way."

"I got it braided at a beauty salon."

"Nice. So I was talking to your daddy earlier. I know I let you down when I left for a long time."

The corners of Corrine's mouth turned downward. "I didn't know where you went."

"I had to figure some things out." She looked up at Red. "But I wanted to tell you that I'm sorry for leaving you. I want you to know that I love you very much and I'm going to be here for you."

"Really?" *Her* baby doll treated her to her beautiful smile. "Are you going to finally marry my daddy?"

She flashed Corrine a smile. "Um, that's a long way off, sweetie. I can tell you that I'm going to be around every day, from now on."

"For dinner?"

"Breakfast too," Red added with a wink.

Corrine flung her arms around Cali's neck, taking her by surprise. "Yay!" she shouted.

Tears pricked Cali's eyes and, for the first time in a long time, they were happy tears. Red leaned down in front of them and squeezed her knee. Corrine wrapped her arm around him, too. "Can we have chicken nuggets today?"

"I think that can be arranged," he said, picking her up.

"Can we go back outside? I want to show Cali my snow angel."

"Sure thing," Cali said, wrapping an arm around Red's waist as they headed toward the front door.

"If you're going to stay here, you need some pajamas," Corrine said.

"No, she doesn't," Red said.

Cali smacked his back. "Stop, Red."

"Hey, I was just being truthful."

Corrine patted her dad's head. "Telling the truth is the right thing to do."

"Don't encourage your father, baby doll," Cali said, helping Corrine into her coat and boots, before pulling on her own.

Red pulled the hat over Corrine's eyes and she screamed in delight.

"You ready?" he asked, kneeling down in front of Corrine. When she nodded, he stood up, turning to Cali. "Are you ready?"

"For everything you have to give me."

He brushed his lips over hers, lingering for a minute before he pulled back. "I'm going to hold you to that."

"Please do."

"Um, wait until we have our private discussion tonight. I'm going to show you a thing or two."

"Please do," she repeated with a smirk. "I love you."

"Oh, it's on now." He smacked her butt and she giggled like a schoolgirl with a crush. "I love you, too, baby."

Engaged to a prominent preacher, Allina is the envy of Ohio. But instead of walking down the aisle, she runs back home to Michigan, and to Kent, the man she'd left behind. One look is all it takes for Kent to know two things: his attraction to Allina is as strong as ever—and there's more to her story than she's telling him…

Please see the next page for a preview of

Her Kind of Man

CHAPTER ONE

The large door slammed behind Allina Parker as she entered the huge church. There was a flurry of activity around her as people scrambled to prepare for the ceremony. The weather wasn't cooperating, her friends couldn't come, and her dress wasn't as perfect as she'd want, but she was getting married to the man of her dreams.

Isaac Hunter was a man of God, the one who'd been groomed to take over the church she was in at that very moment. He was everything she'd asked for. And she'd become Mrs. Hunter before the day was out. She shook off her umbrella and headed for the changing room.

She scanned the foyer, hoping to see her mother. Sharon Parker hadn't had much time to prepare, since the wedding was kind of last minute, but she'd managed to transform the church into an elegant yet whimsical space. If she'd had more time to plan, Allina would have preferred an outdoor wedding. There was something about the natural beauty of a garden that appealed to her—the sound of the wind, the feel of the sun on her skin. This wasn't a bed of grass with beautiful wildflowers, but it was a close second.

What did the venue matter? They'd have the rest of their lives together.

Isaac had convinced her that getting married right away was best. He wanted to be established as a married minister of the church before his father handed him the reins in a few short months. And she'd agreed.

As she approached the changing room, she heard voices coming from the Pastor's study—a woman…and her fiancé. Normally, she wouldn't have given it another thought because there were many women who knew her future husband. Some were members of the church, but most were simply residents of the large community surrounding Christian Dreams Church. The boom of his voice sounded like an echo and she stopped in her tracks. Curiosity got the best of her and she glanced behind her before she tiptoed toward the room.

"You need to leave this alone," she heard Isaac say, a harsh edge to his voice.

"I'll never leave it alone," the mysterious woman snapped. "You don't deserve to live, let alone inherit this great church. You destroyed my life, ruined my chance at happiness. You're an evil man. I've kept quiet long enough."

A heavy feeling settled in her stomach. Leaning with her nose against the door, she waited for Isaac to respond, hoped he would say something that would alleviate the dread that had crept in. It wasn't the first time she'd felt that way, either. As wonderful as Isaac was, as perfect as he presented himself, there was a nagging feeling in her that something was off with him. At first, she'd dismissed it as nerves. After all, it was marriage. Forever. And he was exactly what she'd prayed for in a husband.

But then he'd started getting possessive, controlling. He didn't want her to go anywhere, hang out with anyone but him. She'd exerted her independence by spending a couple of months in Michigan with her friends. Her best friend, Sydney, had just had a baby and she used that as an opportunity to get some time away, think about if this was what she really wanted. In the end, she'd decided that there was more right than wrong in their relationship and she came back to Ohio. Things between them had seemed fine since she'd returned home.

"How much?" she heard him say.

A slight shiver crept up her spine. *Money? He's going to pay her off?*

"I don't want your money," the woman said. "Your father tried to pay me off, and I can't be bought."

The sound of glass breaking startled Allina and she stumbled away from the door. The door swung open and the woman rushed out. Allina scrambled backward, pressing herself against the wall, praying the young lady didn't see her. As the woman stomped to the front of the church, Allina exhaled. She didn't get a good look at her, but the woman didn't look familiar. The urge to catch up to her shot through her and she started after her.

"Allina?"

She gasped, frozen in place. Slow, hesitant footsteps neared her and she fought back the urge to flee. The feel of his breath on her neck made her hair rise. He touched her shoulders and she held her breath.

"What's going on?" he asked, his voice low.

Her heart pounded in her chest. "Nothing," she croaked.

What am I doing? Isaac had never shown her anything more than kindness. He had his faults, but he'd never been cruel.

"Are you okay?" His voice seemed far away, but she heard everything else, from the clang of a hammer to the sound of furniture being moved.

"Who was that woman?" she asked finally.

He turned her around to face him. He looked normal

enough. His short hair was freshly cut. He smelled like Isaac: Gucci Guilty, his signature cologne. But the man in front of her wasn't the man that she'd come to know. This man was a stranger.

"Shouldn't you be getting dressed, sweetie," he said tenderly. He ran a hand down her cheek. "We don't want to be late for the ceremony. I can't wait to make you my bride."

Frowning, she asked, "Are you going to answer my question?"

He paused as if he was thinking it over. Finally, he said, "No. It doesn't matter. She's nobody."

She moved back slightly, put some space between them.

But he only stepped forward, crowding her, hovering over her. Allina was a tall woman, but Isaac had a couple inches on her.

"I don't like this," she admitted. "That woman...I heard her." She couldn't get the woman's words out of her head. Her thoughts scrambled to understand why he would pay someone off if he had nothing to hide. That alone made her rethink everything about the wedding, about him.

"It doesn't matter," he told her again, in a stern tone, like he was talking to his child.

"It matters to me," Allina hissed. "And I'm not going to—"

Marry you died on her lips when his fingers dug into her cheeks. He pulled her to him, his eyes boring into hers.

"Allina," he whispered.

She gasped as he squeezed tighter. If anyone were to happen upon them at that moment, it would probably look like they were sneaking some time in with each other before the ceremony. But Allina was terrified. She pushed against him. "Let me go," she ground out.

"Allina?" The sound of her name on his lips used to make her feel special, but now she felt cold. Tears welled up in her eyes. "You are going to marry me."

"I won't," she cried softly.

"You don't want to play with me. I can make your life ten times worse than you think it is now. I *will* hurt you if you leave me." He leaned closer. With his mouth against her ear, he whispered. "Don't cry. Go put on that wedding dress. And make sure you smile wide for the camera."

Then he let her go, and she rubbed her face where his hands had been. *What the hell am I going to do?* His threat seemed more of a promise. She believed every word of it.

She rushed to the room they'd designated as her changing room. Opening the door, she stepped in and slammed it behind her. Sagging against the door, she ran a shaky hand over her hair.

"There you are," her mother said.

Allina's eyes snapped over to the far corner of the room. Her mother was fiddling with the handmade bouquet.

"I was wondering when you'd show up. Sydney called. She said she was trying to call your cell, but it kept going to voicemail."

Allina wished Syd was here. She needed to talk to someone. Glancing at her mother, she wondered if she'd be able to tell her what had just happened. She wanted to. But Sharon was a worrywart. She'd call her father in and everything would be bad.

"Babe, are you okay? You better get moving," her mother asked, concern in her dark eyes.

Her mother was half Filipino, raised in the United States by her African American mother. She had no ties to her father's side of the family and Allina had grown up thinking she was just light-skinned. She didn't find out about her mother's history until she was a grown woman.

She smiled sadly at her mother. The woman was beautiful from head to toe. Her long, gray dress flattered her small frame, and loose tendrils of her light brown hair framed her face.

They'd been through so much together, shared a special bond. Growing up, her mother always told her she'd do anything for her—and she had. The woman had risked her own freedom to save Allina. Looking at her standing before her with a straight pin in her mouth and a determined look in her eyes as she wrapped gray ribbon around the stem of the bouquet, Allina choked back a sob. Then she embraced her mother tightly.

Her mother's hands stroked her back slowly. "Are you nervous?"

Nodding, Allina stepped back, averting her gaze. "Yes. I just... can't believe I'm getting married."

"Well, Isaac is a good man. The members here love him. Everyone was willing to pitch in on decorations, food. The church is excited about this wedding."

"It looks beautiful."

Her mother reached out and wiped Allina's eyes, gave her a loving smile. "You're going to be happy. I'm so happy for you. I never thought you'd be able to find love."

Allina thought about her mother's words. Honestly, she didn't either. She'd spent years crushing on her friend Kent, hoping he'd actually *see* her. Unfortunately he never did, so when she met Isaac, she figured... *why not*. After all, he'd pursued her—told her that she was the most beautiful woman he'd ever seen. Why wouldn't she go with someone who actually *wanted* to be with her?

She thought about Kent, considered calling him. But they'd had a horrible argument when she told him she was getting married. He didn't believe she was doing it for the right reasons. He'd told her she was making a huge mistake. And he'd refused to come.

"Mom," she said, her voice hoarse. "Do you think I could have a minute? I really need to get my nerves under control."

"Sure," her mother said. "Just call me if you need me."

·

When her mother left the room, Allina walked over to the wedding dress hanging on the closet door. It was one that she'd designed herself for another bride, one who'd changed her mind about getting married. With the short notice, she hadn't had time to make the wedding dress she wanted, so she'd gone with something she'd already had.

Designing wedding dresses was Allina's passion. She'd done so happily for the last several years. She'd had dreams of opening up her own bridal shop. She'd even had the opportunity to take over the one she'd worked in for years before the owner retired. But she'd left it all behind to follow Isaac, to give love a chance. *Now look at me.*

Sighing, she took the dress off the hanger. Her hands shook as she dressed. Could she go through with this? The warning in his tone, the hard glimmer in his eyes, told her he would *hurt* her. She warred with her thoughts. Was this a sign of what was to come? *How can I be so sure he won't hurt me anyway?*

Turning to the mirror, she studied her reflection. She'd straightened her natural curls for the occasion and put a simple, decorative clip at the base of her scalp. The dress was a beautiful A-linc, but it wasn't her. She'd always envisioned a ball gown. Just another sign that it just wasn't right?

A knock on the door drew her from her thoughts. She walked to the door and opened it. Her father was standing on the other side in his gray tuxedo and with his salt-and-pepper hair slicked back, a smile on his face. He ducked as he walked through the door, pulling her into a warm embrace. She took in his smell and she immediately felt at ease. Old Spice. Judge Owen Parker had always made her feel safe. He was tall and slender, but he was strong.

"You look beautiful, baby," he said, tears in his eyes. "I'm so proud of you."

She couldn't help but tear up. The love that shone in her

father's eyes made her feel at peace. She knew what she had to do.

"Where's Mom?" she asked.

"She's running around somewhere," he said. "Probably barking orders at people."

They both chuckled softly.

"Daddy, I love you."

His eyes lit up. "I love you, too. You ready?"

She nodded. "Yes. Can I have a second? I'll meet you out in the foyer."

"Okay. Hurry." He placed a tender kiss to her forehead.

She swallowed past a lump in her throat as she watched him disappear around the corner. Picking up her small purse, she stuffed her phone, her driver's license, a debit card, and all the cash she had on hand into the inner pocket of the clutch.

Taking a deep breath, she walked to the door and down the hall. But instead of heading to the foyer, she turned and rushed down another hallway, leading to the side exit. Her heart raced as she neared the door. She glanced back to make sure no one saw her. Pushing the door open, she stepped outside and took off for the limo. She pulled the door open and slid inside.

The driver turned, his eyes widening when he saw her. "Ma'am?" he asked with a questioning look.

"Just drive, please," she ordered, clutching her purse against her chest when he sped off.

Fall in Love with Forever Romance

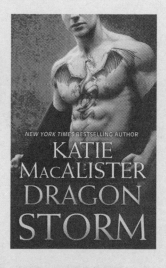

DRAGON STORM
by Katie MacAlister

In *New York Times* bestselling
author Katie MacAlister's
Dragon Storm, Constantine
must choose: save his fellow
dragons or the mortal woman
he's grown to love.

HIS ALL NIGHT
by Elle Wright

In relationships, Calisa Harper
has clear rules: no expectations,
no commitments, no one gets
hurt. She doesn't need a diamond
ring to bring her happiness. She
just needs Jared. Fine, fit, and fe-
rocious in bed, Jared is Calisa's
ideal combination of friend and
lover. But the no-strings status
they've shared for years is about
to get very tangled...

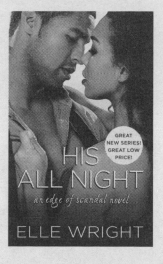

Fall in Love with Forever Romance

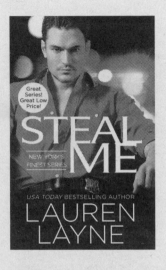

STEAL ME
by Lauren Layne

Faster than a New York minute, homicide detective Anthony Moretti and waitress Maggie Walker find themselves in a perilous pursuit that only gets hotter with each and every rule-breaking kiss.

A BILLIONAIRE
BETWEEN THE SHEETS
by Katie Lane

A commanding presence in the boardroom and the bedroom, Deacon Beaumont has come to save the failing company French Kiss. But one bold and beautiful woman dares to question his authority and everything he knows about love.

Fall in Love with Forever Romance

DUKES ARE FOREVER
by Anna Harrington

When Edward Westover takes possession of his rival's estate, everything that villain held dear—even his beautiful daughter—belongs to Edward. Will Kate Benton fall for the man who now owns everything she has come to know and love—including herself? Fans of Elizabeth Hoyt, Grace Burrowes, and Madeline Hunter will love this Regency–era romance.